A
DEATH
ON
SUNDAY

By

TISH OWEN

A DEATH ON SUNDAY

PRINTING HISTORY
Previously published by Willow Tree Press

ISBN 978-0-9996327-9-6

Published by:
Goddess and the Moon Press

ACKNOWLEDGEMENTS

This book is a labor of love. I am mad for my characters and the story line that just grew and took on a life of its own. I hope that you enjoy reading it as much as I enjoyed writing it.

I'd like to thank my publisher, WillowTree, for having enough faith in me to publish this book; my editor Katherine; my other editor Star Bustamonte (yes it takes a village); the WillowTree publicist Wendy; Chris Franklin for giving me computer information that was crucial to my story; Fekisha who gave me legal procedural information; Barry Archer, my son-in-law who provided stock car expertise and firearm information; Elizabeth Angela who listened to me read sections of the manuscript and cashed my reality checks; my daughter Tanya Gattis who gave me anatomy and medical information; Dr. Christie Diaz who provided medical advice; my cousin Stephanie Simpson Fearman who explained the difference between dislocated and bruised; my daughter Michelle Archer; my son Franklin Gattis who listened to me whine and complain about the torture that is writing even while he was being tortured by his own manuscript; my husband Patrick Owen for giving me information about various poisons; Dorothy Morrison who encouraged me; Billy Center and Debi Fertitta for being my friends through thick and thin; Eric Romberg and Cat Jones for covering for me during my writing sabbatical; my many friends and relatives who have heard me say for over a year: I'm writing a murder mystery, and never told me shut-up; Sydney, Lili, Kaiser, Keller and Acel because you are all so cute; everyone who said, " I can't wait to read it" and everyone who buys it, thank you thank you thank you.

Dedicated with love to my beautiful, ninety-seven-year-old mother, Loraine Simpson Hickman who told me my first story and started my life-long love affair with the telling.
Thank you. I love you.

CHAPTER 1

It was an absolutely perfect spring day. You know the kind of day I mean. The temperature was 75 degrees, the sun was shining, and there were little, fluffy, white clouds floating in the sky. That sky was so blue it took your breath away. The humidity was low and a gentle breeze was blowing just enough to dry any perspiration that might form on your upper lip. On such a perfect day, you looked like you were glowing, not all hot, sweaty and disgusting. All your troubles had been left behind. There was only a long, lazy weekend that stretched out in front of you. No lawn to mow, no laundry to wash, no deadlines to meet, no travel to worry about, just hanging out. Yes, truly a perfect day.

It was such a perfect day that Mommy decided that we'd have Sunday brunch on the back patio. Sunday brunch is a tradition in the Maher household and has been as long as I can remember. I love Sunday brunch. Since most of the immediate relatives—in-laws and out-laws—were over, including a gaggle of nieces and nephews, outside did seem perfect. It's not that I don't like children, but with a herd of them, the acoustics outside are ever so much better. Outside has more space for all that noise to spread out, dissipate and not be quite as deafening.

We all traipsed across the multi-hued Crab Orchard stone patio carrying plates, silverware, cups, napkins, ice buckets, sliced ham, potato salad, green salad, green beans, banana pudding, scrambled eggs, biscuits, rolls, and melon. There were some other things that I didn't care about eating, so I didn't pay much attention to the rest. We looked like a happy food parade. How come they don't have those? You could judge the best float and then eat it. Yum.

One of my brothers-in-law rolled the portable bar out as well. Brunch is just not brunch without Mimosas—for everyone but me. I drink a Bloody Mary at brunch. I love them, but they have to be done right—not a lot of sediment in the bottom of your glass that you have to strain through your teeth like a whale. There must be enough Tabasco to put a burn in the back of your mouth. And lemon, Worcestershire sauce and lots of salt. I don't care for celery, long greens beans, olives or weird flecks of what might be pepper floating on the surface either. I'm a purest.

We settled at the picnic tables, doled out the food and somehow tempted the children to actually take a moment from acting like crazed loons to eat. Never an easy task to perform.

"Whose turn?" Daddy asked as he looked around.

"Mine, Poppy, it's my turn," said seven-year-old James.

The spawn of my sister Moira, he seems quieter than the rest of us. But as my grandmother, YaYa says, still waters run deep. He probably bears watching.

"Go ahead, son," Daddy encouraged.

James bowed his head. The sun glinted off his copper-colored locks, as he folded his hands piously. For a moment he looked angelic, and I decided that YaYa was correct about him.

"Bless us oh Lord for these thy gifts which we are about to receive from thy bounty, through Christ our Lord. Amen."

"Amen," we all intoned solemnly.

I loaded my plate with perfectly baked ham, scrambled eggs, French toast, potato salad and biscuits. Carbs, salt and dead animal— that's the ticket. I savored every bite, taking my time to really enjoy the meal. All around me conversation died off as everyone paid homage to the food. Mommy made the pitchers of Mimosas. Of course, I had to mix my own Bloody Mary. That's what you get for being different.

The children, or the *herd* as I liked to call them, bolted their food and commenced with chasing each other around the yard as children do. They added a sound track of squeals and yells and laughter to the afternoon. There are many members of the herd. Five of my sibs have procreated, and at last count there were fifteen offspring. Mommy thinks that Darlene, brother Brian's wife, may be hatching another one. There's been no official announcement, yet. I noticed YaYa eyeing Darlene closely during brunch, trying to see if Darlene was eating for two, I suppose. She's convinced there's another Maher on the way. YaYa dreamt there was a new baby in the family, and she does have a sixth sense about that sort of thing. When she starts dreaming about babies, all the females in the vicinity pee on sticks just in case.

Usually the dogs chase the herd and add to the general decibel levels, but with food in sight, the dogs sat patiently waiting for handouts. They're mostly better behaved than the kids too. Ahhh, dogs, kids, good food and vodka. All was right with the world.

About two hundred yards from the left side of the patio, the land drops down toward an amazingly beautiful valley. It's one of my most favorite vistas. A river runs down the middle of the valley. Of course, from the patio it looks like a creek. That river is the favored place for youth in the country to swim, drink and make out. Just sitting on the patio looking down at the river brought back many a pleasant memory. I smiled as I drank my perfect drink and thought about my misspent youth while conversation hummed all around me.

The patio is attached to "The House." There's a good reason that it deserves the quotation marks. *The House* is huge—eight bedrooms and a nursery adjoining Mommy and Daddy's room. That room has been converted into a computer room and Mommy has discovered the internet. She claims that surfing the net is ever so much more fun than childbirth. Did I say the house was huge? It's massive. The architecture is a sort of Northern lake house from the century before last.

Here's some perspective. There's a formal dining room that seats twenty-five and a living room where you can comfortably entertain a hundred people in spite of the baby grand piano. Oh yes, we did all have lessons. I can still play *Heart and Soul*, thank you very much. A fireplace dominates one entire wall. It's surrounded by a floor-to-ceiling mosaic of ducks landing on a lake—I don't know why. Adjacent to the living room is a large entry hall with a staircase that runs up one side of the hall to a landing where the staircase splits and continues up both sides to the second floor. Quite grand. That landing is a perfect place for making an entrance. Every one of us had First Communion, Confirmation, winter festival dance, prom and graduation pictures taken on that landing—some wedding pictures too.

The stairs end in a huge landing that is practically a large, open room. The hallways run off the room to the right and the left. The room itself is filled with overstuffed comfortable chairs and sofas, bookcases, and a big screen TV. We use it for a den.

The upstairs bedrooms are on the back side of the house and share a great view of the countryside. My room is at one end of the hall over the kitchen, so I have a window that looks over the side yard too. My grandmother has an identical room at the far end of the house from mine.

The place has more windows than the White House. I know that because when I was a kid and had somehow angered my mother, she made me wash those windows. Mommy believed that if you had so much time on your hands you could cause trouble, then you had too much time on your hands and needed to be busy. Between the seven of us, we had some very clean windows. The house also boasts a full basement and an attic—both great places to spend time on rainy days. During a game of hide-n-seek, one of my brothers crawled into a chest in the attic, fell asleep and became the subject of a manhunt. We all use that against him when needed.

The heart of the house is the kitchen, with a breakfast nook, a huge closet for storage, and a butler's pantry which holds dishes, a coffeemaker and the bar. A lot of problems have been solved at the large, round, oak breakfast table. It was the place we brought our troubles and talked them out. It was the place we brought our joys and shared them, the place announcements were made, dates and proms dissected, comfort sought and given. It was the place we brought our friends that were having troubles. Lots of tears and laughter have flowed through that room over the years.

The house was built in 1919 as a cross between a hotel and a bed-and-breakfast. It was large, roomy and big enough to accommodate visitors but still with a homey feel, not a commercial one. I supposed it made people feel that they were visiting the home of a friend or relative, not spending their time and money with strangers in a business establishment. People visited our town, Medicine Springs, because we had hot mineral springs. We still have the springs but most of the hotels built to accommodate the tourists have closed up or been converted to other uses. The house was built at the height of the "taking the waters for improved health" craze. Even Franklin Delano Roosevelt visited our humble little town. Sadly the tourist health industry lost popularity and the money dried up.

The house was finally put on the market and sat for the longest time. Until Daddy decided it was just the perfect place for him and Mommy, a place that they could fill with children. It was cheap enough that he could afford it on a sheriff's deputy salary.

As I was finishing my last bite of watermelon, Martin, my eight-year-old nephew materialized at my elbow. Cute kid, reminds me of me. The sun glittered on his golden-red hair as his beautiful blue eyes looked up at me adoringly. He grinned appealingly and the freckles danced across his little snub nose. He's his mother's clone.

Well actually, we all look alike. A sometimes annoying and sometimes handy factoid, depending on who you ask. My sister Moira is two years my senior. We look so much alike that we went on each other's dates in high school as a prank. That might be why we both had such a hard time getting dates to prom. Mommy made my brothers, Patrick and Dugan take us since most of the boys in town were no longer speaking to us. I also had a fake ID for several years with Moira's name on it. Even the State of Tennessee DMV thinks we look alike. Mommy did have a fit when she found out about that little prank. Thank God we were in college before she discovered it! Oh well, it was great fun at the time.

"What do you want, boy?" I asked him.

"Well," he drawled, "now that lunch is over, I was thinkin' we might do some shootin'."

Mommy corrected him. "Brunch," she said firmly. "And don't drop your G's."

His grin widened and he looked even more like a little imp. "Please, Auntie Tess."

I pretended to think it over. I put my hand to my chin, rolled my eyes heavenward and made *mmm* noises. As I knew he would, Martin started to jiggle, dancing from one foot to the other.

"Do you have to pee?" I teased him.

"Come on, please, Auntie Tess, please, please, please, please." He was holding his hands folded like an altar boy, imploring me.

By now all the other children had gathered around, sensing some sort of action. The little hooligans are like bloodhounds.

"Okay," I said standing up. "But everyone must abide by the rules. Recite the rules," I commanded.

They shouted in unison, "Rule Number One! Do what Auntie Tess says. Rule Number Two! Never touch a gun unless a grown-up is helping you. Rule Number Three! Never point a gun at a living creature. Rule Number Four! Always clean your gun and restore it to its proper place!"

By this point they were yelling, and the little veins stood out on the sides of their skinny necks. Their faces were red as beets. I loved this part and had to suppress a smile.

All of the adults were staring at us, and Mommy covered her head with her hands. She's always so theatrical!

"Oh my Lord, she's going to break out the artillery—everybody duck and cover."

I rolled my eyes. "Mommy, thank you for the vote of confidence, but for the record, I've never lost a trooper. There'd better be some of that banana pudding left when I get done."

YaYa, my mother's mother, makes the best banana pudding in three counties. She takes the blue ribbon at the Simpson County Fair every year and has since Jesus was in grade school.

I headed into the house with my charges trouping behind me. Only twelve of them are big enough to shoot. There is one tiny girl who has to be restrained from following us to the targets every time we break out the hardware. She cries like her little heart is broken as we leave her behind. I figure she'll demand to come with us next year when she's three. Her name is Deidre and she is fearsome. The last two are babes in arms.

I left the herd vibrating in front of the gun cabinet, which stands to the left of the fireplace, while I retrieved the key from its secret hiding place. You can't really think I'd trust those little monsters with the whereabouts of the key to paradise, do you? Please, none of them can be trusted. I may not be a parent but I was a kid with a big imagination and sibs that would help me implement evil plans, so I know what kids are capable of doing. The door to my parents' room is to the right of the fireplace, and the key is hidden there, high on a hard-to-reach shelf.

I retrieved the key and walked back slowly, swinging it on the sturdy gold chain, taunting them. The herd was waiting for me. Only their eyes moved from the cabinet to the key.

"What shall we shoot today?" I asked.

They danced in place and shouted out answers. "The Magnum!" "The Browning!" "The Mossburg!" "The Colts!" "The Walther!" They shouted over each other and I couldn't make out the rest. It really didn't matter what they wanted, I knew which guns we were going to take. I only asked to make them feel they were a part of the process. I read somewhere that was good for their development. See what a good aunt I am? I held my hands out in front of me in a "stop now" gesture to stem the flow of noise.

"Okay, okay. We'll take the Colts and the Parker twelve-gauge, although none of you can fire it 'cuz you'd be knocked into next week. And the Remington Seven-Hundred. Now watch."

I moved in front of the herd to the gun cabinet. It's big—about six feet tall and four feet wide. Through the beveled glass doors you can see many, many guns. I put the key in the lock, opened the cabinet and pulled out the matching Colt .45s. Such fabulous guns, supposedly antiques. Daddy won them in a poker game in his misspent youth. I went through the process of making sure they were unloaded. The herd watched my every move, their eyes round, staring and unblinking. I wasn't even sure they were breathing. I repeated the process with the other guns. I handed the empty weapons to the bigger children—age has its privileges—so they could be carried outside. The ammunition boxes went to the smaller children, and we all marched back out the French doors and across the patio.

I sent some of the unburdened kids to fetch the targets from the storage shed that sat toward the back of the property. Sometimes it's good to have a large family. You have minions and you can delegate. As we crossed the patio and headed toward the target area, I spotted Deidre in her mother's arms. She was crying and ratcheting up for a good screaming fit. I walked over to her.

"Baby girl," I soothed, "soon you'll be big enough to shoot a gun, and I promise to teach you how."

Her baby blue eyes were filled with tears. Her curly red hair was wet and stuck to her sweet face. I wiped her salty cheek and planted a kiss.

"Now, TisTis, wanna now," she sobbed at me.

I smiled at Darlene as she tried to sooth the fearsome fire-haired creature in her arms and continued on my way. The dogs who had been sitting patiently awaiting scraps from the meal got up and followed me.

My brother Brian caught up to my enthusiastic parade about halfway to the targets. I'm tall but Brian is taller, and I had to look up to talk to him.

"That child of yours is killing me. I guess next year I'll have to teach her to shoot. I don't think she can be restrained beyond that!"

Brian's not just tall, he's lanky as well. He has the obligatory family coloring, though his hair is a darker red than mine and his eyes are a darker blue. He grinned at me and I saw what all the girls who had ever chased him saw—a handsome devil. He thinks so too, of course he does.

"Gonna kill us some straw bales today? Make the world a safer place?" he asked in a smart aleck tone of voice.

I didn't even look at him as I answered, "Yes, so that when the straw bale uprising happens, we'll be prepared and will know what it takes to put the rebellion down. So we can save your sorry asses, so there." I tossed my hair at him like I was twelve.

"Your wife got a bun in the oven?" I asked casually.

"I have no idea what you're talking about. I'm workin' so much I barely see the woman." He was grinning when he said it, so I took that for a yes. They would announce it when they were ready.

In the past they'd lost a couple of babies in the first trimester, and I could see that they'd be nervous about telling. I silently wished them luck and sent a request to the Virgin for protection for all of them. Deidre needed a brother to pick on and boss around. I grinned back at my darling brother. He knew that I knew, and so we were co-conspirators in the secret.

The kids were already dragging the bales to their traditional spot overlooking the valley but in sight of the patio. The setup allows the patio dwellers to observe our antics without leaving the comfort of the patio or the adult beverages. We fired our guns out over the valley. There's not much between us and the river except for some cows. Did I mention that our nearest neighbor is a mile away? That's down the road, not as the crow flies. Good thing too, less chance of anyone getting in our way. The back of the shed is toward the valley, and we set the targets there. The only thing we might hit, if we miss a target, is a bird.

The yard is fairly level from the patio to the shed. Past the shed and to the right of the targets, the land begins to slope down. A football field away from the shed, there's a dirt road. It's an old logging road that's lower than the land on either side of it as if the road bed had sunk over the years. It doesn't really go anywhere. It's just a cut-through from one paved road to another. About once a year the county sends someone out to grade the holes out of it. The road is a perfect "Lover's Lane." Daddy is always bitching about picking up beer cans. Ah, kids these days. At least we were smart enough to hide the empties. The point is, no one travels that road much, plus it's down a hill, and that lessens the chance of an accident. So because of our topography, we have the perfect spot for target practice: the valley in front of us, a low road to the right and the house to the left.

The herd knew the drill. They pulled the table out of the shed to set the guns on and tacked new targets on the bales. In short order we were ready. I saw Daddy ambling toward us. It's hard to keep him away when the guns come out. I could see Mommy mixing a pitcher of adult beverage to help her cope. I don't believe that the shooting really makes her nervous. I think she likes to be dramatic and I think she likes to drink.

"Poppy, we're gonna shoot!" Kevin shouted.

He's eleven, he always shouts. The boy was so excited even his strawberry blond hair was standing on end. He looked like a dandelion. Daddy smiled. I loaded the Colts, and Brian loaded the shotgun. The herd vibrated a bit harder. A gentle breeze blew my hair around my face just a bit, the sun was warm on my shoulders, and I had to squint a little because the day was so bright. Bees were buzzing and I could smell the honeysuckle blossoms. God, it truly was a perfect day!

I shooed the kids behind me, checked to make sure they had complied and only then did I take aim and fire. Six times!

"Good show!" Daddy exclaimed.

Indeed, not too shabby. Most of the shots were touching the bull's-eye, with one dead center. The herd bounced up and down.

"Do more! Do more! Do more!" they chanted as they bounced.

Daddy reloaded for me. Brian took the other Colt, aimed and fired at the second target.

"Uncle Brian got two in the middle," announced ten-year-old Sarah solemnly.

Such is her nature. She's a beautiful girl with long dark, copper-colored hair, a heart-shaped face and a light dusting of freckles. She'd be a much prettier child if she'd only smile more. YaYa calls her "The Judge"—not to her face, of course. YaYa might be old and cantankerous, but she's not cruel to children. Well, almost never.

"Show off," I muttered under my breath at Brian.

I know he heard me. I meant for him to hear me. So it went. We fired and reloaded. The herd cheered us on as we tried to outdo each other with our spectacular marksmanship. Daddy broke out the Parker. The herd covered their ears when he fired it. They loved the noise it made, so they screamed in delight every time he fired. Like Mommy, they liked to pretend that it scared them. Then we helped the kids fire the Remington. Everybody got a turn. The older ones had improved since the last time we had target practice. The younger ones tried hard to do as well as their older cousins. They all loved to shoot—must be in the blood.

When we had finally fired off enough ammo to put down any straw bale revolution that might arise, I called game over. Lots of moans and groans met my announcement, but they started to move to put things away like the good minions they are. Daddy, Brian and I made sure the guns were all unloaded.

"Take your targets home with you," I reminded the herd. "Put the date on 'em so you can compare your skills the next time we shoot."

CRACK! We all jumped and looked around to see who had fired the shot. My heart flew up in my throat. I looked and all the guns were on the table or in the hands of an adult. All the children were standing still as rocks, as shocked as the grown-ups. A movement, high and to the right caught my eye. I turned and saw something, oh God, someone falling from a tall oak tree down by the road.

I started running before my brain engaged. I could hear Brian pounding along behind me.

My father yelled, "CALL CONNELL, NOW! DOGS, STAY!"

I could picture the shocked faces of everyone from YaYa down to little Steven. My heart tried to tear itself out of my chest. I could hear my pulse in my ears. I was terrified but I kept running. I saw pieces of paper, sketch-pad sized, floating gently to the ground like big pieces of snow. Odd how that stands out in my mind.

Brian won the race, his legs being longer. A man lay face down on the ground, a red spot the size of a fifty-cent piece was on his back, right between his shoulder blades. He wore a light yellow tee-shirt, jeans and sneakers. A baseball cap lay nearby. I slid to my knees next to the man and took a moment to catch my breath. I felt his neck for a pulse and found none. Brian knelt on the other side of him. I could hear more footsteps coming behind me. Family coming. Reinforcements. I looked at Brian and shook my head.

"Let's turn him over." I was surprised at how calm I sounded.

We gently rolled him over and both gasped in recognition.

"Chick!" Patrick said from behind me, his voice full of shock and disbelief.

CHAPTER 2

"Oh shit," I moaned. "Oh shit, oh shit, oh shit, oh shit, oh shit!" I couldn't stop saying the word. "Shit! Shit! Shit!"

I slammed my self-control into place and stuffed the grief that was trying to overwhelm me down deep and shut the lid. "SHIT!" I shouted and shuddered all over. I had a grip. I drew in one breath and released it, I had control. I could still feel tears sliding down my face. I couldn't seem to control those. I pulled back from Chick.

"Crime scene, hands off!" I snapped at Brian. He jumped like he'd been goosed.

"GREAT GOD ALMIGHTY! CHICK DONNELLY!" Daddy boomed.

I turned, looked over my shoulder and met his sky blue eyes.

"Baby", he said, anguish filling his voice.

I shook my head again, tears falling hot and fast from my eyes. Most of my relatives and a few of the in-laws had arrived and stood in a frozen tableau just up the rise from Brian and me.

"Children," I gasped.

I couldn't take my eyes from the spreading red stain on Chick's chest. The wound was huge, but it was just leaking blood now that his heart was no longer pumping. For a moment I had the craziest thought that I'd just scoop up the blood and stuff it back into Chick's chest and it would all be alright. I shook my head to clear that thought out of it.

"Mommy," said Moira.

They had left the children with our mother—of course they had. I could hear the screaming of a police siren moving toward us.

"Connell," Dugan said.

God, we were reduced to communication in monosyllables as if we were afraid that if we tried for more we would all just start screaming hysterically. I know that's what I wanted to do. I took one more look at Chick, resisting the urge to touch him. I stood up and stepped back.

Brian stood too. "Why do you think this is a crime scene?" he asked me quietly.

"It's the only thing that makes sense. How could this be an accident?" I replied just as quiet.

I looked up into the tree and saw branches disturbed, a small one broken, some leaves on the ground. "Where the hell did that shot come from?" I pondered.

"Why was he up there?" asked my sister Michelene.

I shook my head, still looking for a vantage point from which a sniper could fire.

Dugan picked up one of the sheets of paper. "Tess," he said, offering it to me.

I took it gingerly by the very tip and held it between my fingers, still conscious of the crime scene protocol, and then damn near dropped it.

"It's me! A drawing of me! What the hell?"

Michelene reached for another sheet of paper close to her feet.

"Mich, crime scene!"

She snatched her hand back.

Patrick walked to the tree from which Chick had fallen and put his back toward it. "If he was looking at the house, he'd be turned this way." He pointed up the slope toward the house.

You couldn't see the house from the ground, but I was sure you could see it if you climbed the tree. I nodded, "He was shot in the back and was sittin' up there where that branch is scraped, I think."

I looked over my brother's shoulder, trying to look down a line of trajectory and found another oak tree on a rise across the dirt road. It was about a hundred and fifty to two hundred yards away. "Bingo," I said and pointed toward it.

"Holy Mary, Mother of God!"

I turned to see my brother Connell standing on the rise, a big gold star on his chest and a look of complete shock on his face. I hadn't realized the siren had gone silent. I took a deep breath and got a grip on my tears. My brother Connell and Chick Donnelly had been friends since birth, actually before. Chick was the son of Mommy and Daddy's best friends, Eve and Paul Donnelly. Our mothers were pregnant at the same time. The babies were delivered within hours of one another. The boys hoped Chick and I would marry one day. We had been involved for a time. He was my first boyfriend. I was five, he was six, and we broke up because he ate my library paste. I wanted to wail and have someone comfort me. But I couldn't lose my shit. There would be time for that later.

"I think he was in that tree," I pointed. "Shot in the back, long range, from there." Again I pointed. "Connell, this was no accident."

Connell finally dragged his gaze from Chick and followed my pointing hand. I saw his "cop" face click into place.

"I got back-up coming. What're these papers?" Connell asked. He bent to pick one up, looked at it then turned a quizzical gaze on me. His eyes held a big question mark.

I shrugged. "No idea," I admitted.

"Okay, everybody move up the hill, get outta my crime scene." Connell made shooing motions with his hands. Everyone took a couple of steps backwards toward the house.

"I'll go check on the kids," said Moira.

Michelene nodded. "They're a little freaked out. You took off like a scalded dog." She paused, "Connell?"

Connell looked up.

"Love you," she said.

He nodded.

Everyone took one more look at Chick. My father made the sign of the cross. So did my sisters and sisters-in-law as they took slow steps away before finally turning their backs to us as they climbed the rise.

"Connell," I said, "I need a minute."

He looked at me and dropped his bag on the ground. "Sure, I'll start markin' evidence."

He rummaged in the bag for a few seconds and moved away from me, dropping little yellow, numbered triangles by the sheets of paper, and Chick and Chick's hat. The hat had "Atlanta Braves" written on it. Chick loved the Braves so much. The last trip he ever took with his dad had been to Atlanta to see the Braves play. They lost, but he didn't care. He loved them fiercely and loyally. Over the years, through thick and through thin, he was a Braves man all the way. When they won the series in 1995, I thought he'd lose his ever lovin' mind. Chick, Connell and I drank that night until we had to be carried to bed since we were all walking on a slant. It was glorious.

I sat on the ground, cross-legged, next to Chick. My heart lurched in my chest. "Chick, oh, Chick, what the hell happened?"

Chick's eyes opened, locking on to mine. *"Whoa!"* he said and sat up.

Rather, a transparent image of Chick sat up. Oh yeah, did I mention I see dead people? Well, I do and have most all of my life. It's not exactly a secret, and I'm used to it. But this was different— the dead person I was looking at, sitting right in front of me, was someone I knew and cared about, someone who had been murdered.

"What happened?" His gaze traveled up the tree.

"Chick! Focus! What were you doing up there?" I asked or rather demanded of him.

He looked at me, chagrinned and hung his head. *"Drawing you"*, he mumbled. *"It was gonna be a surprise."* He stood up and looked down at himself. *"Damn! TisTis, am I dead?"*

I nodded, "Sorry, Chick."

"Well now who the hell would wanna go and do a thing like that? I mean, God damn it! This, well...ain't this a helluva mess! I got a race next week!" he said with frustration.

He sat down next to me and leaned into me. A chill ran down my arm.

"TisTis, I love you, always have, always will. Never could gather the balls to tell you, to really talk about it, to do anything about it. We just always talked around it. Now I tell you, now that it's too late." God, he sounded so sad.

"Chick, I always knew, really, it's alright, I always knew. I love you too." I paused to draw breath.

"Chick, honey, why'd anyone want ya dead? You piss somebody off? Poach somebody's woman? Win too many hands at poker? Do a crummy transmission replacement?" Chick owned Donnelly Repair and Replacement Garage in Medicine Springs.

He shook his head. *"Nope. Nope. Nope. Nope. Now you know I don't hoodoo folks, TisTis, and you know I'm the best damn mechanic in at least five counties, mabbe six."*

I sighed, "I know, Chick. I know. You see anything odd, something out of order, something out of the ordinary, anything weird?"

He shook his head again. *"Weirder'n me being dead, sitting here next to my own body, talking to you, kinda weird?"*

I almost laughed.

"Maybe it was an accident, ya know, some dumb-ass hunter," Chick said.

I shook my head at him, "What would he be hunting? Coon? It's the middle of the day. Magpies? We would've heard 'em."

Chick shrugged, *"Yep, some sombitch murdered me."*

"Tess," Connell called, "back-up's here."

My head snapped up toward Connell and then back to Chick. He was gone!

"ARRRRR! CHICK DONNELLY, YOU COME BACK HERE!" I yelled.

Connell walked over to me, and we just stared at each other for a moment. His deep blue eyes were filled with pain, and his handsome face displayed lines that weren't there yesterday. He held out a hand, I grasped it, and he pulled me to my feet. I wrapped my arms around him and pulled him into a hug.

"Jesus, Connell, I'm so sorry." Tears started leaking again, rolling down my face.

"I'm sorry for him and for all of us." His voice was thick with unshed tears.

"I'm going up to the house, open a bottle of Tullemore Dew. Come help me finish it. After. Okay?"

He looked down at Chick, his face sadder than I had ever seen it. Sadder even than when his wife Carol Ann left him. Chick helped him recover from that. Who'd help him now?

"Yeah. I'll be up," he said quietly, his voice sounding hollow.

Joel and Mark, Connell's deputies, drove up at that moment and parked on the road below us. Behind them an ambulance arrived. The EMT attendants unloaded a gurney and a blanket. I knew somebody would stick a thermometer into Chick's liver to confirm the time of death and someone else would pull a blanket over Chick's face. I wanted to be far away when those things happened. God! Poor Chick! Poor Connell! Poor Me! Poor Everyone!

"I'm gonna touch him," I said. I walked back to Chick, knelt down and kissed him on the mouth. "I love you, Chick Donnelly, now and always," I whispered.

Crime scene protocol be damned! I straightened and nodded to the new arrivals. They all nodded back at me with such sad looks on their faces. Did my face look like that?

I turned and struggled up the rise back toward the house. My sobbing started as soon as I was out of sight of my brother. I had to release some of the grief that was drowning me. I felt like my chest would burst. It was so tight it hurt. I could hardly get enough breath into my lungs to sob properly. I could barely walk, I was staggering. I just wanted to lie down in the grass and scream and pound the ground with my fists.

About halfway to the house I couldn't go any farther. I dropped to my knees and sobbed and sobbed. The horror hit me like a sledgehammer to my chest and took my breath. I knelt there with my hands on the ground for what felt like a really long time. I was crying and sobbing and trying not to scream. This just couldn't be real, could it? How could Chick be dead? How and who and why? This had to be some sort of awful nightmare. Any second I'd wake up and call Chick and he would answer and it would all be okay.

"No, no, no, no," I begged over and over.

Finally, after what seemed to be hours, I dragged myself to my feet and continued to the house. I looked up and discovered it hadn't been hours at all. The sun had scarcely moved. How was that possible? My entire life had been altered and hardly any time had passed. When I got to the edge of the patio, I stopped walking, bent over with my hands on my knees, took several deep breaths and tried to get a grip. I needed to put a game face on in case the kids were still in the house.

CHAPTER 3

I wiped my face on my shirttail and opened the French door off the patio. I entered the place that had been my refuge for my entire life—home. I could hear the soft babble of voices in the kitchen. I crossed the living and dining rooms to go toward those voices. I could only hear adult voices. No kids, thank you, God. I wasn't ready to face them. I had to work through some of my grief before I could talk to them. None of the kids had experienced death yet. Damn. They all loved Chick so much that talking to the herd was going to suck.

Everyone looked up as I entered the kitchen. The dogs milled around my feet. They were upset too. I scratched four doggie heads, and they all sat down and relaxed a bit. Only my sibs, Patrick, Brian, Dugan, Moira, Michelene, and Mommy, Daddy and YaYa were present. I thanked Mother Mary. I love my in-laws, mostly, but right now I needed blood kin. Funny how you draw strength from the people who have known you all of your life, know your faults, your weaknesses, understand your warped sense of humor and love you in spite of your warts. Not because they have to but because they want to. Nothing like family.

Daddy handed me a glass with two fingers of amber liquid. I took a sip and felt the warmth flow through my body down to my stomach, loosening knots in my muscles as it went.

"Ah, thanks," I mumbled.

Daddy topped off all our glasses.

I held mine in the air, "To Chick."

Everyone followed suit. "To Chick", they chorused and we all drank.

Sometime during that long night, Connell joined us. We drank, told stories, laughed, drank, cried, tried to one-up each other with tales and drank some more. Everybody had a Chick story.

YaYa said, "Chick got the nickname 'Chick' because Eve and Paul only had the one child and her mama always said that Eve followed him around and wanted to wrap him in gauze so that nothing bad would ever happen to him. She accused Eve of acting like a mama hen with only one baby chick."

We all laughed at that. I couldn't help but think that his mama had tried so hard to protect him, and still he hadn't lived to see 30. I held my glass up and Daddy refilled it.

"Thanks," I muttered.

"Amanda was a saint for taking that boy in and raising him." Mommy said sadly, her voice rough and scratchy from crying. "She was childless, he was parentless, and so it worked out pretty well. She raised him and loved him. Chick nursed her as she died from cancer. He told me once that he owed her. He was a good son to her and she was a good mother to him. God love them both." She took a healthy sip of her own drink, and I could see the tears glistening in her eyes.

"He was a good boy," Daddy agreed. Then he tightened his lips and shook his head. I knew he didn't trust himself to say more.

"How old was Chick when Eve and Paul were killed?" asked Moira. "Nine or ten?"

"Twelve," said Michelene flatly.

I thought it was time to lighten the mood.

"Chick spent so damn much time here, he was practically the eighth kid in our family." I paused and smiled. "He loved being here. I guess it was because there were lots of kids to play with. Only children just have no idea how good they have it. Guess the grass is always greener. Plus all ya'll didn't pick on him constantly like you did me, so he didn't get the full sibling experience."

"Oh my God," laughed Dugan. "You big titty baby! Every time we said no to you, you went crying to Mommy or Daddy!"

"Or YaYa," chimed in Moira.

"Et tu, Moira? You shaved my favorite teddy bear," I countered.

"We had to practice on something before we started shaving our own legs." Michelene was rather defensive.

"Do you remember when Chick and Connell took all of our Barbie dolls outside and shot them with the paintball guns?" asked Moira.

We all laughed at that memory. The boys had lined the dolls up on the edge of the patio and used them for target practice. They didn't realize that the shockwave from a paintball pellet at close range would practically blow the Barbies to smithereens.

Connell held up his drink. "In our defense," he said, "we did our best to restore the poor things to their original pristine condition."

"Ha, you mean you put the pieces back together, hosed them all off and then snuck them back into our rooms," said Michelene.

"Yeah, yeah, yeah, and you got some of the wrong heads on the wrong dolls and the wrong arms and legs too." Moira was laughing so hard that tears were running down her face.

"You can laugh," I said. "When I came into my room and saw my Barbies all lined up on my bed and Malibu Barbie had fish belly white legs with paint still in her hair, I almost had a seizure! I think I was scarred for life."

"Seizure?!" said Patrick, "You screamed the house down. I thought the place was on fire."

"I thought you were on fire!" YaYa commented.

Connell was smiling a sad smile. "We paid for it. We washed every window in this house, and then we cut yards all summer to get enough money to buy new dolls." He smiled a little wider at the memory.

"I still have nightmares," I said snottily. "I was only seven."

"Here drink more, you'll feel better." Brian poured me and himself another drink.

"Do you remember when we took all the umbrellas in the house and jumped off the barn to see if we could float to the ground like in *Mary Poppins*?" Connell asked.

"Oh, my God," said Patrick. "All the umbrellas turned inside out and we couldn't fix 'em!"

Brian laughed a deep, rich chuckle. "Oh yeah and we panicked because we knew that Mommy would have our hides."

"Right," said Connell. "You two yahoos conned me and Chick into jumping off the barn too. You told us how much fun it was. Like dummies we did it and you two bastards ran when you saw Mommy comin', and left us holdin' the bag!"

"Umbrellas," corrected Brian chortling.

Mommy laughed. "There they were, Connell on the ground with a destroyed umbrella and Chick on the roof just fixing to jump. All over the ground, every umbrella in the house lay in ruins."

"I thought you were gonna skin us alive. I haven't been as scared in my life before or since." Connell grinned at Mommy.

"I was wondering as I walked across the yard, how difficult it would be to put both of you up for adoption, after I jerked knots in your tails." Mommy threw back her head and laughed.

"Hey," said Patrick, "as I remember, we all paid dearly for that one. How'd you know we put Connell and Chick up to it? I know they didn't rat us out."

I smiled sweetly, "Because I told."

"And that," said Brian, "is why we always picked on you."

And so it went. The evening became morning, and it all had such a surreal feeling, like being in a Fellini movie. It didn't feel real. I kept hoping I would wake up to find it was all a bad dream. But when I looked at Connell's face, I knew it was real. Besides, I had never in my life had a dream this horrible. Finally, Mommy decided we needed food, so she made bacon and scrambled eggs. We all helped prepare the meal. About daylight I went to bed. Holmes, the King Charles spaniel, followed me. I motioned him into the bed and snuggled up close to him. I cried myself to sleep as the sun came up.

CHAPTER 4
MONDAY

"Oh Jesus!" I groaned, rubbing my head.

I ran a hand over my face, and it felt crusty from the salty tears I had cried into my pillow. My bedroom door opened, and my mother entered carrying a cup of coffee. The smell finished waking me. Holmes raised his canine head and thumped his tail at Mommy.

My mother was still an attractive woman despite the fact that she had birthed seven children, was pushing 65 and had been up for most of the night. Her hair is fading from blonde to a shade of white that I think she'll like, eventually. Her dark blue eyes, usually so full of fire and fun, were puffy and red-rimmed in the morning light. Even her scattering of freckles seemed muted. She stands about 5'4" and weighs in at 120. I can't understand how that's possible since she loves her chocolate so very much. Of course she's active— walks the dogs every day and is on just about every committee for every club in the entire county.

"Don't take the Lord's name in vain, Tessely Anne Marie Maher." She sat down on my bed and patted my shoulder. "How you holding up, darlin'?"

I closed my eyes and blew out a breath. "Je…gee, I guess, I don't know, I've never been in this place before. I'll make it, I just hate every minute of it. I keep waiting to wake up and find that this is all an awful dream."

She patted my shoulder again. "I know, so do I. I think I cried myself to sleep." She handed me the cup of coffee. "It's cold comfort that Chick is with Eve, Paul, Amanda and the Blessed Mother. But it is all the comfort we have."

She paused and peered at me. "Did you see him?" she asked.

I took a sip of coffee to give myself a moment to collect my thoughts. "Yes and talked to him, he doesn't know who or why. I needed more time and he just vanished." I took another sip and could feel the blessed caffeine coursing through my body.

"They do that, don't ya know. The dead have their own agenda. Ah, poor lad." Mommy's eyes filled with tears.

"Mommy, this was no accident. Somebody murdered our boy." I could feel the pain building up in me again. It threatened to suffocate me.

She pursed her lips, "I know, Connell called, that's what he thinks too."

"I'll give him a call," I promised.

Mommy nodded, kissed me on the cheek and left me to finish my coffee. I sat there on my bed for a time, the misery welling up in me. I had no frame of reference for such feelings. The last time I felt this overwhelmingly sad was when I was eight and our dog Daisy was run over by the milkman. This just couldn't be real. I cried some more for a while.

I sat, tears leaking, sipping my coffee and examined my room, searching for a little comfort. I loved the room. It's big with high ceilings and windows that open up overlooking the back yard. If I open a window and lean out, the valley is to my left. That view is great. I can sit on my bed and watch the sun go down. I felt safe as if this were my sanctuary. I sighed. It didn't feel so safe today, and I couldn't hide here from the awful events of yesterday and pretend that all was well. I could do that as a child—retreat to my own little world to heal from whatever thing was plaguing me. It was the one place that I could be alone. Despite the fact that ten of us had inhabited this house, we all respected a closed door. I wanted to pull the covers up over my head and hide like I did when I was little.

I saw my first spirit in that room. I was four. My father's mother died. She was so very old, and it was no shock to anyone, except me. Young children don't realize that people die, and they don't understand why it happens. Rarely do the adults take the time to explain it, or maybe they just don't know how to explain death to children. After the funeral, I came to my room and lay on my bed. I just could not understand what the priest had been talking about when he said that God wanted Grammy to come to heaven and be with Him. Didn't God have lots of people and angels and saints already there with Him? So why did He need my Grammy. I was really mad at God. And I was really sad and lonely for my Grammy. I am the youngest child in a huge family, and sometimes she was the only one who had time for me. She listened to me, and on many occasions she was my playmate.

That day as I lay there crying, I felt the bed indent as if a weight had been placed there. I looked up and Grammy was sitting on my bed. I instantly stopped crying, I was so happy.

"Grammy! Father Greene said you was in heaben with God and angels!" I exclaimed still sniffling.

She smiled and her face was wreathed in wrinkles. Her bright hazel eyes peered into mine. *"Not yet child, I'll be off shortly, but first I had to see you. I had to know that you'd be alright. I wanted to explain to you why I have to go."*

"Grammy, ya don't have t', you can stay here."

That made perfect sense to a four-year-old. She was here and so she would just stay with me.

"My darlin'," she said, *"folks get old and I've lived for so many years and my parts don't work so good anymore. I've been so very tired and cranky and now I get to go home to heaven where I can rest."*

I started to sniffle again. "Don't you wanna stay wif us? I'll be bery, bery good if ya stay. I'll learn how to make tea the way you likes it," I promised.

She smiled at me. *"Hearts only have a certain number of beats to 'em, love, and all of mine have been counted out and so it's time for me to go to my reward. Do you know that at this minute my old bones don't ache and you know how bad the arthritis plagued me! And look, no cane! My eyes are clear, I can see from here down to the river!"*

I stared at her. She did look different.

"Grammy, that's good. But, you're better, why don't ya ask God if ya can stay here?"

Grammy laughed and shook her head. *"Tess, my body is dead and my spirit needs to go to heaven."* She winked at me.

"In Sunday 'chool, Miz Jeanie told us that in heaben everythin' is perfect and peoples are happy all of the time and 'rounded by all good things. Is that true?"

"Yes, darlin', it's true."

"Is there food there?" I asked, with my chin trembling.

"Yes, darlin', every kind of good food you could want."

I was still not ready to concede. "You could be 'rounded by us and we'd all be good, even the boys will be good if you stay," I pleaded.

She smiled at me. *"You're always good, sweetlin'. But my work here is done and now I go on. It'll be fine, you'll see. You'll all do well and I'll be watching you from heaven. I'll see it all from there. I'll come back to check on you often."*

We talked for what seemed like a good long time. I cried and she comforted. Finally, she sent me downstairs to dinner. Later that night when my mother tucked me into bed, I told her about Grammy and about heaven.

She smiled and patted me. "That's a wonderful gift, Tessely. You know that Grammy is fine and she'll be watching you." I believe that she believed me.

I live in the same house I grew up in with my parents and my mother's mother, despite the fact that I am in my twenties. I sleep in the same room I have always slept in. The décor has changed over the years—no more posters of rock and roll gods, or *Star Wars* heroes. The walls have been a variety of colors, from magenta to bright pink, just like my hair. I went through a phase where everything I owned was the same color. My parents never questioned my color choices, hair or walls or clothes. They're smart and always knew when to pick their battles. With seven kids, you had better know when to fight battles and when to let them lie. Fortunately for me, they had learned plenty on the six sibs that preceded me.

I think my tastes have improved, somewhat. At least I believe the décor is better. The walls have a faux finish in shades of blue and purple, lace curtains, Van Gogh on the walls, distressed white furniture and a state of the art surround sound. It's peaceful, restful. I continue to live in my parent's home because I want to: it's comfortable, my parents don't intrude, we take turns cooking, my grandmother amuses me, there's a pool and I never have to drink alone (I've heard that's bad for you). All of my sibs, except Connell, are married. I'm not, and I see no reason to leave home. When I find someone who intrigues me enough to want to have wild monkey sex with, I go to his place. Simple.

The only reason Connell doesn't live with us too is because he thinks it might look bad for the sheriff of the county to live with his parents. He's probably right.

My mother's mother, YaYa, sleeps at the other end of the upstairs. She swears she will, in spite of the stairs, until she's carried from the house feet first. I believe her. She's still pretty spry despite her years, so I think that it might be a while before that happens. Most days the stairs barely slow her down.

I forced myself to get out of bed, and I threw on some running clothes. As I laced my shoes up, I found myself hoping that the endorphin rush from running would blow some of the pain and anguish out of my head and let a little clarity in. I pulled my hair into a rough ponytail and headed down the back stairs, which are right outside of my room. At the bottom of the stairs you can turn right and go into the kitchen or turn left and go out the door into the back yard.

I called out, "Going for a run," and was descended upon by dogs.

They always think they get to go too. On days when I run on our road I take them. They're well behaved, don't need a leash and run in the ditch, not in the street.

"Come on then," I said and we all went out.

I stopped and did some stretches to loosen my muscles and get some of the kinks out of my spine. I pulled until it hurt and felt better for it. It was chilly, but running always fixed that. I started down the driveway and hit the road in short order. Running makes me feel accomplished, strong and athletic. In truth I don't run for any of those silly health reasons. I run because it makes me feel good, not because it's good for me. I run so that I can eat whatever I want to eat. I run because of the runner's high. I run because I like it. Running lets me be alone in my head, so I can think and go through the crap that needs to be sorted out. Most of the time.

All I could think of that day was Chick. I kept seeing him fall from the tree, kept seeing him lying on the ground broken and bleeding. I ran harder, pounding the pavement, trying to clear my head and purge my grief. The scene kept playing over and over in my head like a movie clip on a loop. I wondered if it would ever stop.

The road that leads to the house is a county road, and there's not a lot of traffic so I never have to worry about dodging cars. Every now and then a neighbor drives by and waves. They smile at me, but I know they think I'm odd because I run for fun not because something's chasing me. Most times I run on the trails by the river. I really enjoy it. It's beautiful there. I can hear the water rushing by, the birds singing, and I truly feel that I'm in a world of my own. That morning I needed to get my run in and get to work. I didn't have time for scenery. I ran my usual three miles and headed home. I walked around in circles in the shaded side yard to cool down, and then I did more stretches. I felt good. The dogs became bored with me and took off after a rabbit.

"Hi, honey, I'm home," I yelled as I came in to the kitchen.

I snagged a travel bottle of cold water from the fridge. Mommy and Daddy are serious about the carbon footprint business, so we have an alkaline water machine and we fill travel bottles with water and keep them in the fridge. It works. You just have to remember to bring the bottle home, wash it and refill it. We have a lot of bottles, mainly because I forget to bring them home.

I headed up the steps. I really wanted to talk to Connell first, but I needed a shower to wash away the sweat of the run and some of the trauma from yesterday. I stripped off my smelly clothes and turned on the water. I showered until the bathroom was filled with steam. I washed the grime off with the delightful lavender scrub I favored. None of that helped, and so I just leaned against the wall and let the spray beat down on me while my hot tears mixed with the hot water.

After an eternity, I decided I shouldn't use up all the hot water in the world, so I shut off the faucets, reached for a towel and climbed out of the tub. The mirror was so steamed up I had to use my towel to wipe it off so I could see to brush my teeth. I caught sight of myself as I wiped the steam away. *Not too bad,* I said to my reflection.

My face is oval-shaped with a dimple on the right side and a small beauty mark over my mouth on the left side. I have wide spaced, almond shaped, two-toned blue eyes. But that morning they were puffy and red like my mother's, and the color was washed out and watery. My rather generous lips were turned down in a frown. I tried smiling at myself but couldn't pull it off. I wondered if I'd ever smile again.

I looked at my nose objectively. It's a rather small nose. As a matter of fact, an ex-boyfriend had once teased me that he didn't understand how a full grown human could get enough air with a nose that small. Could explain why he's an "ex." I like to think that my nose is delicate, although I'll be the first to admit that I don't have much of a profile. My wet, dripping hair hung around my face like rat tails. When it dried it would be strawberry blond and straight as a stick.

I finished with self-examination in the mirror and used the towel to wrap up my drippy hair in a turban. I worked my way through the routine of teeth, moisturizer and a bit of makeup on autopilot since my mind was on Chick. I decided that no amount of concealer was going to hide the outstanding bags under my eyes, so I didn't bother. I wandered back into the bedroom and called Connell while I was towel-drying my hair. He answered on the third ring.

"Simpson County, Sheriff Maher speaking."

He sounded very awake and very official. I admit I was impressed.

I put him on speaker, "Tess."

I heard him draw breath, "Hey, baby sis, how ya doing"?

I grimaced at the phone, "Real shitty, you?"

He replied, "Yep, pretty shitty. You wanna know what I know." It was a statement not a question.

"Yep."

I pulled clothes from the closet and struggled into them.

"This sucks, baby girl, so brace yourself. Old Doc Kochtitzky had a look at him as a prelim to give me an idea of what I was in the middle of here. Chick was shot one time, most likely long range. Doc thinks the shot severed his spinal column between the third and fourth thoracic vertebra. The bullet probably hit his heart on the way out. Poor bastard never knew what hit him. Maybe that's the best way to go, but damn, I want a chance to at least try and take the other son-of-a-bitch out with me!"

I just stopped moving for a second and closed my eyes. Christ, I was miserable. I tucked my Bluetooth device behind my ear so I could finish dressing. I headed down the back stairs, still listening to Connell, but I needed more coffee. One cup would not do for today. Mommy, Daddy and YaYa were in the kitchen.

"He was probably dead before he hit the ground, so no pain." I said to Connell. *Thank you God*, I said in my brain. I waved to the kitchen people as I entered and pointed to my ear.

"Connell?" Mommy mouthed.

I nodded, took my cup into the butler's pantry and refilled it from the pot.

"We recovered eleven sketches of you, the bindings of a portfolio that looks like it broke on impact, various pencils and chalks all over the ground. They fanned out away from the tree toward the house." He paused and I added cream to the cup. "Confirms your theory that he was shot from the opposite side of the road. Also the angle of the path of the bullet agrees that he was shot from a higher elevation. That's all preliminary of course."

"Did you know he sketched?" I asked.

Connell chuckled. "Yep, did you?"

"I did, but he didn't brag about it, so I don't know if anyone else knows."

"True, I think he thought people would make fun of him and think he was wasting his time." Connell sighed.

"How'd he get there?' I asked, stirring my coffee.

"His car was about a hundred yards up Log Mill Road around that blind curve, so it wasn't in sight of the crime scene."

His voice faltered on those last two words.

"We figured the trajectory right to that big oak across the road and up the rise," he continued.

I sat down at the kitchen table and Daddy passed me toast, YaYa passed the blackberry jam.

"What else?" I asked.

"We didn't find much at the sniper site. This asshole was real careful. The bark was scraped in a few places, and the grass was bent around the base of the tree. I don't even know the caliber."

I blew out breath, "It sounded like a thirty-aught-six to me. Have you slept?"

He was silent for a moment. "No."

I took a bite of toast. "Where's Chick?" I knew I didn't want to hear the answer but I had to ask anyway.

"He's in the city. They're gonna autopsy."

"Oh God," I breathed. My stomach clenched, and I had to swallow tears with the toast. The thought of Chick lying out on a stainless steel table with the big "Y" cut in his chest almost overwhelmed me.

"There's more. The state boys are gonna come have a look. Seems like they think that our little Podunk burg can't handle real crime. They kinda insisted that I invite them to the party. Technically, I could've turned 'em down, ya know, but I don't want to appear uncooperative." He sounded irritated.

"They probably don't think you can get your bullet out of your pocket and into your gun all by yourself," I quipped.

"Plus, they want to talk to you as a person of interest."

There was a very pregnant pause. I almost choked on toast crumbs. I shook my head to clear it. "What? Oh, because of the drawings. Okay, I guess that makes sense. So what do I need to do?"

He replied, "Go to work. I'll come by later and get your statement."

Great, that was the last thing I wanted to do—play it all out in my mind all over again.

"Right then, see ya later, love ya, bye," I said.

"See ya later, love ya, bye," he answered and hung up.

I hit the button on the Bluetooth to disconnect, set down my toast and rested my head in my hands for a few seconds. I could feel tears welling up again. No one spoke while I got a grip on myself.

"We know about as much as we did yesterday. Chick's been sent to Nashville, nothing at the sniper scene, the state cops think we're too stupid to pour piss out of a boot with the directions on the heel and I'm a person of interest."

I slathered blackberry jam on my toast and nibbled at it, giving my parents and my grandmother time to absorb this news. They all stopped what they were doing to stare at me.

"Glad I put my hearing aid in this morning!" YaYa said.

"Do you need a lawyer?" asked Daddy.

"A lawyer! Why in God's name would she need a lawyer? She hasn't done anything wrong!" declared Mommy.

"Lots of innocent people in jail!" YaYa said.

I held up both hands and waved my toast at them to forestall any more speculation. "I do not need, at this time, a lawyer. I need to finish my toast, have another cup of coffee and go to my office, do some diggin', and try to figure out who the hell murdered Chick."

Daddy reached across the table and touched my hand. "You'd do well to remember that someone did murder Chick. Be careful."

I took a deep breath, "I'll take the Beretta."

"Take a back-up clip," Daddy said.

CHAPTER 5

I drive a little red Jeep Wrangler Sport with a rag top. It's my pride and joy. It was waiting for me in the driveway. I love my Jeep and usually the sight of it made me smile. But that day it didn't fill my heart with joy as it usually did. That day not even Brad Pitt sitting in the front seat would have filled my heart with joy. It was another perfect day as if nothing horrible had happened. It seemed impossible that the sun was shining and the sky filled with white, fluffy clouds. How could it not be rainy and overcast? How could there be no storm with lightning and thunder. To me it did seem darker than yesterday, the sun not as bright and the clouds less fluffy. I knew that was just my mood. Still it didn't seem fair that the sun could shine as if nothing terrible had transpired.

I decided that a ride with the top down in the Jeep would be good. Maybe the wind would blow the picture of Chick on the autopsy table with his organs being weighed on a scale out of my head. Shit!

The ride to town was only about fifteen minutes long, but it was fifteen minutes with the wind in my hair, my mind clicking away and no one talking to me. Who the hell would want to murder Chick? Everyone, and I mean everyone, loved him. He didn't have much debt—at least I didn't think so. The garage he owned was paid for from the insurance money he inherited from his parents and his aunt. I thought the building belonged to him too. I'd check the county property records to confirm it. He didn't have bad vices besides bad jokes, goofy pranks and drinking with my brothers. He didn't date much, and I figured I knew the reason for that, so no exes who would want to see him dead. There wasn't even a short list of suspects for his murder. Still the shot was too perfect to have been an accident. It felt deliberate. Just because Chick had no idea who might have wanted him dead, I was sure it was murder. That meant that someone had a reason to kill him. There are only a few reasons for a person to commit murder: greed, revenge, jealousy, love and to cover up another crime. Allow me to add crazy. You can never rule out crazy.

I parked in front of my building, a small brick office building off the town square. The building was old—probably built at the turn of the last century. It had been rehabbed sometime in the '80s, and the job had been a good one. The contractors refinished the original wood floors. The huge windows, wide hallways and high ceilings had been retained. The floors had been leveled, air conditioning units had been added on the roof and the plumbing had been updated. All the offices were roomy and well lit from the big windows. It's a solid and attractive building that I share with seven other businesses.

On my way in the door I noticed those huge windows needed cleaning, but I didn't care. The sign on my office door did not inspire me. The sight of "Maher Investigations" fell flat. I unlocked the door—no one home yet, but I was early. Juliet Miller, aka Jewels, my girl Friday was usually in by 9:00. I checked my watch. It was only 8:15. That gave me some more alone time. I walked through the reception area and into my office, turned on the computer and left it to warm up while I made coffee. I figured the first place I should look was Chick's financials. Always follow the money to get the answers you are hunting.

I hacked into the bank records to see how much or how little money he had. Too easy really. This is of course, illegal, so do not try it at home. Usually it's a much harder task, but SunGold Bank was locally owned with about ten branches all told. It was an old-school organization, and there are not a lot of safeguards to keep people like me out. The thought hit me that maybe I needed to offer my services to them to update and protect all access to their system. I made a note to myself to do that very thing.

It was simple to get into the bank and find Chick's account. I opened his account easily enough since I had the password, "Stinks2". He used it for everything. Within a short ten minutes from the start of my quest, the information that I needed was displayed on the screen in front of me. Sure enough, I was right. Just the regular day-to-day running of a well-established and well-off business.

Donnelly Repair and Restoration saw to the needs of the locals: lube jobs, oil changes, and bigger jobs too. The garage could handle any repair. Chick had two boys that worked for him: Sammy Jensen and Billy Jones. Their paycheck info was there too. I swear, between the three of them they could fix a rainy day. In their spare time they rebuilt old muscle cars. Some they raced and some they sold to collectors too lazy to do their own work. Chick himself owned a black and gold '78 Trans Am as his personal vehicle—think *Smoky and the Bandit*.

I poked around to see if I could find more money or assets or big payments in or out. There was a savings account with $200,000 and change in it. Since I saw no monthly payment, Chick appeared to own the building his garage was in. I also knew he owned his house. I could get into the property records when I finished with the bank to make sure I was correct. At that point I figured Chick was worth more than 500,000 bucks. Not bad for an old country boy. None of the money was new. He had built on what his parents and his aunt had left for him. So no big buck payoffs that I could find, no gambling debts, no large amount of money owed. At least that was something I could share with my big brother when he showed up.

I had just started to back out of the bank records when I heard the office door open.

"Tess," Jewels called out.

"On the computer," I answered. "Coffee's made."

I heard her rattling around with coffee stuff.

She semi-yelled at me, "It's all over town, I heard at the hardware this morning. What the hell?"

She wandered in to my office with mugs of coffee. She handed me one that held the perfect amount of cream. Jewels was indeed a jewel: smart, competent, tough, a computer whiz and an arm twister when it came to getting the money people owed us. Cute as a button, big brown eyes, and a little turned up nose, she stands about 5'6" and is slim and trim. She's two years younger than me, usually looks five years younger than me and is happily married to her high school sweetheart. Today she looked sad. She loved Chick just like everyone else in town—everyone except for one son-of-a-bitch with a gun.

"God you look horrible, have you had any sleep? I'm so sorry, Tess. What happened?" she asked.

She hugged me then sat down opposite me. I told her everything that had happened and everything I knew. That didn't take long. My coffee wasn't even cold by the time I finished my narrative.

Jewels shook her head which set her shoulder-length, curly, brunette hair swinging back and forth. "So no mystery money anywhere, no debt, nothing?"

"Nothing, yet. Think I'll call Buzzy and see if he'll tell me anything."

Richard "Buzz" Aldrin is the main lawyer in town. He shares the famous name and got the nickname as a result when he was a small child. He might not be a rocket scientist but he was a brainiac. Everyone from my dad to the local butcher used him for legal work. He was also a prick.

"Hmm, Buzzy's always tight as a tomb." Jewel's dark brown eyes grew round. "Oops, bad choice of words."

I shot her a look and she vacated the office. Good thing too. That way I could tell Buzzy that I was alone and it would be the truth. I finished logging off the bank site before I reached for the phone.

I was sure that Buzzy just didn't like me. He always seemed stiff and formal around me. He barely spoke to me unless he was forced to do so by social circumstances. I'd even seen him duck the opposite way when he spotted me coming. I tell you it could give a girl a complex.

I have it on good authority that Buzzy was fun, told jokes, and could carry on a conversation on just about any subject. He just hasn't proven it to me. I wondered if he still held it against me because I busted him in the nose on the playground when we were in sixth grade. That happened as a result of an argument over a supposedly missed base during a pickup baseball game at recess. He said I missed third. I argued that I had not missed third base but had touched it as I made my dash to home plate. Buzzy grabbed me by one arm and started jerking me down the third base line. I lost my footing and landed on my ass. He continued to drag me along, and I just knew that everyone on the schoolyard could see my underwear as my legs were splayed apart and my uniform skirt was all rucked up. To add insult to injury I was wearing my Wonder Woman underwear that day. I thought I would die from humiliation.

When we finally got to third base he yanked me to my feet and told me to stand on third until the next batter could bring me in to home. I was so mad and so embarrassed that I pasted him right in the nose, in front of most of the sixth grade including Ellen Warner. He was sweet on her. I think she was traumatized by the blood because she started puking. In seconds everyone was yelling and then the nuns showed up.

Sister Mary Assumpta arrived on the scene and surveyed the

situation. Buzzy was bleeding and yelling, Ellen was puking and I was standing right in the middle of it all. She put her hands on her hips and got as pissed off as only a six-foot-tall Dominican nun can get over fighting on the playground and the blood and the puke. She was tore up, trust me. There were phone calls home, Mommy came to school, I got grounded. Which seemed unfair to me since I hadn't started the trouble, but that argument got me nowhere with Mommy or Sister Assumpta. At that point in my development Mommy was still trying to make me into a lady with good manners. It seemed that ladies with good manners do not punch other children on the playground during recess, even if the punchee deserved it.

Buzzy got teased for years over the incident, and for a short while, his nickname became Third Base. Anyway, that episode might explain the attitude. But really that was forever ago. I hadn't punched anyone in years. Besides, he married Ellen and they have two beautiful kids, so he shouldn't hold a grudge.

I put on my best and most friendly phone voice, slapped a smile on my face and dialed. I read somewhere that people can literally tell if you're smiling over the phone, and they're inclined to be friendlier in that case. I needed all the friendly I could get. MarySue Martin answered as I knew she would. I can't stand MarySue and it is so mutual.

"Hey, MarySue," I said so sweetly that she was in danger of developing diabetes. "Tess Maher. Is Buzzy around?"

There was a pause of a few seconds then a cold answer. "Mr. Aldrin is in. Let me check and see if he's available to *you*."

She made "you" sound synonymous with dog poop. I started to thank her anyway and got Muzak in my ear. I sat and hummed along to the instrumental version of "Norwegian Wood" for a few minutes, and then Buzzy clicked on.

"Good morning, Tess," he said stiffly. Of course.

I smiled. "Hey, Buzz, how're you today?"

He cleared his throat, "I cannot tell you anything about the Charles Kincaid Donnelly will or his estate."

Huh, well, well, well. "Buzzy, it happened right in front of me. Someone murdered Chick and I mean to find out who and I don't give a damn who I have to roll over to do it." Dammit I lost my temper. Crap, crap, crap.

"I understand how you must feel, but I have client confidentiality to protect." Then he said in a haughty manner, "And it's *whom*."

I sat for a second blinking like a frog in a hail storm but wisely decided to ignore that comment.

"He's dead. Does the client confidentiality thing still hold?"

"Yes, it does. By the way, since he is dead, and there is no next of kin, who has hired you to work this case?"

Damn, he had me. "No one has hired me, Buzzy. He was my friend and I'm workin' this on my own."

"In that case, get a court order and we can talk. Good day."

The line clicked dead in my ear.

"He hung up on me! That weasel! He freakin' HUNG UP ON ME!" I slammed the phone receiver into the cradle—several times. "And who the hell says 'good day' anyway? Besides Paul freakin' Harvey!"

Jewels came in with the coffeepot and cream. "I take it from the phone slammin', the look on your face and the yellin', that the conversation did not go well."

I held up my cup for a refill.

"Buzzy Aldrin is a sanctimonious, tin-plated, obsessive-compulsive, anal-retentive little bastard with delusions of godhood! He could tell me stuff. Who's gonna get mad at him? I guess I could ask Chick if it was okay for Buzzy to give me info, if I could find him, but that might not hold up in court. And he hung up on me right after he said 'good day'! Bastard! How the hell am I gonna have a good day when people who could help me hang up on me?? Why does he hate me?"

Jewels laughed, "Could be that you broke his nose in front of the entire sixth grade class and brought down the ire of Sister Mary Assumpta on you both."

"I didn't break his freakin' nose! I only made it bleed and it swelled a little."

I looked at Jewels and she was giving me that "Really?" look.

"Okay and both his eyes turned black," I admitted. "But still…"

"Calm down, you're gonna get a case of the hives. Your brother can get a court order in nothing flat, ya know. To further answer your initial question, Buzzy hates you 'cuz his nose is crooked."

I shook my head in denial. "His nose is not crooked! His ugly, freckled-face, carrot-top, redhead is crooked! I just wanted to get ahead of this thing, the TBI boys will hit town before lunch, and they'll take the investigation away from Connell and me, since I am a person of interest."

Now I was sounding pouty.

"WHAT?!" Jewels practically shouted at me. Her brown eyes were huge. She set the coffeepot, her cup and herself down as she glared at me.

"Oh yeah, I forgot that part because really, it's stupid and not important."

She started to open her mouth.

"Hang on, I'm telling."

So I explained about the eleven drawings of me and the whole nine yards at the crime scene. When I was done she just sat with her mouth open.

"Damn, girl. That man has been in love with you all of these years, it's tragic."

I rolled my eyes at her. "I know it's sad, but it woulda never worked out for us. Too many people had too much of a vested interest in seeing us be all happily-ever-after and it was just too much damn pressure. What if we had gotten together and then broken up? Everyone would've been disappointed if we'd failed. They might've chosen sides. That would've been a disaster, for everyone, for me, for Chick, for my whole entire family, maybe this whole town. Chick and I had that conversation and revisited it many time over the years. I loved him, he loved me and we did it from opposite ends of the couch, because it was safe." Holy Crap! I was crying again. "At least I thought we'd settled it, but he said we always just danced around it."

She reached over and patted my hand. "Honey, I'm so sorry."

The phone rang and we both jumped. Damn!

Jewels answered the phone, "Maher Investigations. How may I help you?" She sounded so professional. "Oh, hey Connell. Sure I'll tell her." She hung up. "Your brother's on his way. He sounds miserable."

"Would you make more coffee, please?"

She got up, taking the pot with her as she exited.

About a minute later I heard the door open and the unmistakable sound of my brother's boots walking across the floor.

"Hey, Connell," said Jewels, "I'm so sorry about Chick."

I knew she was hugging him. Because that's what you say and do when someone dies. You say "I am sorry for your loss" or "I'm so sorry" or "What can I do for you?" and you hug. You do not spout a lot of bullshit about heaven, and better places, and Jesus taking him home. God I HATE that shit and there'd be a week or more of well-meaning people talking such drivel. Not that I don't believe in heaven or that I hate Jesus. But Jesus had nothing to do with this, some bastard with a gun did, and to imply that this was somehow the will of God would just make me crazy. Besides, the aftermath of a death is not about the dead guy. It is about the people he left behind, the ones that now had an enormous hole torn in their lives. Boy, I was in a pissy mood.

"Hey, sis, you look like hell."

I laughed in spite of my crummy mood. "And you look like a mule kicked you, Sheriff. You eat yet?"

Connell looked confused for a second as if he had forgotten what food was, and then he shook his head. "Not yet."

I could hear Jewels on the phone out front. She was ordering breakfast from Tilly's. Good girl. That piece of toast and dab of jam was starting to seem like a long time ago.

"Okay, Sheriff, let's get this over with," I sighed.

Connell had taken my statement by the time breakfast arrived. Tilly Holsmer, herself, made the delivery.

"Hey, Jewels honey," she said as she entered the office.

She swept into my office and put the tray down on the desk. Then she reached over and hugged Connell. When Tilly hugged you, well brother, you knew you'd been hugged. Tilly is about 5'10", weighs in somewhere around 300 pounds and has amazing padding, if you know what I mean. Her coal black hair is always pulled up in a ponytail, there's lots of makeup, and she is perpetually dressed in a 50's coffee shop waitress uniform. I hear tell she sleeps in it. She's the chief confessor, counselor, ass kicker, matchmaker, fundraiser, cheerleader, comfort giver and all around town mom in our little burg. Her meat-and-three serves the most wonderful food in the county—maybe the entire state. She must be a hundred, but don't tell her I said so. She let go of my brother and I was next. I stood up to receive my hug. I felt my spine pop.

"Now, you babies, I'm just s' sorry 'bout Chick. I loved him and I know ya'll did too. He was always such a good boy and takin' care of his aunt Amanda when she was dyin' with the cancer, *mmm mmm mmm*. God just don't make 'em no better'n Chick Donnelly." She paused and sniffed. "If there's anythin' I can do, ya'll let me know." She smiled and I almost lost it.

"Yes, ma'am, you know we will," I said.

She patted my cheek. "I'll get Jeff and the girls working on food for the funeral home."

She was referring to her staff. Jefferson Davis Hinkle was about three days older than dirt, a long tall drink of water with dark black skin and a ready laugh. Jeff was married with six kids, and he had a tattoo on his left arm of an anchor from when he was in the Navy. It fascinated me when I was a kid. He was the only person I knew back then who had a real tattoo. My brothers swear that he has a naked dancing girl on the bicep of his left arm, and he can make her dance by flexing his muscles. He never showed that to us girls. Besides being fascinating, he's a great cook. His onion rings would make you sell your soul to the devil. I prayed that he had the recipe written down and stashed somewhere, so he didn't take it to his grave with him.

"Thanks, Tilly, that'd be wonderful. You know it might be a while until we can have the service?" Connell asked.

She turned and patted my brother. "I know. I also know that lots of folks'll be bringin' food, but you know I wanna do him proud. Besides you're gonna be needin' food out to your house too. "

With that she was gone.

"Damn," my brother said, "that woman is like a force of nature."

I flipped back the cloth napkin that covered the tray to reveal covered plates of eggs, bacon, biscuits, hash browns, gravy and a little pot of blackberry jam—all on real plates with real silverware. Nothing plastic from Tilly's.

"Do you reckon she understood that it might be a few days till there's a proper lying out," I said.

Jewels stuck her head in the office. "Yum, I hope there is enough for three."

There certainly was more than enough, and I motioned for her to have a seat. We ate mostly in silence just taking comfort from the delicious food and full bellies.

Finally, I asked, "Reckon what the TBI'll do once they get to town—besides take over?"

"Hell," said Connell as he wiped the blackberry jam off his face, "they'll do the same things we'd do—look to see if there's a money trail, any arguments, old lovers, grudges, recent fights—the usual. But they'll do it with big city style."

I scoffed, "How can they hope to come in here and do a better job than the locals who know everyone involved?"

"In the city, they start cold. Not everyone knows everyone. They look for clues and follow them to the logical conclusion," Connell said.

"And they get to throw their weight around and show us up with the fancy toys they'll be bringing," Jewels chimed in.

"As a bonus they get to question the sister of the local sheriff, which should spice things up for them," I grumbled.

The meal had lifted my spirits. I found that I didn't dread that prospect quite as much as I had before. I still didn't relish the idea. No one likes to be questioned in an investigation. I also figured they would not be nice to me, but with Tilly's breakfast in my belly, I knew I could face anything.

"Bring 'em on." I made little prizefighter punches into the air.

As if to conjure them, Connell's radio crackled.

"Connell, there's some TBI agents here'n the office t' see you," Mavis Mays declared.

Mavis, the county dispatcher, is just a bit younger than God and had worked at the sheriff's office since we were a territory. She is a tough, crusty old bird who doesn't take shit from anyone. She's also damn hard to impress. The TBI agents would not enjoy cooling their heels as she glared at them over the top of her purple-framed, half-moon glasses. Mavis Mays could glare like nobody's business. She'd raised six sons and could stop stampeding Angus cattle with one look. The agents would not be offered coffee either. Mavis was only hospitable to folks to whom she wanted to be hospitable. I was sure the TBI agents didn't fall into the correct category.

Connell stood up and leaned over to kiss me. "Well, time to go see the big boys. I'll let you know if they want to interview you here or at the office. My guess would be the office—more intimidating, ya know. Either of you want that last piece of bacon?"

Jewels and I shook our heads.

"Hey, I checked Chick's financials. It all looks ship shape and above board. I called Buzzy too and he blew me off. Looks like you'll have to get a warrant," I said.

"And so I will."

Connell winked and sauntered out chewing on the bacon strip. Jewels refilled our coffee cups while I stacked the dirty dishes back on the tray.

CHAPTER 6

I got the call of doom about twenty minutes later. The TBI agents did indeed want to see me at the sheriff's office. I sighed as I hung up the phone. Jewels was standing in my door.

"Put a little more makeup on. You've cried most of what you were wearing off. You look pale and wane and streaky. You don't want 'em to think you're nervous or scared of 'em."

She went back out front. I retrieved my emergency makeup bag from my bottom desk drawer and set about trying to restore order. I was sure I had raccoon eyes. I used a little bit of shadow, a little bit of blush, and lip gloss with a little bit of color. I didn't want to look like I was trying too hard to impress the boys from the big city. Five minutes later I called her back in for a critique. She came to my office door.

"How do I look?" I asked.

Jewels looked me over. "I hereby deem you fit to meet the city-slickers." She smiled and winked at me.

"I wish I hadn't quit smoking," I grumbled as I left.

There were butterflies the size of Rottweilers duking it out in my stomach. Maybe that big breakfast hadn't been such a good idea after all. I took a couple of deep breaths to ground before I went in the door. Mavis was at her desk. I nodded to her.

"Hey, Miss Mavis, how you doing today?" I asked, trying to sound cheerful.

She was already looking in my direction. She was such a tiny thing that she practically needed a booster seat to see over the counter she perched behind. With her grey hair pulled into a tight bun, she looked stern and formidable despite her diminutive size. She peered over her glasses, frowned, and a million more wrinkles showed up.

"It's a sad day, girl."

She lowered her voice to a whisper. "Them TBIs gonna try and give you a hard time. Heard 'em talking. They think you got somethin' to do with this awful thang. They're wantin' to solve this and get back to the city, PDQ." She winked and smiled at her eavesdropping skills. "Don't take no guff now."

I smiled back. "I'll be fine. They in Connell's office?"

She nodded and I wandered down the familiar hallway. It hadn't been painted in a coon's age. Or maybe it was just painted the same shade of sucky slime green every time, and I only thought it hadn't been painted in years. Maybe the county got a deal on that color because no one else wanted it. Or maybe someone actually made "Institutional Suck Bile Green for County Buildings" paint color. Something to think about—better than thinking about what was waiting on me.

The door to Connell's office was partially open, Connell was standing at his desk, and two people were sitting in the chairs in front of his desk. Hmmm…a man and women, I hadn't expected that. I wondered which one was the good cop and which was the bad cop. I feared I'd find out shortly. I pushed the door open and stepped inside.

"Agents," Connell said, "this is Tessely Maher, my sister."

I prayed my hands were not sweating as I reached out to shake while Connell introduced the agents.

"Tess, Agents Diane Lyle and Phillip Boyd."

We all murmured "how do" to each other—not very sincere ones either. Both agents had a bone grinding handshake. Man, I hate it when people do that. It's a power play to show you who's boss, how strong they are and so forth. That made me immediately dislike them. Not that I was inclined to love them anyway, I felt like they were intruding on us as if we weren't competent.

"Do you want me present for the interviews, Agents?" Connell asked.

My brother hadn't moved from his side of his desk.

Boyd spoke up first, "No, Sheriff, this might go smoother if just the three of us are present."

Lyle nodded her head in agreement as she eyed me up and down. I sure wanted to hear her voice. It would help me judge how she intended to treat me. I examined her while she and the men did a little verbal sparring. Have you ever walked into a room and met a person for the first time that you immediately took a dislike to for no discernible reason? That was how I felt about Lyle. She made the hair on the back of my freakin' neck stand up. She put me in mind of an unfriendly pit bull.

She was dressed in a dark pantsuit with an unflattering cut, modest heels and no jewelry other than a unisex wristwatch with a faux leather band. Her unattractive hair was an oddly colored reddish brown, and she had pulled it back into a severe and painful looking chignon. I bet she had a hell of a headache at the end of the day. I knew she was trying to look professional and be one of the boys, so to speak. All she had succeeded in doing was to look "frumpilocious". That wasn't the problem. I'd seen ugly before. I could practically feel dislike and resentment rolling off her in waves. I thought she had prejudged me. She just set my bells and whistles off, big time. I turned my attention back to the conversation at hand.

Connell said, "That's fine. I'll go ahead and start the machine so that my office can have its own copy of the interview." He reached into his desk, pulled out a digital recorder, placed it on his desk and turned it on.

Agent Lyle looked at the recorder like it was a dead rat lying on the desk and then looked at my brother with narrowed eyes. "Don't trust us, Sheriff? Or is this because the interviewee is your sister?"

So that was how she was going to play it—fair enough. Her role was to be the antagonist in the drama. I was surprised she tipped her hand so soon into the game. Her question confirmed my gut on her. She was going to be a bitch.

Connell smiled his poker smile—the one that made you wonder what he had in his hand. "Not a matter of trust, Agent Lyle."

Well you could take that anyway you wanted. He walked out the door. Add to the caution, "never get involved in a land war in Asia", this one: never play poker with my brother for anything other than matchsticks. It always ends in tears.

Agent Boyd pulled up a third chair for me and reclaimed his seat. Then he and Agent Lyle turned their chairs to face me. That position made me feel like they were closing ranks against me. It was supposed to make me feel that way—intimidating, you know. Agent Boyd pulled out his own digital recorder. It was much fancier than Connell's machine too. He snapped it on and placed it on the desk. He spoke the date, investigation numbers, my name and both of their names, and then got right to business.

"What was your relationship with the victim?" he asked in a

severe tone.

"We were childhood friends," I answered calmly.

"Was there a physical relationship between the two of you, now or ever?" asked Lyle.

"No! He was like a brother to me, one of my best and oldest friends, but nothing romantic."

Thinking of Chick made me want to cry. Never cry in front of the TBI. Another good rule.

"And yet there were eleven drawings of you in various poses found with his body. One was in process of being drawn, so there's no doubt about who the artist was. Did you pose for him? Did you know he was drawing you? Why do you think he was drawing you? To what purpose do you suppose he made these drawings? Did you take his stalking as a threat?"

Lyle ticked her questions off without a pause for breath in between. Wow, I disliked the woman more by the moment, and it seemed to be extremely mutual. What the hell was her deal? I was trying to be cooperative. I felt like I was reacting to her antagonism, but maybe she was reacting to mine. All I knew was, I needed to be careful in giving these people the answers, so I took a moment.

"No. No. I do not know. I do not know. I do not know. I was not threatened by Chick."

"I don't think you're being cooperative, Ms. Maher," said Boyd. He leaned forward in the chair to get closer to me, looking me straight in the eye, his body language saying he was concentrating on only me. Goody. I just love being the center of attention.

I looked him straight in the eye and copied his body language. "I answered all of the questions, even the redundant ones. How am I not cooperating?"

"Come on Ms. Maher," Lyle said sharply. "The man died with eleven pictures of you in his possession. Pictures he had drawn over a period of time. He was obviously over the moon for you, and you just as obviously were not interested in him. Now you give us these yes and no answers with no real information. Stop playing games and tell us what happened."

Boyd took his turn. "Did you get tired of him chasing you, harassing you, stalking you? Or is there another man, one who was jealous of Donnelly's attention and interest in you. Is that what we have here, a lover's triangle?"

I was trying to keep my temper, but I felt like my head was swelling up and was ready to pop clean off my shoulders.

"Wow. My oldest friend has been murdered and you two sit here and ask me asinine questions. Questions that get us no closer to the *who* or the *why* of Chick's death. Is this how ya'll operate in the big city? 'Cuz if it is, I'm surprised you solve any crimes at all." I probably shouldn't have said any of that, but hell, my nerves were on edge.

"Did you kill Charles Donnelly?" asked Boyd in his best Law and Order voice.

"No."

I was no longer nervous. Those two yahoos didn't have a clue, and they were just doing the case by the book. The book said, "Throw it all against the wall and see what sticks." In my house that's how we see if the spaghetti is done! But here I was seeing it in real-life crime solving. Wow.

"You have a license to carry and are certified on almost all weapons. It would seem you certainly know your way around guns," said Lyle in a snotty tone of voice.

She acted smug as if she had me or surprised me with this information. Since it was a statement of fact and didn't really require any answer, I didn't give her one. I bet she didn't know how good I was with a Thompson sub-machine gun. Computers don't tell you everything.

"Do you know who killed Charles Donnelly?" asked Boyd.

"No."

"You always score marksman on your weapons certification for your license. I'll bet you could have made the same shot that killed Mr. Donnelly from two hundred yards away," said Lyle.

She had her head cocked to one side and reminded me of a sparrow who was examining a tasty worm. I had definitely pissed in her Wheaties. Careful, careful, don't say anything rash, I warned myself.

"I have not yet mastered the art or the science of bi-location," I told her.

"But you're not denying that you could make that shot, right?" Boyd's steely grey eyes tried to bore a hole through me.

"I have no idea. You're askin' me a question that I can't possibly know the answer to. It'd be pure speculation on my part. I could only make conjecture."

"So you are saying that you could make the shot," demanded Lyle.

I restrained myself from rolling my eyes at her, but God Almighty, the woman was really annoying me!

"Nope I don't think I could. That was a hell of a shot."

"You admire the ability of the shooter to make such a difficult shot?" demanded Lyle almost jumping out of her seat.

I looked at her and could feel my right eyebrow rising toward my hairline.

"You win," I said simply.

"I win?" she said. "Does that mean that you could've made the shot? You're admitting that? Or are you telling us that you are holding back vital information on this case?"

"No. No, that's not what I meant. I meant that you're the winner of the dumbest-damn-question-I've-ever-heard contest. There ought to be a trophy for that, I reckon."

I didn't take my eyes from hers. I sat and watched as her face grew redder and redder. I fully expected to see steam shoot out of her ears any second, just like in the cartoons.

I can't explain my reaction to Lyle. I should've been working real hard to get her to like me, even be sympathetic toward me. But the woman rubbed me all kinds of wrong. I just wanted to smack the fire out of her. She asked ignorant questions when she ought to be out finding the asshole who murdered Chick. Even though she was playing bad cop I couldn't help but feel she truly didn't like me either. I couldn't find it in my heart to be nicer to get her to like me better even though I knew I should. Sometimes I cut my nose off to spite my face.

"It could be made out of Silly Putty and depict a head firmly up an ass." I egged her on. To my disappointment, smoke didn't occur.

"Tell us again what happened," she snarled at me.

So I told it again and again and again. I actually lost count, but I think it was six more times, with Frick and Frack getting testier with every telling. Lyle took notes, and occasionally the two of them would share a sardonic look as if they were communicating about my guilt telepathically. I knew they were trying to throw me off my story, hoping to find holes in my narration, or slip-ups in the retelling. They might be hoping that some of my details would change and show that I was making the whole thing up.

You might wonder why they pounded me for almost three hours when there were thirteen witnesses to the murder, not including minors. But of course, those people were all related to me, and family will lie for you. I have it on good authority though that in some families they will also lie against you. Maybe they really believed that I knew something about the murder and were trying to trip me up. That didn't help give me warm feelings toward them. Finally, I decided enough was enough and I was done. I looked from one agent to the other.

"If you need me to tell it again, I'm gonna need to get Miss Mavis to bring me a bottle of water. I'm dry. After that I'll need to pee."

They just stared at me for about 60 seconds. I refused to blink.

"We're done for now, but don't leave town. We'll have more questions for you in the next few days. Keep your nose out of this case, and don't discuss it with anyone," said Boyd.

"Don't think that we will neglect to look under every rock you've ever owned just because you're the sister of the current sheriff and the daughter of the former," Lyle sneered at me.

She was agitated. Her over-processed-not-a natural-color-on-this-planet hair was trying to come undone and stand on end like a pissed off porcupine.

I stood up. God, my butt hurt. Connell needed to do something about his chairs.

"I wouldn't dream of thinkin' that, 'cuz I'm positive you like to turn over rocks. You probably eat what you find."

I smiled sweetly and made my exit. I thought it was a good one. I passed Connell in the hall. We winked as we passed. Wow, I was tired. I gave Miss Mavis a thumbs-up as I left. She smiled at me. I really needed to get back out in the fresh air and sunlight. Those two jerkoffs just sucked all the oxygen out of the room. I would hate to be stranded on a desert island with them. I'd die of starvation 'cuz I sure as hell wouldn't eat either one of them.

CHAPTER 7

Jewels was on the phone when I got back to the office, and she was wearing her serious face.

"No, we have no more information about the murder than has been reported in your paper." She paused for a moment. "You'll have to call the sheriff for that information." She paused again, held her left hand out in front of her and examined her nails. "Well, I am sure there are a lot of cars in town with government plates on them. Uh huh. She's out of the office right now."

I stepped back over the threshold. I didn't want to make a liar out of my girl.

"I don't deal in rumors. Uh huh, you can camp out down here and bring your dog for all I care, but it won't get you any more information. Someone's coming in. I need to let you go. Bye bye." She hung up.

"Eddie Murdock," she said.

I rolled my eyes. Eddie's daddy, Sterling, ran the Noon Day Times, our local paper. Sometimes referred to as the "No Duh Times" due to the fact that they seemed to print stories that contained information that everyone already knew. Sadly, it's a daily publication. Usually the paper had nothing more exciting to report than who was elected president of the garden club or details of the fistfight on Friday night down at the Springwater. But now with Chick's murder, they had a real story, and Eddie was going to aggravate the living hell out of all of us until he got every detail.

"Eddie's such an annoying little shit under the best of circumstances. He's gonna be a royal pain in the ass now." I exhaled loudly.

"Now, now. I always thought that Eddie's problems were due to improper toilet training," Jewels said.

I cocked an eyebrow at her.

She grinned at me. "I believe that his momma put the wrong end in the toilet."

We both laughed for a long time—much longer than the comment warranted. I guess we just needed to laugh at something. Eddie was as good a subject as anything else. I finally got a grip on myself and poured a cup of coffee. I could feel my muscles relaxing as the hot liquid hit my stomach. What I really wanted was an adult beverage and a nap, maybe some chocolate.

"So, how bad was it? Did they bring out the thumbscrews?"

"Well, they were not nice, and they tried to scare and intimidate me."

Jewels snorted. "How did that work out for them?"

"They asked me stupid questions such as, did I kill Chick, when I was in plain sight of thirteen adults at the time. Did I know who or why and so on and so on. Asked me about my relationship with him."

I added extra cream and sugar to my coffee.

"They have a murder-case-solving checklist, and they're moving down it. It just pisses me off that they got no fire about 'em. They're doing this by rote, and this is Chick we're talking about. They suck."

"What else?" Jewels asked.

I pointed at the pot. "Want some?" She did and I poured.

"Stay in town, stay out of the case, don't think I'm special because my brother is the sheriff and my daddy used to be the sheriff. Man and a woman. I was surprised at that. And they were both the bad cop. Doesn't anyone respect tradition anymore?"

"Woo-hoo, I can't wait for them to question your momma. I sure wish I could be a bug on the wall for that session. She'll chew 'em up and spit them out." Jewels laughed.

The office door opened and Eddie Murdock came in. He must have called from the freakin' sidewalk. He didn't so much walk as he sauntered. That was the only way to describe his walk, except maybe strutting. He was big, about 6'5" and fat, like the Pillsbury Doughboy. He walked like John Travolta in *Saturday Night Fever*. It was just weird, all that fat jiggling and him grinning like he just knew that you wanted him. It was weird and creepy. I truly believe that Eddie thinks he's handsome, sexy and desirable. He's grown a little "soul patch" under his bottom lip, and he must think it adds to his sexiness level. I assure you it does not. It just makes him even weirder and creepier. I had to work not to laugh or make gagging sounds.

"Hey, girls," he drawled in what I am sure he thought was a come hither voice.

"Eddie," I said. I tried not to let my distaste show on my face. It's a less than stellar idea to piss off the press, even when the press is Eddie. "What can I do for you?"

"I just had a conversation with the lovely Juliet here. I think that she may have left some details out of our conversation. Thought maybe you could fill me in." He grinned at me and tried to look charming.

He has this sing-songy way of talking that made me want to punch him. Ick!

"Eddie, I know you know that this is a murder investigation. As such, I'm not telling you anything. Talk to Connell."

"Oh now come on, Tess, throw me a bone," he said cajolingly.

"Not even a piece of gristle, Eddie. I've been told to keep my mouth shut and shut it will stay. I got squat for you," I said firmly.

"Did the TBI question you?" He cocked his head to one side and raised an eyebrow at me.

I made the age-old hand motions of locking my lips and tossing away the key. Then I just smiled at him. I knew he wasn't going to take "no" for an answer so I might as well have a little fun with him.

Eddie stepped closer to me, leaned over me, invading my personal space. I could smell his Hai Karate aftershave. Eddie is one of the few people I know who can loom over me since I stand 5'10" in my stocking feet.

"Tess, everybody knows that you and Chick were…close." He caressed the last word, making it sound dirty. "Give me details and I can paint you in a good light."

That put me in overload. It was just too much to bear and I didn't bear it.

"Fun's over! Eddie, get the hell out of my office, out of my sight and away from my side of the street. Do not come anywhere near me, write about me, talk to me or talk about me now or ever. Do not call, email or so much as send Post-it notes to me. If you make me have to repeat this list to you I will stomp a mud puddle in your worthless ass and walk the son-of-a-bitch dry! Then I will sue you, your father and your rag of a newspaper for slander or libel or just aggravation! Got it?" My voice was raised—okay more than raised. I knew they could hear me yelling down at the A&P, but I didn't care. I wanted to bite him!

His face turned red—not a good color for him. It made him look like he was about to have a heart attack. I hoped he did!

"You've always been a bitch!" he snapped.

"You'd do well to remember that!" I snapped back.

Eddie made his exit and slammed the door behind him.

The rest of the day was uneventful. Jewels and I went over paperwork, updated the website and looked at the cases that were active. Most of our cases are not very exciting: a divorce here and there; background checks for prospective employers and occasionally, for a smart prospective bride; missing persons searches; and cyber investigations to follow the money trail. A lot of our work is done on the computer, but still legwork is legwork and the hours are billable. I've followed folks, taken notes and taken pictures too, just like in the movies. Most of the time, the fieldwork is uneventful. Most people don't pay attention to their surroundings and never know they're under surveillance. Every now and then I get made, and there have been confrontations. Usually I can talk my way out of the jam and diffuse the situation. Sometimes not. That's why I carry a gun. For the record, I have never shot anyone, yet.

Eddie could be my first. This is where Auntie Tess's fifth firearm rule comes into play: never draw your weapon unless you mean to pull the trigger. I knew I was capable of shooting another human being. I had no doubts on that score. My sense of self-preservation is extremely well developed. So I was very careful about pulling my weapon. When the herd is a bit more mature, I'll add rule number five for them.

Jewels and I concluded that there was nothing on the roster that she couldn't deal with, and I decided to go home. Ye gods and little fishes, but I was tired. As a bonus, a tension headache was starting at the base of my skull. I gathered my stuff, hugged Jewels and walked out.

I ran into three people on the way to the car, which was only parked a half of a block away. Debi Fertitta crossed the street to speak to me. She's a cute, dark, well-dressed, well-coifed Sicilian, and tough as nails. She runs the only Italian restaurant in town. She would be a walking cliché except she's about five-foot-nothing and weighs in at around a buck-oh-five. She made me promise to eat and sleep. She hugged me, gave me condolences, and told me she'd have a mass said for Chick at St. Mary's Catholic Church. I loved her for that and told her so.

Doris Remington owns the antique shop next door to my office building. She is about 70, eccentric as all get out and spends most of her time chasing men and hunting bargains. Sometime those two things coincide and usually explode. She recently went to the city and had a little work done. Now she looks startled all of the time. Bless her heart, and I do mean that in the Southern way. Doris hugged me as well and said all the right things: Chick was such a good person, how loved he was, how no one ever had a bad word to say against him. It was good to hear.

Jim Leach, the insurance guy, hailed me too. Jim's a nice guy who will look for the right insurance for the right price and actually cares about his customers. He's fortyish, with sandy-colored hair and a big smile. He's still in good shape because he jogs every day. I know this because I see him many days on the running trails around town. He expressed condolences over Chick's death, hugged me, asked after Connell, told me to be careful and made me promise to call if I needed anything. I figured that Chick's life insurance policy was with Jim, but I didn't ask. I'd know that soon enough, I hoped.

I like living in a little town. True, everyone knows your business five minutes after it happens, but most of them give a real damn about you too. I felt uplifted as I climbed into the Jeep.

I took the fifteen minute car ride to get my thoughts in order. I didn't know any more about the circumstances surrounding Chick's death at the end of the day than I did that morning. That made me feel sort of like I had wasted the day. All I knew at that point was that I could find none of the regular reasons that people became victims of violent crime. No one owed him money, he owed money to no one, there were no vengeful exes, and the boys who worked for him were loyal and nonviolent.

Okay, so maybe Billy was a hothead, but he worshipped the ground Chick walked on. They would also have to know that if Chick died, they'd be out of a job, right? I'd have to ask Connell about that. Who would run things now? There were jobs that were unfinished surely, and how would the boys get paid? Maybe Buzzy would take charge for now. Lord, I was sure he didn't know a spark plug from a dipstick.

What if Connell couldn't get a court order before the TBI told him to go sit and spin? That would certainly suck. Crap. Crap. Crap.

At that point a little light went off in my head, and I decided that I needed to talk to Sammy and Billy at Donnelly's Repair and Replacement. I felt like I should go at that moment, but I was beat and my head felt like it was going to explode any second. I promised myself that the next day I'd go straight to the garage and poke around. Not that I was investigating or anything like that, God forbid. Didn't want to piss off the good ole TBI.

CHAPTER 8
TUESDAY

The sun had been up for a while before I decided to join it. I pulled my lace bedroom curtains aside and looked out. It was another beautiful day. Of course it was. I could smell coffee from the kitchen and decided that it was time for me to get my ass in the wind. I needed a fast shower since I had plans for my morning. I'd need to be clean and caffeinated if I was going to outsmart the TBI agents. But first I made myself put on running gear and go out and log in three miles before anything else. I've found that if I try to put my running off until later in the day, it usually doesn't happen. I'm easily sidetracked and I know it.

After my amazing, exhilarating, sweaty and dog-infested run, I climbed into the shower and let the hot water pound on me for about five minutes. A quick scrub was all that I could allocate time for. There was just too much to do. I hurried through my daily routine of cleaning and scrubbing and drying and moisturizing. I threw on jeans and a Motley Crew tee-shirt, pulled my hair into a club at the nape of my neck and felt ready to face the world. Or I would be as soon as I had coffee.

Mommy and Daddy were both in the kitchen reading the newspaper, drinking coffee and, I felt sure, waiting for me.

"Morning," I said as I bent to kiss them on their cheeks.

"Morning, honey," Daddy said, returning my kiss.

"Coffee's made," said Mommy, "and there're waffles in the oven." She took in my attire and cast a fish eye at my tee-shirt. "Motley Crew, Tess, really?"

"Hey, I was told to stay out of this investigation, so I'm not working, I'm just hanging out. I'm dressed to show that."

She rolled her eyes at me.

"Where's YaYa?" I asked. She was usually in the kitchen at this time of day, and I was sure that she wanted to hear all the news too. Not that there was much.

"Did she run off with a drummer?"

Mommy laughed. "She's outside deciding where she wants to put the gardenias. She'd like a little help when you get done with breakfast."

I made myself a plate of waffles and poured a cup of coffee. Carefully, I made my way to the table to prevent spilling.

"I need to get into town and do some snoopin'. I don't have time to dig holes in the ground for plants that won't live to see spring."

Daddy looked at me. "So tell us what happened yesterday."

"Tell us about the TBI," Mommy prompted.

"Ugly as hell, and that was just her suit."

Mommy raised a brow at me.

"Just trying to lighten the mood," I said, holding my hands up in mock surrender. "They were threatening, and they don't have a clue about this situation. They're doing this by the Murder Investigation One-O-One Handbook. They also either really don't like me or they're very good actors. I can tell you I really do not like them. *Agents Boyd and Lyle.*" I said in a snotty voice and wrinkled my nose.

"So did they actually accuse you of the murder? Or were they just on a fishing expedition?" Mommy asked.

I laughed. "I bet Miss Mavis called you before I got out of the parking lot. She has good hearing for someone who's a hundred and seventy-two years old."

Mommy frowned at me some more.

"Okay, okay. Both. They were sure as hell fishin', and they asked me point blank if I killed Chick. They told me not to think I was special or that they would go easy on me because of my relationship to the law in this town, essentially that Daddy nor Connell could save me if I was on the wrong side of this. I was also warned to keep my nose out of the investigation and not to leave town." I shook my head.

"They were just assholes to me, I know they were tryin' to shake me up, but, man oh man, it felt personal. The woman agent just set me off. She made me feel like she thought she was superior to me, lookin' down her nose at me, that kind of thing."

"They're just doing the job, Tess. Figure out the players and then shake the trees, see what falls out," Daddy said.

"I know that. I guess I thought we'd all be on the same side. Colleagues, you know. And we'd work together to find out who did this thing. They treated me like…well like a suspect. It pissed me off, and I guess it hurt my feelin's too. I snapped back and probably made the situation worse, but I'm not gonna be pushed around. I will be the first to admit that I showed my ass."

When no one spoke, I took the opportunity to tell them about the financials, the total lack of anyone who hated Chick enough to put a bullet in him, then about Buzzy and Eddie.

"Well, not surprised about Chick's money," Daddy said, "and Buzz is still mad 'cuz you embarrassed him."

"Eddie is a puffed-up-pop-in-jay in long pants, always has been. He doesn't like you either, honey," said Mommy.

Daddy got up from the table. "More coffee?" he asked.

Mommy and I both nodded.

"Don't talk till I get back," he said.

I just laughed and ate a couple of bites of waffle. Daddy returned with the coffeepot and poured for all of us. I poured cream and sugar into my cup and stirred.

"I think they like me for this, Daddy."

Mommy gasped and started to say something. I held up my hand to stop her.

"Just listen. These are big city cops, and they think they know all the reasons why people do murder. It's too good that Chick had drawings of me, and everyone who can talk will tell them that we were some sort of star-crossed lovers or some such bullshit. The conclusion is that I got tired of him pursuin' me, or there was another lover that wanted him out of the way. It makes a compellin' argument. Either way I am involved to their way of thinkin'."

Mommy looked at me so sadly. "But it's all a lie. You loved him and he loved you and you'd never do anything to hurt him. Plus I know you couldn't kill anyone in cold blood."

"You know it because I'm your daughter. You raised me and instilled values in me. You're pretty sure I haven't been hidin' a murderous nature from you all of these years. You love me. Look at the situation from their point of view, and it looks sorta bad for me." I returned my attention to my waffles.

Daddy took a sip of coffee and shook his head. "It may be true that they'd like to pin this on you and have done with the investigation. If that's the case then they have a big problem. They're gonna need proof, which they don't have. They can bring charges against you, move the trial to a different venue and paint you as black as night. But, they have to convince a jury of your guilt with almost no evidence, and I don't think they can do that."

"Is that the cop or the father makin' that pronouncement?" asked Mommy.

"The cop," Daddy said firmly. "If I was workin' this case I sure wouldn't bring it to the DA."

I felt the knot in my stomach loosen a bit.

"What really chaps my ass about this aren't the accusations, or the fact that they're hell bent to build a case on me, but that they're not out tryin' to discover who really murdered Chick!" I felt tears well up behind my eyes and took a deep breath.

So," Daddy said, "what are you going to do about that?"

"I'm gonna go to the garage and pay a condolence call on the men who worked for Chick. I'm gonna commiserate with them over the death of an old friend and see what I can find out. But I am definitely not investigatin', no-sir-ree-Bob, not-me." I smiled.

"Right after you help YaYa with the gardenias," Mommy pronounced.

I quit smiling.

I found YaYa on the back patio looking out over the valley. "Morning, darlin'," she said without turning around.

"Morning, YaYa, I come bearin' gifts," I said.

I offered her a cup of coffee, prepared exactly as she liked it. When I was a little girl I delighted in making her coffee. She said I was the only one in the house who knew the exact way she liked it. Probably not true but it was high praise to a five-year-old. She turned and took the cup from my hand and motioned me to the glass-topped table.

"I've been thinkin' that this patio needs gardenias to surround it. They'll look beautiful and will perfume the air all summer long."

I sat next to her. "Why gardenias, YaYa, really?"

She smiled at me, and it took twenty years off her face.

"Because child, I find that I think better when I have a project. I just carry on doin' a set task and let my mind wander, and sometimes a solution comes to me. And they smell nice."

"Oh, YaYa, this is all so awful. Someone murdered our boy, and I don't even have time to mourn for him. I have to find the killer. Now the TBI agents think that I did it. I..." I choked on the words and couldn't finish my sentence.

"Murder's different." YaYa reached over and patted my hand to comfort me. "When someone dies of disease or in an accident, you grieve and mourn and you're sad. If the death is one of a young person, your grief is boundless for the waste of a life, for all the things they'll never do or see or become." Tears streamed down my face as images of Chick ran through my mind. YaYa took my hands in hers. They were old and wrinkled and the veins stood out, but they were strong hands, and I felt some of that strength flow into me. "But when someone you love is murdered, you add hate and the need for vengeance to all the other emotions. You can't help it, you're only human. Now it's not God who has called your loved one home, but some treacherous human monster that's snuffed out a life, stolen someone's fate."

"Yes," I sobbed, "that's it. I want to find the bastard who did this and kill him slowly. I want to hurt him, make him bleed, watch him die an inch at a time. And I want Chick back!"

YaYa cupped my face in her hands, and my hot tears ran over her fingers.

"You can't let vengeance cloud your judgment. You can't make good decisions from a place of hate or anger. You have to have a clear head so you can find the person who took our boy from us and bring the bastard to justice."

"I hate him. I want him to die. He stole Chick's life, and he stole Chick from us, from me. I feel like I can't breathe, and I wake up in the night thinkin' this is all a nightmare. But it's not. It's real and Chick's dead. Oh God, YaYa, what am I supposed to do?" I wailed like a lost child.

"You are supposed to find the killer and bring him to justice, so you can mourn and so Chick can rest. It's the last thing you can do for him." YaYa leaned over and kissed my forehead.

I closed my eyes and tried to breathe through the pain. "Yes, and I will. I'll do those things for Chick and for all of us." I sighed. "I keep expectin' him to drive up and want to go fishin', or him and Connell to show up with beer so we can watch the game on the big screen. I want to tell him so many things, YaYa. Maybe he and I were wrong, maybe we made a mistake. I want to tell him that, I want to tell him that." I couldn't stop crying.

"Then tell him, honey. You'll get your chance to tell him." My grandmother looked so sad.

I nodded and wiped my face on the neck of my tee-shirt. "But first I'm gonna catch a killer." I stood up and kissed her on her soft, wrinkled cheek. "Thanks, YaYa, I love you."

"I love you right back. Good huntin'."

I walked around the house, climbed into my Jeep and headed to the garage. I had one moment of worry over the TBI jerks telling me to stay out of the investigation, but I was just going to check on my friends and see how they were doing. Not exactly a federal offense. Right? A state offense maybe, but not a federal one, said the little voice in my head.

Twenty minutes later, I pulled in the garage parking lot and parked to one side of the pumps. I climbed out of the Jeep and walked into the garage. Both the boys were working on cars, of course.

"Hey, ya'll," I called out.

Sammy looked up, and there was sadness in his grey eyes that I'd never seen before. He was working under the hood of Mrs. Stratton's 1967 baby blue Oldsmobile. It was old, but it was in tip top shape, thanks to the care that Chick, Sammy and Billy gave it. Sammy was about 6' tall, but today he was slumped over and looked shorter. His long brown Billy Ray Cyrus hair looked unkempt and was plastered to his head, as if he hadn't taken the time to style it. He always styled his hair. Usually, he had a merry little twinkle in his eye like he knew a good secret. Today he didn't have a twinkle for me.

"Girl," he said.

Sammy put down the wrench, wiped his hands on a rag, stepped over to me and hugged me, hard. He smelled like car grease, gasoline, cigarettes and sweat. Honest smells. He pulled back and looked me in the eye.

"How you doin', honey?"

I mustered a smile for him. "Horrible, awful, terrible, shitty, miserable. Hell, Sammy, I can't find a word bad enough to describe how I'm doing. I'm gonna have to make one up. How 'bout you?"

Before he could answer, Billy rolled out from under the 2009 Mustang to my right. He stood up and hugged me as well. Billy is about twenty years old—a natural blond or so I've been assured. He has ice blue, Paul Newman eyes, very cute, very muscular. Most of the girls and some of the boys turn their heads as he walks by, that was for sure. He'd been a little wild in his teens, but between Chick and Connell, he never did any real time in jail and finally calmed down. Again, thanks to Chick and Connell. His blue eyes had a watery look today.

"Who the hell could've done such a thang?" he demanded.

"I wish I knew, and we'll find out. Right now there're no leads. But somebody somewhere knows something. It's just a matter of time."

Billy looked so sad I wanted to pet him like you do with a small child who's in pain.

Billy had serious hero worship for Chick and with good reason. Billy was such a hell-raiser that no one in town would hire him, his own momma threw him out, and he had been headed down a real bad road. He needed a job and some guidance. Chick was there to give it to him. Chick promised to teach Billy all about cars, if Billy would straighten up and keep his nose clean. Connell promised him that he would pound him into putty if he screwed up. Billy said he would try. They all kept their promises.

"Come in the office and take a load off, Tess. Y'ant a coke?" Sammy asked.

I nodded. He reached into the ancient cooler where cold drinks and lunches and sometimes beer were stored. It was old, red and banged up. The lid was hinged on the back side and lifted up like an ice chest. You put money in the coin box, slid the bottle down little metal avenues, and there was a release at the end. Chick had loved it. It was the first thing he bought for the garage, after all the tools.

"What kind of coke y'ant?" he asked. In the South, "coke" is the universal name for a cold, carbonated, sweet drink. Don't ask me why, it just is.

"Coke-a-Cola would do me fine," I said.

Sammy looked at Billy, who nodded. Sammy pulled three Cokes out of the box. Billy snagged three bags of peanuts off the shelf next to the cold drink machine, and we all went into the office. We sat around Chick's desk. No one sat in Chick's chair. No one was ready to fill it yet.

We opened our drinks and clicked our bottles together. "Chick," we all said and took long pulls of the sweet, cold liquid.

"Whaddya think?" asked Billy.

He began to add one pack of peanuts to his Coke. I was busy with my own peanuts. The trick is to pour all the peanuts and the salt into the narrow mouth of the bottle without spilling any crumbs. I made a cone with my hand and poured the peanuts slowly and carefully into the bottle, perfectly.

I shook my head at Billy. "I don't have a clue, Billy. I kinda wondered if ya'll had seen anything out of the ordinary in the past few weeks that might have set you to wonderin'. Chick been acting different, any arguments with anyone, anything?"

They both took another sip from their bottles and both shook their heads.

"Everything's just 'bout the same as always, a bit more business lately. We was getting the Grand National ready for the races this next weekend. I don't rightly know what we should do about that now," Sammy said sadly.

"I think we should run it, for Chick. His last race," said Billy fiercely. "Why the hell not. Who's gonna stop us?"

He sounded angry and sad. He squeezed the bottle in both hands until the veins stood out on his arms. In one fell swoop, he had lost a friend, father figure, mentor and boss. He had every right to his emotions. My heart just went out to him. I was worried about what would become of him.

"Buzzy might stop us if he knew we was gonna do something with Chick's property." Sammy winked at us. "I think we just won't tell him."

I thought about the first thing Chick had said to me yesterday— that he planned to race the next weekend. "I think you should race it. That sort of takes care of the last piece of business Chick had. He'd want you to do it," I encouraged.

"Besides," said Billy, "we all own a piece of that car. We all chipped in and bought it, we all worked on it, we got a right to race it."

Billy turned to me, his face full of anger and pain. "Tess, I sure hate this jackleg son-of-a-bitch what murdered Chick. I wanna see 'im get what's comin' to 'im, ya know." His voice was low and menacing. You could call it a growl.

"Billy, he will. You don't need to go thinkin' like that," I cautioned him.

Silently I hoped we found the bastard and put him under the jail before Billy found out about the arrest. We were all silent for a moment with our own thoughts.

That's when the TBI showed up. Holy Crap! Caught dead to rights! Busted! Agents Lyle and Boyd frowned at me as they pulled out their badges and flipped them open for Sammy and Billy. They must give seminars on badge flipping at police school, and they all must practice, a lot. I was willing to bet that these two took top badge flipping honors. They were particularly good.

"Agents Boyd and Lyle. We'd like to speak with you about the death of Charles Donnelly," said Boyd.

"Ms. Maher," said Lyle, "I thought you were told to stay out of this investigation."

I took a big slug of Coke and smiled as if I had good sense. "I'm here visitin' my friends. Sammy and I went to school together, and I have known Billy since he was in diapers. We're havin' a cold drink and talkin' about the tragic death of an old friend. I'd hardly call that investigatin'."

Boyd raised one eyebrow at me. "You can go now."

Assholes. I took my time standing up, and I finished the rest of my Coke. I put the bottle on Chick's desk.

"I'll see ya'll later. I'm sorry for your loss," I said nodding to Billy and Sammy.

"Likewise," said Sammy frowning.

"Later, Tess," said Billy. He looked nervous and even more unhappy than he was when I first arrived. He didn't like the cops.

I didn't make any good-byes to the TBI agents. Screw 'em.

CHAPTER 9

I was speeding as I sometimes do when I am pissed off. Who the hell did those two assholes think they were, ordering me around, telling me who I could and could not speak to, where I could and could not go? I lived in this damn town. This was my damn town! My oldest friend was lying on a morgue slab in Nashville with his organs labeled and stuck in little jars! They were throwing their weight around and getting nowhere!

"Bastards!" I shouted.

I beat my fist on the steering wheel. Those bastards could just pound sand! Damn, I was crying again. Driving and crying is not a good idea. I wiped my face on the back of my hand and took deep breaths to calm down. The phone rang at that exact moment. Oh goody, I would sound all snotty and tear stained. I reached up and hit the answer button.

"Tess."

"Hey, baby," said a velvety voice.

It was Marcella Price. She is my best friend: the one person in the world who will cash my reality checks, hold my hand when I'm scared, kick my ass when needed, lie about how fat my butt is, and match me tequila shot for tequila shot. She knew all of my secrets and I knew all of hers. We'd been through everything together. I loved her real real good, and I had neglected to call her.

"Oh God," I gasped. My breath was coming so fast I thought I was going to hyperventilate. "Chick's dead, he's dead, oh God, Mars! Oh God, help me." My chest hurt, I was afraid I was having a heart attack.

"I know, sugar, I know. You drivin'?"

"Yes," I hissed through closed teeth.

"Where are you?"

"On the road home, but I don't want to go home." When would I ever stop crying?

"Meet me at the Springwater. Can you drive there? I know it's noisy, and I know you don't want anyone to see you like this. But I'll get our orders, and we can sit at the picnic table out back. Okay?"

"Yeah, sure, okay." I nodded even though she couldn't see me. I had the hiccups too. Wonderful.

I broke the connection and pulled a U-turn just before the turn-off to the house and went back toward town. Ten minutes later, I drove into the gravel lot of the Springwater Bar-N-Grill and circled around to the back. There sat Marcella at a picnic table with a couple of Fat Tires. I had never been so glad to see anyone in my entire life. She was just the most beautiful woman I had ever seen, and she smiled her amazing ten-million megawatt smile at me. I jumped from the Jeep and ran to her. She stood up and held out her arms to me. She hugged me long and hard and let me cry all over her. She just hugged me, did not shush me or pat me or tell me it would be alright. I never loved her more than at that moment. She always knew the right thing to do. Finally, I pulled back from her a bit.

"You look good," I said.

She always looked great. That day she was wearing a dark hunter green suit with a cream-colored silk blouse, gold jewelry— understated but professional. Her bag and shoes were black leather and costly. She also had a stunning body, so the outfit looked perfect on her. More importantly, she had a magnificent heart.

She always looked this good, and I always looked like an unmade bed. We'd been friends since kindergarten. We met on the first day. I remember being fascinated by her dark, velvety skin and the tiny cleft in her chin. I thought she was so beautiful. I was and will always be jealous of her hair. Mine is as straight as a stick and defied any means I took to curl it or style it. Her shoulder length hair fell in ringlets around her face, perfectly. I shared my lunch with her that first day so long ago, and we have been best friends ever since. (She even helped me track down Chick when we discovered that he'd eaten all of my library paste.)

I stood drinking her in with my eyes. Whatever happy genetic mix created her, the fates should be thanked. I felt better just being in her presence.

"I think I got some snot on your collar," I said wiping at her a little.

"Wouldn't be the first time and probably not the last," she said.

"You smell good too," I said sniffing.

She grinned at me as she smoothed my hair back from my face.

We sat down, and I swallowed a serious amount of my beer.

"Wow, that's good and cold! Just what the doctor ordered. Your timin' as usual is perfect. Thanks."

Marcella smiled a sad smile at me. "I'm so sorry. I know you loved him your whole life. What are we gonna do about this?"

I shook my head. "Don't know. I mean I want to find out who murdered him. There're no leads right now, no suspects, no clues, no nothing. How the hell do you murder someone in this day and age and not leave a single clue? It's almost impossible to do ya know."

Marcella took a pull of her own beer. "I'm sure of that."

"Mars, some coward shot him in the back. It's all so unreal. He was up in the big oak on the back of the property, sketching me. He was gonna surprise me with the artwork. That's what he said. I can't believe this is happening."

Mars looked me in the eye. "There's nothing I can say that will make you feel better. Only time can do that. But I will promise you that I will do everything in my power to help you find the bastard who did this and make sure justice is done."

Mars relaxed and sat back. "Now, tell me everything you've done so far. I know you've checked out all the financials and found nothing, or you'd of told me. What else is there?"

"I couldn't get Buzzy to talk to me. I'm sure there's a will. From what I know, Chick was thorough about that type of thing. Let's see who he left everything to. There's a sizable inheritance with the savings, the business and the house. I think there're several cars too."

"No clue as to who gets it all? Connell getting a warrant?"

"I don't think that he'll be gettin' it. There are two TBI agents in town, and it won't be long till they tell him to go piss up a rope."

"You met them yet?"

"Met 'em and been interrogated by them. A man and woman, both assholes. To be fair, they don't like me any more than I like them."

"I don't understand what brings the TBI into this. How is it their jurisdiction?"

"Here's how I figure it. The murder happened on our property, the victim and I had a history, the man who would be investigating the murder is my brother and might overlook anything that connected me to the murder. I mean it makes sense." I took another sip of beer.

"Since this is murder, they have to be invited into the case. They put some pressure on Connell. He gave them a green light. Looks better, I reckon. More innocent."

She cocked a bright green eye at me. "Give."

I did. It took about ten minutes to explain the whole thing from beginning to end. As the most dramatic thing that had ever happened in my life, I would've thought it should've taken longer than that to tell the story. I didn't leave out the part about seeing and talking to Chick. She knows all about that.

"I can't believe Chick doesn't have any idea who killed him. I thought that things were much clearer on the other side."

"Chick's not on the other side yet. He's still here and he's as baffled as we are. I can't get him to come back either. I tried for the last couple of nights, or rather mornins', before I fell asleep. Nothing."

"Well, don't give up. I'm sure he'll show up for you again. Do you really think you'll need a lawyer?"

"I don't reckon. I don't know. Damn, I can't believe he's dead, Mars. I keep thinkin' I need to call him and tell him the latest news. We could laugh about what assholes the TBI agents are and what crappy clothes Agent Lyle wears. I feel like he's only a phone call away." I started to tear up and took another swig of beer. I turned the beer bottle around and around in my hands. "I feel like a big hole's been cut out of me."

"Oh baby, I'm so sorry. I wish I could make this better, but I know I can't. I can only love you. It sucks and there's nothing anyone can do to make it suck less. You just gotta keep rockin'." Marcella reached over and squeezed my shoulder. "How's Connell holdin' up?"

"Worse than me I think. I may look like hell, but he looks like he just climbed out of the deepest pit in hell. I don't think he's slept, and I only know he's eaten 'cuz Tilly brought us breakfast yesterday mornin'." I paused for another sip of beer. "God has it only been two days? Seems like weeks ago."

"You eaten since?"

"Oh yeah, you know I can't get out of the house without being fed. I also had a Coke and peanuts at the garage with Sammy and Billy."

Marcella made a face. "Ick, I cannot believe you still ingest that mixture. It's so nasty. I also wonder that your blood pressure is not four hundred over three hundred!"

I laughed. "My blood pressure is just finer than a frog's hair split three ways, thank you very much."

"I'm going to go and place an order. What do you want? Never mind, some kind of dead animal, rolled in white flour and fried within an inch of shoe leather. No nutrition, no vitamins, no veggies and no redeeming qualities. I gotcha covered."

She placed her bottle on the table and headed inside.

"Hey," I said to her back, "potatoes are vegetables! So are fried pickles! They used to be cucumbers!"

She completely ignored me as she sometimes did. I had to admit, I felt better than I had in about 48 hours. Nothing like a dose of Marcella treating me as if nothing bad had happened to wreck my world. My chest felt less tight and I sighed with relief. I knew it would be short-lived relief, but I'd take anything I could get at that point.

I could hear the juke box and the patrons talking over the loud Garth Brooks music. Cars were coming and going out front. I could hear them churn up the gravel. I was surrounded by humanity, and I was all alone. I polished off my beer, hoped Mars would bring another one and started to hum with Garth. Mars appeared with two more Fat Tires.

I sang out loud, "I've got friends in low places where the whiskey flows and the beer chases…"

Mars joined me and we sang the rest, loudly, badly, and laughing as we did. We were halfway done with our second beers when Andy showed up with dinner. He placed the hot plates on the table and pulled two more Fat Tires out of his pockets and put those on the table too.

"I'm s' sorry Tess." He patted me clumsily on the shoulder. "Chick was good people, one of the best I ever knowed."

"Thanks, Andy. You know that means a lot coming from you. Chick thought the world of you too."

Andy Fitzgerald just stood there staring at me. He had big tears in his light brown eyes. He's about as country as you could find—big, about 6'4" and around 285 pounds. His straw-colored hair was almost always unkempt, but his round, open face usually boasted a crooked smile. Andy played football in high school and college. He was drafted by the pros and played for about fifteen minutes, until his knee blew out. He might not be too bright, but he came back home with a lot of money. Andy knew how to cook, people couldn't help but like him, he liked bars, so he bought one.

Seems that he knew how to keep a bar running, he could bust heads when necessary and lead the singing if that was what the night called for. His mama, Pam, kept the books, took care of the bills and made the orders. Andy's sister, Erin, ran the bar and delivered the food. Actually she yelled at you, and you had to come get your own food. It was a system that worked.

Andy nodded at me once, turned on his heel and went back inside. I saw him raise his apron to his face and knew he was wiping tears away.

"Shit, I think that if he'd started crying in front of me, I would've fallen on the ground and had a seizure."

"Yep,' said Mars. "Eat your dinner and let's bounce around some ideas so we can figure out who murdered Chick before the TBI does."

I dug in. I talked between bites, which wasn't easy because I found that I was starving.

"Okay, here's what I know. Chick was shot at long range, about two hundred yards out, with a high power rifle. I think it was a thirty-aught-six, but we won't know until they finish the autopsy. He was taken out with one shot to the spine. The bastard that shot him knows his business. You don't get that lucky accidentally or if you're a lousy shot. There was not one clue left behind, not even a thread on the tree bark."

I wiped my chin and sighed. The fried pickles were perfect and put me into a foodgasm.

"Chick owed no one, no one owed him, his bills were paid, he had money in the bank, had no girlfriend that we know of, seemed to be in perfect health, everyone loved him, he got along with just about everybody, had few bad habits and no friends in low places, unless you count my brothers." I ticked off the points on my fingers until I ran out of fingers. The food revived me, and I felt pretty content.

"I'd say the bastard that shot him hated him, but that doesn't feel right. This is too clean and too tidy. Pro?" Marcella looked at me.

That idea stopped me in my tracks. "That could be, it could so be. Why?" I answered my own question. "Cuz Chick saw something out of place and rattled someone's cage."

Most people are murdered by someone they know, usually a spouse, loved one or a family member. A sad, little statistic and all too true. That had been the vein I had been mining until that moment—that Chick had been murdered by someone he'd pissed off in some way. But maybe it wasn't personal. Maybe I needed to broaden my horizons.

"Thanks, Mars."

"You think I could be on to something?"

"Yep and so do not breathe a word about this conversation. If someone murdered Chick for reasons unknown, that person is still out there and is probably willing to kill anyone who discovers whatever it is that he or she is hiding." That was a vague statement, or maybe convoluted. Still I thought it was a true one. "Let's don't make targets of ourselves."

Marcella nodded at me. "You going to tell Connell?"

"He'll probably drop by the house tonight, and I'll tell him then. I'd rather tell him in person. With the TBI sniffing around I'm feelin' a bit paranoid. I'm not willin' to share with them, and they might be listenin'. You wanna come home with me and spend the night?"

"Sure, can we stop off at my place, so I can get some clean underwear?"

I stood up. "Why not. Even in the middle of a murder investigation, a girl has to have fresh undies."

CHAPTER 10

Mommy was glad to see Marcella because Mommy loves her some Marcella. I get compared to Mars regularly and have since Jesus rode a school bus. I get all the "Why can't you be more like Marcella? She always looks like she just stepped off a runway, she has a profession where no one ever shoots at her, and she's never sullen and does not argue." There's more, much more, but you get the drift. It's all true, so I can't argue with any of it. But in my defense, I've only been shot at once. I was tailing an estranged husband. Besides, he missed.

Marcella is a real estate agent. She makes good money even when the economy sucks, drives a cute little silver Thunderbird, dresses like a woman in a magazine, always has makeup on her face, gets her hair and her nails done every week, and no one has ever taken a shot at her. She can also pound down more tequila shots than anyone else I know, including my brothers. That just makes me smile.

"Marcella, you look so wonderful, I love that color on you." Mommy gushed all over Mars. That suit was definitely going to have to make a trip to the dry cleaners.

Mars moved into the kitchen and hugged Mommy.

"You look great too, Ms. M, younger every day."

Mommy laughed and made a shooing motion with her hand to brush away the compliment, yet I knew she secretly loved it.

"What are you girls up to?"

I laid my non-matching, non-magazine-cover bag on the kitchen counter. The Beretta made a loud *thunk* sound as I did, and Mommy rolled her eyes at me. I smiled innocently at her and took a seat at the table.

"Well, we thought we'd discuss Chick, bounce around some ideas and see if we could come up with anything new."

Mars pointed to the butler's pantry. "Coffee?"

"Just made a fresh pot, thought we might need it this evening. Help yourself."

Mommy turned her attention to me. I quickly filled her in on the rest of my activities of the day. She nodded at the appropriate places.

"Ya'll want coffee"? Marcella called out.

"Sure," I answered.

"Yes, darlin'," Mommy answered then turned her attention back to me. "Aren't you worried over the TBI agents catching you at Chick's garage? What can they do to you?"

"I'm not real worried. It isn't like they caught me pickin' a lock, destroyin' evidence or hackin' into bank records." Thank God for that, I thought, but wisely kept my mouth shut.

Mars entered with three coffee cups, spoons, cream and sugar balanced on a tray, which she deftly set on the table within easy reach.

"Thanks, Mars," I said and began doctoring my coffee. "Where're Daddy and YaYa?" I asked Mommy.

"They've gone to the Plant Place to get gardenia plants. I don't think they'll do well here during the cold weather, but she has her mind set on trying it. You know how she is when she gets a bee in her bonnet," Mommy answered.

"I think I already mentioned they won't live, but I'm sure she'll get all the info on gardenias from Sue. Actually I'm sure that YaYa will suck all the information Sue has in her head, right out. YaYa will be an expert on all things gardenia by the time she and Daddy leave the shop, and Sue will be brain damaged."

I felt a bit sorry for Sue. YaYa could worry the tits off a boar hog when she set her mind to something. I sipped my coffee for a moment, and a thought hit me in the head.

"Why must she conceive of projects that cause me physical labor?" I asked no one in particular.

Mommy just smiled. She got up and checked on something in the oven. I vaguely knew meat was cooking, but because my stomach was so full of lunch, or whatever meal I had just eaten, I wasn't interested enough to identify the smells.

"Pork loin," she answered my unspoken question.

I don't know if she can actually read minds or not, but sometimes it seems likely. Mommy closed the oven door, grabbed a notepad and pen from the counter by the phone and rejoined us at the table.

"Let's see what we know so far," she said.

I went through everything from the beginning. Mars injected comments. I gave Mommy the cliff notes of the conversation that

Mars and I had at the Springwater.

"Mars made me rethink the way I'd been looking at this whole mess. We think that maybe Chick was murdered by a pro."

Mommy stopped writing and looked back and forth at us. "Dear God, do you really think so?" Her voice held shock and disbelief.

"There's nothing in his financials, his business dealings or his personal life to give anyone reason to kill him, and let's face it, there are only a few reasons why a person commits murder," I answered her.

Connell came into the kitchen at that moment. "Jealousy, love, power, revenge, rage, greed, to cover up another crime, and crazy. Hello, Mommy. Hello, Mars. Hello, sis."

He walked around the table and deposited kisses on all of our cheeks, then headed into the butler's pantry. He emerged with a mug of coffee a few seconds later. He joined us at the table and started to put sugar into the cup.

"It's a short list, and almost every murder falls into one of the categories," Connell assured us.

Daddy and YaYa arrived at that moment, and we spent the next thirty minutes finding out more than we ever wanted to know about the care and feeding of gardenias. Finally, YaYa ran out of information on her new favorite flora.

"So who the hell murdered Chick," she asked.

I was about to answer her when the front doorbell rang, and all the dogs in the house lost their collective minds. They came running from four different directions, barking like the end of the world had arrived. I was a bit surprised. Not at the dogs, they always go nuts when someone knocks or rings the bell, but at the idea that someone had come to the front door. There's a long sweeping drive that makes a circle in front of the house. There's also a parking area at the side of the house by the kitchen. Almost everyone parks at the side and uses the kitchen door when they visit. No one ever knocks, except for traveling salesmen and Jehovah's Witnesses.

Mommy got up from the table and headed for the front door. The dogs, running in circles and barking loudly enough to make a person deaf, ran behind her. Before they could all descend on the front door, Daddy whistled them up, and after a moment I could hear them thundering back toward us. Connell got dog treats from the pantry, and the next minute or so was occupied by handing out the treats and telling the dogs what good dogs they were.

"Now sit," Daddy said sternly.

Four dog butts hit the black and white tiled kitchen floor.

"And stay," he admonished them.

They all looked at him for the next command.

"Eat."

The canines slid into reclining positions and started working on their treats. Mommy entered the kitchen with a false smile on her face, and agents Lyle and Boyd following in her wake. Surprise, surprise. I reached over and scooped up the notebook Mommy had been writing on—damn if I'd share any ideas with these two morons. I thought Boyd caught my movement. Those steely grey eyes were pretty sharp. Let him wonder.

"This is Agent Lyle and Agent Boyd from the TBI," Mommy announced.

She was going for "gracious Southern hostess", and she was hitting the mark perfectly. I bet the two agents didn't realize that more than anything in the world, Mommy wanted to turn the dogs loose on them. I couldn't help but smile into my coffee cup. Mommy introduced everyone around the table.

YaYa cast a jaundiced eye on the two agents. "Welp," she said, "you two carpetbaggers solved this yet?"

I snorted. Marcella pinched me, and Mommy cut me a withering look.

"Agents, would you like to join us for coffee? I just made some fresh."

Agent Boyd smiled. "Well, we don't mind if we do. I haven't had a decent cup since I left Nashville."

He was going for the "Ah shucks, I'm just a country boy" act. I expected him to pull out a piece of straw and start chewing on it. He chose the chair next to Daddy. Lyle sat opposite him and one seat over from me. Cozy. She didn't smile or break out any act of her own. I silently thanked God for that little favor.

Mommy scooped up the tray that we'd been using, shot me another look and jerked her head toward the butler's pantry. "Tess, will you give me a hand with the coffee things, please," she said sweetly.

I left my seat without a word and followed her. She came to a halt just inside the door and put the tray on the counter.

"What the hell are we going to do about these two? What do you think they want?" she whispered fiercely.

"I know where there's a nice deep rock quarry," I whispered, shrugging. "In truth, I think we talk very little, and let's see what they want. If either one of them asks for directions to the bathroom, one of us will show them the way and wait until they get done. We don't want them wanderin' around on their own." I paused and giggled. "I thought I would choke over YaYa."

Mommy smiled. "I love it when she acts crazy. Now help with the coffee and hurry. We don't want to miss a word. We better start a fresh pot while we're at it."

Mommy poured the remains of the last pot into the serving carafe while I threw grounds and water into the coffeemaker.

We emerged in record time to hear Agent Boyd say, "No, Mrs. Morgan, sadly we haven't solved the murder of Mr. Donnelly at the present time. But we're following a few leads."

"Fresh coffee, and I hope y'all like homemade blueberry muffins," Mommy announced.

She placed the full tray on the table, and I added the sugar bowl and creamer. I love the creamer—it looks like a cow, and the milk pours out of her nose. My sibs and I were fascinated with it as children. It's just horrible and so much fun. I thought the TBI agents needed a bit of fun, which is why I chose the cow instead of the pitcher. This choice had absolutely nothing to do with me comparing Agent Lyle with a bovine. Really.

Mommy and I settled back into our places at the table, and the coffee was served all around. Agent Boyd accepted a blueberry muffin and took his coffee black. Agent Lyle was also a coffee purist. She declined a muffin.

"Ah, delicious coffee, Mrs. Maher."

He bit into the muffin and made a sighing noise. I rolled my eyes. Agent Lyle was content to keep her mouth shut and sip her coffee. I did notice her shooting me surreptitious glances when she thought I didn't see. She didn't know that I have the peripheral vision of a freakin' rabbit, and so I saw her every time.

"Well since we have opened the subject of the investigation, I'd like to know how everyone in this county knows about the murder." Boyd said this in a very low voice and in a conversational manner.

I wasn't fooled. He was conducting an interrogation. He was paying careful attention to his coffee, but Lyle was watching all of us for a reaction. I gave them one. I laughed.

"Well that just means that the Hillbilly Telegraph is in good workin' order and in full swing." I took a sip of coffee, still smiling.

"The what?" Lyle was staring at me.

"This is a little town. Not too much excitin' happens here. Chick's death is big news because everybody knew him. It's even bigger news because he was murdered. There are several ladies who listen to the police band as a form of entertainment. Mostly so they can gossip about who gets carried home drunk, or domestic situations. They love those the most." I reached for a muffin. Boyd looked up and to the right, clearly digesting the information.

"Okay, but why would they think he'd been murdered?" Boyd asked.

"Because nothing is in season right now," Marcella informed him.

The man looked at her like she had grown an extra head.

"It couldn't have been an accident because no one would have been out shooting. Except maybe for rabbit, and they almost never roost in trees." She cocked her head at him and held her hands out in a "get it?" gesture.

He still looked puzzled. Maybe he just didn't expect anyone who looked like a model to know about hunting. Looks can be deceiving. She's almost as good a shot as me. Maybe he was an ignorant city boy and didn't realize that there were different hunting seasons for different game.

Daddy took up the explanation. "Someone heard the report and called her friend or sister or cousin and passed the info along. From there it spread like wildfire in August—to the gas station, to the hardware store, to the barber shop and so on. Before you folks up in Nashville even knew there'd been a murder down here, just about everyone in the county knew and had formed an opinion." He reached out and snagged a muffin.

"That hardly seems a likely scenario," said Lyle.

Wow, she can speak in whole sentences. How unfortunate.

"Lot of people out this way don't have cable or satellite. They have to do something to entertain themselves. Nothing's more fun than bad news, I reckon," I said.

I gave Lyle back the hard stare she was giving me. I swear the longer this mess went on, the less I liked the woman.

"Are you making a joke out of this investigation? You think this is funny? You think murder is amusing?" She snapped at me, her muddy brown eyes shooting fire.

I wanted to slap the snot out of her, but I took a deep breath instead. "Oh hell no! I do not think the death, the murder of my oldest friend is a joke. But I do think that you and your BFF here, and the way you're runnin' the show sure is, sister."

She stood up and placed her hands on the table, leaned over and invaded my personal space, her little pinched nose almost touching mine. "You do realize that we could arrest you right now for obstruction of an investigation? Give me one more reason." Her voice was cold like a snake on a spring morning.

I cocked one eyebrow at her. "I think you're a bitch and you have a shitty hair dresser who might be color blind. That's three, the last two are freebies."

"That's it," she snarled. She grabbed a pair of handcuffs from her tacky, cheap, knock-off bag and shook them in my face. "You get to spend the night in your brother's jail. I hope you like it there."

"Love it there. Bring it," I snarled back at her.

At that point all hell broke loose. Everyone started talking at once, telling us to calm down, be reasonable. You know all the stuff people say when other people are fixing to square off and beat the hell out of one another. The dogs added to the noise level. The humans were upset, and so the dogs went a little crazy, barking and running amuck.

Through all of it, TBI girl and I just stared at each other. If only we had penises, we could've pulled them out and had a pissing contest right there in the kitchen. After a minute when neither of us spoke, everyone else gradually calmed down.

Daddy called the dogs to order, "Dogs! Sit! Now!"

The Master had spoken, so the dogs thought all was well, and they settled down. None of them sat, however.

I stood up slowly, placed my hands on the table and leaned

toward Lyle to match her threatening posture. "I'm not sure what your beef is with me. But I suggest that we step outside and settle it now so we can get on with the business of findin' the bastard who murdered Chick Donnelly. Whaddaya say?"

"I say you haven't got the balls to be a real cop. You play cop, and when the chips are down you run and hide behind your brother's badge!" Her mouth was twisted up in distaste, and her beady little eyes looked even more beady and squinty. She was the poster child for hate. Most of the time people had to know me longer to hate me so bad. Another record broken!

"That's your malfunction? That I'm a PI instead of a *real cop*? Really? Really? For your information I decided not to be a real cop because I hated how the uniform made my amazing butt look so fat."

I looked at her butt. "Guess that wasn't a problem for you, huh?" I smiled my ugly eat-shit-and-die smile.

I thought she'd take a swing at me. Before she could, Boyd intervened. "Let's sit down and calm down. We need to be mutually beneficial to each other. Fighting won't get this solved." He held up a hand toward each of us as if he were holding us apart.

No one else in the room made a sound for a good thirty seconds. Lyle and I continued to stare daggers at each other. Then my brother pushed back from the table and stretched his long legs out in front of him. "So this is how you folks from the big city run an investigation? You piss off the locals who could help you, direct you and give you information. You throw your weight around and threaten to arrest people, and you're downright insultin' to boot. You develop theories and then collect the facts that support the theories. Hmm. Guess that's why I stayed here. Here we all help each other, try and fix what's wrong and solve the problems. It's not about who stands the tallest, who wins the biggest prize, or who solves the most cases. It's about workin' together and helpin' each other." He leaned back in his chair and waited.

"Right," snapped Boyd. "The locals who have secrets they don't share, misdirect and outright lie to us? Run us around in circles? That the kind of help you talking about?"

Lyle chimed in, "Besides, we like your sister more and more for this." She gave me a smug look. I saw Boyd give her a funny look.

My mother opened her mouth, and Connell held up a hand to

shush her. He leveled a look at Lyle that should have turned her to stone.

"That. Dog. Won't. Hunt." He shot an equally ugly look at Boyd. "And you both know it."

TBI Girl got an odd look on her face and cocked her head to one side like a dog looking at a ceiling fan. She didn't get the reference— where the hell was she from? "If what you're saying is that we are incorrect in the conclusions we have drawn, I'd like to hear your reasons."

"Motive," Connell said.

"In that your sister does not have one?" Lyle countered. Her voice was suddenly silky and seductive like she knew something we didn't know. I decided I was going to have to stomp her into putty.

"Let's hear your theory," said Connell.

Lyle cleared her throat. "Your sister and the victim had a history, a *romantic* history. Your sister spurned the victim. He wouldn't leave her alone but continued to harass her and pushed her to the tipping point with his advances. The day of the murder, she was presented with the perfect way to get rid of him. She saw him in the tree. It is in line of sight from where we think the practice targets were set up. We'll question everyone who was here and have a forensics team in from Nashville tomorrow to prove it and to search for the bullet if it's not in the victim. Your sister took the opportunity to shoot her stalker while everyone else was focused on the children and the other shooters. It was busy, lots going on. Or, your sister was involved with another man who got tired of the victim's advances and removed him."

She smiled like a self-satisfied child who had given a good report to the teacher. I stole a look at the teacher and he didn't look so happy. No one spoke for a moment.

Daddy broke the impasse. "It's time for you to leave my house. The next time you come out here, you'll need to bring a warrant. If you plan to question everyone, set up appointments at City Hall." Daddy stood and stared at Boyd. His stare made me remember that he had been the sheriff of our county for 35 years, and he knew how to command attention.

"I'll show you out." Daddy turned on his heel and walked toward the front door. The TBI agents really had little choice but to follow him. Oh, they could have protested, tried to throw their weight around, but that would have meant a call to the TBI headquarters, and Daddy would have climbed up the chain of command, right after he put on his ass-kicking boots. Both agents nodded good-bye as they left, but didn't speak, and no one spoke to them. Neither did anyone move until we heard the front door slam, then everyone sighed with relief.

Everyone but me. I ran through the house like a rabbit and nearly collided with Daddy as I hit the intercom by the front door. I looked at Daddy and raised a finger to my lips. Agents Boyd and Lyle were having a rather heated argument on my front porch. Daddy and I leaned in and listened.

"Have you lost your goddamned mind?" Boyd said in a low menacing voice. "We wanted this bitch and her entire family to be ignorant of our suspicions. We wanted her to not feel threatened enough to lawyer up. We need much more evidence before we can charge her, and it's too easy for her and her whole damn family to hide evidence. They're hiding something. She tucked away a notepad when we came in, and I'd love to get my hands on that. Just remember, there are a lot of them and only two of us. The bureau doesn't want to send more agents here at this time because the prevailing wisdom is that such action would spook them. Then you sit in her house and threaten to arrest her and lock her in her brother's jail. So I repeat, have you lost your goddamned mind?"

"She just pisses me off so much. She thinks she owns this town and can do anything she wants. You've read her file. She's not a cop because she doesn't think she should have to follow rules. She's above the rest of us poor suckers who do. She acts like she was born with a silver spoon in her mouth, like she's better than everyone else. She makes every woman in law enforcement look bad and like fools because we choose to carry a real badge."

"So you're letting your personal beliefs and issues get in the way of the proper handling of this case. Do I need to take you off this case? Send you back to Nashville?"

"No."

"I think you're pissed because you're down here in the ass end of nowhere working a very low profile case. So let me put it to you this way. If you could control your mouth and your manners, you would be somewhere important working some high profile case. Do you think that you can behave, so we can find out what the hell happened around here and go home?

"Yes," she answered sullenly.

"Good, because tomorrow we're going to talk to every person in this hell hole until we find someone willing to throw Tess Maher under the bus. That means we have to find someone who has an ax to grind with her, which given her attitude shouldn't be hard. And you're going to behave, got me?" Boyd sounded pissed off.

"I'll behave. But when we arrest her, I get to put the cuffs on her."

"Deal."

"So why are you here?"

"Somebody had to ride herd on your bad attitude, and I lost the bet. Now get in the fucking car."

I listened until I heard the car doors slam shut. I had a file? Who knew?

We walked back into the kitchen to find a rather stunned bunch of folks sitting at the table.

"Are they insane? No one could believe this!" Mommy said.

Daddy walked over to her, leaned down and wrapped his arms around her. She was shaking with rage.

"Maggie, honey, we will all get through this. It'll be alright."

He cut his eyes at me, so I didn't dispute him. But I knew I was in trouble. Deep trouble. As ridiculous as it seemed, these big city cops had decided to pin the murder on me. That meant that they would only look for evidence that would help them build their case. They wouldn't be looking for the person or persons who actually murdered Chick. I felt the cold icicle of fear lodge itself in my stomach. Mars reached over and grabbed my hand. She didn't say a word. She didn't have to. I knew she had my back. I knew a lot of people did.

YaYa looked at me. "Don't worry, squirt, I'll start a novena to St. Jude right now, and he'll set this mess straight."

Good old St. Jude, the saint in charge of impossible causes. He and St. Anthony, the saint of lost things, were big guys in my house when I was a kid. We prayed to St. Jude to help us pass the chemistry test we had not studied for, at all. We prayed to St. Anthony when we absolutely could not find page 3 of the term paper, or Mommy's diamond earring that I was not supposed to touch. That's a whole 'nother story.

"Thanks, YaYa." I smiled at my grandmother.

I looked at Connell. "Think now would be a good time to get a lawyer too, just to give the saints a little earthly help."

"And figure out who murdered Chick," said Connell.

No one felt like eating dinner that night.

Mars spent the night. When I woke up, the sun had risen and birds were singing. I lay there for a minute remembering all that had happened the night before. I opened my eyes and saw that Mars was looking at me. I smiled.

"Jesus, Mary and Joseph on a pogo stick! What the hell? I was hopin' I'd dreamt all that insanity."

She chuckled. "It's been a crazy few days, my dear. I still can't believe that TBI bitch wants to nail you for this. I think they have squat and are tryin' to impress their bosses in Nashville with a speedy conclusion."

"Huh, that's all fine and good, and no one else wants to solve this any faster than I do, but Holy Crap! This isn't good police work, and I know something about good police work, even if I am a weaselly PI. You think that's really the reason she hates me so much?"

"Have you seen her hair? If I had hair like that I'd hate everyone who had good hair too."

"She doesn't appear to hate you, and you have the best hair ever."

Mars smiled. "I do, don't I? She'll get to me. Right now she's still fixated on you. She hasn't even really looked at me yet. She's like a dog with a bone with you, girl."

"Yeah, thanks for that image."

I got up on my side of the bed and very calmly hit Mars in her beautiful head with a pillow. Then I ran into the bathroom and locked the door behind me. I was just about to brush my teeth when Mars tapped on the door.

"Yeah?" I said as I opened the door.

"Better call Connell before you do anything else. He has news. You might have to postpone your run this morning."

She took my place in the bathroom and turned on the shower. I speed-dialed Connell's cell, and he answered halfway through the second ring.

"Hey."

"What's up, Connell?"

"How soon can you get to your office?"

"Thirty minutes if I speed. Why?"

"Make it twenty. I'll tell you when I see ya. See ya later, love ya, bye," he said and hung up.

Okay that was cryptic. I opened the bathroom door.

"Just wash the important bits, we gotta go."

Mars was fast. I jumped in the shower as soon as she was out of my way. Ten minutes later I emerged, feeling a bit better, at least clean, and my fabulous strawberry-blonde-straight-as-a-freakin'-stick hair was clean too. I swiped at myself with a towel, struggled into my clothes and grabbed a hair tie as I exited my room. Mars was still painting her face.

"Hurry!" I yelled over my shoulder.

I took the back stairs two at a time and hit the kitchen at a run. Mommy, YaYa and both of my sisters turned to stare at me.

"I don't know," I said to their unasked question. "Connell wants me at my office as fast as I can get there. I'm going to fix a roadie for Mars and for me."

Moira came to me and hugged me. "We got your back on this. You know that, right?"

Michelene nodded at me. I smiled at both of them.

"I know. It's just that this horrible thing has happened, and in the midst of my grief I'm accused of being Chick's murderer. It sucks. On a scale of one to ten, this is a fifty-seven."

I walked into the butler's pantry and grabbed two travel mugs out of the cabinet. There was a fresh pot of coffee. I filled both mugs and doctored them with the appropriate amounts of cream and sugar.

Michelene said loud enough for me to hear, "We've told the children. The boys have told theirs too."

I closed my eyes for a moment. "Ai, yi, yi."

Mars and I entered the kitchen at the same time from two different directions, she with her makeup on and hair looking fantastic, me with coffee. She was fast! I waved the coffee at her.

"Brilliant," she said and took her cup.

"You going with?" I asked her.

Mars nodded as she sipped her coffee.

"Same car?"

Again she nodded.

"Whose?"

"Mine," she said. "It's faster."

We hugged and kissed our way out of the house and patted all the dogs who looked disappointed at being left behind. We jumped into Mars' adorable silver Thunderbird and blazed a trail to town. Good thing I have an in with the law in this town, or we might have risked a ticket. Mars drives like a demon with her horns on fire. Only a teleporter is faster.

Jewels had beaten us in to the office and smiled as we entered.

"Morning, Boss. Morning, Marcella. I see you have coffee, need a refill? Whatta we know?"

I nodded. "Mars got us here so fast, I still have coffee, but I'll take a warm-up. The TBI loves me so good that they want to pin a big metal on my chest and give me a parade 'cuz I am such a doll."

"Oh shit, they think you did it! What are we gonna do?" Jewels asked, her eyes big as dinner plates.

"Connell's on his way here. Time for a war council. We need to find out who really did it. Jewels, will you confirm that Chick owned the building his garage is in, please?"

I was stumped on the next step. I had no real power to investigate, and as a matter of fact I had been told to butt out. I needed to step back and investigate this as if it were a regular case, and that meant I needed to take all the pain and fear and anger out of the equation. This was just like when I had to dissect a pig in physiology in twelfth grade. I had to forget that I was cutting up an animal and look at the parts as individual pieces in a puzzle. Except this time I wouldn't have to breathe formaldehyde. I took a deep breath. I could do it.

"We need records of every phone call that came or went from Chick's garage and house for the last, I don't know, six months I guess."

Jewels said, "I'll call my friend at the phone company. She always comes through for us. She'll get me some records off the record. I know we can count on her."

"Right, only this time, she can't fax them to us. We'll send someone for them, and we'll pay her in cash. Let her know that she'll be crossing the TBI. That might make her think twice about helping," I said.

Jewels shrugged. "I still think she'll help us."

"I've got my laptop. I can see about the property," Mars volunteered.

She grabbed her bag and headed into my office. I was right behind her. She took over a corner of my desk. I called the garage on my cell while she was logging on to the internet.

Sammy answered, "Donnelly's."

"Sammy, it's Tess, you alone?"

"Yep, you okay? And what the hell is up with them TBI folks? They was rude and mebbe stupid too."

"They're givin' me a real hard time, and I'm not supposed to poke my nose into this case, but I think I'm in serious trouble and I need your help."

"I reckon you're right, girl. Them agent assholes asked lots of questions, but mostly they asked about you. You and Chick and your relationship. They're huntin' you sure as mushrooms follow rain. What can I do to hep?"

"You realize you could get into trouble too?"

Sammy laughed. "What're friends for? Now what can I do?"

"You got receipts for work ya'll have done, gas sold, that kind of thing?"

"We got credit card receipts and some work orders too. Cash sales, well you know how that is, no names, just amounts."

"That'll do. Can you make copies of everything that came in over the last month? Sammy be careful, don't let anyone know what you're doing. I don't want you to get into trouble over this."

"Don't worry 'bout me, I invented sneaky. How do I get this to ya?"

"I think that Marcella needs to have her oil changed." I looked over at Mars and she nodded at me.

"Oh yeah, I do love to work on that little buggy."

"One more thing. This is my cell phone number, and if you have caller ID, erase it. Write it down and call me on it, not my office phone."

Sammy laughed, clearly enjoying this. "Got ya covered."

"Hey, where's Billy?"

"Oh, he's takin' a few days off. Them state folks made him nervous as a long tailed cat in a room full of rockers. He's gone fishin'."

"Good, I want him as far away from all this as possible. Sammy, thanks, I owe you."

"You don't owe me nothing. This is for Chick," he said and hung up.

I heard Connell enter the front office and exchange greetings with Jewels. He looked flushed and just plain weird when he came into my office. Jewels came in right behind him. I caught the look on his face.

"What the hell is wrong?" I asked. He looked so horrible that I stood up as if I might need to catch him or at least break his fall.

"I got warrants from Judge Smiley for the financials. I slipped right under the wire too. The TBI agents called to officially tell me to go practice my knittin' right after I left the judge's chambers. I knew the judge wouldn't rat me out, so I went ahead to the bank." He stopped talking and just stared into space.

"Connell, then what?" I prodded him.

"Oh, then I went to see Buzzy to get a look at the will and anything else he had. You won't believe who inherits everything." He stopped talking again.

"Connell, out with it!" I demanded. I was ready to get a pair of pliers and drag the news out of him.

"Sorry. I am just in shock. Me. I get everything."

"Holy Crap!" Mars, Jewels and I all said in unison.

I had to sit down again. My head was spinning from the news. Jewels ran out of the room and returned with the coffeepot, cups and other coffee accoutrements. I only wished I had a pint of Jack in one of my drawers.

"Sit down and let's lay this thing out," I said.

Connell sat and then slumped into the chair as if his spine was no longer working.

"The way I see it, you're now gonna be seen as a co-conspirator with me. You got an alibi?" I asked.

He sat straight again. "Not really. I mowed the yard, showered, changed into my uniform and went into the office to catch up on some paperwork. Mavis's good, but she can't do everything, and there are some things only I can do." Connell shook his head. "No, wait a minute, I saw a couple of people on the street as I walked into the office."

"Drink this coffee. Maybe it will help you think. While it's on my mind, Tess, our friend is willing to send the phone dump. I'll go get it later. She and I are going to have lunch today," Jewels said.

"Thanks, Jewels. Connell, we got a phone dump comin' and the receipts from the garage. All under the radar, of course. We just gotta get ahead of them, 'cuz they'll shut us out just like they almost did with the financials." I held my cup out for Jewels to fill.

"The agents are going to be pissed. Will they know we got to any of the information before them?" asked Mars.

"Well, they'll know about the bank soon enough and Buzzy too, 'cuz someone'll tell it not thinking there's any harm. The phone dump and the receipts, I doubt it," said Connell. "My argument is that I got the warrants and the info before they shut me down, and technically that's the truth."

He paused and ran his hand across his face.

"I can't believe he left everything to me—the house, and the cabin down by the river. He left the garage to Sammy with the provision that if Billy keeps his nose clean for five years, Sammy'll make him a partner."

"Wow," I breathed, "he really had it all worked out. Bless his heart. Oh shit! This gives Sammy and Billy motive too. Sammy is libel to hurt anyone who suggests that he might've killed Chick, and Billy is out of pocket. That sure won't look good."

"The agents already talked to them both before. You think they'll want to see them again?" asked Mars.

"For sure they will now. We better give Sammy a heads up and find Billy and quick," I said.

"Billy'll be down at the river house, I guarantee it. He knows where the key's stashed," Connell said. "I'll go and get him. I'm pretty good at calming him down, and he'll have to be calm to deal with the TBI. He hates cops. they scare the hell out of him. Present company excluded of course." He added ruefully, "I just don't know how I feel about this—weird and sad, I guess. He won't be here to share it with me. So none of it even matters."

I got up and walked behind Connell's chair and hugged my big brother where he sat. He looked so sad and so lost that he broke my heart. I put my head next to his.

"Brother, I love you, and we'll get through all this together. We'll find the chicken shit bastard that murdered Chick, and then we'll mourn Chick and celebrate his life and be thankful that we had him for as long as we did. We loved him and he loved us and nothing, nothing, not even death can take that away from us. Okay."

"Okay," he nodded. "I know you're right. When you see him, tell him I love him, and I'll meet him on the flip side." He stood and hugged me hard. "I'm gonna go find Billy and try to talk him through this thing."

Jewels hugged Connell too. "I'm going to have lunch and incidentally get copies of the phone dump. I'll warn my friend that she might want to make it look like no one has been looking at Chick's phone records. I'll make you a copy too, Connell."

"Good, thanks," said Connell.

Mars stood up and gave Connell a bone crunching hug. She looked him straight in the eye.

"I have a strange knocking under my hood, and I think I better go and have Sammy look at it. While I'm there, the garage receipts will somehow fall into my purse. You'll get copies of them too. We're going to solve this, Connell." She sounded very determined, and I suddenly remembered that Mars never failed to get what she set her eye on, so the killer better beware.

Connell smiled, "Yes'um."

He started to leave.

"Connell, wait!" I called.

He stopped and turned to me with a question mark on his face.

"Last night in all the crazy, I forgot to tell you something. Mars and I were talking yesterday, and Mars said maybe the person that killed Chick didn't hate him, like I'd been thinking all along. Ya know, the usual suspects? Maybe the person who killed Chick killed him because Chick knew something or saw something. Maybe Chick didn't even know what he saw, but the person couldn't take any chances and killed him to keep him quiet. Maybe we've been barking up the wrong tree."

"That's a reach." He cocked his head to one side like he always does when he's trying to figure out a puzzle. "Yep, a reach, but it's possible." He nodded.

"Connell, it feels right to me. So I think that we all better act dumb as stumps and not draw any attention to this theory. Let the TBI lead the chase, and us act worried like they're zeroing in on me and maybe you too. Meanwhile, we work behind the scenes, quiet as little church mice and find out what the hell really happened."

"Agree," Connell said.

Mars and Jewels nodded in agreement.

"So, how do you want to play this?" I asked.

"Mars goes to get an oil change, and Jewels goes to have lunch with a friend. You do whatever it is that PIs do, and I'll wander on down to the office and pretend to be surprised when the TBI agents show up and raise hell with me for ignorin' their wishes. Then I'll go find Billy."

"Hey now, I works hard for the money!" I said in mock indignation.

"All to the good," said Marcella. "How do we get the information back to each other?"

"Text," said Jewels and Connell at the same time.

I groaned. I really hated texting. For me it's a slow ponderous process, and I have to keep backing up and correcting myself. Even then I usually don't impart what I wish to impart. I had to agree with them though. It is too easy to use eavesdropping surveillance equipment to overhear cell phone calls.

"If we do much of this kind of thing I guess that I'll have to come into the twenty-first century and get a phone with a real keyboard or touch screen or something. Or risk arthritis of the thumbs."

"And as we all know, without thumbs you'd be a talking dog," Marcella said with a smirk.

"You're mean today," I said in response.

"Today?" Connell joked.

Mars stuck her tongue out at him. That was just about all the playing we got in because the day got busy. My partners in crime all took off for their assigned tasks. They left at intervals and in different directions as if they had not a care in the world.

"Oh, I feel just like Jane Bond!" Jewels said over her shoulder as she left.

I was reminded of the old television show, *The Beverly Hillbillies*. Someone would ask Jethro what he wanted to be when he grew up, and he'd say, a double naught spy. That is kind of how I felt—like a not very bright spy trying to figure out all the gizmos of the trade. I'm a PI and a damn good one. I can follow an ant's trail through a snow storm, but I cannot for the life of me figure out text messaging!

CHAPTER 12

I sat down at Mars' laptop and looked at the property records she had been working on before our impromptu war council. She had the info on Chick's garage already pulled up. Sure enough, he owned the building, and it was worth $255,000.00 according to the tax assessor. Wow, I'd have to raise my evaluation of the worth of the estate. Ugh! The estate. I put my face in my hands for a moment and sighed. Then I kicked myself in my own ass and went back to work.

While I was in the county property records, I thought I should look around and see what my building was worth. I don't own it, so it was just idle curiosity. I found that my building was worth $372,000.00—more than I thought. Furthermore, the building had changed hands last week. Wow, I had no idea. I hadn't gotten a notification about different owners, changes in contracts, rent or anything. That was odd. The name of the new owners was not familiar to me either—Aggroco International Inc. That was quite a mouthful and who were they? They weren't local. I'd never heard of them. I decided to see if they owned anything else in the county, so I punched the name in. Lo and behold, they did.

Most of the properties had been bought up in the last few weeks. I smelled something. I just wasn't sure what. Most of the recently acquired property was out of the city. I couldn't put my finger on what was making me twitchy about this, but I went with it. I pulled up the map, so I could see where the properties were located. The parcels were all along Coleman Cove, an area of the county that was sparsely populated. It was out beyond the valley where we swam in the river as kids, in the back of beyond. A few old timers still lived out there, I thought, but the farms were mostly abandoned and allowed to go to rack and ruin. It was kind of an eerie place, like a ghost town. It was a lot of land that no one seemed to want. From what I could see, some of the properties had changed hands a few times, but the properties always came back to the state or the bank. Most of the properties had reverted to the county by way of unpaid property taxes years ago. Hmm, curiouser and curiouser.

I'd be damned if I'd put all that information into a text. Besides I didn't really have anything to tell, just a hunch. I decided to copy the records and print off the map. Besides, it might not be important— just a bright sparkly thing that grabbed my attention. I'm kind of like that. YaYa called me a magpie when I was a kid. But really, this gave me a strange feeling in the pit of my stomach, and I felt that somehow it was related to Chick's death. I didn't know how or why, but I always listen to my gut instincts. It's kept my head attached to my body on more than one occasion.

Speaking of my stomach, I realized that I'd missed breakfast. I reached into my desk drawer and grabbed an energy bar. It didn't taste bad, just not good, but it would have to do.

I texted my spy team: got something interesting maybe any1 else?

About ten seconds later, my phone made weird little chirping noises to indicate an incoming text message. I got several more in rapid order.

Mars sent: Still at garage.

Jewels sent: Lunch was perfect.

They were cagey with their answers just as good spies should be. I smiled. The one from Connell was a bit more ominous.

Connell sent: TBI on warpath, beware. No Billy yet.

Crap. I wanted Billy where we could produce him in a heartbeat for Boyd and Lyle. Under no circumstances could any suspicion fall on him. He'd lose his tiny, little mind, and that would only make him look guiltier. Crap! What a mess.

I texted back: war council @ the house?

I got affirmative answers from everyone.

Next, I texted my siblings: War council @ the house 2nite do not call text only.

My phone started to buzz and chirp immediately with responses. All my siblings would be present. Good, the more brains on this the better.

I texted to everyone: Someone drive 2 house 2 give Mommy heads up do not call her or each other no phones repeat no phones erase all messages!

Sixty seconds later Moira texted: Gone 2 Mommy.

Good. I was delighted that she volunteered to make the drive. Which made sense—she was the closest. Mommy didn't text, didn't read the ones sent to her and really ignored the entire phenomenon. She said that her fingers where too fat and her eyes were too bad to bother and that she was old and damn well didn't have to do it. Maybe this would bring her into the twenty-first century.

I decided I'd better do some work that actually paid the bills. I shut down the laptop and stowed it in the carry bag. I sure as hell didn't want that sitting out if uninvited pests showed up. I turned back to my computer and brought up the list of things to do. There was a background check, several prospective clients with questions, a cheating husband, and a couple of reports that needed to be typed up and mailed.

The background check was for a store manager of a furniture business over in Spot. He wanted me to check out a potential hire for warehouse and delivery work. It looked pretty simple and straightforward. I didn't think I'd have to do any personal interviews on it. The applicant was young—just out of high school. If he had any kind of criminal record it would be juvenile, and unavailable to me. Easy peasy.

I'd hand over the prospective clients to Jewels. She could contact them and give them my fees and get the details on the investigations. One person wanted a background check and the other was for a missing person. A background check is usually pretty standard. You check credit scores, voting info, look for accidents, active lawsuits and then check for a criminal record.

A missing person is anything but standard. Most missing adult people are missing because they don't want to be found. They may have changed their name, or gotten a false social security number, or moved to another country. I'd have to check births, deaths, marriage records, criminal records, hospital records, in short, every record I could find to run the person to ground. Even after all that work, there was no guarantee I'd be successful. I still had to charge for the hours I put in looking. It takes longer to do the missing person investigation and costs more money. If the potential client accepted my terms, Jewels would contact them again, get all the necessary information and mail them a contract to sign. We ask for a deposit of half the estimated cost of the job. When we got the check and it cleared the bank, we'd get started.

The cheating husband investigation had to be dealt with today. I had to email the wife to tell her that, indeed, her husband was cheating on her with a much younger, much blonder, much more cosmetically enhanced woman. That email would take awhile to compose. I wanted to break the news gently, even though it wasn't really news to her, or she wouldn't have hired me in the first place. Women always know. Up until that point, we'd done everything via email. She'd bought a laptop which she kept in the trunk of her car and created a new email account just to communicate with me. She might not make such a bad PI herself. She had the stealth part down. Now I had a conclusion to report and pictures to deliver. I needed to know how she wanted that done: courier, mail, email or in person. Can I just say that I love it when cheaters pose for me! My client had a pre-nup with a fidelity clause. There was a lot of money involved. I hoped the blonde bombshell was worth it.

I also had to gather notes in several investigations and give them to Jewels so she could type up reports for the clients. You have to keep the client informed every step of the way on an investigation because that is the professional way to do business. You also do it so that the client will feel they are getting the most bang for the buck.

I decided to start with the background check first. It was easy, rather mindless and would occupy me for several hours. I had to think harder for the others. Not that I don't have to think to run a background check, but once I plugged in all the facts in the right places, the computer would spit out the info I needed, generally. I just have to know where to look, and I do. If I have to hunt hard for information, that usually means that someone is hiding something. Almost no one is off the grid these days unless they want to be. Go ahead, Google yourself and see what you find.

Jewels showed up about an hour or so later with burgers from Fat Mo's. Oh, they are the bomb! And the fries will make you weep.

"Don't worry, I got extra ketchup for you," she said as she set our food out on my desk.

"Thanks, Jewels, you're the best. Gimme the dirt on the phone dump," I said.

Quick as a bunny, I saved my work on the computer, so I could get to my burger. Man oh man, it smelled like I imagined heaven smelled.

"Well," she said, unwrapping her own burger, "I just glanced at it, but I didn't see anything out of the ordinary. The house phone showed calls to the garage, the Sheriff's office, your house and your cell phone. The garage phone showed mostly local numbers, folks probably calling for repairs and services. Calls out went to Chick, Sammy, Billy, Connell, Tilly's and you."

I drew a sharp breath. "Wow, I've saved the last message on my cell phone from him." I stopped talking and scrubbed my hand across my face and took a deep breath. "I can't believe I'm never gonna get another one."

"I know." Jewels brought her burger toward her mouth and stopped. "Hey, what about his cell phone?"

"Didn't have one. He thought that if anyone wanted to get hold of him they could call him at the garage or at his house. If he wasn't in one of those places, he didn't want to be found. He didn't have a land line at the river. Said that if he was there and someone wanted him bad enough they could damn well drive out and talk to him while he was fishin'."

I chuckled remembering how adamant he was about not having a cell phone. *"Hell, TisTis, if it's important, then people can leave me a message on the two phones I do own. I don't see no reason why I should buy two more phones for other people's convenience!"* he'd groused.

"So that was a waste of your time. I apologize, but we can't afford to let any lead slip through the crack. Too much is at stake."

"Nothing's a waste of time in this case, Tess. You're right, there's just too much at stake. We have to run everything to ground. There was a chance we'd find something."

She took a bite of burger and I did too. We immersed ourselves in gastronomic delight for a few minutes.

"Yum, this stuff should be illegal!" Jewels said.

"It probably is in many places. My mouth and my stomach thank you and sing your praises. My hips, however, curse you."

Jewels laughed. "Run an extra mile tomorrow."

"Speaking of, I thought you already had lunch with our girl at the phone company. You eating for two?"

Jewels smiled. "No on both counts. I had an ice tea and dessert with her, so I could have Fat Mo's with you."

I chuckled. "You know the only consolation that we have on the time you wasted is that Boyd and Lyle will have to waste even more time getting the same non-info because they'll have to get a warrant first."

"Oh that is very satisfying," Jewels said. She reached in her bag, pulled out the phone records and handed them to me. "Take a look and see if anything strikes you."

I took a few minutes and scanned the records while I polished off my fries. I couldn't see anything wrong with her logic.

"I don't see a thing that sends up any red flags. Crap, I was hopin' for something." I tossed the papers down on my desk. "Don't file those. Put them in your purse, and let's take them...where the hell are we gonna take them?"

"Huh? Oh yeah, they may think we are hiding evidence and obstructing an investigation. They'll be able to get warrants to gain access to all of our houses and all of our businesses, plus this is the tiniest bit illegal."

I laughed at that. "Hell, they may get warrants to toss all our places anyway just for the annoyance factor. Besides, I like to think that we're not really hidin' evidence. We're just not sharin' it. I'm sure they won't see it that way. OH! Got it, if there's anything important in this pile, I'll mail everything to Derek."

"You sure about that? Won't they know about him? Won't he have to turn anything you send over to the authorities?"

"Jewels, he's a fireman not a cop. Besides, the only people outside of the family who know about him are you and Mars. I think the secret is safe."

"You better hide the Four Alarm Fire calendar then. Lyle and Boyd can put two and two together, eventually." She grinned.

"Yep, I'll take care of that tonight."

Mars finally texted: Got receipts, coming 2 office.

After that Jewels and I buckled down and got some real work done. We were falling behind in reports and billing. I finished the background check on the eighteen-year-old future hernia patient. He was as clean as fresh snow. I wasn't surprised. Jewels walked out to check the mail.

"Good news," she said when she came back. "We have checks!"

"Thank God, now we don't have to sell the milk cow. What did we get?"

"The rest of the money from the Spearman job and the deposit on the Marsden job."

Oh, the Spearman check was hefty. Mrs. Spearman was a concerned mother in Nashville who wanted me to look at her prospective son-in-law. The Spearman family had money, property and Ivy League schools. It was old money by the way. The possible groom, Marvin Smithson Hill the 3rd, had a story. It was a good one as stories go. His daddy was a Texas oil man, and his mama was a socialite. They spent a good deal of time in Europe. Marvin had pictures of his parents, his siblings, the house, the summer house, the vacation house in Aspen, the yacht and so much more. He had a Facebook account with all his many Texas relatives, his entire history since birth and more pictures. He had stories about going to Texas A&M, and he had a great job in Nashville. He invited the girl, Mary Lee, to his office in the Bat building on several occasions, met her in the lobby and walked her to his office. It was a richly appointed office. His condo was fabulous as well, with a view of downtown Nashville that would knock your socks off.

But Momma just didn't buy it. She smelled a rat. She called me because I'm great at my job, and she thought that I was far enough removed from Nashville that no one would recognize me. She was right, no one did. I followed the boyfriend for three days. During that time he never darkened the door of the Bat Building. A simple phone call to his supposed employer revealed that he did not work for the Premium Investments Corporation, who rented space in the building. I was able to slip into the Bat building during lunch time and wander around. I found many office doors unlocked and unattended during my tour. In the entire 45 minutes that I was in the place, no one challenged my right to be in the building. When I found a human, I showed Marvin's picture and my license and no one knew him. Neither was I asked to leave.

The condo he supposedly owned was actually a model in the Terrazzo, a rather fantastic, fully furnished condo in the Gulch, the hot new area in town. Marvin was friends with a realtor—a female realtor, I might add. I tried to run down all the relatives he had on his Facebook account and none of them existed. The criminal records told me there had been a name change—he wasn't a 3rd. There was so much pay dirt there: fraud, grand theft, grand theft auto and bad checks. All the victims were women. The boy was a flimflam man and a damn good one. There were lots of arrests and many complaints on record, but not many convictions and not much jail time either. Did I mention he was smoking hot?

I made my report to Mrs. Spearman, and she asked me to come to the house and give it to Mary Lee in person. She was afraid her daughter wouldn't believe her, and I had credentials. I also had pictures, police reports, arrest records and a marriage certificate to a young lady in Texas. There was no record of a divorce. It was a very ugly night. It culminated with Mary Lee phoning Marvin and crying and screaming at him. When he found that he couldn't talk her into believing his side of the story, he hung up. Much hysterical sobbing followed that, and I slipped away into the night. Mr. Spearman promised me a bonus for my work.

"Is it a lot?" I called out to Jewels.

Jewels walked into my office waving the check. "Ten thousand dollars."

I know my eyes nearly bugged out of my head. "Holy shit! Let's run off to Cancun!" We both laughed.

That was a lot of money. I wondered if the Spearmans had any more daughters.

Jewels and I worked through the afternoon without much disturbance—a few phone calls, but otherwise quiet. Until Agents Lyle and Boyd showed up. They caught us working on PI stuff, not sneaking around and interfering in their investigation. Thank God!

I heard the door open and the lovely Agent Lyle speak to Jewels. "Don't bother. We're here to see your boss."

The agents walked into my office looking for all the world like a death squad.

"Agents, what can I do for you today?" I asked.

"We're considering charging you with obstruction of a TBI investigation and tampering with evidence on top of murder one. Your fate is being decided in Nashville right this minute," said Lyle, obviously delighted with herself.

"My fate?! Wow! I've been here all day working on several investigations, writin' reports, sendin' emails, gettin' paid and talkin' to prospective clients. Juliet has been here too except when she went and got lunch. What's your problem, what do you think we've been doing?" I tried to look innocent and affronted.

"Your brother may be in some hot water too," said Boyd. "Of course it doesn't have to go down that way."

The subtext was that I could save my brother any harm by admitting my guilt. I didn't think they had one shred of evidence, or they would've handled this different—as in, handcuffing and the reading of rights would have been involved.

"Do your best. I'm not guilty of murder, I'm not tamperin' with or withholdin' any evidence. Neither is my brother or anyone I know. So if you're done tryin' to scare me, I think I'll go back to makin' a livin'." I met Boyd's stare and did not back down.

Lyle screwed up her face at me. "We'll get you," she said.

"And my little dog too?" I said in a bad impersonation of the Wicked Witch of the West. I couldn't help it. The words just fell out of my face. I wondered in that moment if a person could have filters installed between the brain and the mouth.

Lyle opened her mouth to speak, but Boyd touched her arm. "Know that we're watching you," he warned.

He turned on his heel and walked out. Lyle followed him and spared an ugly glance over her shoulder for me. The front door slammed.

"I cannot believe you said that to her," Jewels said. She dissolved into laughter, walked into my office and collapsed into the chair next to my desk.

"I gotta buy some filters before I get into trouble."

I really did. But instead I went back to work. Occasionally, I would chuckle over my retort. It really had been perfect.

About 5:00, I decided I was whipped like a rented mule. I turned off my computer, said goodnight to my plants and fish, stretched and turned off the lights. In the front office, Jewels was still hunched over her computer.

"Jewels, go home, see your husband, do dirty things to him and then get some sleep. I'll see you in the morning."

"Yes, Boss," she saluted me. "But before you go you might want to take the phone records with you." She reached down into her blouse, pulled the papers out and smiled at me. "I was afraid they might've had a search warrant on 'em. I figured if they did, it wouldn't cover a personal search."

"Girl, I love how you think, you rock." I took the papers from her. "Now git." I made shooing motions at her.

She saved her work, turned off the computer, picked up her purse and went out the door. I grabbed Mars' laptop, turned out the lights and followed her. As I walked toward the Jeep I sent Mars a text: Laptop with me.

Her response: K

I jumped into my Jeep and pointed it toward the house. Immediately, thoughts of Derek filled my brain. A slow rush of heat started in my nether regions and climbed upward. Derek was just yummy. He fought fires on his day job, and as a sideline took his clothes off for money. It isn't what it sounds like, really. The Nashville Fire Department did runway strip shows for charity. Women lost their minds whether the guys were wearing full scale firefighting gear or tuxes. Derek was built for the job: broad in the shoulder, narrow in the hip, an honest-to-God six-pack and a beautiful butt. He reminds me of the New York batter, Derek Jeter, except my Derek can't play ball. But he has other talents. I nearly broke out in a sweat just thinking about him.

I wasn't in love with Derek, but I was in big like with him and had a huge case of lust to boot. We met at a convention about a year ago, where he was stripping and I was pretending to sell invisible bras. Actually, I was staking out the pretzel booth woman. Her husband just knew she was cheating on him and was convinced that she was using the convention as a cover to meet her lover. I watched her non-stop for three days, and I followed her to her hotel every night. She wasn't getting any action that I could see, unless she was keeping some guy in the closet.

On the last afternoon of the convention I took in the strip show, only because I was following the pretzel woman. Honest. The stage sat in the back of the convention center. The lights are on, of course, and it's not like a sleazy strip club. My guess, it's because it was a convention geared toward women who might be put off by a real strip club. No one that I saw was put off. Most of them jumped out of their seats to stuff dollar bills in g-strings. That was when I first saw Derek. He was gorgeous: dark hair, perfect features, café au lait skin, great teeth and a smile that lit up the room. I couldn't see his eye color because I was too far away. I stood near the back of the crowd and at one point during his routine our eyes met and I decided that I didn't care what color they were.

After the show I went back to my booth, and ten minutes later Derek showed up. He had clothes on, street clothes, and I discovered that his eyes were an odd blue-grey.

"Hi, my name is Derek Martin." He reached out and shook my hand.

"I'm Tess Maher, pleased to meet you. That was a great show."

He blushed a bit. "Well it's fun and it's for a good cause."

"And women putting money in your underwear is a bonus, I suppose?"

He laughed. "I know you don't know me, but since you just saw me mostly naked, I was wondering if I could buy you dinner after the place closes."

I sighed with real regret. "That is an original pick-up line and I'd love to, but I have to break down the booth. I also have an appointment later."

No way was I going to break cover for a pretty face. He looked disappointed.

"But, I could stay in town an extra day, and we could have dinner tomorrow night," I counteroffered.

"That works. Shall we exchange numbers?" He smiled like I had just given him a prize.

"I am staying at the Hyatt," I told him. I had no idea why I felt compelled to share that information with him. I pulled out a business card that only contained my name and cell phone number. It's the one I used when working undercover.

He handed me a card with the NFD logo, his name and number. "I'm off for the next few days, so we can do dinner and not have to worry about a late night."

"Perfect, I'll call you around lunch time. I should have all my loose ends tied up by then."

"I look forward to hearing from you."

He shook my hand again and walked off to join some of his fellow firefighters. They all waved at me. I felt like a senior in high school—weak in the knees and silly and sort of pleased with myself.

I helped the real owner of the booth pack up, all the while watching the pretzel lady. When she left, I followed. The booth owner knew the deal, and besides I had paid her for the privilege of hanging out in her booth. I had even sold some bras. She came out ahead in the deal.

The pretzel lady made the short walk to the hotel. No one approached her, no one met her at the hotel, and according to my listening devices cleverly planted in her room, no one joined her in her room. The pretzel lady did not get lucky. I was glad. I could give the suspicious husband some peace of mind.

I slept late the next morning. Then I showered, dressed and spent two hours composing my notes for the report. I ordered room service. If the man was suspicious of his hard working, pretzel-selling wife for no reason, he could pay for it. At five minutes past noon, I called Derek as promised. He answered on the first ring.

"I was hoping you'd call," he said.

I felt flattered. "You promised me dinner, and I never turn down a meal. So where are we goin'?"

"I thought we could go to the Painted Ox. It's a great little place on Third. You do like steak, right?"

"Only if it is so rare that a good vet could get it back on its feet, and there's a loaded potato to keep it company, and beer, there must be beer."

"You're my kind of woman! So what say I come over to the hotel and meet you in the lobby? We can walk over to the Painted Ox from there."

"It's a date. How's seven for you?"

"Works. See ya then."

I spent the rest of the day working on reports, but I did manage to get out and do a little shopping. I never waste a trip to Nashville, especially when I needed new boots.

Derek met me in the lobby at 7:00 sharp. He was dressed casually, but he looked so damn good, my heart beat a little faster. I too looked fabulous in my new boots! Derek brought a present for me—the Nashville Fire Department calendar, called Four Alarm Fire. He was Mr. July, and oh, he was hot!

It was a great night. The Painted Ox did a mean steak. The potato was perfect and the beer on tap was cold and plentiful. Derek and I hit it off like a house on fire. Couldn't help it, that's the truth. Dinner was wonderful. During dessert we had a serious discussion about life, birth control, condoms, general health and the fact that we were both consenting non-attached adults.

As soon as I finished my last bite of chocolate mousse, we headed back to the hotel and promptly lost our minds. The post dinner festivities were phenomenal! The man knew his way around the female anatomy, and then some. The pretzel lady had not seen any action that weekend, but I certainly did. He liked my boots too. Those memories carried me all the way home.

CHAPTER 13

The house smelled of pork loin when I came in the kitchen. The gang was all there: siblings and spouses, parents, YaYa and Mars. God it was so good to be home. I blew kisses all around the kitchen. Everyone seemed engaged in the dinner operation.

"Where are the many children?" I asked.

"Many of the minis are upstairs playing on various electronic toys," answered my brother Patrick. "You want a drink?"

"A beer would be good."

He reached into the fridge and pulled one out for me.

"Some of the children are having a Wii tournament upstairs," said Moira.

"And Grace is here to chase the little ones," said Dugan.

"Thank God for Grace!" we all said.

Grace is a high school girl that our entire family employs as a babysitter. She's kind, conscientious, smart, good in an emergency and always available. That's not because she has no friends or is ugly or hunched-backed or goat-footed. No, it's because her parents would not let the girl date. We all thanked heaven for that rather archaic decision.

"The TBI agents have set up appointments with the family at Connell's office tomorrow," said Michelene.

"Good God above! Can we get dinner in our mouths before we discuss anything about this, please?" Mommy exclaimed.

"Okay by me," I said. "What can I do to help the process along?"

"Toss the salad."

So I tossed the salad within an inch of its life, and shortly, dinner was ready. We moved into the dining room, so we could serve everyone, and Sarah said grace for us. Grace joined us, of course. She needed to keep her strength up. We had pork loin, cheesy potatoes, asparagus, green beans and tomatoes. It was lovely and we did not talk about the case once. Instead, we discussed Patrick's job over at Public Works, where there was a hiring freeze. We all commiserated with him. As head of Public Works, all the crap rolled up hill to him. He couldn't hire more people, the needs were expanding, the workers were over worked, and not everyone got the services they needed when they needed them. Everyone who was unhappy bitched to Patrick.

"Some days, being a wino under a bridge is looking good to me," he complained.

His wife Elaine swallowed a sip of iced tea. "Sure it does, but John, Michael, and Steven would have to live under there with you, and they would be no fun at all. Now if we could live in a tent at the park that might work. They see camping as an adventure."

"Only because they never really had to live in a tent," quipped YaYa, who then turned her attention back to her asparagus.

"You never had to live in a tent!" said Mommy.

"You don't know everything about me. I had a life before I married your father and started having babies and keeping house, you know."

YaYa tried to look mysterious, but we all knew better. She had worked as a secretary, rolled bandages during World War II for the American Red Cross and went to USO dances. She spent one summer in Chicago with her aunt where she modeled hats for a department store. But if she wanted to be mysterious, far be it from me to take that away from her.

"Are we gonna live in a tent?" asked Michael.

"If Michael is gonna live in a tent, can I live in a tent too?" asked Shawn.

There was a fifteen minute discussion to explain why no one was going to live in a tent and why living in a tent in general was a very bad idea. The herd failed to get the message.

Finally, I said, "If you lived in a tent, there'd be no place to recharge your electronic gizmos and computers and other stuff."

They all looked at me as if I had lost my mind.

"We'd get car chargers," said Sarah.

You just cannot argue with that kind of logic. From there the discussion turned to a camping trip. There were many great ideas and some not so great ones. No one wanted to go to the desert and see prairie dogs, which was Kevin's idea. Art museums were ruled out too; we'd have to put on clean clothes to go. Finally, we decided on a state park, but not which one.

"Can we just please go before it is four hundred degrees?" begged

Moira.

"Aunt Tess," said Mary Katherine.

"Yes, ma'am."

"Mama says that Uncle Chick is dead."

Movement at the table froze. I looked at Moira and Bobby with a question mark on my face. They both nodded at me. It was a sucky conversation but it had to happen at some point.

"Yes, love, Uncle Chick is dead and we're all very sad."

"Well why do people have to die?"

Oh God, out of the mouths of babes.

"There're a lot of reasons that people die, baby. Some people are sick and they can't get well and the doctors have done everything for them, or they're very old and they just wear out."

"Just like the TV at our house—it wore out," said Kathleen.

I smiled, "Yeah, baby, like the TV, people wear out too."

"Cept we got a new TV," said Patricia.

"But, Auntie Tess, we can't get a new Chick," said John. His bottom lip was trembling.

"Then what are we gonna do?" Michael asked.

"Well," I said, "we are gonna remember all the good times that we had with Chick, all the silly tricks that he pulled on you, all the places we went and all the things he taught you. We are gonna be sad, and we are gonna love him."

"But Auntie Tess, here's the good thing. Now Uncle Chick is in heaven and he gets to see his mommy and his daddy for the first time in a long time and he's so happy. We should be happy too," offered Sarah.

Beautiful, solemn, practical Sarah. I wanted to hug her for that statement. I breathed in through my nose and smiled at her.

"Oh, yes, he's with his mommy and daddy and they're all so happy. Even though we miss him so much, we know that he's happy, and we're glad for him."

I reminded myself that I just needed to keep my shit together for another five minutes. Dinner would be over, and we could send the kids to play in the other room.

It was longer than five minutes before we cleared the table and loaded the dishwasher. It was more like fifteen. Kevin cornered me as I swept the dining room for missed plates.

"Auntie Tess, I know that Uncle Chick wasn't sick or old. I know someone killed him, and I know that you're not happy no matter what you say. I know you're sad and I'm sorry and I'm sad too."

Tears welded up in his big blue eyes. He was trying so hard to be brave. Bless him. I leaned over and wrapped my arms around him.

"Kev, thank you. To get through times like this, we have to stick together, lean on each other and love each other. This is hard times but we'll get through it. I meant what I said about remembering the good times with Chick and how much we love him. That's all that matters, baby, love."

"I won't say nothin' 'bout how sad you are. I know that Mom and Dad are sad too, I heard Mom crying." He looked me straight in the eye. "When I grow up I'm gonna be a cop so I can catch bad guys like the one who killed Uncle Chick."

"We're gonna catch him, Kev, and when we do, he'll never be able to hurt anyone else. I promise."

"I know you will." He hugged me hard. "If you need a shoulder to cry on, I reckon mine's big enough."

Then he picked up a dirty plate and headed into the kitchen. I drew in a deep breath and resisted the impulse to bend over and put my head between my knees. Damn. What a kid!

I entered the kitchen and shooed the remaining kids away. Grace herded them upstairs. The adults settled in around the kitchen table.

"Before we get started, I hope I didn't step on any toes by havin' that discussion with the kids," I said.

Several of my sibs shook their heads.

Michelene spoke up, "Often we don't discuss death with children. We try to protect them. They can feel left out of the process and they can become frightened and can even develop phobias."

I nodded. "Kevin knows that we're all sad, so you might want to have further discussion with him. He heard Chelsea cryin'."

"Oh God," she said rubbing her forehead. "I've tried to be careful so they wouldn't see and get upset."

"Chelsea," said Michelene, "don't hide it. Let them know that you're sad, that it's okay to be sad when someone dies. It's normal."

"Okay, I will. I just didn't want to upset them, you know."

Dugan wrapped her in a hug, and she put her head on his shoulder for a moment. That was good to see. I was glad they had each other.

"Now," said Mommy changing the subject, "What do we have?"

Dugan said, "I wanna make sure I understand the need for texting and no phone calls. We're texting so that we can keep our movements under the radar of the TBI, correct?"

I answered, "Right, the beauty of text messaging is that once you read and erase the message, most carriers don't retain the actual message longer than seven days. After that, it can't be traced or recreated. They might retain the fact that a text happened but not the content."

"You're pretty smart for a dumb ole girl," Patrick quipped.

"Then I won't tell you it wasn't my idea. I'm thinkin' that we need burn phones so that even with a warrant, the TBI'll find zip. I'll send Jewels out for them tomorrow. If some of ya'll could stop by the office in the afternoon and pick 'em up, that would be lovely."

"The TBI scheduled interviews tomorrow, starting with Mommy and Daddy and going down the line," Connell said.

"Wow," I said, "that's pretty ambitious of them. That's thirteen interviews."

Connell grinned. "Yep, they're holdin' Friday open to finish them up. Plus they're tryin' to talk to every single person in town. That's proven frustratin' for 'em."

"How so?" asked Darlene.

"Most people don't want to talk to them at all, and so give 'em short answers and no help. They're gettin' aggravated as hell." Connell smiled.

"Good!" said YaYa. "I hope they brought the Pepto for the sour stomach this is gonna give 'em." She grinned.

"The phone dump of Chick's house and the garage gave us nothin'—no unusual numbers or many from out of the area. Most seemed to be durin' business hours at the garage, and the only ones to his house were familiar. So, dead end," I said sadly.

"Can't win 'em all, baby sis," said Brian.

"Yeah I know, still I was hopin' for somethin'," I muttered.

"Mars and Connell were telling us about this idea that Chick was murdered by a professional," demanded my brother-in-law, Bobby. "It's just too crazy for words."

"Maybe not. So far we have absolutely no motive for his murder—not the usual ones anyway. Everyone loved him. But what if he saw somethin' or heard somethin' that compromised him?" I said.

"Mommy says Chick has no clue as to who or why either," said Patrick.

"None, but if I could get him to contact me for more than three minutes we might be able to figure it out!" I raised my voice. "Sorry," I said looking around the table, "I'm just very frustrated."

Michelene reached across the table and patted my hand. "Honey, we're all frustrated and miserable, but I know we'll find out who did this and make the bastard pay."

I almost laughed. My rather angelic, almost nun-like, big sister hardly ever said shit with a mouth full. To hear her cuss was a rare treat.

I smiled. "I know we will. I just want this over now so we can bury Chick and mourn him properly."

"One thing for certain," said Mars, "if this was a professional hit, we all need to play this very close to the vest—don't tell a soul what we think, be careful of having discussions where the children can hear, that sort of thing."

"No land lines or cell phones either," Connell cautioned. "Text or face-to-face only."

"Good advice. If indeed Chick was murdered over the need to keep somethin' quiet, that unknown suspect won't hesitate to kill again. We all need to watch our backs, if for no other reason than Chick was close with us, and the murderer could believe he divulged information to any of us."

"Daddy, you're scarin' me," said Moira.

I knew she wasn't afraid for herself but for her children.

"We'll get it figured out, Moira, but in the meantime I think it might be Tess who's in the most danger. She was close to Chick. Everyone in town knows it. She'd be the most likely person he'd confide in about anythin'," said Connell.

"Or you," I said quietly.

Connell smiled, "Or me, and fortunately, we both carry guns. This'll come out right. I have faith."

Mars pulled out the receipts she had gotten from Sammy. "While we're all here, we can look these over and see if we can spot anything odd. The more eyes on this the better." She divided them into piles and handed them out to everyone at the table.

"We can pass them around and let everybody look. Maybe one of us will spot something that the rest of us missed," suggested Connell.

"How did you get these? I thought the TBI told you to butt out," Elaine asked.

Connell smiled, "They did. A concerned citizen just happened to drop these in my lap today and I couldn't turn them down."

"Anyone want a beer?" I asked. I got up and walked to the refrigerator. Five hands shot up around the table. I fetched and distributed bottles.

"Anybody else need anything while I'm up?"

Heads shook as everyone bent over the receipts. I settled back into my seat and looked at my own pile. We didn't seem to find much—gas, tires, oil changes, brake jobs—the usual fare that a full-service garage sees. Most of the receipts had the customer name written across the top. Most of those names were local.

"I think we can toss the locals out of the mix," I said.

"Why?" asked Mommy.

"If we're lookin' at this as a professional hit, then I doubt that Junior from the Acme Feed and Grain is a suspect," I answered.

"I agree," said Connell.

"So we look through every receipt, then cull the locals and put them in a pile in the middle of the table," Daddy said.

The process took awhile. Donnelly's was a pretty busy place. The handwriting on the receipts was not the best either, and some of them had to be deciphered. Finally, we had a few receipts that might fit our criteria: no name, or from out of the area. One that grabbed my attention was for a tire repair. There was no name on the receipt. If it was a repair for someone local, Chick would have written the name of the customer on the receipt out of habit.

"Did everyone see this receipt for a tire repair? No name and Chick wrote 'looks like a piece of metal' across the bottom. I think this is the kinda thing we're looking for. The more I think on this the more inclined I am to believe that some person or persons unknown came into the garage for somethin' or another. I think that Chick made a remark in passin' to the unsub that made him or them suspicious that Chick had some secret knowledge about them. They killed him rather than take a chance."

"That is a lot of maybes and unknown suspects," said

Michelene's husband, Danny.

"True," I said, "but find me somethin' better. I'm drownin' here. We've explored all the other angles and come up empty. Hell, the TBI has no answers either, and so they're gonna pin this on me or maybe Connell. Unless you think that some crazy son-of-a-bitch just decided to commit murder on a Sunday afternoon, and the first person he ran across was Chick, then this was a hit!"

I stopped and ran my hand over my face. I had no business mouthing off to my brother-in-law. This wasn't his fault. "Sorry, Danny," I mumbled.

I pushed back from the table, but before I could get up, Connell cleared his throat.

"I need to say somethin'," he said quietly.

Everyone looked at him.

"First, this is info that needs to stay under your hats." I was pretty sure I knew what was coming. "I sort of beat the TBI agents to this info and they suspect it and don't like it. So I never told you and you don't know anythin', okay?

"For Christ's sake, Connell, out with it!" Dugan said.

"Chick left me the house, the river house, all his savings, life insurance, damn near everythin'. He left the garage to Sammy and to Billy."

No one spoke. What can you say? Congratulations! Wow, that's great! Nope, you can't say anything good because the circumstance sucked so very much. Daddy reached over and squeezed Connell's shoulder and Mommy hugged him.

"I'm gonna text Sammy and see if he remembers this particular repair. It's a long shot, but what the hell else do we have," I announced.

I wandered through the living room and went out on the patio. Not for the first time did I regret my decision to give up cigarettes. God I missed them! I didn't realize Michelene had followed me until she spoke.

"How can you do this?"

"Do what?" Her question puzzled me.

"How can you be so detached? You act like this is any other case that you've been hired to solve. I know how you felt about him. You loved him, so how can you act as though he was a stranger?" She stared at me, hard.

If she'd hit me in the gut, I couldn't have been more surprised.

"Jesus Christ, Mich, if I'm not detached I'll go crazy. I'll lie in bed all day and cry, I'll wander around in my pajamas, I'll start to collect cats or jelly jars or some damn thing, and I won't be able to do my job. If I don't do my job, the asshole who murdered Chick will get away with it!!! Add to that the fun fact that I'll probably go to prison, and you and the kids can visit me once a month. Oh yeah, and Connell will share a cell with me. I have to be rational in order to solve this. That does not mean I do not care or that I did not love Chick. I love him, present tense. But sitting around cryin' in my God damned beer is not going to help!" I said rather loudly.

"Okay. Okay," she said and held her hands up in surrender. "I was just afraid that you might be disassociating."

I just looked at her.

"Believe me, Mich, the only thing that would help me disassociate would be a frontal lobotomy. Do not try and shrink me. I don't need a shrink, even though I know you're a good one. I just need to get this solved."

"I'm here for you, you know that, right?"

Oh yes, I knew it. I nodded my head.

She stepped over to me, hugged me and kissed me. "I love you."

"I love you too. Just be my sister, not a psychologist."

Michelene quietly slipped back into the house, and I could see her moving through the living room. Sometimes she blew my mind. I recognized that I would need grief counseling when this was all said and done. I further recognized that it would not be with my sister. I whipped out my cell phone and began the laborious process of texting Sammy.

Sammy

Hey girl whatsup? he replied.

U remember tire repair chick wrote on invoice looks like a piece of metal?

Yep on account it was a big black hummer

Get a look?

Nope he stayed inside Chick used big jack. Windows dark

Tag?

No sorry

Thanks man hang loose

Always u got something?

Maybe keep you posted

Well it was something. I headed back into the kitchen.

"This one receipt just pegged my meter. I can't explain why but I know it's important. Sammy remembers the customer because the vehicle was a black Hummer. The customer stayed in the vehicle." I sat back down at the table.

"That's luck," said YaYa.

"Yes it is. Thank God for big ostentatious consumption and penis size compensation," I said with a laugh.

"You have such a smart mouth sometimes, Tess, it just breaks my heart," mourned Mommy.

I just laughed harder.

"Well as much fun as it's been to be in on the crime solvin', it's time for us to round up children and head for the hills," said Brian.

I looked at my watch. It was after 8.

"I'll help you. I like how they scream when you try to throw 'em in the car," I offered.

"God you are just awful!" Moira said. Since she was laughing, I knew she didn't mean it.

"Wait, wait, wait!" I said. "Today I was looking in the property records for Chick's building, and I looked my own building up and saw that it has been sold recently to a company called Aggroco International. Anybody ever hear of it?"

Heads shook all around the room.

"Me either, and they've bought up lots of property around here, most of it down in the Coleman Cove area."

"How much land?" asked Mars.

"Most of it," I answered.

"Funny I haven't heard one word about that, Very funny." She looked puzzled. "I usually hear when something gets bought or sold, especially when it's such a big sale."

"We need to find out who these folks are and what they're up to, 'cuz I got a gut feelin' this land deal and this company are both tied to Chick in some way or another. So keep your ears open."

Thus ended the Maher war council and began the rounding up of screaming, wiggling children who did not want to go home and bathe.

CHAPTER 14
THURSDAY

Another sunrise. Well it was kind of a sunrise. The sun was up, but it was raining. That didn't bother me. I like running in the rain. It cleanses me somehow, it isolates me from the rest of humanity and I'm alone in my bubble. Whew! God, I sounded like a philosopher—or a junkie. I threw on running clothes and tied a scarf on my head to keep the rain from running into my eyes. I added a hoodie since it felt a little chilly.

The dogs were all waiting for me at the back door, but I had to disappoint them. I cannot stand the smell of wet dog, so I do not create wet dogs for me to smell. Call me crazy.

"Sorry, boys, but there'll be no running for canines today. It's raining and I know you'd rather be here where it is warm and dry, right, good dogs?" I tried to sound enthusiastic. They all just stood there and stared at me hopefully and wagged their silly little tails.

"Daddy! Can you call the furry ones, please?"

Two short, sharp whistles and they all turned tail and trotted off to get treats. I slipped out the back door and headed to the road. Before I got to the end of the drive I decided I'd better do some stretches or I'd be sorry. I was stretching out my hamstrings when I heard a vehicle coming down the road. It sounded like a big vehicle moving slow. The little voice in my head told me to take cover, so I did. Call me paranoid but I try to listen to that little voice. It's saved my ass more than once.

There's a huge hedgerow of honeysuckle across the front of the property that's probably three feet high and three feet wide. It provided plenty of cover. I crouched down and waited. About fifteen seconds later a big Hummer came tooling down the road. Damn! It was black with dark tinted windows that prohibited me from being able to see who was in the vehicle. The dark windows gave the big vehicle a creepy vibe. I knew the people inside could see out well enough, and I was sure I didn't want them to see me. The Hummer was moving at about ten miles an hour. I thought this was probably a scouting mission of some kind because I sure as hell don't believe in coincidence.

The Hummer drove by the entrance to the driveway even more slowly. It was practically crawling, and I couldn't shake the feeling that I was being hunted. I felt like the field mouse when the shadow of the hawk passes over her. My heart was beating so hard I could feel it thumping in my chest. My lack of a weapon weighed heavily on me. It would be too easy to come at me here, out of sight of the house and isolated. The only defense I could muster would be to throw rocks at the bastard. Shit. I broke out into a sweat. I hunkered down a little lower and waited for the Hummer to get out of sight before I moved. I knew it could come back by the house, but the road looped around to the highway from either end so no guarantees that it would. I decided to change my plans. From now on, I'd do my running in town and shower at the office. I'd stick to main streets and watch my back. I'd carry a small caliber handgun in my waistband too.

I listened for the sound of the big engine to fade off then I hot-footed it back to the house. I may be a little crazy, but my momma didn't raise no fools. I ran like hell.

I pulled out my phone as I ran toward the safety of the house and dialed Connell. I was so shook up I forgot to text.

"Simpson County Sheriff's office, how can I help you?"

"Miss Mavis, this is Tess, may I please speak to my brother?" I tried not to sound too winded or too scared even though I was both.

"Sure, honey, I'll put you right through. You doin' alright?"

"Yes, ma'am, I am hanging in. It takes more than a couple of big-shots from Nashville to get my goat, ya know."

"Heh, heh, good girl."

The line went silent and two seconds later Connell picked up.

"What's up so early in the day?"

It occurred to me there was no way to have this conversation in code. Damn."Let me get right back with you."

"Sure." Connell sounded a little puzzled.

I hung up and texted: Big hummer just drove by house

Tag?

Nope, 2 worried about my hide

Good call. Think I'll take a cruise through town c if I can find big Hummer. Where the hell could they hide the thing it's as big as a house?

? vehicle like that here would draw all kinds of attention surely someones seen it did you find Billy?

At cabin. Filled him in after he calmed down & quit cussing. Swore him to secrecy & took him to my house. Orders r 2 keep his nose inside, do not answer phone, no charges 4 porn on my account

Only because yr account is past spending limit for the month

Cute. Try and have a little respect for the law. Go 2 work touch base later and watch your ass

Yeah think I will run in town 2day

Great idea, see ya later, love ya, bye

Ditto

I stuck the phone back in my pocket and came in the kitchen door still shaking.

"Oh that was a quick run," Daddy said.

"Where're Mommy and YaYa?" I asked.

"Don't know," Daddy said. He folded the paper he was reading over to the next page. "They're somewhere doing something. God knows what but as long as they don't make me work, I ain't asking."

I chuckled, then sobered. "Daddy, the big black Hummer we talked about last night?"

He put the paper down. "What about it?"

"It just cruised past the house."

"Hmm, checking us out or maybe looking for you. Getting the lay of the place I'd say."

"You got any ideas why?"

"Well I'd say you or Connell have made someone nervous, and now they're doing a little recon, tryin' to see how hard you are to get to, how the place is set up."

"Shit!" I said and sat down. "So we've rattled a cage or two. Good, that means they will come out into the open and we'll nail 'em."

"I'm gonna talk to your mother and grandmother about this and text the rest of the kids. Everyone needs a heads up. Before, the idea of a hit was just a theory. I think this pushes the idea firmly into the reality column. This is no coincidence." He looked me straight in the eye to drive his point home.

"Yep, that's great. Okay, I'm going to the office, do my run in town and watch my back. Connell's gonna do a little pokin' around and see if he can spot the Hummer. He'll get back to me. I'll get back to you."

I got up and kissed Daddy. He caught my arm as I turned to go.

"I know it's stupid to tell you to be careful, but be careful."

I kissed him again, ran up the stairs, grabbed clothes to change into later and hit the road for town. Every inch of the way, there was an itch between my shoulder blades. I kept remembering that Chick was shot in the back from long range. I drove a little faster all the while expecting a black Hummer to appear and give chase. Okay, that was a little fantastical, but I knew they were somewhere close. They'd checked out my house and who knows what else they were up to. I intended to be vigilant.

Thankfully, the ride into town was uneventful. I arrived at the office unscathed and unshot. I put one in the "win" column for me. It sure seemed like the longest ride into town ever though.

"Morning, Boss," Jewels greeted me.

"Morning," I returned. "I had a moment this morning as I began my run. A big, black Hummer came cruising down the road and past the house."

"Holy Crap, you think they were scoping you out? Has this got something to do with Chick?"

Jewels was quick on the uptake.

"That's what I think, and Connell and Daddy both agree. This is tied to Chick somehow. He did a repair on a Hummer three days before he was murdered. So I want you to be especially careful, understand?"

"I do. So do you think that somehow we have tipped our hand to these bastards? I just don't know how. We've been so careful in gathering our information." Jewels frowned.

"It could just be that they're looking at all the players, and we came up at the top of the pile. So we walk very small from here on out. I think that I'll take the time to do a search on Aggroco and see what I find on them. I just can't help thinking that somehow they're tied to this mess."

Jewels looked at me funny. "More info, please," she requested.

"Oh sorry. This company Aggroco, has been buying up land, including our building. A big black Hummer gets a repair at Chick's,

Chick gets dead. The Hummer cruises my house. I feel suspicious of these Aggroco folks because they showed up about the time the murder happened. They're the newest kid on the block and that trips my triggers. I'm gonna try and connect the dots."

"Wow! Okay, while you do that I'll do some work that'll pay my salary around here." She smiled.

I went into my office and fired up the computer. It didn't take long to find Aggroco. Their website was impressive. They were a multibillion dollar fruit and vegetable company, owned farms all over the country and shipped to all fifty states and several foreign countries. They were HUGE and powerful. The company started out a couple of decades ago as a family-owned farm in the fertile farmland of the Central Valley of California, but as they grew and got government subsidies and more and more money came in, they incorporated. Now a board of directors ran the show, and it looked like most of the remaining family members had been given figurehead jobs and quietly moved out of the way of the actual day-to-day running of the business. The website didn't say that, of course. It was just an impression I got from the pecking order on the board of directors.

The business was expanding by leaps and bounds, growing lots of food and making lots of money. The food grown on Aggroco lands not only went into just about every grocery store in the country but many fast food places, and much of it went to feed the United States military. Wow. These were big guns in every sense of the word. But were they big enough to murder someone without fear of getting caught? Maybe. But why?

I clicked around and looked at some of the other websites with the Aggroco name. Most were owned by the company and praised the company as being fair to workers and only growing the best food for people to eat. There was one entire website dedicated to the story of the food as it was grown, processed, boxed, shipped and finally ending up on plates for our fine young service men and women. That website had a waving American flag on every page. Hmmmm, people who wrap themselves in the flag always make me skeptical.

Then I got to some websites that were not owned by the corporation, and they told a far different story of Aggroco. These sites claimed that the farming giant paid small wages and treated workers poorly. There were also claims that Aggroco knowingly hired illegals and paid them even less and treated them far worse than American workers. Still other websites claimed that the agriculture giant polluted streams with chemicals and fertilizers, forced small farmers who were having hard times to sell their land to the conglomerate, and implied that maybe Aggroco was the reason for the hard times the small farmers were having. Many lawsuits had been launched against the company, but no one had ever won in court. Those websites painted the corporation as an evil empire whose only goal was to make as much money as possible. I felt a chill run up my back.

If Aggroco bought the land out at the Cove, why did they want to keep that a secret? Since Mars hadn't heard a word about it, then someone had kept it quiet. Was it to keep the land prices down? Keep anyone from knowing there was a big sale happening and you would keep others from buying up some of the land too in hope of making a big profit. You might also want to keep any of the private owners in the dark about the huge land grab. Possibly the answer was D, all of the above.

A company that was buying a lot of land for a low price would want to keep it quiet until all the sales were completed and the ink was dry on the contracts. But would any company risk murder to keep such a secret? That was a stupid thought, of course. If a junkie would kill you for the twenty dollar bill in your pocket, then a giant corporation would murder for millions. I stopped reading and rubbed the space between my eyes. I needed to find that Hummer, get a tag number and find out who it was registered to—the sooner the better. That might be a dead end, but maybe these guys were arrogant enough to actually have the vehicle registered to the company. Maybe that was just a pipe dream and had nothing to do with Chick's death, but I couldn't shake the feeling that I was on to something. I bookmarked every website I had looked at, left all of them open and got up from my desk.

"Jewels, I'm going for my run. No one gets in my office while I am gone. I've got a bunch of websites opened, and I would just as soon keep my research a secret."

"Do you think the TBI agents might show up with a warrant?"

"Oh, someone nosey could wander in and have a look. As a matter of fact, I think I'll lock my office door and take the key. If anyone shows up with a warrant they'll have to wait. I'm taking my cell phone and my twenty-five too, just in case a big Hummer starts chasing me."

"Be careful."

"Yep."

I tucked the gun into the pocket of my shorts. It was still raining as I emerged from my building—just a slight spring drizzle really. I pulled up the hood on my jacket, stretched and took off at a slow jog. I didn't expect to be molested on the streets of Medicine Springs, but I kept a sharp eye out as I ran. More than anything, I wanted to see if anyone was following me or paying special interest to me. I only saw locals as I ran. Most waved and smiled, I returned both.

As I ran around the square, I saw Donna Maples emerge from the property tax office in the back of the courthouse. She looked up and saw me, frowned, then shot me the most hateful look ever. Then in an eye blink that look was erased. So fast, in fact, that I wondered if I imagined it. She smiled her famous beauty contestant smile at me and waved. I did the same but I was perplexed. She'd always been friendly before, but in that moment when she saw me, I saw not just unfriendliness but malevolence. Another little chill ran down my spine. I decided that was enough exercise for the day and headed back to the office. I arrived just in time to meet Connell on the sidewalk.

Since it was still drizzling a bit, I stepped into the hall where it was dry to stretch out my muscles. Connell leaned up against the wall to watch.

"You got anything," he asked.

"Maybe," I said as I touched my toes. "I've found out some interesting things about Aggroco. Lots of websites that praise them to the heavens, and lots more that say they're the devil. The truth is probably somewhere in between."

"Probably. How big are they?"

"Big. It seems they squeeze out little guys, little farms, and then buy the property at bargain prices. It's all on my computer. Come have a look and see what you think."

We walked down the hall to my office.

"Connell, there was an odd thing that happened while I was running…maybe odd, I can't decide. I could just be imagining things, jumping at shadows."

"More information would be helpful."

"Right. Well I ran past the courthouse, and Donna Maples was coming out of her office, and for about two seconds she shot me the most venomous look I've seen since I flipped pig brains on Janie Hartley in twelfth grade physiology."

"God, I remember that. You got grounded and had to wash windows at home and up to the convent." He chuckled.

"Ugh, Janie was a stuck-up bitch. I just threw a little bit of brain on her, and you'd thought I'd beaten her with the whole damn pig. I've never heard so much screaming and crying. Good Lord!"

We were both smiling as we entered the office. Jewels looked up at us, not smiling.

"What's up?" I asked, immediately on guard.

"Connell, you left your radio at the office. Miss Mavis just called. She said there is trouble at your office."

"She say what kind?" he asked. I saw his hand move instinctively toward his gun.

"Trouble with your grandmother. She's about to get herself arrested by the TBI." Jewels looked very worried. Connell and I laughed.

"Oh Jesus," I laughed harder, "they deserve her."

I dissolved into giggles. In my head I could almost hear the conversation that YaYa was having with the TBI agents. It was one-sided, opinioned and probably mean. I knew she was casting aspersions on them, their mamas, daddies, their upbringing, every lover they'd ever had and their dogs. They'd need therapy when she was done with them.

"She's giving 'em hell, and saying terrible things to them about them. Nothing they can threaten her with will scare her, and they don't really dare arrest her. I say let her have her fun," Connell explained.

"Come on," I said and laughed a little harder, "I want you to see the websites before you have to go and save the poor TBI agents from YaYa."

I led him into my office, leaving Jewels with a perplexed look on her face. I pointed to the computer.

"You explore while I get a quick shower."

I gathered my change of clothes and headed out. Jewels stopped me.

"Hey, Tess, are you truly not worried about your grandmother. I mean, she's old and this is upsetting to her, I'm sure. They could be hard on her, scare her, you know how intimidating they can be." Jewels stopped talking, her brow wrinkled up and she looked totally distressed.

"Honey, you are talking about the toughest little old woman I've ever known. She's almost died six times from disease and injury, spent six months in bed with a broken leg, had spinal meningitis before there were antibiotics and almost died in childbirth, twice. She birthed nine children and buried one. She's had three husbands, all of whom she's buried. She was the first person in her family to graduate high school and the only one who has ever lived above the Mason-Dixon line. She had two dresses for an entire year during the Great Depression, she washed one and wore one every day. She cried and prayed when Pearl Harbor was bombed. Both her brothers, most of her friends and her first husband spent four years fighting Hitler. She danced in the streets on VE Day and lived through the cold war, the Korean War and Vietnam. If you think these two yahoos can scare her or even make her uncomfortable, be assured, they cannot. She's worn tight shoes that were more of a pain in the ass than these two. I'm gonna go take a shower."

I closed the office door behind me. Fifteen minutes later, I felt like a new woman. My hair was still wet, but it would dry. I opened the office door but didn't see Jewels. I could hear voices coming from my office. She and Connell were bent over the computer lost in the information that was on the screen.

"You find something interesting?" I asked.

"Maybe more questions that anything else. One thing for sure, these are not nice people," Connell said looking up from the screen.

"I think I'll be looking at labels on all the food I buy from now on. It makes my skin crawl to think that I've been eating food that these gangsters produce." Jewels shuttered.

"By the way, we've had two more calls from Miss Mavis," she said.

"Agents Lyle and Boyd ready to confess to the Hoffa murder, are they?" I chuckled.

Connell smiled. "I reckon I better wander on down to my office and rescue somebody."

"Connell, I had a thought while I was in the shower. Donna Maples is the county tax assessor, and she'd know who all the land in the county belongs to, when it changes hands, how much it sells for, the taxes on the land, if the taxes have been paid, everything, right?"

Connell nodded. "Yep, she knows it all or at least she has access to it all. Why, what has your convoluted little brain come up with?"

"Well, she must know that a lot of land has just changed hands. She knows all the details of the sale. How do we get her to tell us those details?" I said.

"You can't ask her. You've both been told to butt out. You could tell the TBI agents what you suspect and get them to ask her," Jewels argued. She looked back and forth between me and Connell to see if we agreed with her.

"We could do that," said Connell, "and they could tell us to go suck eggs. There's absolutely nothing that ties this land deal or this company to Chick."

"Except a receipt from Chick's for a Hummer tire repair—the same Hummer that drove past the house this morning," I countered.

"And your gut," Connell said.

"When you put it that way, it sounds mighty damn thin," I admitted.

"True that, but I can put it to 'em and see what happens," Connell said.

He kissed me on the cheek and walked out.

"And if they won't listen, I can get Mars to poke around and see what Donna will tell her," I said.

Jewels and I smiled at each other and did a little fist bump.

CHAPTER 15

I sent Jewels off to the store with a list of goodies to buy while I spent more time on the World Wide Web with my new favorite company, Aggroco. As I studied them, Miss Mavis called with an update from the sheriff's office—the TBI agents had sent my grandmother on her way. I was just getting myself another cup of coffee when the front door swung open and YaYa stomped in, mad as a wet hen.

"Those bastards!" she declared.

She slammed the door behind her. It re-opened immediately and Jewels walked in with a shopping bag. She looked a bit startled since the door had practically hit her in the nose. I smiled to myself as I stirred my coffee but wiped the grin from my face before I turned to my grandmother. My amusement would only serve to piss her off even more.

"Hey, YaYa," I said and gave her a kiss on the cheek. "How bad did they sweat ya?"

"They've got no raisin', none t'all. The things they suggested! How dare 'em!? I'm gonna call the governor!" YaYa was on a roll.

"Are you alright, Ms. Morgan? I'm so sorry they upset you," said Jewels. She set the bag down behind her desk and immediately got busy making YaYa a cup of coffee.

"Upset me? Hell, girl, I'm not upset, I'm pissed off! Put extra cream in that cup, if you will."

YaYa marched herself into my office and sat at my desk. I came along behind her with coffee for both of us. I set her cup in front of her and took my seat behind the desk.

"So, what'd they want to know?" I asked.

I sipped my coffee and YaYa took a careful sip of hers.

"Ah, let me see. If you had ever shown any temper, how did you feel about Chick, did you have a current boyfriend, and they wanted a blow by blow of the day that boy died. I should've given them the 'I'm old and I can't remember what I had for breakfast' routine. That woulda chapped 'em, I'm thinkin'." She chuckled.

"You really gave 'em some shit today, didn't you? You almost make me feel sorry for the agents, YaYa, but just almost."

YaYa looked over the rim of her coffee cup at me. "I'm worried for you, Toots. These two peckerwoods mean to railroad ya. They're not gonna listen to anyone who has any other ideas about anythin' but that you murdered Chick. They got a real bone with you. I reckon there's a bunch of reasons why. The girl don't like you 'cuz she believes you think you're better than her, and you made 'em look stupid, you don't have proper respect for 'em or their badges and you don't kiss their backsides. I reckon they're used to folks bendin' their necks for 'em." She nodded her head for emphasis.

"Yep, if you kick me I kick back, can't seem to help it. Even when I know I should lie down and shut up. My mouth has always caused me trouble."

My cell phone made that weird text-message sound. I dug in my bag, located it and flipped it open.

Sup? It was from Mars.

Come 2 office, I texted.

K

YaYa looked at me with raised eye brows.

"That was Mars. She's on her way here. There're a couple of questions I'd like to ask her."

"Hmmm, I reckon them TBI people are gonna want to talk to her too, after they talk to everyone else in the family. I tell you what, it ain't no 'talk', it's an interrogation pure and simple and that's a fact."

I sighed, "I know YaYa, and I know there's nothin' we can do about 'em except grin and bear it. The only hope in all of this is for us to figure out who killed Chick. I think if I can figure out why he was killed, then maybe I can figure out who did it. Oh God, I don't know."

The front door opened and I heard Mars greeting Jewels.

"Get a cup of coffee," I called. "This is gonna take some time."

Thirty seconds later Mars strolled in. As always, she looked like a freakin' fashion model. Today her suit was a champagne color with a black lacy shell under it, accessorized by cute clunky black jewelry and black shoes and black bag. They matched, of course. She made me feel like a truck driver. I decided I hated her.

"If I liked girls, I'd marry you," I said.

She grinned, "You should marry me anyway, I can cook." She

took the third chair in the room, but not before she leaned over and kissed my grandmother on the cheek. "How you doing, YaYa?"

"I've seen better days, girl, and that's the God's truth. How 'bout you?"

"Me too." Mars turned to me. "So what do we know? Before you ask: no, I have not heard anything of importance, just the usual small town fascination with something new happening. By the way, if I was a CNN pollster I would tell you the general opinion poll is running ten-to-one against you being guilty."

I grinned. "Well that's nice to know."

"So whacha got?"

I turned my computer monitor around so that Mars could see it. "Take a look at everything in my history today. All of it is about Aggroco, and most of it isn't good."

"Who's that?" asked YaYa.

"That's the name of the company that's been buyin' up all of the land down at the Cove in the past couple of weeks. We talked about them at dinner."

"Oh yeah, I remember now, big outfit from somewheres else. So they look like bad news, do they?"

"California is where. And they look like a multibillion dollar company that has poor business ethics or at least questionable ones. I need to do some more research on them before I totally throw them under the bus, but it ain't lookin' good for 'em right now."

"That reminds me. Hey, Jewels," I raised my voice a little, "what's the name of that PI in San Diego that I worked that skip trace with a few months ago?"

There was silence for a moment, and I knew she was looking him up.

"Sandy Ford. Want me to get him for you?"

"Were you able to get the items that I sent you for?"

"Yes, Spy Master, I did. Shall I use one?"

"Oh, yes, please do."

Mars and YaYa both looked at me.

"He lives in California, and I just thought he might know a little more than I can get just surfing the net."

"Is he cute?" asked YaYa.

"Is he straight?" asked Mars.

"Is he married?" asked YaYa.

I laughed. "Don't know, don't know, and don't know."

"Some PI you are," sneered Mars.

"Please hold on for Ms. Maher," Jewels said as she entered my office. She handed me a brand new cell phone. I put the phone to my ear.

"Hey, Sandy, how are ya?"

"I am fine, just fine Tess and I hope that you are too." His deep, sexy voice traveled through the phone line and gave me a little moment.

"Truthfully, I have a situation here, and I sort of hoped you might be able to shed some light on it for me."

"I owe you big time for that last catch, so if I have in my power to help you out I will. What ya got?"

"You ever hear of Aggroco?"

Sandy kind of snorted, "Oh yeah, I've heard of them, investigated them, given testimony in court cases on them, watched dirty money change hands between their bag men and had the hell scared out of me by them. If you got them, then you got big trouble."

"So, if I asked you, were they capable of dirty land deals and murder, what would you say to me?"

"I'd say, yes ma'am they are. Watch your cute little tukhus, take a shower fully armed, and if you want to make vacation plans in New Zealand, now would be a good time to do that. Although, that might not be far enough away."

"Holy Shit, Sandy, are they really that bad? They grow vegetables for Christ sakes. They're a publically traded company that feeds the freakin' military, and they have to answer to someone. Nothin' happens in a vacuum. Someone besides you knows all this too."

"Well, a lot of people know a lot of things, and the devil's in the details. You have to prove it. They have, I have been told, an enormous slush fund to pay off the likes of you and me. They have politicians in their back pockets, and they make it their business to have dirt on all those politicians so they have leverage. They employ about a zillion people in this state, and that gives them a lot of clout too." He paused for a couple of beats. "This isn't the first time that I've heard the word 'murder' connected to them."

I drew a long breath and blew it out. "Thanks, Sandy. By the way, this call is brought to you by a burn phone. When this is over, this phone will disappear and so will this call."

"God, I love a devious woman. You wanna marry me? The weather is good here all year round and I'll teach you how to surf. Whadusay?" I could hear the grin on his face.

"Sadly, I have to turn you down. Not that it wouldn't have been great fun. But I gotta catch me a killer and then I have to bury my best friend."

"Oh, Tess, I'm sorry for your loss. I didn't realize this was a personal matter for you. Please listen to me, Tess. Be careful, be more than careful, be paranoid. These are some mean bastards. A prosecutor went missing two years ago. He's never been found. Everybody knows he's dead, and everybody knows who killed him but there's no proof. They are big league bad guys."

"I hear ya. I'll keep my head down. Thanks for the info, Sandy. No one'll ever know where it came from, you have my word."

"I look forward to working with you in the future."

"Likewise."

I broke the connection and looked around the room at the worried faces. They were worried just from hearing my side of the conversation. Great.

"Well I think we got a little more now than just my gut feelings. Sandy's had dealings with these fellas before, and it seems they're big bad trouble. He suggests that we be careful and cover our butts."

"You think his information is reliable? And by the way, I'm impressed by the burn phone, Double-O-Seven." Mars smiled at me.

I chuckled. "Yeah, I do. Sandy has a good rep in the business, with twenty years experience, and he treated me fairly on the case we worked together. Man, this is bad."

"You have a theory based on all this information about Aggroco that you've dug up. So what do you think is happening in our little corner of the world?" asked Mars.

"I think that a big company that grows lots of food has bought up a shit ton of land that no one else seems to want. The question is, do they want it to remain a secret or is that just my paranoid delusion? Or if I'm not crazy, why do they want it to remain a secret? At this moment, the land deal is done, the ink is dry and there is no reason that I can think of to keep it quiet. But I'd bet my entire re-mixed and re-mastered Beatles CD collection that they do want to keep it quiet. So quiet that they murdered Chick over it. Why?"

My regular phone made the text-message chirp and I picked it up. This phone thing was going to get confusing.

Connell texted: Tbi tells me 2 go peddle my snake oil somewhere else

Crap! I texted back.

"It's from Connell," I said. "Today I had a weird encounter with Donna Maples. She looked at me across the square like she hated me. I know I haven't done anything to her, so it was odd. It struck me that she would know all about these land deals, so I told Connell about the encounter. Since we've been told to butt out of this investigation, he said he would pass the info on to the TBI and see if they would like to go have a conversation with her. They don't."

Mars smiled that "butter wouldn't melt in her mouth" smile. "Well, I think that I'll go down the street and pay Donna a friendly visit. Maybe she'll tell me something about this land deal. I'll act like I smell real estate money and see if that gets me anywhere." She turned to YaYa. "So, who do you want to ride home with, YaYa?"

I noticed the Southern accent had grown deeper as Mars talked. She was going to lay some charm on Donna. Mars could be very charming when she chose to be, and when she was charming she was very hard to resist. I could hardly wait to see the outcome of this venture.

"I do like your sporty car, Marcella, but when we get to the house you'll probably have to pry me out of it with a crowbar. But it'll be worth it," YaYa answered. "You know, Marcella, if you're going to see Donna now, I'll get you to walk me over to Tilly's. I can have a nice cup of tea while you go and have your visit."

"Good idea," I said.

"You come on home too, Tess. Don't you be here by yourself workin' late. It is too dangerous," said my grandmother.

"You know I have a gun, right?" I asked.

She just stared at me with "the look."

"Okay, not a problem. Jewels and I have a few more things to do, and then I'll call it a night and head home. Alright?"

"Alright," she said.

"Anybody ever tell you that you were bossy?" I asked.

"Only everybody," she said.

"Mars, get a new phone from Jewels."

"Can I be Double-O-Six?" she asked.

She was still laughing at her own wit as she and YaYa walked out.

"Jewels, will you finish the billin' on that Workman's Comp case, please? I'd love to get the money from the insurance company for that ASAP. The sooner we bill them the sooner we get paid."

"You've got some messages you need to return—people who were not content to talk to your lackey." She walked in and handed me a bunch of message slips.

"You are not my lackey; you are my minion."

"Then I should get a raise," she said.

She went back to the front office, and a moment later I heard the click, click, click of her keystrokes. Good minion.

I spent the better part of an hour making phone calls and answering questions that Jewels could've answered, but some people have to talk to the boss—makes 'em feel more important I suppose. I resent it because it feels like a waste of my time. It usually pays off, so I suck it up. That personal touch is important in business.

I laid out paperwork to be filed and typed up a report for Jewels to pretty up and send off to the client. I felt very accomplished. There's something about getting all your ducks in a row that makes you feel virtuous.

"Hey, Spy Master," Jewels said. She was standing in my door. I hadn't heard her moving around.

"It's about quittin' time. What do you say we quit?"

"You go on ahead. I got a couple of things to do here first," I said.

Jewels stood her ground. She even folded her arms at me.

"Really, go home. I won't tell YaYa you left me here alone."

"Promise? Because she scares me."

"Promise."

"Okay then I'm going. See you in the morning." She turned to go.

"Hey, Jewels."

She turned back toward me. "Yes?"

"Tomorrow when you come in, don't touch anything in my office, okay?"

"Yes, Spy Master, you're going to set some Double-O-Seven type traps, aren't you? This would be fun if it weren't so damn scary, ya know?"

I laughed. "I know, see you tomorrow, now git."

She got. I reached into my desk, retrieved a thumb drive, plugged it into the computer and copied all the info from every website I'd pulled up about Aggroco. Then I snagged my laptop out of my bottom desk drawer. When I got home I could pull it all up, and we could have show and tell. I wanted everyone to be on the same page as far as how nasty these boys were. I could show them a lot easier than I could tell them.

After that, I spent a few minutes scattering salt around my computer and a bit of powder right inside my door. I arranged papers on my desk in an exact manner, got out my cell phone and took pictures of the desk.

I got my newest toy out of the closet. It was a tiny lipstick cam, and yes, it is the size of a tube of lipstick, hence the name. I looked around for a place to hide it and decided the window sill would do just fine. I moved the vertical blinds just a touch and set the camera on the sill pointed toward my desk. I turned it on and covered the little red light with some electrical tape. With any luck, if I had nocturnal visitors they would never know they were on candid camera. Last, I set a voice-activated recorder in my ficus plant and left the office feeling very 007ish and sneaky as hell. I chuckled all the way home.

CHAPTER 16

I got home and parked at the kitchen entrance next to Daddy's car. Marcella was parked out front behind Dugan. I walked into the kitchen and took a deep breath. The smell of lasagna filled the air. Wonderful! I realized that I'd missed lunch. My stomach growled right on cue.

"Hello, family!" I called.

No answer. I wandered through the dining room and spotted everyone sitting on the patio. Looked like it would be family drink time before family dinner time, which was alright with me.

"Hello, family," I said again as I stepped out onto the patio.

"Oh, Tess," said Mommy, "you're just in time. Dinner will be ready in twenty minutes, so you have time for a drink." She held up a frosty silver pitcher to me. "Sangria."

"Lovely and thank you," I said graciously. I took the glass she poured for me, perched my butt in a chair and settled into the cushion. "So are we discussing this mess before dinner?" I didn't want to go against the protocol of the evening.

"Well, Mars and your grandmother have been filling us in on their day. Your brother, here, met the TBI agents today and so did his lovely wife and your brother Patrick, and Elaine," Daddy said.

"Wow, those two are ambitious. So where are my brother, his better half and your wife?" I asked Dugan.

"All at home with headaches and in very bad moods. Chelsea might become a Libertarian after this," said Dugan.

I laughed. "Lots of us might decide to convert to other things before this is all over."

"Mars has been tellin' us about this Aggroco company that you've been researchin'. She says that you got a theory," Daddy said.

"Well, I may be crazy, but not about this. I think they've bought up all the property they could get out at the Cove. For some reason they want to keep everythin' quiet about it. I think that Chick stepped in the middle of this mess and that got him dead."

"Hello to the house!" Connell called.

Dugan stepped to the French door and yelled, "We're on the patio gettin' drunk!"

"Dugan!" Mommy admonished.

We all laughed. Connell joined us, walked straight to the Sangria pitcher and poured himself a drink.

"This may not be enough alcohol, but it's a start!"

"Rough day?" Daddy asked.

Connell threw back about half of his drink and then refilled the glass.

"If I can get through this disaster and not get my ass in a sling for beltin' a fellow officer in the mouth it will be a miracle! Really, I'm not sure who I want to hit worse, him or her. He's just a hard ass doing his job, as he sees it. But her, she's an egotistical bitch with a chip on her shoulder the size of a redwood. I guess I'll hit her first."

"Oh no, if anybody is gonna hit that bitch, it'll be me," I said. "You can have what's left." Connell and I clinked our glasses together to seal the deal. "Besides I've brought something to take your mind off the TBI. I've been doing a bit of research on Aggroco today, and I brought my laptop home for a bit of show and tell. You've already seen most of it, so you can help with the presentation."

I pulled my laptop out of my bag, inserted the thumb drive and before you could say "Bob's your uncle!" all the info that I wanted to share was in front of us.

"This company bought up the land at the Cove, and they're some serious players. I talked to a PI in California today who told me that we'd better be careful. Look, here's the map of all the property they've bought at the Cove."

"Wow," said Dugan, "that's a lot of land!" He leaned over the computer for a better look. "Is that all that empty land where we used to play when we were kids?"

"Yeah," said Connell. "Remember there were some Quonset huts that were fallin' down. It was a great place to play army."

"I told you about a million times not to go down there. You'd come home covered in red clay. You ruined more outfits than I can count. I could never get the clay stains out," Mommy said in a long-suffering voice.

YaYa pointed at the screen. "You know, during the war, the Army had a set-up down there. It was all fenced off, and they patrolled the place in a real serious manner. You couldn't get in. Some of the boys tried and got caught. The Army kept 'em for several days until the mayor finally appealed to the big brass to get 'em released. They didn't hire locals to work either. It was all Army men as near as we could tell. If they gave those boys leave, none of 'em spent it in town. We never saw a single Army man on our streets the entire time that place operated."

"What were they doing out there, YaYa?" I asked.

"Don't know. It was all very hush-hush; most people didn't ask. In those days we all thought there was a Nazi under every bed and that the Japanese would be killin' us in our sleep. We just figured that the Army was doing something to protect the country, and we left 'em to it. Now the two boys who did manage to get in said the place looked like some kind of factory. They didn't tell much cause the Army men put the fear of God in 'em. "

"Then they just went away?" asked Dugan.

"Sure enough," said YaYa. "Not long after VE Day they were just gone. Some of the buildings were left behind—you know, those funny lookin' ones, look like a big barrel someone cut in half?"

"Quonset huts," supplied Daddy.

"Yeah, them. We all went out and looked around, but they didn't leave nothin' else behind."

"What were they doin' out there?" I mused.

"Maybe they were doing something secret, like in Oak Ridge, building weapons of mass destruction," said Mommy.

"You might not be far off," said Daddy.

"Then what happened? They left and the land just sat there empty for this entire time?" Dugan asked.

"Well, after the war, folks moved in and set up farmin' down there. But you know it was like the place was cursed. Crops didn't do well, cows died, women and livestock miscarried and lots of blue-babies were born out there," YaYa said.

"Blue babies?" I asked.

"Babies that was blue. Old folks used to say that they was born with their hearts on the wrong side of their chests and the blood didn't flow right and so they was blue. I guess really more like a light purple, but their lips and their fingernails was blue. It was pitiful."

"What happened?" asked Connell.

"Well they died, of course. Finally, folks just gave up and moved away. Folks are superstitious, you know, and the local lore said the place was cursed. No one bought the land and it just sat empty."

"Till now," said Mars.

"What could they be hiding out there? I mean there had to be some reason that the land sale is so hush-hush. Maybe there's some sort of minerals under that land," I speculated.

"Like what? Uranium, gold, silver?" asked Dugan.

I shrugged my shoulders. "Beats me, but something's rotten in the state of Medicine Springs."

"Can you pull up the tax map?" asked Mars.

With a few clicks, the map appeared on the screen. Mars leaned over to study it.

"Okay, now get us the sales of the property," she directed. "Go back to the other screen. It looks to me like there is one parcel of land that hasn't been sold yet. It's this one right here." She pointed to a parcel on the map. "Let's see who that belongs to."

I pulled the info up. "John T. Harrington? That's not anyone I know, anybody else?" I asked.

Heads shook all around.

"Accordin' to the address, this Harrington lives in Massachusetts. Maybe that's the reason this land deal needs to stay on the down-low: there's a hold out. That sheds a bit more light on this thing," I said.

"That's not all of it, at least I don't think it is," said Mars. "Look on the, oh never mind, let me drive for a minute, will ya?" Mars held her hands out to me to indicate I should give her the laptop, which I did. "I can do this faster than walking you through it."

She typed at a rapid clip. She clicked through some more screens until she found the one she wanted.

"I want to see when the closing on the properties happened—if they were before or after Chick was murdered. I just need to type in my password to bring it up and voila! Okay, according to what we know from the map, there are seventeen separate parcels of land. Look, the sixteenth property did not close until Wednesday, three days after Chick was murdered."

"We have motive," said Connell.

The timer in the kitchen went off, and we all headed for supper. We set the table, retrieved the salad from the refrigerator, cut up the bread and poured the wine. Daddy said grace.

"Wow, this whole thing is crazy! Mars, how did your meeting with Donna Maples go?" I asked.

"Not much of a meeting." Mars frowned and her eyes narrowed. "Donna was curt and short and practically rude. When I told her that I was just tryin' to scare up a little business for myself, she told me that I should go and find my own property deals and not try to horn in on other peoples' deals."

"Holy cats, then I didn't imagine that ugly look she turned on me today. I was really surprised by her nasty attitude. This tells me she knows somethin' about this whole deal."

I looked at Connell for confirmation. He nodded at me. Good to know that he didn't think I was building castles in the air.

"I think we need to find out more about this blue-baby thing that might give us more clues. I've never heard of it but it sounds just horrible. Poor little things." Mars sounded so sad.

It was sad—worse than sad to watch your baby grow sicker and sicker and finally die, while you sat helpless. I hated to even think about such a thing.

"As soon as I finish eatin', I'll call Moira and see if she has any idea what this condition is and what causes it to happen. Let's put her education to work."

Mommy said, "I got new movies in the mail today. Would you like to watch one after you talk to Moira?"

"Sure, pick somethin'," I answered.

I tried to eat slowly but I was anxious to talk to my sister. I wiped my plate with the last of my bread, drank my wine and excused myself. I deposited my plate in the sink and stepped out on the patio to call Moira. The phone rang three times before she picked up.

"Hey, honey, what's up?"

"Moira, what do you know about blue babies?"

"Wow, that's an ice breaker!" She paused for a moment. "Why?" she asked.

"YaYa said that a lot of the babies that were born on farms at the Cove were blue babies and I'm scratchin' an itch."

"Hmm, well I know a little, but let me do a bit of research to make sure I know what I'm talkin' about. You home?"

"Yep, we're gonna watch somethin' Mommy's picked out.

Connell, Dugan and Mars are here too. I think I'll drink beer until I fall asleep."

Moira laughed. "Okay, I'll call you in the mornin'. Hang in there, honey."

"Yes, ma'am, I be hangin'. See ya later, love ya, bye."

"See ya later, love ya, bye."

I hung up and sat for a few moments just staring into the darkness and mulling all the information around in my tired brain. I finally gave up and went back inside. The kitchen was silent, so I walked up the stairs to the second floor and into the den. I took a seat and settled down to watch the flick Mommy had picked out for us. I couldn't concentrate on the show. I can't even remember what it was. My mind was a thousand miles away as the colors flickered across the screen in the darkened room. Dugan, Connell and Mars stayed to be entertained too. I heard laughter in several places so I guess the movie was good. All I could think of was acres and acres of empty land, sad farmers, sick cows, pathetic dying blue babies and Chick, my darling, dead Chick.

I was asleep and my dreams were of beaches and perfect boat drinks with little umbrellas served to me by pretty, well-oiled, tanned, finely-muscled, young men. It was a wonderful dream, but the burglar alarm and the howling dogs snapped me awake! What the hell!

My hand snaked under my pillow and grabbed the Beretta. I slapped the clip in and rolled from the bed. All in under ten seconds. I crouched low as I ran down the full length of the upstairs hall to YaYa's room. She was still asleep. I moved from her room to the little room next door to hers that sits under the front eaves of the house. Its windows look over the front yard. I stole a glance outside and didn't see a soul. There's a set of stairs in the room that come out downstairs in the computer room adjacent to my parents' bedroom. I took the stairs low and quiet.

"'Tess coming down."

"By the alarm panel," answered my father.

I moved that way as well. I wanted to see that panel and find out which door had been breached. I didn't think anyone was actually in the house. The dogs were making high, hysterical, someone-is-here barking sounds—warning barks. They would be making far different noises if someone were actually inside. Then there would have been growling and biting noises, and maybe there would also be some screaming human noises.

Daddy had the panel open, and the light from it seemed very bright in the mostly dark house. Everything was blinking red. Our lines had been cut. Daddy tapped in the code and the alarm claxon ceased—thank God.

"Daddy, I think he's still outside. I'm gonna go out the patio door and circle around. Give me three minutes and come out the front. Maybe we can surround him. Does that work for you?"

"I think you're taking a chance. Go out low, use the patio furniture as cover. As long as you're careful going out, you should be okay. It's dark and it's hard to hit a moving target even in good light. Just keep your head down."

We moved out of the computer room and through my parents'
bedroom.

"Maggie, call Connell on your cell and stay put. We're gonna go
have a look see."

"I love you," Mommy said as we passed the bed.

I knew Daddy was armed. I'd take bets that he'd gotten his gun in
his hand every bit as fast as I had. Second nature for us both, I guess.
My parents' room is off the living room behind the fireplace. When
we exited their room, the front door in the entry hall was to our right.
The French doors were to the left. It was a short distance to either
door, but it didn't seem like a short distance. It seemed like a mile
walk. All the while I waited for someone to jump me or to shoot me
even though I knew in my gut that there was no intruder inside the
house. It was irrational, but my heart beat faster with every piece of
furniture that I passed. I couldn't help but imagine that someone
might be crouched in wait for me. The grand piano seemed a
particularly good place for an ambush. I began to sweat, my stomach
felt sour, and there was the taste of copper pennies in my mouth.

I could hear the dogs in the kitchen raising hell. So that was the
direction the bastard took—good to know. The location of the dogs
further confirmed my belief that there would be no one waiting
outside the French doors to get the drop on me. The dogs had tracked
him as he circled around the outside. I was convinced of it.

My plan was to slip out the French doors and come around to the
kitchen end of the house in hopes of getting the drop on the intruder.
My hand reached out to open the door and a thought struck me. Why
the hell would anyone come here? What would be the point? To shoot
all of us in our beds? That would only raise the bar of the
investigation even higher, even if it were made to look like a home
invasion. It would deprive the TBI of their number one suspect, and
they'd be required to find a new suspect. It would just be stupid. Of
course, we'd all still be dead. I crouched there in the darkness for a
moment and tried to puzzle it out.

It hit me like a lightning bolt! Someone wanted me to step outside
where I would be gunned down by a person or persons unknown.
Shit! That was pretty smart. One murder is easier to get away with
than four. My death could be passed off as random violence or night
hunters or some damn thing, or maybe it would look like I shot

myself. I guess someone figured I knew too much. Pretty funny when you think about it. I knew next to nothing. But I wasn't laughing. Someone wanted me out of the equation. I'd rattled cages for sure. Guess my reputation as a rush-in-where-angels-fear-to-tread kind of girl had preceded me. I had to admit that my reasoning made me feel a little better. He wasn't here to murder my entire family, just me. Well he could try.

"Daddy?"

"Front door."

"Don't open it."

"Okay, whatcha thinkin'?"

"I think that's exactly what he wants us to do. I think he's here for me. I'd really like to disappoint him."

"Good, I like disappointing assholes. Stay put, I'll be right back."

I heard him move away from the front door and back toward his bedroom. Then I heard him and Mommy have a low conversation. I hoped he was telling her to contact the rest of the family. I didn't think that they were in harm's way but better safe than sorry. Besides, calling everyone would keep Mommy busy.

Of course I didn't stay put. I had a plan of my own. I moved through the dining room and into the kitchen. The dogs were all clustered around the door by the pantry at the far end of the kitchen. That door opened into the driveway where the family usually parks. I kept my head down as I moved beneath the kitchen windows. I'd be a great target there even in the dark house. I got all the way to the end of the kitchen counter just before the pantry door. Very mindful of my head, I rose up and peered out the window. There in my driveway was a big black Hummer. I hadn't been able to see it from the other end of the house. The bastard. How dare he come on to my home turf? I looked around as well as possible from my vantage point and saw no humans. I crawled past the kitchen door and into the pantry where I grabbed some dog treats off the shelf.

"Come on, good dogs," I said.

I moved back into the kitchen and shook the bag. That got their attention. They all looked at me and whined and looked back to the door and growled.

"I know, I know, there's a bad guy out there. But you need to come with me. Come on, come on."

I moved out and gave the bag another shake as I went. After ten seconds the dogs were all behind me. They still growled non-stop as we moved through the house back toward my parents' room, but they came.

"The dogs and I are coming your way," I said in a low stage whisper.

We invaded the bedroom, me in a crouch, the dogs behind me growling and snarling, their hackles raised. I bet we were a sight. All the dogs jumped onto the bed with Mommy.

"There's a big black Hummer parked behind where the three of us are parked at the kitchen door, so our cars are blocked. I can't get a head count, could be more than one person, but this sure as hell ain't no social call."

Agreed," said Daddy. "My thinkin' is they want to see how protected we are, and they might want to try and flush you out so they can solve one problem."

"That's what I think too. So what's our next move?"

"Well, let's go upstairs and make some noise. Let's let 'em know that we know they're here."

"I checked on YaYa and she's asleep—maybe she'll stay that way. If you could keep the dogs in here, Mommy, I'd feel better. I don't want 'em getting hurt if we draw return fire."

I walked over and shut the bedroom door that led to the living room.

"Tess," my mother said sternly, "you be careful and don't take any chances."

"I won't, Mommy, cross my heart. So, Daddy, is the idea to move from window to window and take some shots at them."

"Yep, we keep movin' and fast. We never give 'em a good shot at us. Maybe we can keep 'em pinned down until help gets here. Got it?"

"Got it. You want the back of the house or the front?"

"I'll take the back of the house through the bedrooms, and let's hope for some good hunting." Daddy grinned and I could see his white teeth flash in the near total darkness.

"I like it," I said.

"Maggie, finish your calls, and tell Connell to be very careful when he comes in since there'll probably be gunfire."

"Saints preserve us," said Mommy.

She picked up the phone and began to dial. We left her there with a bed full of dogs and moved back through the computer room. I shut that door behind us. We moved up the stairs.

"I'll meet you on the other end," I said.

We split up. I moved to the window in the little room. Daddy moved out into the hallway, and from there he would enter the bedrooms on the back side of the house.

Upstairs, all the bedrooms are on the back of the house overlooking the valley. They're all joined by bathrooms in between, so you can go from one end of the house to the other without ever going into the hallway. The exceptions are the two little rooms on the front of the house under the eaves. There is one on each end of the house. They look out over the front drive. They're small pokey rooms with a slanted ceiling. I call them the servant rooms.

Those little rooms served me well that night. I carefully crept up to one window and poked my nose above the window sash. I saw no movement in the yard, but I knew someone was out there. I opened the screen which swings in and lifted the latch on the window which swings out. I performed the same maneuver on the other window.

I left that room and moved as fast as possible to the far end of the hall and into the twin room of the one I'd just vacated. That room was over the kitchen and next to my bedroom. I looked down and saw the Hummer below me. I decided that was as good a target as any. I opened the screens and the windows, just a little. I was very quiet. I drew a bead on the Hummer and shot it in the grill. WOW! The gun discharge almost deafened me in the small room. No one moved out in the yard. Good nerves—they were trying to see where the shot had come from. I decided to see how long their nerves would hold out—I shot the truck again. I heard the whine of a bullet and dropped down below the window sill. My heart hammered in my chest. He had a bead on me but where the hell was he?

I rose up slightly and shot the Hummer again, then moved to the next window on the other side of the small room, so I could try and see where the return fire had come from. I saw a flash in the Forsythia bushes on the passenger's side of the Hummer and heard the *thunk* of a bullet hitting the window sill. I took aim and fired three times into the bushes. I didn't wait to see if I had scored a hit but scrambled out of the room and down the hall. I heard Daddy's service revolver open fire. He was in the far end of the house from me, probably over the living room. He was moving from room to room looking for targets, and it seemed that he had found one. Good. That also meant we had more than one assailant. Bad.

I went into the hallway and walked to the den, where only a few hours ago we had sat and watched a movie. From that vantage point I could see out the window on the landing below me. It dawned on me what a great target I was in that spot. I crouched very low and tried to think small thoughts. Down the steps I went, to the window on the landing. Below me, the stairs descended to the main floor of the house right next to the front door. The landing is large—the width of the French doors at the top of the stairs. On the landing there's a table built over a long old-fashioned radiator with chairs at either end of the table under the 10' long window. The main, middle part of the window doesn't open; however, there are small windows on each end that do. It was a great place to sit and read a book in comfort.

I moved a chair out of my way so that I could get to the small window on my left. I rose up with great care and looked out the window. Now there were dark shapes moving across the lawn. Jesus, I counted four shadows. These bastards meant business. I opened the screen and window then leveled the Beretta on the windowsill.

"*Careful, TisTis, there's more of 'em than you think.*"

"JESUS CHRIST!" I hissed.

I almost squeezed off a shot in my shock. It was a testimony to my training that I didn't. Crouched in the chair at the other end of the table was Chick—he kind of glowed in the dark and was easy to see.

"Chick! Holy Crap! You scared me out of a year's growth!" I whispered.

"*Hey, I've seen that Hummer before, I think those boys came into the garage last week with a slow leak in the left rear. And I fixed it for 'em too. I shoulda made more holes.*"

I forgot the gunfight for a moment. "You remember anything else about them?"

"*When I was fixin' the tire, I noticed there was some good red clay in the tires, and I commented that they must've been down to the Cove, since that's the only place hereabouts that has clay that color. I asked 'em if they was hunting out there, but they didn't look like hunters, ya know. Guess I was right about that, unless you call this huntin'."*

He continued to peer out the window, but for me a bright light went off. I wanted to cry or scream or curse, because now I understood that Chick was killed because he was simply in the wrong freakin' place at the wrong freakin' time. I rose up and took a shot at the Hummer and dropped back down. The whine of a bullet came toward the window, and there was a loud *thunk* as it buried itself in the sash. Mommy was going to shit Twinkies over the damage. Somebody out there had a bead on me and it was time to move.

"Come on, Chick."

I ran in a crouch back up to my room and scrabbled in my nightstand for the two extra clips I kept there. My room's on the very end of the house, and my side windows look down on the side yard. I sneaked a peek and saw no one. I ran all the way back to the room over the computer room on the other end of the house, opened that window and started to shoot up the front lawn at random. I ducked just as more bullets hit the window sill, and one took out the glass and buried itself in the wall behind me. I closed my eyes and shook my head to get glass off me, stood up and ran back to the stairs. I was scared shitless, but I was also as exhilarated as a drunken loon. And pissed—God was I pissed off!

I went back to the windows over the table on the landing and fired two wild shots, and then I just kept running from window to window, at random. I wanted them to think that we had a fair number of shooters that stood in defense of the property. I also wanted to scare the living hell out of them. I was scared as hell and I wanted them to be too! I like sharing. I sat with my back to a wall in one of the small rooms for a moment to get my wind back and my heart back in my chest. I'd never experienced anything like this before. Everything seemed to happen so fast, yet it seemed that I had been at it for hours. My breath was labored and my mouth was dry. It was then that I realized that Chick had disappeared. Shit!

I heard the report of Daddy's gun. He was in the middle of the house. The bastards had us surrounded. Okay, time to shake things up. I rose up just enough to poke my gun out the window and I emptied the clip in all directions. More shots came my way, and I scurried out of the room and back to the landing. I scouted out the landscape—everyone had gone to ground, nothing was moving out there.

"*TisTis*," Chick whispered.

I jumped out of my skin. "Chick, stop sneakin' up on me!" I growled at him.

"*It ain't like I can stomp my feet.*"

I laughed, I couldn't help myself. It was probably inappropriate or maybe hysterical, but I laughed anyway. "Okay, sorry, you just scared me and I'm already scared enough to pee on myself. I may even have peed myself already."

"*It's okay.*" He pointed toward the formal gardens. They were almost directly across from the window where I crouched.

"What am I looking at?"

"*Right there,*" he pointed, "*behind the purple bush, there's one of the bastards. He's on his knees so aim low.*"

I did and squeezed off three shots. I was rewarded with a loud yelp, and then I saw the bushes move as if someone had fallen. A shadow detached itself from the garage which set at a right angle to the house and moved across the drive toward the fallen bad guy. I drew a bead on him and squeezed off three more shots—he kept moving. Damn! Daddy was right. It is hard as hell to hit a moving shadow in the dark. Try it sometime.

At that moment I heard a siren and knew that the cavalry was on the way. "Yahoo! That's Connell!" I shouted.

Man, I felt sort of lightheaded—must have been the adrenalin rushing through my body. I also heard Daddy moving toward me.

"On the stairs, at the window, keep low," I said.

"Coming," he answered.

In a moment Daddy joined me, and we both peered out the window. "What's the situation?"

"Well I got one who was hiding in the Rose of Sharon bushes, thanks to Chick who spotted him. There's another guy who crossed the drive from the garage to get to the wounded guy. I took several shots at him but missed. They're both just about right in front of us."

"Hard to tell."

"Yeah, a sliver of a moon would be appreciated the next time we're under siege. Wonder which saint's in charge of that?"

Daddy chuckled. "So now we decide, do we shoot at 'em and

keep 'em here for Connell to deal with, or do we let 'em go? Since they're outside the house, if we kill one of 'em we might be prosecuted."

"That's a happy thought. How about if we just fire at 'em and keep 'em pinned down until Connell gets here? If we kill anyone, well if they're dead, they can't argue."

"True enough," Daddy agreed.

We poked our heads up and fired at the Rose of Sharon bush, then ducked back down. I heard the whine of incoming and cringed. You can't duck or outrun or dodge a bullet no matter what you see on TV or in the movies. Human nature makes you try though. Your best bet to dodge a bullet is to put something solid between you and the other guy. The walls of the house are thick and I wasn't real worried. Still it will rattle your brain to take fire and not run from it.

Daddy and I rose up, shot back and ducked some more. The sirens were at the driveway now. The next time I popped up, I saw lights coming down the drive.

"Help's here!" I shouted.

I was excited and relieved for about ten seconds, then I got scared for Connell. All the different emotions and the adrenalin made an unpleasant stew in my stomach. I felt a bit queasy.

I rose up just enough to see out the window. I saw that Connell was coming up one side of our circle driveway. There was another squad car just entering the other side of the drive. The shadow men in the yard made for the Hummer, including one shadow that was helping another shadow along. They all fired shots at Connell. At least I was pretty sure it was Connell in the first patrol car in the drive. He returned fire. The engine of the Hummer roared to life, and the huge vehicle lumbered off, away from Connell and toward the other squad car. The Hummer picked up the pace while Daddy and I held our fire and just watched as the bad guys made a break for the road. There were shots from the Hummer and some return fire from whoever was in the other squad car. The huge vehicle didn't stop but plowed into the squad car head-on and pushed it back out the driveway. Damn! We could hear the tortured screeching of metal from our vantage point.

Connell's car followed the Hummer which cleared the drive and the wreckage of the other squad car and took off. Connell stopped, got out of his car and ran around to the driver's window of the other car.

"We've probably got a man down," said Daddy.

He moved down the steps with me right behind him. He opened the front door, and we ran up the drive toward the cars. I could hear Connell talking, his voice low and urgent. I threw "thank yous" at the Blessed Mother, and anyone else who might be listening, that my brother was unharmed.

When we reached Connell, he had the squad car door open and was applying pressure to Mark's chest. Mark's head was bleeding too, and he was unconscious.

"Got an ambulance on the way. This looks bad to me, but I'm no doctor. Everybody here okay?" He didn't look at us as he talked, keeping his eyes on the task at hand.

"We're all fine. I'll go back in and let Mommy know where we stand. Glad you're okay, Connell."

"Likewise, baby sis." His voice was strained and that told me how bad Mark's wounds were.

I high-tailed it back up the driveway to the house. "Mommy," I shouted as I came in the front door, "we're okay!"

I went into the bedroom and found her getting dressed. The dogs were milling around her feet, whining and impeding her. She handed me a flashlight.

"What's happened?" Mommy asked.

"The Hummer crashed into Mark's car, he's shot in the chest and he was hurt in the crash too I think. Connell's giving him first aid, and there's an ambulance on the way. He's bleeding pretty badly. I'm gonna go check on YaYa."

"I'll take some towels and see if I can help Mark."

She turned and headed into the bathroom.

I ran up the stairs to my grandmother's bedroom and found her still asleep. She had taken her hearing aid out before she went to bed, and this just proved how deaf she really was. I was tempted to leave her in peace, but I knew she'd be mad as a hornet when she found out she missed all the action. With great reluctance I touched her shoulder.

"Mmm, what?" she asked sleepily.

"YaYa, we had intruders, they're gone, Connell's here, Mark's hurt, but the rest of us are fine," I said loudly. I practically had to yell.

"Jesus, Mary and Joseph! Did I sleep through all of that commotion?"

"Yes, Ma'am, it appears that you did."

"I hope you paid attention, I wanna know every detail. Why is it dark?"

I smiled there in the dark as I knelt beside my grandmother's bed. I was so relieved I wanted to cry and so keyed up that I wanted to laugh and so scared that I wanted to vomit.

"The lines to the house have been cut. I paid extra special attention, YaYa. When I tell you the story you'll think that you'd actually been there."

"Damn right," she said. "I hope you shot somebody."

I kissed her on the cheek. "I love you," I said.

I helped her get up, find her glasses and her bathrobe and put in her hearing aid. I got her flashlight from the bedside table, and we made our way down the front steps. We stopped so that she could survey the action from the window.

"How bad is Mark?" she asked.

We stared down at the cars and lights and moving figures.

I shook my head. "I don't know, YaYa, I only saw him for a split second. He was bleeding pretty badly and he was out cold. Connell was applying pressure to his chest and that's never good. He was bleedin' from his head too."

"I'm gonna go on down to the kitchen and make coffee. Will you be a good girl and run back up to my room for my rosary?"

"Sure, YaYa."

By the time I made the round trip to her room and back to the steps, the ambulance was in the driveway and more people were running around in the flashing red strobe lights. I decided that more light would be helpful, and it might be a good idea to switch on the front flood lights. God, why didn't I think of that before? I did and then laughed at myself because I'd forgotten there was no power. Despite what you have heard, adrenalin does not make your brain work better. I headed for the kitchen.

"Ambulance is here," I announced.

"Coffee's cooking," said YaYa. She emerged from the butler's pantry with a lantern.

I laughed. "Thank God for gas!"

"Yep, I dug the old aluminum coffeepot out of the emergency supplies and got on with it."

I handed her the rosary. It was a pretty, silver thing with an ornate crucifix, and it was older than dirt. I left her to her prayers and headed out the kitchen door toward all the activity.

The EMTs were loading Mark into the ambulance. He was still out and looked so deathly pale on the gurney.

"How bad?" I asked.

"Not good," one of the EMTs answered. "We'll get him stable and then LifeFlight him to Nashville if we have to." My heart sank. "We'll keep the sheriff informed."

The other EMT never said a word. He just kept working on Mark with a dogged and determined look on his face. They got Mark squared away and hooked up to lots of tubes and wires. The EMT closed the doors, ran around to the driver's side, jumped in and took off.

"I've called Mark's wife. She'll meet 'em at the hospital," said Connell.

We all walked back to the house together. I realized that Mommy carried an arm load of blood soaked towels.

"Let me help with those, they must be heavy," I offered.

God, Mark had bled so much. The smell of coppery blood just about overwhelmed my olfactory senses as I took the towels into my arms. My stomach rolled a bit more sharply and I gagged. Please, please, I begged, do not let me puke.

I walked toward the house and saw how beautiful it looked lit by lanterns and candles—odd but lovely. YaYa had been very busy. When we got inside, even by lantern light I could see how much blood was in the towels. I had to swallow several times to force the bile back down. How could he still be alive after he had lost that much blood?

"Mommy, I think we need to trash these towels. They're beyond salvaging."

She looked at the towels in the light and blanched. "Yes," she said.

Daddy rummaged under the sink and came out with a lawn and leaf bag. He brought it to me, and together we stuffed the towels in and tied the sack off. Daddy took the sack out the kitchen door to the trash cans. I looked around the kitchen. Everybody looked like hell. YaYa sat quietly in her chair at the table. The silver beads moved steadily through her bent fingers. Her lips moved silently in prayer. Her eyes were closed. I sure hoped that God was listening tonight. Man, I was so tired.

Mommy caught my attention and pointed to my hands. I looked down to discover my hands and arms were covered in Mark's blood. I went to the sink and washed. The water became a bloody pinkish color as it ran down the sink. I stood and watched it flow away in a pink ribbon. My shirt was bloody too. Mommy nudged me over so she could wash too. I saw more headlights coming down the drive.

"Incoming," I observed.

"That'll be Joel. We've been in touch by radio. He was looking for the Hummer, I guess he didn't find it," said Connell. He stepped to the kitchen door and yelled for Joel to come in.

"I'm going to call the children and let them know the situation here—that we're all alright and that Mark's hurt," Mommy said.

She removed her cell phone from her pocket and moved into the dining room to make her calls. Connell, Joel and Daddy entered the kitchen.

Joel nodded all around as way of greeting. "Evenin', ya'll. Glad to see that everyone here is okay."

"Joel, have a seat and a cup of coffee," Daddy offered.

Joel sat down and Daddy took the pot off the stove, put it on the table then went to fetch mugs. He returned in a moment with coffee mugs hanging off his fingers. Connell snagged the cream from the fridge and the sugar bowl from the counter and placed both on the table. I got some spoons from the silverware drawer and we were set.

YaYa gathered her rosary into her hand and slipped it into her pocket.

"Evenin', Joel, glad you're here and safe."

"Thank you, ma'am," he answered.

"So let's discuss what we know so far," suggested Connell.

"We were awakened at 3:17 AM by the alarm and the dogs. The intruders had cut phone and electric to the house. We drew fire and Tess and I moved from window to window and shot at anything that moved in the yard. We drew return fire. Tess apparently wounded one assailant. I counted at least four on the grounds. I think they were here in hopes of drawin' Tess outside so that she could be killed." Daddy's account was precise and delivered without emotion.

A chill ran down my spine at his words. Then I played Daddy's words back and realized he was covering for us. I just needed to remember the party line was—they fired first.

"I would agree. Nothing else makes sense. You've done pissed in somebody's mess kit, baby sis." Connell frowned at me.

"I don't know how. I've been so careful in making any inquiries. I've really tried to stay off the radar. Of course my concern was staying off the radar of the TBI, not homicidal maniacs who wanted to murder me in my sleep."

"Why kill her now, wouldn't that just cause more heat on this case?" asked Joel.

"Good question and one we better find an answer to and fast before they succeed. I think I'll spend what's left of the night here. Joel, patrol as usual, but if you see anything out of the ordinary, don't approach, call me. You understand?" Connell looked at Joel to make sure he understood.

Joel nodded his head. "Yes sir, I got it. These boys are armed and considered dangerous. I'll be careful."

"Finish your coffee before you go, I don't think there's any rush to go running off into the night. I bet these boys have gone to ground somewhere and are lying low. Let's don't forget one of 'em's hurt, maybe bad. Depends on how good a shot my sister is." Connell grinned at me.

I stuck my tongue out at him and took a big sip of my coffee. Coffee in the middle of the night, after an adrenalin-charged running gunfight that lasted an hour or so—what a good idea! I was sure the caffeine would keep me up the rest of the night. Funny thing though, it didn't.

CHAPTER 18

I awoke the next morning, or rather the same morning. Sounds from downstairs floated up the back steps and right into my room. They were regular, ordinary household sounds: the coffeepot being filled, water running, the clink of cutlery, voices talking softly. There was a phone ringing somewhere, too. I could hear people outside talking. I supposed they were the crews here to restore the electric and the phone lines.

I lay in my bed and thought over the events that had transpired in the middle of the night. Given the number of shots exchanged, we were all pretty lucky—except for Mark. I swung my feet onto the floor and leveled myself into a standing position. God Almighty, I hurt everywhere! My gluts were in agony, and my hamstrings were burning like fire. I had a hell of a workout during the gunfight. Gunfight. You hardly ever get to use that word in a casual conversation! Now I could.

I didn't bother to get dressed. I just threw on my robe and headed for the kitchen. I needed coffee. I glanced at my phone on the way out. It was only 7 a.m. Ugh! I'd need lots of coffee in order to make it through the day. I decided on my way downstairs that this could possibly qualify as a coffee emergency. I chuckled and was stunned to realize that I was feeling pretty chipper, even happy. I guess that's what happens when lots of bullets come flying at you and none of them hits you. Weird, I should be shaking in my boots, but I kind of wanted to sing or at least whistle. I took the stairs with a little pep in my step.

"Good morning, Glory!" Daddy called.

"Morning," I said.

I rounded the corner into the kitchen. We had a little extra company. Mars and Connell were both sitting at the table.

"I was in a gunfight last night."

Everyone stared at me. I shook my head.

"Well, I was and I've never gotten to say that before, I just wanted to try it out."

Mars laughed, "Girl, you are crazy!"

I smiled back at her.

"How's Mark?"

"He's still hanging on, but it's a real touch and go thing right now. Grab some coffee, sis, we got lots to discuss," said Connell.

I quit smiling. "That sounds ominous," I said. I got a cup of coffee and sat down. "But I guess that once you've been in a gunfight everything else is relative."

Again, everyone just stared at me.

I sighed. "Okay, trying for a little humor here which looks like it fell flat. Gimme the dirt."

Mommy sat down at the table with us. I was surrounded by the people on this earth that I love and trust the most. Whatever it was, I could face it. I was so glad to be alive and thankful they all were. I was overwhelmed with gratitude for a moment.

"Well," said Connell, "to start with, Mark is pretty bad off. He has a concussion and a hole in his right lung. He's had surgery, he's drugged up to his eyeballs so he'll stay out, and he's lost a lot of blood, but the doctors are hopeful. They're gonna keep him here unless he takes a bad turn."

"I've started a novena to St. Catherine for him, he'll be fine. Don't you worry," piped up YaYa.

"Next, I just got off the phone with Agent Boyd. I thought I should give him a call and fill him in on the events of last night. Seems he'd gotten an anonymous phone call yesterday afternoon. Actually, the call came into the TBI headquarters in Nashville and the information was sent to him."

"And I give a shit, why?" I asked.

"You give a shit because the call was about you," Connell answered.

"Okay, now you have my undivided attention." I took a sip of coffee and then another, it was heavenly.

"Seems that someone called the TBI yesterday to report that you and Chick are drug dealers and have been running drugs all over this part of the county. You also screwed somebody in a big drug deal for a lot of money, and the aggrieved party is out for blood, literally. That's why Chick was murdered, and that explains why they came after you last night. At least that's what Agents Lyle and Boyd think. As a matter of fact, he didn't even turn a hair when I told him what happened," Connell said.

He leaned back in his chair. I could tell he was mad as hell but he was trying to keep his cool.

"Wow, that's brilliant! It explains not only why Chick was murdered but also why someone came gunning for me. The caller expected me to get my brains blown out last night. Glad to have fooled 'em, by the way. Oh, but it would've been such a tidy package. I wouldn't be around to dispute it, and the TBI would direct their attention to finding these mythical drug dealers, who of course would never be found. Holy crap! Someone has put on their thinkin' cap for this one." I blew breath out and made a motor boat sound.

"Tessely! This is serious. You're in even worse trouble than you thought," my mother admonished me.

"Mommy, I am taking it seriously. I haven't forgotten that an unknown suspect, amend that, several unsubs tried to kill me last night. I don't think those guys were here to sell me magazine subscriptions. I know if I'd given them a target, I'd be dead. Really, I'm taking this seriously. I won't do anything stupid, I promise."

"The TBI still likes you for Chick's murder," said Connell.

"What are you freakin' kidding me?! How is that possible? Someone came here last night and shot the house up and tried to kill me, and Daddy too, and they damn near did kill Mark. I'm a known drug dealer and I still killed Chick? These are two of the dumbest sons-of-bitches that have ever drawn a breath! Sweet Baby Jesus on Christmas! I've seen boxes of hair that were smarter. DAMN!"

"You finished?" Connell asked.

"And don't take the Lord's name in vain," my mother snapped at me.

I almost laughed but decided that it wasn't worth the trouble it would bring me. I huffed out a breath. "Yes. Okay. I'm finished."

"Here's how they see it. You two were running a big drug operation, he screwed someone big time, you got mad about it and shot him, or you got someone else to shoot him."

I rolled my eyes but kept my mouth shut.

"Now the guys that he screwed are gunning for you for payback. Boyd and Lyle are gonna start looking for a drug stash or someone to confirm that you're a dealer."

"This just gets better and better. I know that all big-time drug dealers live with their parents and drive a three-year-old car. I saw that on CNN." I shook my head. "So what the hell do I do?"

"The most important thing is that you cover your back-side at all times. These shooters aren't finished with you. I know it in my gut. They have to believe that you know something and are just gatherin' info before you blow their entire deal sky high," Daddy said.

I didn't doubt my father's lawman instinct.

"Which is true," said Mars.

I cut her a look, and she shrugged her shoulders at me.

"They don't mean to let that happen," Daddy finished his thought.

He looked tired and he looked scared, which scared the hell out of me.

"So I don't go anywhere alone, I don't walk down dark alleys, I don't stay late at the office, I don't go anywhere without telling someone where I am, what else?"

"Be armed at all times," said Daddy.

"Without a doubt," I said. I looked around the table at the people I knew and loved. "So given all that, who's gonna go out to the Cove with me and poke around?"

That's when everybody started yelling all at once.

Showers are good—you get to stand in the steamy, hot water and shut the rest of the world out. Except when that world follows you into the shower. My mother, YaYa and Mars all invaded my space and were yammering at me. They were all standing in my bathroom, yelling at me through the shower curtain.

"Have you lost your rabbit-assed mind? These bastards come here to try and kill you and you want to go out and play in their backyard. Are you sure that you didn't take a blow to the head last night?" Mars was actually yelling.

"Really, Tessely," said my mother much more calmly, "you can't really mean to do this. I'm sure these horrible men will be waiting for you. You're going to get yourself killed."

I poured some vanilla cream shampoo on my head and lathered up. God, it smelled good. I was trying to remain calm myself. I didn't think it was a stupid idea or a crazy one. I just knew there was another reason, besides timing, that the land buyer wanted that deal to be kept quiet. I was positive the answer was on that land.

"Ya know, kid, usually I agree with you, but this time I think you're dead wrong and you need to leave this to the TBI and your brother."

Wow, even YaYa was against me—she always sided with me.

I rinsed the suds out of my hair while I tried to decide if I should lie to them and make them shut the hell up or tell them I was going to go through with my plan? To lie or not to lie? That is the question. I came down on the side of lying.

"Okay, okay, you win, it's a crazy idea. Now will you all kindly get the hell out of my bathroom and let me finish my shower?"

After a few seconds I heard the door close. Who says lying is bad?

I peeked out of my bathroom door, and no one was in sight—hooray! They believed me. Good. That gave me time alone to think and figure out how I was going to get on to that land and live to tell about it. I towel dried my hair and pondered. I couldn't ask anyone in this house to go with me. That was right out. They'd handcuff me to my damn bed to prevent me from going. A light bulb went off over my head—Billy! He'd go with me to scout out the land if I could convince him that we were doing it for Chick, and he'd keep his mouth shut. No one would miss him since he was supposed to be lying low at Connell's house. I'd have to drive out there and get him because Connell told him not to answer the phone. I could invent an errand and tell that to Jewels. Or could I tell her the truth? Would she rat me out? I didn't think she'd rat me out on purpose, but she's a terrible liar. I threw on some clothes, added a snub-nose .38 to an ankle holster, tucked my Beretta into the back of my waistband, reloaded both the extra clips and hit the stairs.

"Going to work, love ya'll," I said.

I practically ran through the kitchen, none the less, Mars caught up to me as I started the Jeep.

"You gave up entirely too easily. I know you, girl, and I know you're fixing to do something stupid. I can smell it." She glared at me and leaned in the driver's side window. "Pinky swear you're not going to do anything stupid." She held up her little finger.

I sighed, "Good God, Marcella, you have got to be kidding. What are you five?"

She just continued to stare at me with her hand up in the air.

"Fine." I reached out and hooked my little finger on to hers. "I swear not to do anything stupid." I lied.

Her eyes grew narrow and she stared at me for a few more seconds. Then she turned on her heel and left me there in the driveway. I admit I felt a certain level of discomfort about lying to her and then doing a fake pinky swear. There is probably a special place in hell for people who break that oath. I felt I had no choice. Connell couldn't go out to the Cove. The TBI were keeping tabs on him, and he'd need a warrant. Anything he did that even smelled like he was working Chick's case could put him in a world of hurt. That left me. What was the worst they could do to me? I could be charged with obstruction of an ongoing investigation. They'd already threatened me with that. If I didn't bust this case wide open, I could be charged with murder and God only knew what else. If that happened, I believed that I'd eventually be exonerated, but, it would cost time and money to get me off and it might ruin my career. That wasn't a joke. I didn't know how to do anything else. I'm not gorgeous like Mars. I'm really not a people person, so retail was out. I didn't think that I should advertise as a hacker although I'm pretty good at it. That left being a PI. Plus the bottom line is that I had to find out who killed Chick and make sure they paid.

I hooked my Bluetooth over my ear and headed to the office. I could hardly wait to see if the place had been violated, although that seemed sort of anti-climactic now given the gunfight. I zipped along lost in thought when the phone rang. I hit the ear thing.

"Go."

"You have amazing social skills," said Moira.

"Funny you would say that, I was just thinking it myself," I quipped.

"Self-examination is good for the soul I hear. You okay?" She sounded worried.

"Weirded out and strangely giddy, so yeah, I guess that I'm okay. Thanks for asking. You got something for me?"

"As a matter of fact, I do. I did a bit of digging. I'm going to read you what I found, but I already sent it to you in an email. Quote: Blue Baby Syndrome is known as methemoglobinemia. It is caused by the ingestion of high concentrates of nitrates in its inorganic form, inhibiting the oxygen-carrying capability of the blood. If the concentration of methemoglobin becomes too high, the infant will become cyanotic and may die of asphyxiation. This condition especially occurs in infants below six months of age on a pure milk or infant formula diet. At present, this is not frequently diagnosed since it's not a required reportable disease, and today's medical students are not trained to connect the symptoms of the disease with its possible source. In many instances it is no longer recognized by young doctors. End quote."

"Can you break that down into English for me, please? I prefer easy words that are under two syllables."

Moira laughed. "The nitrates are in the soil and in the water, the baby formula is made with the water or the mother drinks the water and breast feeds the baby. Either way, the baby ingests the nitrates, and the blood stream is affected so that it is unable to carry enough oxygen to keep the baby healthy. A human has to have a certain amount of oxygen in the blood stream. Without it the organs begin to deteriorate, and eventually the affected person dies from lack of oxygen."

"Holy shit! What an awful way to die. Does it affect grownups?" I asked.

"Yep. Research shows that it can cause migraine headaches, miscarriage, possible stomach problems and even leukemia."

"Where does this stuff come from?" I felt like my head was spinning from this horrible information.

"Most nitrate pollution comes from farm and animal production. It's in the fertilizer used on crops, and it's produced by the animals— it's in their waste. A small amount can come from poorly treated human waste. Since so much of it comes from farming, you normally only see it in rural areas."

"This poison comes from cows and growing corn?"

"For the longest time, no one realized what was happening. As we've gotten smarter, we figured it out and most commercial food or meat producers take steps to make sure this no longer happens."

"Okay, but the farms came after the Army, so where did the nitrate stuff come from?

"There're several other ways. It can actually be present in the rocks. Sometimes during lightning storms atmospheric nitrogen is converted to nitrate and deposited in the soil through rain. Weird, huh?"

"Very. Anything else?"

"Did I mention weapons manufacturing?"

"What?!" I yelled and damn near wrecked the Jeep.

"God, calm down, you're so high strung. I swear. Hang on, let me find it." She was quiet for a moment. "Oh, here you go: Nitric acid was used to make fertilizer, propellant for rocket engines and the manufacturing of trinitrotoluene, also known as TNT, between 1940 and 1965."

"So when they got finished and didn't need the factories, or relocated the factories, they just dismantled the buildings, carried away the machinery and the land got turned into farmland or developed into real estate tracts." I got so excited I was practically vibrating.

"Like I said, no one knew the dangers. Rocket fuel, or perchlorate, the main component in rocket fuel, can contaminate water, vegetables and dairy products and can cause attention deficit learning disabilities, thyroid dysfunction, birth defects, lower IQ, cancer of the digestive tract and blue baby syndrome."

"Moira, I don't say this enough, I love you. I am so glad you are my sister. You may be the smartest person I know. I LOVE YOU!"

"So I guess that's what you needed?"

"It explains one of the reasons that the land deal was so hush-hush. If the land is tainted, Aggroco wouldn't want anyone to know. They must have done a soil and water sample test—it's kind of standard—as well as a perk test and who knows what else. Mars would know that, I'll ask her. So they knew the soil was poisoned, and they didn't care because the land was so cheap. They probably figured that no one would get sick or any sickness couldn't be traced back to them. Isn't that information worth killing over?" I took a deep breath.

"I think so. Now your problem is going to be proving it. If you can prove the land is tainted and that it poses a health hazard and that Aggroco knew it, you have your motive."

"Maybe they needed extra time to get rid of the nitrates, or can that even be done?" I asked.

"It can be, but it's a very long and difficult process called

Phytoremediation. You have to plant certain grasses and trees that will remove the nitrogen compounds and release them in to the air. It can take years to accomplish. With a faster method called biodenitrification, you pump nitrate-contaminated ground water into a specially designed tower and inject bacteria and a carbon source to stimulate the denitrification process."

"Wow, Moira, you're so smart that I'm in awe of you. Now I'm gonna be a little paranoid. Send me everything you have and then erase all of it. Erase your history so that no one can see where you've been without working hard for it."

"Sweetie, after last night, I don't think you're being paranoid in the least. Consider it done. Please be careful. I'm so thankful that you're safe. I love you."

"I love you," I answered.

I hit the button to disconnect before we both got too mushy. My brain was reeling. I knew the answer was on the land, I just didn't imagine that the answer was poison. These bastards were willing to take the risk of poisoning people with the fruits and vegetables they planned to grow. They shipped food everywhere, so if someone got sick in Iraq or Ohio, it would be hard to prove that the food came from tainted ground in Tennessee. They were gambling with the health of millions. Yes, it was a secret worth killing over. I drove a little faster.

Jewels was waiting for me when I got to the office. She looked anxious and excited.

"I haven't opened your door just as you asked. But can we do it now? I'm about to break out in hives from the anticipation."

I laughed at her. "Sure, come on."

I laid my bag on her desk and locked the front door. I didn't fancy anyone coming in and catching us. I slowly opened my office door, and there in the powder were footprints.

"Oh, oh, you did it! I'm vibrating!" She was staring at the footprints.

"We gotta get you out more, girl."

I walked over to the computer, and sure enough, the scattering of salt was disturbed. The papers I'd left on my desk were in slightly different positions than where they were last night.

"So you put salt, is that salt?"

I nodded.

"Okay, you scattered salt around your computer, and now it's kind of scattered around more or differently. What else?"

"The papers are not exactly as I left them last night. I took a picture of them after I arranged them, and I think they look different." I pulled my phone out of my pocket and brought the picture up. "See?"

"Yeah, they're different, but just the tiniest bit. This is so cool. What else did you do?"

I walked across to the ficus tree and retrieved the recorder. "I recorded them." I picked up the lipstick cam. "With any luck we have their pictures too."

"Oh goody!"

Jewels actually clapped her hands. For me, the pictures were the most important part. I really wanted to put faces on these bastards, which would make them much less frightening to me. That's silly, I know. But a faceless adversary is just scarier—think of all the faceless villains you've read about and seen in movies. I'm right. I plugged the camera into my computer, turned it on and started the movie. It was dark in my office. There was a bit of light from the streetlight outside the window but not enough to give good definition to the pictures. One guy was big, as in muscled up. The other guy was little. Clichés, anyone?

"Crap, crap, crap. I had hoped for so much more!" I exclaimed in frustration.

"At least you know all the places they searched. That's something, right?" Jewels looked worried.

We watched the rest of the recording in silence, not a lot more enlightened when it ended than when it began.

"Let's find out what they said. Maybe that will be helpful," I grumbled.

If you've ever recorded an entire night of sounds on a voice-activated recording then had to listen to it, you would be bored to tears. You mostly hear dogs barking, car engines, cars backfiring, people taking out the trash, cats fighting and similar night time noises. But every now and then you hit pay dirt. I hit the play button and heard all the regular noises of the town winding down, but then we heard footsteps in the front office, my lock being picked, the rustling of papers, drawers being opened and closed, more footsteps, my computer coming on, mouse-clicking sounds, then a loud *thunk* noise and a loud crash.

"GODDAMN IT." It sounded like someone had run into something solid in the dark.

Then a different voice, which was lower in timbre, whispered. "What the fuck is wrong with you? Are you trying to get us caught? Shut the fuck up!"

"I tripped over this rug and hit the chair, it hurt. Are we done here?"

The first voice answered but quieter and still very pissed off. "Yeah, I don't see nothing that helps us. Come on, we got more business with this bitch tonight."

There were sounds of them leaving, then more dogs and cars and then Jewels coming in this morning.

"Wow," Jewels breathed.

"Yep. Wow. Pay dirt. We now have their voices, and this may prove handy when we actually catch 'em. The 'more business tonight' comment can possibly tie them to the shootin' at the house."

"What?"

"Oh yeah, I was in a gunfight last night." I smiled.

CHAPTER 19

It took over an hour for me to give Jewels all of the details on the previous night. She was blown away and kept making me go over the confusing parts.

"You really think they came to your house to kill you? That's the craziest thing I've ever heard."

"Connell and Daddy think so too, so not so crazy."

"No, not the part about believing it, the part about them wanting to do it. I mean, really, it's so hard to murder someone that you know in this day and age and actually get away with it—the statistics are overwhelming. It's just crazy."

"Yeah, but, they don't know me. I don't know them. They're probably hired hitters, or at least hired muscle. They've already dropped a great story on the TBI—one the TBI really likes and wants to believe. They could conceivably murder Chick and murder me and get away with it. Except, I'm gonna do everything in my power to make sure they don't get away with it." I smiled a nasty little smile.

"What's the next step in your evil plan?"

"I can't tell you," I sighed.

"What?? Why can't you tell me? You tell me everything?" Jewels got a sad look on her face. "I can't believe that you don't trust me."

"Oh, Jewels, it's not that I don't trust you. I trust you with my life. I know if I tell you a secret, the secret is safe and you would take it to your grave. But, you couldn't lie about it 'cuz you're the worst liar that I've ever seen. You can't even lie to a three-year-old."

She looked indignant for a second. "You're right. That's why I don't play poker and always let my husband do the car shopping. Lies show on my face. I totally blame my grandmother for it. She always said that lies show in your eyes so that the devil will know and take you below."

"How charming. Have you had therapy?" I wondered aloud.

"Plenty, that's why I'm so well balanced and healthy." She smiled.

"But you still can't lie."

She stopped smiling, took a deep breath and sighed. "Yep. So what do I tell people when they come callin'?"

"That I am out runnin' down a lead, that I have my phone, my gun, mace, actually two guns, and I am not doing anything dangerous."

Jewels rolled her eyes. "Wow, I'll try. But even I don't believe that. When will you get back?"

"Don't know." I smiled at her and took off.

On the way to my Jeep, I took stock of the situation. I was going to go into what could only be considered enemy territory, with just Billy as back up. Billy was a scrapper, but that was in bars and alleys. This was different. Still, if I didn't want to do this alone, he was my best bet.

Before I went to Billy with my crazy idea I had to stop at the local hardware store. There were a couple of items I needed and couldn't take the risk of bringing from home. That would've given me away. My shopping only took minutes, and I tucked the items into the backpack that I keep in the Jeep.

I hurried to Connell's before I lost my nerve or someone caught me. Connell's house is not far from town, so the ride only took me ten minutes. I kept checking my rear view all the way to make sure no one was following me. I pulled into his front yard and parked under the big walnut tree. As I got out of the Jeep I crossed my fingers that this would turn out alright and I wouldn't get either of us killed. Shit, maybe this really was a bad idea.

I walked up the stone steps, but Billy opened the front door before I ever set foot on the front porch.

"Hey, Tess," he said. "I heard the car and thought it was a Jeep, but I checked just to make sure. I seen it was you so I come to the door. Figured that would be alright, seeing as how you was you."

I had to smile over his convoluted sentence. "Hey, Billy, how you doing?"

"Okay I reckon. 'Cept I feel like I'm hiding out and I ain't done nothing wrong. But I know that Connell is trying to protect me. He don't want me to get crossways with the TBI agents."

"True enough."

I walked into my brother's house and took a seat on the couch. I always liked Connell's house. It has a wide front porch with columns. It's an American bungalow, I think. The living room is big with a fireplace at one end, and the dining room is opposite that through an archway. He kept it neat and tidy too. The living room was lined with bookcases—big surprise. There was also a big plasma TV as well. I took a deep breath and looked at Billy.

"I got a favor to ask you."

Billy sat down opposite me in the recliner. "You look all-fired serious and that's for sure. Whadaya need me to do, Tess?"

"I think that Chick was murdered by some fellas who are buyin' up the land out at the Cove. I think there's something wrong with the land—that it's poisoned. I think they also wanted to get all the parcels of land bought before anyone found out the deal was going down. I think Chick fixed a rear tire on a Hummer last week that had lots of red clay in the treads. I think that he mentioned in passing that the tires must've picked up the clay from the Cove. I think they were afraid he knew something about the land deal and killed him to shut him up. I think that I need to get some soil and water samples from that land to prove all this. I need a wingman."

"Whoa!" Billy leaned back in the recliner. "Ain't that some shit, that strangers could come here and do such thangs. I remember that Hummer." He shook his head in disbelief. "I'll sure as hell be your wingman if it'll help catch these bastards."

"Billy, you gotta stay calm, no matter what we see or hear. We're going on a recon mission only. These boys are dangerous—really, really dangerous. If I think for one minute that you can't keep your cool, I'll leave you here and go by myself. You understand?"

Billy cocked his head at me. "So you don't want Connell to know what you're up to? That's why you got me as a wingman instead of him?"

I nodded slowly.

"I figured that but how come?"

It was a fair question. I was about to put him in harm's way, and he had a right to know why.

"Well, it seems that someone thinks that I know too much about this business that got Chick killed. Some fellas in a Hummer came by the house the other day or maybe yesterday. God, too much has happened in too short of a time. Turns out they were scoping the place out and came back last night and shot the house up. I think I hit one of 'em, but no one has reported a gunshot wound or Connell would've told me. Anyway, I mentioned that I thought that I'd go out to the Cove and get some soil and a water sample to prove my theory about the land. All hell broke loose. There was lots of yelling, and even YaYa threatened to tie me to the bed post. Connell needs a warrant to go out there, and he can't get one now because the TBI agents have taken over the case. That leaves me and you."

He looked at me for a full minute before he spoke. "I understand. You're asking me to go on account of everyone else has told you to stay the hell out of it. You want a witness in case something happens to you. You want somebody to have your back in case things get rough."

He narrowed his eyes and looked so serious I almost didn't recognize him. In that moment, I realized that the young man I had always thought of as a boy might indeed be a very dangerous individual in his own right.

"I reckon I can do what you need me to do. Don't never think otherwise."

"Okay then. Let's do this thing."

We locked Connell's door, climbed in the Jeep and backed out of the driveway.

"We're gonna drive out to the Cove and park a little distance from where the Quonset huts are. You familiar with them?" I asked.

Billy laughed. "Every kid who grew up here knows where those things are. We all played out there and came home covered in red mud."

"I think that's where the bad guys are. I don't want them to see us. I want to get in there, get soil and water samples and get the hell out of Dodge."

"Simple, I got it." Billy nodded.

"Billy, these guys came to the house last night to try and kill me. Between the alarm and the dogs, we were warned. There were at least four of them, maybe five, and they came packing plenty of heat. My point is, they came to the house of the former sheriff of the county, in a strange town, to do murder. They aren't afraid of anything. They'll kill us if they spot us."

"I got ya, Tess, I get it, really. This is dangerous. I'll be quiet and cool. Do I get a gun?"

Oh shit, if this went south and he didn't have a gun, we could both die. But if I gave him a gun and he shot someone, heads would roll. Mine being the first.

"Yes, you get a gun. You don't use it unless someone is firing at you. If we play our cards right, that won't happen. I've got a thirty-eight in an ankle holster, and I'll give it to you when we get there. You know how to shoot one?"

"Are you serious?"

Okay, it was a dumb question. We drove the rest of the way in silence, each thinking our own personal thoughts. I was scared. These thugs had tried to kill me once already, and now I was delivering myself right into their hands. Maybe everyone was correct and I was crazy. But I just knew this had to be done, and there was no one else. I kind of wondered what Billy was thinking.

"You're quiet, whacha thinkin'?"

"Thinkin' that I hope you're right and we get the proof you're lookin' for, that we can slide in and back out without bein' caught, that this doesn't bring your brother down on me like a ton of bricks, not to mention the rest of your family."

I laughed. "Yep, that's pretty much what I was thinking too."

I pulled the Jeep over and edged it down in the brush on the side of the road so it would be harder to spot.

"This is about as close as I want to get on wheels. We walk from here— actually we sneak from here."

I got my backpack out of the back seat and struggled into it. I propped my foot up on the bumper and took the .38 out of its holster. I offered it butt first to Billy.

"It's loaded and the safety is there." I pointed.

"Got it," he said. "Let's do this. Hand signs from here?"

"Hey, who taught you hand signs?"

"Chick and Connell." He grinned.

We moved off the road and took to the woods where we went into stealth mode. My woodcraft is pretty good—it was necessary growing up. The sibs kept me in the dark because I was the youngest. If I ever wanted to know anything I had to sneak up on them to eavesdrop. We're also a family that hunts. You learn how to move quietly in the woods so you can approach your target and not piss off your brothers because you stepped on a stick and spooked the deer.

I spotted the top of one of the Quonset huts off to my right. I touched Billy on the shoulder and pointed. He nodded back at me. We crouched down and moved to the right, giving the Quonset hut a wide berth. Billy touched my shoulder and made signs for going to the building to see if there was anyone inside. I thought about it for a moment, but as tempting as the idea was, I shook my head and pointed straight out in front of us. I wanted to get some red clay into the Mason jar I had acquired and get the hell out of there. I hoped to find a water source someplace where I could grab a water sample too, which would be a bonus. It was also one hell of a long shot.

I removed one jar and a garden spade from my bag, made the hand sign for "keep watch" and moved out of the woods, low and slow. I needed to get to an open area for my soil sample. I reached the field and as I bent down to dig, I heard a vehicle start up—a big vehicle. I turned tail and ran back to Billy. We both dove behind the nearest trees.

The Hummer backed out of a broken down Quonset hut, turned around and headed toward the road. I was worried that if they turned left they'd see the Jeep and come back in here to look for us. There was no happy ending to that scenario. The Hummer moved out of sight, and I ran back into the open field. I shook out the contents of my bag, sweating like a whore in church. Billy ran across the field and joined me.

"Hold that jar," I demanded.

He did. I scooped up a shovel full of dirt, tossed it into the jar, and then we ran back into the trees like rabbits.

We hunkered down for a few minutes and listened for the Hummer. I could hear it moving off to my right. I let out a breath that I had been holding. Thank God for big, loud vehicles! I didn't know how long they'd be gone, but at least it should be long enough for us to make our escape. I felt we needed to move since we had no way of knowing who might still be on the property.

"Let's go," I said.

"I thought you wanted a water sample too." Billy laid a hand on my arm.

"I'd love one, but I have no idea where a well might be out here, and they may only have run down the road for a pack of smokes." I wanted to flee.

Billy smiled. "I know where a well is. When I was a kid and the old man was on a rampage, I used to hide out here for days on end. I found a well. It ain't far from here." He pointed past the hut. "Come on."

I followed him. "Did you drink the water from the well?"

"Nah, I usually stole as much beer from the old man as I could carry and drank that. The well was boarded up, and I just took a look in it and dropped rocks down it. Good thing I liked beer better'n water, huh?"

I laughed in spite of myself. I decided to risk it since no one had come running out of the Quonset hut to shoot at us. "Okay."

The well was a good hike from where we started. The farther away from the Jeep we walked the more nervous I got. Then I saw it—a simple concrete pad just standing out in the middle of nowhere.

"That's it?" I asked.

"Yep."

We ran toward it. I dropped to my knees and pulled the ancient boards off the concrete. In the middle was a 6" diameter pipe coming up from underground. I got one of the jars, opened it, and then tied a long piece of kite string around the neck of the jar. I had no idea how far I'd have to lower the jar to get to water, which was why I brought a ball of kite string. Billy remained standing and acted as lookout for us. He seemed as steady as a rock.

I lowered the jar into the pipe and kept playing out the string. I wanted to hurry but made myself go slow. I wanted a decent size sample and didn't want to drop or spill anything in my haste. It seemed like it took a week before the jar bounced a little and I knew it had hit the water. I let it sink for a good thirty seconds then pulled it back up. Funny, the water was clear as glass. I guess I thought it should look nasty and slimy. I untied the string and capped the jar. Billy gathered the string, and we headed back the way we'd come. All in all, our little excursion had taken less than thirty minutes. Now if we could get back to the Jeep and get away clean, I'd be a happy woman—as well as one who was still breathing.

We ran like the hounds of hell were chasing us and made it back to the Jeep in record time. There was no sign of the Hummer—that damn thing was going to haunt me in my dreams I just knew it. God, I wanted to see inside that Quonset hut so bad, but we didn't dare linger. I started the engine, threw it in gear and we were gone. We were about a mile away when I started to laugh.

"Whew, shit! I was scared! I thought we'd been had." My hands were shaking on the steering wheel.

Billy grinned. "Yep, me too. I knew we was outnumbered, and I ain't that good of a shot. That was a hell of a rush though, I gotta admit. Now we got the samples, what're we gonna do with 'em?"

"We are not doing anything with them. I'm takin' you back to Connell's, and you are going to act as if you never left the place, and I'm gonna take this stuff to a friend of mine who's a chemistry teacher over at the high school. He'll analyze it for me and tell me if and what kind of poison is in the dirt and the water."

Bully chuckled, "Who says school is a waste of time."

I stopped at Connell's, and Billy opened the door of the Jeep to get out. He stopped with one foot on the ground.

"I'm real glad that you took me with ya. Makes me feel like I'm doing something to help. I reckon as how you'll be wantin' this back." He reached behind him and got the .38. He hesitated for a split second before he handed me the gun. "I don't think it's a good idea for me to hang on to it."

"Billy, you gotta promise me you won't go back out there."

He looked me straight in the eye. "Tess, I swear, I won't go back out there unless you or Connell goes with me. Okay? I wanna kill somebody real bad, you know I do, but Chick would want me to do this right."

"You're right about that. Billy, thank you. Today you put your life on the line for me. Thanks."

"I done it for Chick."

CHAPTER 20

I hated to involve anyone else in this mess, but I felt I had no choice. I hightailed it out to the high school. My old friend, Jeff Tompkins, was the chemistry teacher there now. I knew I could trust Jeff to keep his mouth shut, but I also felt that I was endangering him by asking for his help. I hate moral dilemmas. I parked in the familiar parking lot of Simpson County High School and hurried inside. I had to check in at the office and state my business, or rather, lie about my business. I actually said that I was going to go see the teacher in charge of the yearbook to talk about buying ad space for my company. Damn, now I would actually have to do that.

I left the office feeling a bit guilty and headed down to the chemistry lab. School was in session and I hoped to catch Jeff between classes. I opened the door. There were no students, but Jeff was there, studying a big stack of papers.

"Hey, Jeff."

He looked up and got a surprised look on his face. "Well. Ms. Maher, to what do I owe the pleasure of this visit?" He grinned at me.

Jeff has a great smile. His teeth are white as snow and perfectly straight too. He should be the poster child for braces and good dental hygiene. A dimple shows up on the edge of his mouth and his eyes sparkle. Jeff is handsome, with blonde hair, light grey eyes, a rugged square face and nice build. Very nice, also very gay. Not a lot of people in town know that, or they pretend they don't know. Those of us who do know, don't tell. This may be the 21st century, but we are still a small town in the South. Lots of folks would take exception to a gay man teaching their impressionable children. It's bullshit, but there you are—prejudice is everywhere.

I walked over and gave him a big kiss on the mouth—couldn't hurt either of our reputations.

"How's your life, anyone new in it?"

"You didn't drive over here to ask about my love life. What's up?"

"Jeff, I have a huge favor to ask of you, and you can't tell anyone."

He smiled and took my hand. "I'm pretty good at keeping secrets. Why don't we sit down, and you can tell me all about it."

We moved over and sat at one of the chemistry tables. It had been a long time since I had sat there. God help me, I was a terrible chemistry student. I was only interested in the stuff that blew up.

"I'm not sure how much I need to tell you so that you can do the job and still have plausible deniability." I shook my head trying to decide. "If I tell you too much I might be putting you in danger. If I don't tell you enough you won't know what you're lookin' for."

I blew out a breath and ran my hands through my hair. This was frustrating. I wasn't accustomed to dancing around an issue.

"Okay, you need me to do something that involves chemistry?" Jeff asked.

"Right."

"What?" He prodded me.

"I need you to run some tests on the soil and water samples that I have. I want you to look for poison, heavy metals and nitrates. Really anything that's dangerous." I pursed my lips and frowned at him.

"But you don't want to tell me where you came by these samples?"

I shook my head.

"You're in trouble."

I laughed. "Yes, I am. Listen, Jeff, if you do this for me, you can't tell anyone about it. No one. You'll put yourself in danger if you do." I held my hands up in "stop" gesture. "Before you ask, I can't tell you anymore. I'm just tryin' to keep you safe. It's not a matter of trust, please believe me."

I willed him to understand. Jeff smiled a sad soft smile at me and he patted my hand. "Okay. This'll take a while because I run a rural high school chemistry lab, not the TBI lab, so be patient. How do I get the results to you? I assume you don't want me to phone them in. Speaking of the TBI. I can only assume that your request has something to do with that whole mess."

"They been out here to talk to you yet?"

"Oh yes, they're talking to everyone who ever knew you as far as I can tell. I gave you a glowing report, in case you're worried."

"I would expect no less of a teacher. Thanks and I mean that. These two are all over me like white on rice. They seem to hate me as a person, like they have some vested interest in this case, or I shot their dog or something. The female agent indicated that her problem with me is that I think I am too special to be a plain ole cop, but really it has to be more than that. It's a real bad personality clash. I think they are worried about solvin' this, plus I didn't make nice with 'em. They're talkin' to everybody in town, harassin' my family and in general making a nuisance of themselves. Meanwhile the bastard that murdered Chick is out walking around scot free." I drew a big breath. "Sorry, I get all wrapped around the axle."

"Tess, I'm so sorry about Chick. He was one of the best men I've ever known."

Tears sprang into my eyes. I seemed to have no control over that these days. "Yes, he was and thank you."

"I had a big crush on him when we were in high school you know." Jeff laughed.

"How could you not? He was so cute." I laughed at the memory of Chick at sixteen, tall and gangly with a crooked smile.

"He was always a good friend to me. He knew that I liked boys, probably before I did. He didn't care. He never allowed others to treat me bad when he was around. My high school years could have been a lot more difficult if it hadn't been for Chick."

"He was a stand-up guy. Everybody loved him."

Jeff squeezed my hands. "Everybody liked him, admired him, and looked up to him. You loved him."

I started to cry in earnest. Jeff wrapped his arms around me and let me cry on his shoulder for a good long while. Jeff was a good guy too.

When I came dragging into the office, Jewels took in my appearance.

"Do I even want to know what you have been doing? You're a mess. Your clothes look like you have been dragged through the mud, and your makeup is ruined. You have raccoon eyes and it's not even noon."

I held up my hands in mock surrender. "Probably not. Is it only noon? Damn. By the way, you are gonna go to the Piggly Wiggly in a bit and accidentally run into Jeff Tompkins. He's doin' a favor for me."

Jewels raised an eyebrow at me. "Give."

"He's runnin' an analysis on some soil and water samples for me."

"Jesus Christ! You went out to the Cove! Didn't you? Oh my God, oh my God! You could've been killed. No wonder Connell had a fit when he came by here and you were gone." She stopped to draw breath. "Tell me everything. No wait." She picked up the phone and dialed. She paused then said, "Tell him she's back."

I rolled my eyes. I knew that message was for Connell.

We got cups of coffee and made ourselves comfortable in my office. I looked in the mirror that I kept in my desk. Jewels was right. I looked like a big raccoon. I set to work repairing the damage, and while I did that I told her everything that had happened. She was breathless with the adventure that Billy and I had survived.

"Oh my God, they almost caught you, weren't you scared spitless? I hope the risk was worth it and Jeff gives you something you can use. I just love him. I had a big crush on him for the longest time."

I just smiled. That wasn't my secret to tell. I repaired myself as much as possible as Jewels left me to my work. I lost patience with my sad appearance because I had a bee in my bonnet to do a little research on my own about nitrate poisoning. So I gave it up as a bad job, went to Google, typed in nitrates in water, and quick as a bunny I had dozens of places to look. I opened Moira's email and read through it. She must have been surfing the same websites that I was looking at.

Basically the information was horrible—and scary. One described affected cows as having chocolate-colored blood. Yuck! I kept digging and found a website that detailed the nitrates in water and soil due to weapons manufacturing, and there was my proof:

Nitrogen is a major element in the manufacture of explosives, which primarily utilized ammonium nitrate and diesel fuel. Without proper management and treatment, waste streams that contain high concentrations of ammonium nitrate and diesel fuel can cause ground water quality degradation. In some instances, this waste stream, along with improper handling of the ammonium nitrate, has created nitrate contamination. Presently, most explosive manufacturers have taken pollution prevention steps to reduce or eliminate this waste. Waste streams from explosives manufacture contain nitrogen concentrations ranging from 200 mg/1 to over 1,000 mg/1.

Ordnance testing grounds and weapons manufacturing, loading, packing and transportation sites that were operated by or for DOE or DOD have historically used nitrogen compounds... These compounds pose many environmental concerns...*

It was like a script for a horror movie! There was even a map of old weapons manufacturing plants that were still being cleaned up in America. Five of them were in Tennessee. I sat in stunned disbelief for a minute. I was right. The ground and water poisoning were real. Medicine Springs wasn't listed on the map, but two clean-up sites were very close to us. I buried my face in my hands. How did the land at Coleman Cove fall off the radar and not get cleaned up? Could it be possible that because the installation was so hush-hush, it was built off the books? All I knew was that when this case was over, I'd be calling my congressman and asking him to take a long hard look at our issue.

The text warbling of my cell phone shook me from my reverie. I reached over and grabbed the phone.

On way 2 piggy, Jeff texted.

Agent 99 on way, I texted back.

"Hey, Jewels, time to make the Piggly Wiggly run," I called to her.

She appeared at my door a few seconds later. "Do you want me to buy something to keep up my cover?"

I snickered. "Yep, get some office stuff. You know, coffee, filters, cream and some of those good cookies that have chocolate in 'em. You know the fancy ones I'm talking about?"

"Yeah, the ones your momma always serves at Christmas. I'll get some of them. Is there anything else that we really need?"

"Nope, not really."

The front door opened and we both waited to see who it was. I knew immediately it was Connell. Who else would stomp into the office. Shit, this was going to be unpleasant. What was I going to tell him? He walked in with a big frown on his face and it was all for me.

"Jewels, honey, would you go on down to the store and get those things for us?"

"Sure will. Hey, Connell."

She scurried away like a rat deserting a sinking ship. I couldn't blame her. Connell looked like a hanging judge. He just leaned on the doorframe and stared a hole in me. A serious ass-chewing was about to be delivered, and I deserved it, kinda.

"You want some coffee?" I asked sweetly.

"No!" Connell snapped. "I do not want any goddamned coffee! What I want is to shake you until your teeth rattle. After that, I wanna know where the hell you went and what the hell you thought you were doin'!"

He stomped in and slammed himself into a chair. He was in a royal snit over this. Crap! It had been a long time since I'd seen him so pissed and even longer since he was so pissed off at me.

"I went out to the Cove and got soil and water samples and took them to Jeff Tompkins and asked him to run tests for nitrates and other poisonous substances. And I am sorry I scared you, really I am." I said it all very fast and with great sincerity.

"Jesus Christ on a bicycle, Tess! Have you lost your mind? Are you insane? You could have gotten killed. These bastards are playing for keeps!"

That's about when I got tired of being yelled at. I can only do so much penance.

"Hells bells, Connell, do you think I don't know that? What else could I do? You sure as hell couldn't go out there. I couldn't ask anyone else to do it without tellin' 'em why, and that may have blown this whole thing up in our faces. What would you have had me do? Sit on my ass and do nothing, wait for the TBI to slap cuffs on me, let the bastards that murdered your best friend walk away clean? Which of those options do you like the best?" I drew a big breath.

Connell glared at me for about ten seconds and then he shook his head. "Tess," he said quietly, "I was scared when I came by here and you were in the wind. All I could think of was that I couldn't lose you too." I could see him swallow hard. "I drove out to the Cove and looked for the Jeep since I figured that was where you went. But you must've been long gone by then. Jewels called me when you got back. She didn't want me to worry. Nice that somebody didn't want me worryin'. Honest to God, you cannot take chances like that."

"Connell, I was careful. I went in, got the samples and scooted right back out. I did not linger, did not investigate the Quonset huts— as much as I wanted to—I just skedaddled. If anyone had been there, I'd have snuck away. I was armed. I had two guns, mace and a cell phone. I got away without being seen."

I thought I'd wait until he calmed down before I told him I took Billy with me. Seemed prudent.

"Jeff's run all the tests and he's meeting Jewels at the Piggly Wiggly to give her the information. We thought that would look natural and better than him coming here. I don't want anyone to tie him to this case."

"Right, you'll protect everyone but yourself." He just stared at me.

I decided that comment did not deserve an answer. "Do you want to wait and see what Jeff has found out?"

"Sure, why not? My office is filled with TBI agents and most of our relatives. I can't get anything done, and if a crime spree breaks out, Mavis can raise me on the radio. Now tell me all the stuff you left out of your narrative the first time."

"Damn, you really are a cop, aren't ya?"

He didn't answer but just continued to stare at me, and then he began to tap his index finger on my desk.

"Okay, I took back-up."

"Are you going to tell this piecemeal?"

I sighed. "Okay, I took Billy with me." Connell's eyes grew big, but before he could start shouting I started talking fast. "He was the perfect choice. I could trust him not to tell, and he wouldn't be missed since you're hidin' him from the TBI."

"I'm not hidin' him. I am just keepin' him out of the way. When they go lookin' for him, I'll make sure to produce him. Go on." He made a hurry-up motion with his hand.

"We parked on the side of the road and walked in. They were there, at least some of them. I heard the Hummer start up. We hid until it was gone. I couldn't tell how many bad guys were in it because my face was in the dirt. They are hiding it in one of the Quonset huts, so no wonder you couldn't find it. Just so you know, we didn't go anywhere near the huts. We just got samples and ran like thieves in the night."

He closed his eyes for a second or two. "I'm gonna have to bell you like a damn cat at this rate. You took Billy? Those assholes were there and you stayed anyway? Never mind. I wanna go out there and take a look see. Someone'll have to report some strange activity out there that the sheriff needs to see about. There's gonna have to be an anonymous call to the office. Maybe Jewels will do it after she returns from her spy mission."

"While we're waiting on Agent 99 to get back, I bugged my office last night and got film and audio. You wanna listen?" I shifted the display so he could watch the show. "In my defense, how could I know there was anyone out at the Cove? The Hummer was hidden in a Quonset hut. How could I see it? I can see dead people but I can't see through walls!"

He began to tap the desk with his index finger again—a sure sign that he was annoyed.

"The video is not so great. I used my new lipstick cam. Which is a wicked cool tool! The light was low, so the quality is poor. But the audio is pretty good."

I cued both the audio and video so they would run more of less together. We watched in silence. When we reached the part where the bad guys left my office, I turned it all off.

"After that, you only get cars backfiring and dogs barking. I think we have good voice stuff here. We could definitely get a voice match from this. Once we get our hands on 'em anyway. I think the last comment could tie them to the ambush at the house. The defense might argue that it's not admissible since I recorded them without their knowledge. I think it could be argued that I bug my own office all the time 'cuz I'm paranoid and accidently caught them ransacking my place in the middle of the night."

Jewels showed up about then and she was excited. She rushed into my office waving paper at us. "I got it! That was exciting and fun." She plopped down and spread the papers out on my desk. "Take a look. This proves your theory, Tess."

I looked over the paperwork from Jeff and she was right. The water samples contained nitrogen concentrations ranging from 200 mg/l to over 1,000 mg/l. According to several websites that I studied, safe levels should not exceed 10 mg/l NO_3-N.

"Wow, this is it! This is our smoking gun. Good work, Agent Ninety-Nine." I gave Jewels a high-five.

Connell nodded. "Now all we have to do is prove Aggroco knew about this and bought the land anyway and intended to cover up the toxic levels of chemicals in the water and ignore the potential health risk of growin' vegetables on that land. Further, we need to prove that they murdered Chick to keep the secret. That might be a tall order."

My good mood evaporated like a soap bubble.

CHAPTER 21
SATURDAY

It was Saturday and I slept late. I was tired and sore and sad, and I figured I deserved to lie in bed, so I did. About ten o'clock my empty stomach refused to let me pretend to sleep anymore, so I got up and got ready to face the day.

When I came into the kitchen, the room was empty except for YaYa.

"Morning, YaYa. Where's everybody?"

"Getting ready to go to the Catfish Festival. You going?"

"Holy crap, is that today?" I looked at the calendar hanging on the wall and saw that today was marked in a big red circle. "Crap."

YaYa just looked at me and waited for me to get a grip. She was a patient woman. I got coffee instead.

I cannot stand catfish. They're ugly, and scary and slimy. They're bottom feeders, and in case you don't know what that means, think about what is on the bottom of the river. Let me give you a hint: other people's garbage, slime and fish shit. Catfish have horrible bulging eyes and long, ugly whiskers—kind of like a cat and hence the name, catfish.

When I was about twelve, my brother Dugan caught a huge catfish that probably weighed somewhere in the neighborhood of 30 pounds. He wanted to show it off to Daddy, so he decided to keep it alive in the bathtub. That bathtub was in the bathroom I used. Meanwhile, I innocently went in to take a shower, pulled back the curtain and damn near had a seizure. The ugly thing was swimming around in my tub and shitting in my tub too. GROSS! I pitched a hissy fit, screaming and yelling and jumping around like something insane.

Everyone in the house came running, thinking I was being killed, so everyone got to see Dugan's big fish. The boys all laughed at me for being freaked out by a fish and congratulated Dugan on his great catch. Mommy made Dugan scrub the tub until all trace of fish poop was gone. Everyone but me had catfish for dinner that night. I contented myself with hush puppies, home fries and slaw. I just couldn't bring myself to eat anything that had been so ugly in life. I have since seen an even uglier fish, the beluga sturgeon. I don't eat caviar either.

"I want to go, YaYa. It's fun, there's great food besides catfish, there're rides and games and I get to see everyone in town. I love the Catfish Festival. I'm just not in the mood for a party and seein' everybody, and people givin' condolences over Chick and askin' questions about him." I sighed.

"On the other hand, if you don't show up, might make people wonder why. A guilty person would lay low and stay out of the public eye."

YaYa eyed me. She was pretty smart. I couldn't afford for anyone to be looking at me crossways right now. I bet the much lamented TBI agents would be wandering around the festival, poking their long noses in everywhere.

I ran my hands through my hair. "Yep, guess I need to go get ready. You goin'?"

"There's Bingo," YaYa said with a wicked little smile.

When all the people who live in our house go off at the same time, there are logistics that have to be considered. First, all dogs have to be let out so they can do doggie business outside. Then they all have to be gathered back up. If we left them to run loose, chances are they'd follow us into town. It's happened before. They all have to be fed. This takes longer than you might think. They get excited and mill around you and food gets spilled and there's yelling. The doors to all the bedrooms have to be shut, unless you want to come home and find that canines have taken over your bed. Clouseau, the French bulldog has to go out to pee one more time before you leave. He has a little bladder and gets excited very easily. That's a bad combination. Last but not least, the burglar alarm has to be set. There is no such thing as getting away in a hurry. You just have to start way early.

Daddy, Mommy and YaYa rode together in the Expedition. I decided to take the Jeep, so I could have some autonomy in case something exciting happened and I needed my own wheels. Truth to tell, Daddy's driving scares the living hell out of me. He drives like a Chihuahua on crack with an espresso chaser. He talks with his hands as he drives and yells at everyone else on the road, whether they deserve it or not. It is the only circumstance where I find him to be irrational.

I tapped the Bluetooth and called Mars.

She answered on the second ring. "Hey, gorgeous, you heading into town?"

"Why, yes, I am. You are comin' to the festival, right? It's the event of the season after all." I grinned at my wittiness.

"I'll be there with bells on. I hear there're some great items in the auction that are well worth bidding on this year."

I laughed at her. "I bet that means there're shoes in the auction."

"Damn right."

"See ya there."

The Catfish Festival is held in early spring each year. All the businesses in town have booths set up, and lots of individuals rent space as well. You can buy anything from a handmade baby blanket to clothes to tie-dye tee-shirts for your dog or cat or kid. I thought my sister-in-law Elaine would have a booth for You're Invited!, the calligraphy company she owns.

You can also get every kind of sweet, tooth-rotting, hip-expanding goody you can imagine. I began to drool just thinking about it. My particular favorite is the deep-fried Twinkie. It'll make you see Jesus and that's a fact. I think it's the sugar, preservatives and hot grease that cause the mystical experience.

All the restaurants in town set up a food court in front of the courthouse. That meant my brother Brian and his better half, Darlene, would have a booth for the Red Dog Restaurant. It's a pub with a higher class clientele than the Springwater, and the food's a bit more upscale too. They love being in the food business and constantly create new dishes for the menu. I could hardly wait to see what new specialty they had dreamed up for the day.

Last, but not least, there's the catfish. Each restaurant fixes the nasty creature in different and inventive ways, with secret ingredients in the batter and different kinds of side dishes. But at the end of the day, it was all still just catfish, and no matter how fancy it was cooked, I couldn't eat it. Good thing for me there were plenty of other things to munch on at the festival.

There were all kinds of games of skill and chance to play, and rides too. There were also the catfish races. Yep, I'm not kidding. Who could make something like that up? Each ugly, slimy monster got outfitted with a waterproof number, and then dozens of them are let loose in a quarter-mile long canal created from black garden plastic and filled with water. You can bet on which one you think will win. The entire downtown square looked like a carnival midway. There's always dancing and fireworks after dark.

All the gaming money went to charity. The Simpson County Retirement Home was the recipient of the funds. It's a privately owned nursing home and a good one. The extra money the festival brought in allowed them to hire skilled techs and therapists and to pay everyone a decent wage. The money also bought extras for the residents, like a big screen TV and parties. All in all, it's a win-win.

I knew Mars would be at the auction site, so I parked and walked over to the auction. Mars was already there drooling over shoes. What else is new?

"Hey, babe," I said.

"Oh my God, look at those Italian, calfskin, gold slingbacks!"

I kissed her on the cheek. She never looked in my direction but continued to stare at the object of her adoration. They were cute, but could I run down a bail jumper in them? Not without risking serious injury. I smiled and shook my head. I looked over the other items being offered. I spotted a hand tooled leather holster. It looked like something a gunslinger in the Old West would wear. Except this was a shoulder holster, and pretty. I fell in serious lust in that moment. I knew what I would bid on. I sighed.

"The holster," Mars said.

"Oh, hell no. I'm gonna out bid you on those shoes."

"Then I'll have to kick your ass."

"When does this hoedown start?" I asked.

"Three-o'clock."

"Let's get some food. I skipped breakfast to save myself for the food here."

"God, you're getting fried Twinkies, aren't you?"

"For dessert." I grinned.

We wandered the food court, greeted my sister-in-law and bought lots of goodies from everyone. We carried all of our waxed-paper-wrapped bounty to one of the picnic tables set up close to the food court and spread out our plunder. There were fried clams, fried cheese sticks, onion rings, lasagna, chili, corn dogs and some kind of an hors d'oeuvre thing from Darlene made with black olives, cream cheese and sun-dried tomatoes. I was in heaven.

"Where's your momma and daddy?" I asked Mars between bites.

"They're here. You know the entire staff from the high school volunteers to help run the catfish races."

"Ick, do they have to touch those monstrosities?" I could not for the life of me imagine tiny, beautiful and fastidious Nancy Price handling catfish.

"No, she makes Dad do all the handling. She only supervises." Mars laughed.

Marcella's dad, Jack, is a large man. If you want to understand how big a guy he is, walk over to your refrigerator and introduce yourself. His presence is very commanding. He teaches Math, and his students give him very little trouble. He has a stunning Barry White voice too. I'm convinced that Nancy fell in love with Jack because of that voice.

"What do you want to drink?" I asked Mars.

"Oh, lemonade, I think."

"Good choice."

I took a five from my wallet and went to fetch drinks. The lemonade at the festival is the real deal, made by squeezing lemons, adding them to water and pouring in enough sugar to make your teeth itch. Heaven! I was waiting for our glasses when I spotted Donna. My first impulse was to wave, but after the weird reception I'd gotten the other day, I hung back. She was standing at the door that led to her office and looked as though she was waiting for someone. As I watched her while trying not to let her see me staring, she was joined by two men I'd never seen before. That wasn't what struck me as odd. No, what I thought odd was their behavior. They all looked, to me, clandestine and sketchy, and they were trying too hard to act normal. Know what I mean?

Remember when you were a teenager and you'd been out drinking. You came home, and tried to act normal, and sober. You talked slower so you wouldn't sound stupid, and you moved slower so you wouldn't fall down on your drunken face. Of course, your parents knew damn good and well you'd been drinking, and there was hell to pay the next morning. You couldn't for the life of you figure out how they knew! You were so careful trying to hide the fact that you were hammered, that you looked like a dumb-ass—you just didn't know it.

These three were acting the same way: really working hard at being normal, smiling, and being friendly to each other. But their body language screamed nervous, uncomfortable and trying hard for invisibility. The two guys were dressed very down-home comfortable: John Deere tee-shirts, jeans and boots—all brand new I might add. The jeans still had creases. I'd bet they had never eaten catfish in their whole lives. I wanted to get closer so I could hear their accents and see if they were from the area or anywhere within 100 miles of where I was standing. My Spidey senses were tingling to beat the band. I got my two large lemonades and wandered across the street.

"Hey, Donna! How ya'll doing today? Isn't this fun? I can't wait for the catfish races, can you? You got a favorite? Who're your very handsome friends here?" I was being so friendly and sweet that butter wouldn't melt in my mouth. I batted my eyes a bunch as I rattled off my inane questions and smiled like a loon.

Donna stared at me for about 10 seconds before she got hold of herself. "Uh, well uh, this is my friend Bill...uh...Green and my other friend Al Smith." She stammered and broke out into a sweat despite the fact that it was a very mild day in April.

"Please to meetcha," I said and nodded to each man in turn.

They looked very uncomfortable with the encounter. Good on 'em.

"I'd shake but as ya'll can see, my hands are full. I sure hope you fellers have a good time today, Donna, you make sure they do now." I stood there for a good twenty seconds waiting for one of the thugs to speak. Neither did and I figured I'd worn out my welcome. "See ya'll later."

I spun on my heel and headed back to the table. Damn, I was really hoping to hear their voices.

"Who are those two with Donna?" Mars asked. She was frowning over my shoulder at Donna and her two new friends.

"Well I can't say positively, but I think based on body type they're the two bastards who searched my office. I got 'em on my new fabulous lipstick cam."

"Holy shit!"

"Indeed. What say we eat up and keep an eye on Donna? We'll

give 'em enough time to settle in, and then I'm gonna sneak over and see if I can hear anything interesting."

Mars started to open her mouth and I held my hand up to forestall her.

"You're gonna sit right here and keep watch. If I don't come back or you see them carryin' me out feet first, you can yell for the posse."

"Oh goody, I get to be the faithful sidekick. If I'd known that, I would've dressed differently, more in keeping with the second banana role. Something with a cape and thigh high boots." She dug into the food.

"Smart ass," I mumbled.

I ate just enough to fill the burning hole in my belly, wrapped up the rest and made it look as though I'd just purchased it. I retrieved my lock pick kit and my very discreet listen-through-walls device from my purse and stuck them in my pockets. They are both "don't leave home without it" items, at least in my profession. I felt too conspicuous standing in the middle of the town square to transfer my gun from my purse to my waistband.

I sighed, "No gun today."

Mars looked at me with a worried expression. "Be careful," she said.

I nodded to my cohort in crime and walked back across the street toward Donna's office. A big part of being a PI is listening to conversations that other people would rather you not listen to, so you have to be creative. I carried the food as if I were bringing it to someone inside the courthouse building. As long as you look as though you belong in the place where you are, most of the time no one will question your presence. Handy to know, right? There were other offices that shared the hallway with Donna's office. My plan was to see how close I could get to her door and put my big ears on.

I confidently entered the hallway. It was empty and I couldn't hear any sounds either. I was pretty sure that everyone was outside enjoying the festival, everyone but Donna and her two friends. I quietly made for the bathroom where I deposited the remains of my brunch. I picked the county surveyor's office right next door to Donna's office and picked the lock. Fifteen seconds and the door gave up—that's because I'm a fantastic lock picker. Grow up with four brothers and you'd be an expert in breaking and entering too. They only thought they could hide their secrets from me. The second reason for such ease is that I own a state of the art lock pick kit. The third reason is that state and county buildings are built by the lowest bidder; and therefore, the locks are very cheap.

I slipped into the office, silently closed the door behind me and locked it. I went directly to the wall that stood between me and Donna. I retrieved my handy dandy listening device from my pocket. It's tiny and compact and electronic. God, I do love my job! The toys alone make it so worth doing. I fastened the device to the wall and put the headphones on. For a few seconds there was no sound, and I began to doubt my technology. Then I heard voices. Angry voices.

"I never signed up for this. Ya'll are crazy and you jumped the gun. Now we've got a murder hangin' over us. You've made me an accessory to murder!"

Holy shit! That's when I knew I was right. I almost hyperventilated! Ohmygod! Ohmygod! Ohmygod! These sons-of-bitches murdered Chick, and this homegrown, traitorous bitch helped them. Donna sounded mad and scared. I didn't blame her. If she was involved in this mess, she was in big trouble.

My hands started shaking and my breathing got ragged. I took some deep breaths to keep from passing out, but I think it was a near thing because my vision got black all around the edges.

"Bitch," I whispered, "I'm gonna see you fry."

I had a vision of me rushing into her office and beating them all to death with my fists. I did some more deep breathing to calm down. The assholes were still talking, and I decided I'd better listen. I didn't want to miss anything important.

"You've been paid plenty to take a very small risk. This is covered. We tossed this PI bimbo who's been sniffing around, under the bus. She's the perfect fall guy. The TBI are running around chasing their own tails. In the meantime, we get the last holdout to sell, finish this deal, and we all go home happy."

The speaker had a Yankee accent. He sounded like someone had called central casting and ordered a thug, very large and in charge. I tried to decide which guy he was, but I thought he was the smaller of the two men.

"You have no idea what you've done, the can of worms you've

opened here." Donna was getting more and more agitated. "This *bimbo* is the daughter of the former sheriff and the sister of the current one. Her entire family and most of the people in this county will go to the wall for her. You murdered one of the most well-liked men in town. We're not in the big city where people are all strangers to each other. Everybody here knows everybody else here. This isn't going away just because you say so or because you think you've handled things. Let me tell you how this ends. This bitch is gonna turn over every rock and stump until she discovers who murdered her boyfriend and she'll find you and then she'll find me."

I leaned my head against the wall and tears swam in my eyes. She'd called Chick my boyfriend. Shit. Maybe I had really screwed up. Maybe the one person in the world that was right for me, who would love me to the end, and always have my back, was Chick. What if I'd been wrong, and I should've just bitten the bullet, taken the risk and married him? I drew a ragged breath and got a grip. It was hard, but I did it. I had to keep my head and listen to those assholes, even if tears were running down my cheeks.

"Look, this Maher broad was close with him. She's a goddamned PI, and she's been nosin' around like you told us. We needed to get her outta the way. So the TBI got an anonymous tip about her and her boyfriend being drug dealers. Now it don't matter what this bitch knows or finds out. The TBI ain't listening to her. They don't like her. I'd say she rubbed 'em the wrong way, given some comments me and Rick overheard at the local watering hole. But they do like her for the murder. So alls we gotta do is keep our heads down and get this job finished. Then the suits move in and make nice with the locals, get the soil and water test falsified, and like Joe says, we all get to go home with a fat paycheck."

The other guy was trying to be reasonable and calm Donna down. I thought he was the bigger guy. Who the hell was Rick, I wondered?

"I don't get to go home, you idiot, I am home, I live here and I have to continue to live here and live with what you've done!" Donna sounded like she was talking through clenched teeth. Oh no, she was not calming down one little bit.

"Then I suggest you find someplace new to live," said Joe.

He was a real charming guy. I heard the scrape of a chair and someone collapsing into it.

"When I was first approached on this land deal, it seemed so easy. All I had to do was get the information on the parcels of land at Coleman's Cove and give your bosses the names of the owners. Nothing illegal, not really, just usin' the knowledge I had at my fingertips to help a big company move into the area. There'd be new jobs. The county owned most of the land, so the local government would get lots of cash. It was all so easy."

"It's still easy if you keep your head," said Joe. "In a few days this will all be over. Why don't you go home and take something for your nerves."

"Listen, you asshole, you have no idea what Tess Maher knows. She may be on to this whole deal. You don't know who she's shared her knowledge with. That entire family is thicker'n thieves. She's probably told them everything. It's a pretty simple trail from the land sale to Chick's death and back to me. She just has to be able to put two and two together, and she's always been good at that."

"I told you, we got this covered. If it'll make you feel any better then we'll find out what she knows and who she told. Then I can put that fire out too, just like with the boyfriend. Calm the hell down. You don't gotta get your hands dirty so what're you bellyaching about?" Joe growled.

Joe was a prince among men. I bet he had to fight the women off with a stick.

"You've got it covered? What are you going to do, kill the entire Maher family and anyone else that Tess may have confided in? You've gotten me involved in murder and you act as though it were nothing! You're a monster!"

"I don't know who the hell you think you're talking too, but I'm warning you, watch your fucking mouth," snarled Joe.

"Get out of my office." Donna's voice was low and hard. She didn't sound scared anymore. She sounded dangerous.

I decided at that moment it was time for me to pack up my tent and steal silently away. I turned from the wall, stumbled and slammed into the desk. I sucked in air. That hurt, and worse—I made noise.

You hear that, Marty?" said Joe.

I froze in mid-step.

"Sounded like it came from next door," said Marty.

I knew I only had seconds before those two were on me. Quickly,

I scanned the room. There was a desk, some filing cabinets and a closet. Not many options for a place to hide. The windows looked as though they hadn't been opened in a century, so that was out. A good rule is never hide in a closet—it's the first place the bad guys look—unless there is just no other option. I stuffed my equipment into my pockets and moved to the closet. It had double doors. I opened one side and scouted it out. The space was full of big maps and some office equipment. There was a high shelf that ran the length of the closet with a lot more maps and what looked like giant rolls of paper.

There was just enough space for me to close the door. I stood on a filing cabinet and pulled myself up on the shelf. I wiggled back behind the rolls of paper, unrolled some of it to cover me like a blanket and willed myself to be invisible. I could hear the lock being picked as I settled down. I was having trouble with my breathing. My body wanted to gasp in huge amounts of air, but my brain told me that was too noisy and I shouldn't listen to my lungs. I concentrated on breathing quietly and being calm. Zen, I was Zen. It wasn't easy. I was scared and my heart was hammering so hard I was sure the bad guys would hear. Then there were footsteps in the room.

"Maybe you was hearing things," said Marty, "'cuz I don't see nobody here."

"You heard some kind of noise from in here too, so shut up and look around," Joe demanded.

Someone pulled the chair away from the desk. Thank God I didn't hide there. The closet door was yanked open. I almost screamed in a knee jerk reaction. There were sounds of items being moved around a bit below me.

"See if those windows open," Joe commanded.

I heard more scrabbling noises. I guessed that was Marty trying the windows.

"These windows look like they're painted shut. Nobody went out this way. Maybe the noise we heard came from outside. There's a lot of people out there you know. Could've been kids playing around, huh?"

"It sure as hell sounded like it came from in here. But maybe you're right, it could've come from outside. It could've been that damn PI sneakin' around too. She's a problem. The sooner we find out what she knows, the better. We're done here. Push that closet door shut like it was, and let's get the hell out."

My hiding space got dark again, and I refrained from breathing a sigh of relief. I was grateful to whatever saint was in charge of hiding from bad guys, since I was fairly positive I wasn't really hidden very well.

I heard the door to the surveyor's office shut and Donna's office door open again. I scrambled out of the closet and reattached my big ears to the wall.

"You'll be hearing from us," said Marty. His voice was loud and threatening.

The door slammed and I heard the unmistakable sounds of Donna sobbing. For one nanosecond I felt sorry for her. Then I shook it off. Maybe using her position to give Aggroco information was not illegal, I didn't know. But she took money from them, and that was at least questionable.

The part that was unforgivable was that she knew her cohorts murdered Chick. Tennessee still has the death penalty. We administer it via the electric chair, whose nickname is "Old Sparky." She was gonna get a guided tour of the procedure if I had my way.

While Donna was having her pity party I slipped out of the building. I walked back to Mars as if I didn't have a care in world. She was faithfully waiting for me at the picnic table and stood up when she saw me coming.

"God Almighty, I was fit to be tied. I saw those two gangsters walk out and you didn't. I was ready to go and find Connell." All of this was exclaimed through her clenched teeth.

"Did you know that your Southern accent gets thicker when you get agitated?" I asked.

She stared at me and blinked like a frog in a hail storm for several seconds. "Are you kidding me, that's all you have to say? You were in there forever and I was scared to death and you make jokes?"

"Calm down and sit down. They murdered Chick over the land deal. I heard her say that she was working with them. One of them is named Joe. I think that's the smaller guy and he implied that he killed Chick! The other guy is Marty. There's some guy named Rick too. Donna was raising hell about how this whole thing was not supposed to be illegal and now they've done murder. She didn't sound the least bit sorry they'd murdered Chick, just that they'd committed murder and now they were all in deep shit. The thugs were trying to calm her down and did a poor job of it I might add. She's an absolute powder keg, and the slightest thing is gonna set her off." I stopped to draw a breath. I was agitated and spitting out words like machine gun fire.

Mars smiled an evil smile at me. "Then let's light her fuse," she said.

I smiled my own evil smile right back at her. "I wonder where my brother, the sheriff is right now."

"You mean your brother who is going to shit a squealin' worm over the little adventure you just had? That brother?" Mars said. Terribly snotty tone she used too. In all fairness, she was still pissed at me for scaring her, and she had a right to be.

"I said I was sorry for scarin' you, which was never my intention. I just saw an opportunity to get some information and I took it. You would've done the same thing in my shoes," I said earnestly.

Mars looked down at my beat up running shoes. "Ha, I wouldn't be caught dead in those shoes."

"That was just mean." I tried to look hurt but I knew I failed. Luckily, Connell showed up at that moment. "Thank God, I was looking for you!" I said.

"What have you done now?" he asked.

"Why would you say that to me?" I asked defensively.

"You won't believe what she's done now," said Mars. She proceeded to tell him all about it. "She followed Donna Maples and two strangers into Donna's office and eavesdropped on them. She could've been killed! She's lost her ever lovin' mind, Connell!"

"Jesus Christ, Tess! I know you own a cell phone, did you ever think about callin' for back-up?"

I held my hands up in defense. "I thought someone might notice you in your sheriff's uniform skulkin' around the courthouse in broad daylight. Which by the way, since it is broad daylight I figured that I should be safe enough, plus I did have Mars standin' lookout. I knew she'd call the cavalry if anything bad happened to me. Besides all that, it was an opportunity that just fell in my lap and I had to act. Connell, I heard her say they murdered Chick over the land deal at the Cove. I heard her admit it!"

I was so frustrated and agitated that I shook my fists at him. Connell sat down beside me and took my fists in his hands.

"They could've killed you and stuffed you in a bathroom stall. Tess, you aren't usin' your brain here. I know you heard her admit the murder, but it's your word against hers. We need proof. Right now all we have is a theory."

"I could beat a confession out of her," I suggested.

Connell and Marcella both gave me a disgusted look.

"Fine, make a better suggestion."

"Well, in a regular investigation I'd take this information you've brought me, and I'd haul Donna Maples in for questionin'. We have two problems with that. The TBI would hang me by my thumbs, and she's the mayor's sister-in-law. Again, we need proof before we can move on her."

"Is it illegal for a county employee to help someone with a special interest in exchange for money?" I asked.

"We call it a bribe, and we still need proof," Connell said stubbornly.

I blew out a breath at him and we all sat there for a minute thinking.

"I have an idea."

I did have a great idea, but I didn't intend to share it with Connell since it was illegal as all get out. I intended to break into Donna's office and go through her computer records to see if I could find anything that showed she'd been offered money to help broker the land deal. That would be something we could use against her. I knew if we had a wedge we could break her. She was on the verge of cracking up. She just needed a little help. Connell and Mars were both staring at me waiting to hear what I was thinking.

"Oh sorry, I got lost in thought. I was just thinkin' that we need to keep an eye on her as much as possible. Maybe she'll do something stupid. She is the weakest link."

I still liked my idea of beating a confession out of her.

CHAPTER 22

The Catfish Festival was a huge success. If you've never been to a celebration in a small town then you must understand that an almost magical excitement infuses the very air after the sun goes down. For the children it's the opportunity to be free and play and eat all the things they're usually denied, to run with their friends and family like lunatics, to stay up way past bedtime and to believe the evening would never end. For adults it's the opportunity to give the children that fun and to be kids themselves for a few hours. The night is filled with music and the sounds of the games ringing and clanging and the laughter of children. There's a light dust in the air stirred up by many feet, and the bright, colored lights that surround the entire grounds of the carnival make it sparkle like fairy dust.

The rides spin you around and around in the dark, and you feel transported to another time and place. You forget for a while all the problems that you usually carry around with you: the house note, the asshole boss, the lack of love life or too much of one, problems with your significant other, crab grass, that odd noise your car has been making. You just let it all go and revert to your childhood.

I played all the games that were set up, from the bean bag toss to the rings on the bottle game to the rifle range. Most of the herd followed me from game to game, and I won prizes for them while they stood and cheered me on. I paid for all of them to play the duck game. I love that one. There are rubber ducks that float by, and you reach down and grab one. Each one has a number on the bottom that corresponds to a cheesy prize. The kids loved it. Everybody played twice. Several trips were made to the Jeep to deposit the booty.

We ate cotton candy, funnel cake and caramel corn. It's a wonderful feeling to get kids all sugared up then return them to their parents. I guess I'm just mean that way. I even cheered for the catfish races, which are silly and funny. The catfish are all trapped behind a gate in the water, then the gate opens and they race to the finish line. Maybe "racing" is the wrong word. Some hurry, others meander and some swim back the way they came. Everyone has a favorite, and so there is much yelling and cheering. There're even trophies for first, second and third place that are awarded to the winners—the human winners. They're cheap plastic little statues with a fish on top, but the people who get the dopey things always give them a place of honor in their homes. We have a bunch, as my father and grandmother have quite an eye for winners. The prize for the fish is that they get to be dinner. Good times.

I rode rides with the bigger kids: tilt-a-whirl, the bumper cars, the roller coaster and the Ferris wheel. I stood and waved as the little ones rode the carousel. Everyone got balloon animals and a tee-shirt with a big ugly catfish emblazoned on it.

I danced my feet down to nubs that night. I love to dance. There was a country band first and a rock and roll band after that, so I danced with just about every male I could find. Daddy and all of my brothers are good dancers, but I also danced with Billy, Sammy and Jeff. I didn't turn down a single offer.

We all oohed and aahed over the fireworks. Mars had the winning bid on the Italian calfskin slingbacks and I won the holster. I don't want to admit how much either of us spent, but we were happy none the less. YaYa won a new electric blanket at bingo. We were all as pleased as punch with ourselves.

All the while, under the surface, I was thinking about Donna and the vengeance that I intended to visit on her. Funny how I hated her so much more than the hired thugs who'd actually pulled the trigger on Chick. I guess that was because she was local, she knew Chick, they were friends. I guess that made her a traitor in my book. I meant to make her pay for it. So I smiled and ate and danced and hid my dark, ugly thoughts.

In all my wanderings during the rest of the day and the night, I never once saw Donna. I suppose that was for the best. I wasn't sure I could control myself if I came face to face with her. I didn't see Agents Boyd and Lyle or the hired muscle either. I just knew they were all out there in the dark watching. It was a creepy thought, and it made the hair on the back of my neck stand straight up.

Finally, it was time to pack up and go home. Mars and I helped my family members break down their booths and load out. I saw Mommy, Daddy and YaYa heading to the car with a bunch of the herd in tow. I guessed several of the bedrooms at the house would be occupied by short people. Good, that meant they wouldn't miss me for hours. By the time anyone came looking for me, I'd be finished with my night's work and safely home. I walked Mars to her car.

"You okay?" she asked.

"I'll do for now."

She didn't need to know what I planned to do because she'd try to talk me out of it or she'd tell Connell. I hugged her and she hugged me back much more fiercely than usual.

"I love you," Mars whispered in my ear.

"I love you back," I said.

I released her and climbed into the Jeep. She started the Thunderbird. We left the parking lot together and headed in our opposite directions. I drove toward home for about sixty seconds before I made a U-turn and headed back into town. I thought about where to park. My fire-engine-red Jeep is pretty distinctive, but it's the license plate that really makes it stand out—PI4U. In case you're wondering, whenever I run an investigation I rent a car for the occasion.

If Connell saw the Jeep, he'd suspect that I was up to something, and then he'd start poking around. I decided to park behind the Red Dog. I figured that if he saw my car there, he'd assume that I had ridden with Brian or Darlene for some reason. I parked in the alley, tucked my gun in my waistband and my other equipment into my pockets. I slipped across the deserted square to the courthouse.

Of course, it's illegal to break into the county courthouse, but then it's illegal to break into any building that you don't own. The trick is not to get caught. I stayed in the shadows, trying to look innocent and reached the same back door that I had walked through earlier in the day. I looked around and was satisfied that there was no one watching me. I pulled on my latex gloves—yes, I am paranoid. I got the lock pick kit from my pocket and set to work. It only took about a minute to get the tumblers to fall into place, but I was sweating by the time I accomplished it. I was feeling terribly exposed in the open. I breathed a sigh of relief when the door opened. I closed and relocked the door behind me and went straight to Donna's office. That door, like the county surveyor's door, practically opened itself. That door got closed and locked behind me too.

I slipped my miner's light over my head—they are so awesome, although I suppose they were never intended to help facilitate burglaries. First things first, the blinds were open and I closed them, then switched on my head lamp and got my bearings. I fired up Donna's computer. I was sure that the info I wanted would be there. At least I hoped it would be there, otherwise I was risking a jail sentence for nothing. I laid my thumb drive next to the computer. I meant to copy everything relevant. The computer woke up and the little password box opened. I'd anticipated this and so I'd been thinking about what word she would use. Most people use familiar words or dates that they won't forget, like their birthday or anniversary or their children's names. That's a bad idea. If anyone knows you fairly well they can crack your code. Most people don't change their passwords very often either. Passwords are like underwear—you should change both often.

Donna was three years older than me, and she was in the homecoming court every year of high school and queen in her senior year. It was an award she had aspired to since she was in the 6th grade. She campaigned for the award and made lots of promises to lots of people for the votes. There was some ugly talk about some of those promises, I can tell you. Donna was nothing if not ambitious. Hey, it's a small town. You can't get away with much. She also did the pageant circuit from the time she could walk, and she brought home lots of trophies. I promise you that the crown she wore the night of homecoming was the most important prize ever. Go figure. She had the plaque, the crown, the pictures with her court and the dried flowers in a glass case on the wall of her office. The pictures of the special night had their own album on her Facebook page. It's even in her bio there. I typed "homecoming queen" in the password box with confidence, and the computer opened up like a present for me. I grinned with a smug satisfaction. It was good to be me.

I searched through file after file until I nearly fell asleep. Donna had lots of hobbies, and they all had their very own folder. It seemed like I went through a bazillion folders with names like: Oriental Flower Arranging, Cheese-making, Origami and Historical Japanese Kite Construction. She had a bucket list that was equally exciting. I had to open every one and take a look at everything. I had no idea where she might have hidden the information I wanted.

She even had an enemies file. I couldn't resist, I had to open it. There were lots of names on that list and the reasons she thought of them as enemies and the date she had added them. Two of the county judges were on the list, the courthouse secretary, three of the teachers at the high school—and my brother. My eyes went wide at that. Most of the people on the list had been added because they had snubbed her in some way or wouldn't give her something she wanted, but Connell was on the list because he wouldn't sleep with her. Ewww. She had actually typed "spurned my advances" next to his name, and there were several dates next to that entry. She had also typed the word "BASTARD" in capital letters. She'd obviously hit on him more than once. Holy crap! I wondered if he knew how she felt about him and the crazy bullet he had dodged.

Donna's not ugly, goat-footed or hunched-back. She has no reason to throw herself at men. She's tiny and petite, her ash blond hair is chin length and stylishly arranged, she has a nice body and she's cute as a button. She could probably still twirl a baton like nobody's business too. She's also a cold, heartless bitch. I closed that file and kept looking.

I started looking in her email. She had a lot of folders there too. Finally I came to one labeled "Retirement". I clicked on it and sure enough it was a folder filled with emails between Donna and several people from Aggroco. The emails had lovely letterhead and official signatures. The first email was a fishing expedition to see if Donna might be willing to help the company gain the property. The second email was Donna's answer: she would be delighted to help, but given her busy schedule working her fingers to the bone for Simpson County she could not guarantee how much time she could actually devote to them and their enterprise. A senior vice-president at Aggroco offered to compensate her for her help and she accepted. The original correspondence was dated eighteen months earlier. I was surprised this deal had been in the works for such a long time and no one had caught wind of it. This bitch knew how to keep a secret.

There were maps of the Cove, each parcel marked with the name of the owner as an attachment on one of the emails. Most of the parcels were owned by the county. There was one email that was labeled "my island". She had sent it to herself. I opened that file and the only thing it contained was a string of numbers. I would bet my ass and my hat that the numbers were for a bank account. The smart money said it was an off-shore account. Donna may have been the homecoming queen and a beauty pageant winner, but she wasn't stupid. If she'd been paid and put the money into an off-shore account then she had no intention of mentioning her windfall to the IRS. When all was said and done, Donna was looking at murder, conspiracy and tax evasion too. A trifecta!

Important safety tip: if you are going to do something illegal such as taking outside money to do your job as a county worker, then you shouldn't keep the emails that outline the illegal activity. You certainly shouldn't keep them on your work computer. Maybe I was wrong and she was stupid or just arrogant. Maybe she just couldn't conceive of anyone suspecting her much less that anyone would break into her office and hack into her computer. I would've erased the emails and driven a nail through the freakin' hard drive. But that's just me and reflects my level of paranoia.

I plugged in my thumb drive and transferred the entire file into it with a grim determination. Here was everything I needed to tie Donna to Chick's death, but what the hell could I do with it? Who could I show it to? What I was doing was illegal as hell. I could go to jail for it. I wasn't even sure the information would stand up in court since I had stolen it. I ran my hands through my hair and sighed. There was an answer. I just didn't have it yet. I needed to think hard and be right. I couldn't have this bitch get off on a technicality.

I was almost finished copying the files when I heard the outside door of the building rattle as if someone was checking the doorknob to see if it was locked. My heart stopped for a beat or three. Did I lock it behind me? I was almost positive that I had. Still I froze like a deer in the headlights. The door rattled again, and then I heard nothing. I closed my eyes and took a deep and silent breath. It had probably been Connell or Joel checking to make sure the building was secure. Just a regular night patrol, I tried to convince myself. I finished with the files and put the valuable thumb drive in my pocket. I erased my footprints so they wouldn't show up in the history, turned off the computer and my miner's light. I sat in the darkness for several minutes and gave whoever was walking around the courthouse time to move on. I was as nervous as a long-tailed cat in a room full of rocking chairs. I couldn't get caught. Jail wouldn't agree with me— orange makes me look sallow.

I got up from the desk and opened the blinds. Carefully, I took a good long look. Not a creature was stirring. If I was going to make a break for the safety of my car, I had my opening. I locked the office behind me and moved down the hall. I opened the outside door a crack and peered out. Again I saw no one—my luck was holding. I slipped out the door, locked it and moved into the shadows. I peeled the gloves off as I walked and stuffed them into my pocket.

My luck held right up until I put my hand on the Jeep's door handle when a hand clamped on my shoulder.

"What the hell are you up to?"

I didn't need to turn around to know that Connell had snuck up on me. I was pretty proud of myself for not jumping and shrieking, I have to say.

"Holy shit, Connell!" I turned toward him. "What are you doin' sneaking up on me like that?"

"I saw your car and because I know you so well, I called the house to see if you'd ridden home with someone else. Of course they hadn't seen you, so next I called Mars. She told me that ya'll had parted company, and you were headed home the last time she had seen you. So I decided to sit here and wait."

He stood there and stared at me, silently demanding an answer.

"Why do you always think I'm up to somethin'? You make me feel like you're pickin' on me." I tried for angry and defensive.

"Tess, get down off the damn cross, we need the wood for somethin' else," he snapped back to me.

Okay, so he wasn't buying my martyr act—not surprising really. I tried lying. "I was stakin' out the courthouse to see if Donna and her new friends came back for another meetin'."

I can't lie to my family for some reason—I guess they know me too well— so I was truly glad it was dark in the alley and Connell couldn't see my face.

"Hmm, nope not buying that either. Give it up, baby sister."

Bastard, I thought. "Get in the Jeep, take a load off." I said as I opened the driver's side door.

I was stalling for time. I needed to decide how to phrase my next statement.

We settled in and I turned to Connell. "What if there was proof in writin' that Donna was in league with these Aggroco guys. Not proof that they had anythin' to do with Chick's murder, but at least a conspiracy to smooth the path toward a land deal for the property in the Cove in exchange for a kickback. What could you do with that?"

"Jesus, what have you done?"

"Me? Work with me here, Connell. What if?"

"Well if I could say that I got a tip about this land deal, and the pay-off scheme, it would have to be a fairly convincin' tip that could be backed up. Then I could investigate those allegations without bringin' down the wrath of the TBI, I think. After all I'm still the sheriff in these here parts, and I am duty bound to investigate crime.

"Wow, that sounds impressive. So much so, that I could actually believe it. Maybe you can convince Boyd and Lyle of that when the two investigations collide." I smiled at him.

"If we had enough evidence, the only person I have to convince is a judge."

He waited for me to say something.

"Okay, some evidence has come into my possession. The damnedest thing really. It just sort of fell into my lap. Sorta out of the sky. Crazy, huh?"

"Crazy," my brother agreed.

"But I'm pretty sure it was obtained illegally, and as such it probably couldn't be used in court. But could it be used to open an investigation?"

"Maybe if someone sent a copy of this alleged information that proved there was a deal between Donna Maples and Aggroco where she promised to help them and they promised to pay her for the help, I could probably get a warrant to seize her computer. County officials are not supposed to take payoffs you know. That copy had better be sent anonymously, of course."

"Probably be best if it was a hard copy, sent in the mail, or better yet dropped through the mail slot of the sheriff's office in the dead of night, huh?" I asked.

"It might be better yet if whoever sent it wore gloves when handling the paper and the envelope. That's how it's done in the movies," Connell offered.

I leaned my head back on the headrest and closed my eyes."Yep, that'd probably be best. That's how they do it on all those crime shows. I sure hope somethin' like that happens soon. We need a break."

"That's the truth. Tess, there'd better not be anything that can tie you to this evidence in any way, shape or form, or it's both our butts in a sling."

I took a deep breath. "There's not, I'm sure that whoever originally got the evidence was extremely careful."

"So, you headed home for real now? Promise me, and I'll call the house and Mars and let them all know you're okay."

"Shit, Mars is gonna be mad at me."

Connell laughed. "Gonna be, baby sister, she is royally and totally pissed."

"Crap, get out of my car, I gotta go home."

CHAPTER 23
SUNDAY

I stretched. I yawned. I was still tired from yesterday. But it was a good tired. I did an inventory and discovered that my feet hurt most of all. My gaze traveled over to my brand new hand-tooled leather holster that was lying on my nightstand. God, it was pretty, covered with little green ivy vines and tiny blue flowers that wound all over it and up the strap. I'm not much of a girly-girl, but this rather ostentatious creation made me happy. I glanced at the clock display and realized I had two hours to get ready and be in a pew for twelve o'clock mass.

As I showered, I thought about all that I had seen and heard and stolen yesterday. I decided that I'd make copies of the emails that offered money to Donna in exchange for her helping Aggroco buy the land that the company wanted. After church, I could slip the envelope through the mail slot at Connell's office. I was pretty sure I could do it sight unseen. That Sunday was race day, and most people who went to church would hurry home to eat some lunch and get out to the track. In our town just about everybody went to the races: rich, poor, black, white, male, female, tiny babies and little old ladies. Truth to tell, in the South we just seem to like watching cars go round and round a track at stupid high speeds. Of course, it could be the allure of the beer that brings us out, or the wrecks. Billy and Sammy would be racing Chick's car, and I'd be there with bells on. Wild horses couldn't keep me away.

The coffee smell perfumed the air as I went downstairs.

"Morning, all," I said.

Mommy, Daddy, YaYa and members of the herd were all in various stages of breakfast and paper reading.

"Morning, honey," said YaYa. "Some day, huh? I think I did better at bingo than I've ever done. That dadgum Earl Spivey tried to beat me on every card, but I smoked him!"

"That's awesome, YaYa. So have we opened an orphanage around here?"

I looked around at four members of the herd—John, Michael,

Deidre and Steven—who were sitting at the table.

"Auntie Tess," said eight-year-old John, "we spent the night, but we're not gonna live here forever."

"Me will," declared Deidre.

I laughed. "Did we have fun yesterday?"

I was answered with much cheering and spoon banging. The dogs joined in by barking and my mother cut me a look.

I shrugged my shoulders. "I was just asking. Okay, eat up you evil lot, we have to go visit Jesus," I commanded.

I got a cup of coffee and a biscuit with ham. There were eggs too. We don't usually have a large breakfast before church on Sunday, but there would be no brunch on race day.

"I've got a few things to do before church," I said.

"Fine, their parents are coming over to help get them ready," said Mommy, "but hurry."

I waved at the kids and scooted upstairs. I popped the thumb drive into my computer and set about picking which files I wanted to print. I nibbled at my breakfast as I worked. I wanted the most incriminating emails for this task. In the end I chose four: the initial contact asking Donna to aid Aggroco in purchasing land, her acceptance and rather clumsy fishing for a bribe, their offer of a bribe, her jumping at the offer. At first glance, it took my breath. One point five million tax free dollars is a lot of money. But ultimately, it's a cheap price for your soul. As an afterthought I added the bank account number.

I copied those emails into a separate document then printed it. I slipped on a pair of latex gloves and put the documents in a manila envelope. I weighed out the pros and cons of addressing the envelope. I decided not to, Mavis would know to take it straight to Connell. I went into the bathroom and used a little tap water to seal the envelope, then I tucked it into my purse. Yes, yes, yes, I am paranoid!

I put on my new holster and stuck the Beretta inside. I practiced drawing it to see if it was easy or if it was stiff because the leather was so new. It was so easy. I practiced in front of the mirror several times. I might not be the fastest draw in the West, but I was satisfied. I threw a light jacket on over my floral sundress to hide the gun. I added white sandals to my ensemble, and I thought I looked good enough to satisfy even my mother's sense of propriety. If she only failed to notice the holster. Truly I don't usually go armed to church, and I would leave the gun in the car for mass, but I wasn't going to be without my piece until this nightmare was settled.

I ran up the stairs to the attic and hid the thumb drive in my favorite hiding place, an open compartment behind a loose brick in the chimney. I've been stashing stuff in there since I discovered the hidey-hole when I was seven. We were playing hide-n-seek on a rainy afternoon, and I decided to hide in the attic. I soon discovered that treasures stashed up there were ever so much more interesting than my siblings. No one has ever discovered it, and I've never told. Back down the stairs I went.

"I'll drive myself this morning. See ya'll at church," I called out.

I went out the kitchen door and jumped into the Jeep. While I was skulking around in the attic, I had decided that I'd drop off the envelope on the way to church. I was just too nervous to sit in a pew listening to Father Sherman with an information bomb in my bag. I knew I'd look guilty.

Fifteen minutes later I pulled to the curb in front of Connell's office. With Mark still in the hospital, Joel would be on patrol and the office should be vacant. I stayed in the Jeep while I checked out the sidewalk and the street. My plan, if anyone saw me, was to say I was looking for Connell. That seemed reasonable, and not suspicious. The street was totally deserted. Everyone in town must have had better things to do than hang out and spy on my activities, that included the TBI. Satisfied that I could pull off my delivery, I got out of the Jeep and walked over to the building. Casually, I peered in the big front window and saw nary a soul. Taking one more look around me, I saw the street was still empty. I reached into my bag and caught the envelope between my fingers to avoid leaving prints and slipped it into the mail slot. My fear was that somewhere down the road, the TBI would get into this and investigate who initially stole the email files. They could whistle for that information. I calmly walked to the Jeep and drove to church where I prayed that my plan worked.

Mass that day was said for the repose of Chick's soul. During the homily, Father William Sherman talked about Chick and his kindness to people, how everyone loved him, and his willingness to always help others in need. Chick wasn't a Catholic; he was a Methodist. But

I knew Father Sherman loved him and had secretly hoped Chick would convert. I tried to see the humor in that as I sat in the pew with an aching heart.

After church, we got trapped on the steps by Father Sherman and members of the congregation who wanted to offer condolences. St. Mary's is not a large parish—probably about two hundred souls altogether. It seemed like everyone was present and had something to say about Chick that day. Which was nice, but it was hard. I had to keep smiling and saying thank you, when really I didn't want to talk about it at all. But those people were not random strangers. They were friends, neighbors, past classmates, and they were hurting too. They were trying to give us comfort, but they needed comfort as well. So I stood there and talked, shook hands, got kissed and hugged, tried not to cry—instead I smiled. I knew it was only a dress rehearsal for the funeral.

When the last well-wisher had departed, Father Sherman put his hand on my arm. Bill Sherman was young and handsome. St. Mary's was his first parish and everyone loved him. He was a good guy—kind, sincere, good with old people and young people too. He was truly a man who had dedicated his heart to the service of God. I looked into his lovely grey-green eyes and smiled.

"Nice homily, Bill. I bet Chick enjoyed it."

"Tess, if you need anything, to talk or just to sit with someone who's sympathetic to your loss, please call me. Chick was my friend too."

I smiled at his comforting words. "Oh thanks, Bill, I appreciate that, really I do. If you could talk to your boss and ask him to help me catch the person responsible for this, I'd be eternally in your debt."

"I'll be talking to him tonight, and I'll ask as my first order of business."

I kissed him on the cheek and walked with my family to our cars. I took the opportunity to distribute the bounty from the games of skill and chance to the rightful owners. They all squealed and jumped around all over again as if none of them had ever seen the prizes before.

"So," I said over the yelling children, "are we all going to the races?"

"Hey, you lot, cool your jets," said Dugan to the herd.

They did not cool their jets but continued to laugh and yell and chase each other around the parking lot like Chihuahuas on crack. I wondered for a moment why St. Joseph's Valium for Children in colorful animal shapes was not bottled and sold everywhere. Illegal to drug the little buggers, I suppose. Still I was willing to wager that it would be a big seller.

"FREEZE!" Mommy's voice cut through the mayhem. "BUTTS! IN! CARS! NOW!"

She used the dreaded "Mommy" voice on them. They all froze and turned to look at her for about 1.5 seconds, then they all walked calmly to their own cars and climbed in. The bigger ones helped the little ones. None of them spoke a word or made a sound. It was amazing and a little eerie—truth be told, rather Stepford-esque.

"I believe that we're all going to the races," said Mommy in her normal tone.

There were nods all around. Then all the adults calmly went to their cars, climbed in and drove to the race track. I was barely out of the parking lot when the phone rang.

I hit the button. "Tess," I answered.

"I will kick your ass when I see you!" said Mars.

"Who is this? Is this JoAnne from the A&P? No matter what you've heard, I did not say your boyfriend had a wart on his penis. I only said it felt like he had a wart on his penis, I swear to God."

I thought levity was the best route here because she was pissed. Her anger radiated through my Bluetooth and singed my earlobe.

"Not funny! You really are crazy. I think that you're at least a half a bubble off plumb, girl. What the hell where you thinkin', goin' back into town alone? I thought you weren't going to go anywhere without tellin' someone where you were? Are you tryin' to make it easy on these bastards to kill you? And you pinky swore that you wouldn't do anything crazy!"

"Yes, I am funny, am not crazy, more like three-quarters, thought I would break and enter as I need the practice, of course alone, I had to on account of it being illegal, and no I will not make it easy. If they plan on killin' me they'd better pack a freakin' lunch! I do feel bad about the pinky swear. I'll make it up to you."

"God, I give up. You cannot die. You promised to be the godmother to my children and I haven't even had them yet."

"I'm being careful, I'm fully armed, and I do not underestimate my enemy. Are you gonna name one of your kids after me?"

"Good God, no! I don't fancy having a child named Crazy Bitch. Are you headed out to the track?"

"You suck. Yes, ma'am, I'm en route. The entire wreckin' crew is headin' out there, except for Connell. I didn't see him at church. With Mark in the hospital, they're shorthanded, but I can't imagine Connell missing this race."

"Me either. How's Mark?"

"Hanging in like a hair in a biscuit from what Connell tells me."

"Not funny, still mad."

"Are you coming?"

"On the way now."

"I'm here. See you in a short."

She didn't say bye to me. She just hung up. Okay fine, she could just be that way. I arrived at the track a little early, but even so the place was packed. I had to park at the far end of the lot from the gate. I got my ticket and searched for the family. They were easy to spot— all that red hair blowing in the breeze. I spotted Connell too. I was so glad he was there.

"Hello, fellow race enthusiasts. Save Mars a place. She's on her way. Are we doing food and drink orders yet?"

Patrick shook his head at me. "Do you ever do anything besides eat?"

I raised both eyebrows at him. "Is that a dig at me? Is my butt getting bigger?"

He grinned. "Yep, I been meaning to talk to you about that."

"Can you talk to me about it while you take my food and drink order? 'Cuz I'd like a burger with all the trimmings, fries and a beer. Please."

"At least you're polite when you demand something. Okay what about the rest of you?"

Patrick whipped out his Crackberry and became too busy taking orders to give me any more grief. He commandeered several of the older kids to help him carry food back from the concession stand. It was only then that I noticed it was another perfect day, just like last Sunday. My mood darkened considerably. Connell came and sat down beside me.

"How you doing?" he asked.

"Everybody at church wanted to talk about Chick. It was a stone bitch. I bet I was hugged and kissed at least a hundred times."

Connell laughed at me. "Poor baby," he teased.

I gave him an ugly look.

"Did you know that Donna Maples has a big thing for you?"

He took a deep, long suffering breath. "I'm aware of that. Sometimes it gives me nightmares."

I laughed. "Now that we know she's a murderous, larcenous bitch without a conscience, I can understand the nightmares. Before we knew that, she seemed normal, and she's cute as can be, so why?"

"Why'd I turn her down?" he asked. "Because I always got a crazy vibe off her. She's too perfect, too perky, too friendly and too precise—almost manically so. She hit on me several times and with a very determined attitude. I guess I thought she was hunting for someone or something to replace the glory days of high school for her. I knew I wasn't the guy and truth to tell she just doesn't appeal to me. She kinda reminds me of a Barbie doll. I was right to run when I did."

"Wow, I never had a lot of dealings with her, so I didn't have an opinion. She really hates you, I think. There's an 'enemies' list in the files on her computer, you're on it, my darling."

Connell shrugged. "Not surprised."

Patrick, food and Mars all showed up at the same time. Mars greeted all my family members but me. She sat on the other side of Connell away from me and began to converse with everyone around her. So, that was how she wanted to play. Fine, two could play that game. She'd get over it soon enough. Meanwhile I contented myself with my lovely, greasy, fully-loaded cheeseburger.

There were several races on tap for the day: the Powder Puff race, which was an all-female race; the Teen Challenge for sixteen to eighteen-year-olds; and the Run What You Brung race. The main race was the modified stock car event. Think, General Lee from the *Dukes of Hazard* TV show and you have the right image.

All the others races went first so that there would be a build up to the main event. First things first, the national anthem was sung by one of the girls from the high school chorus, who did a pretty credible job. We all stood and most of us sang. It always surprises me that people don't sing the anthem like they do in other countries. If you don't believe me, watch a soccer game sometime. After the singing, it was time for the qualifying race, or heat, with the modified stock cars. The heat was a three-lap race to see where the cars would be placed in the pack for the actual race. The better time a driver got in the heat, the closer to the front he'd be placed and the better his odds to win. Of course, you could do poorly in the heat, get placed in the back of the pack and still manage to take the checkered flag. It wasn't very likely but it's happened.

I could hear the cars warming up, and I knew the heat was about to start. I spotted Sammy's wife Jeanie and her daughter. I waved. She waved back, but her little girl was too excited to see anything but the track. I figured that Billy would be driving today. He's smaller and lighter than Sammy, plus the man can drive. One of the things that got him in trouble as a teenager was boosting cars and drag racing.

The cars lined up at the starting line. They all looked amazing, and the engines sounded so extremely powerful that my heart beat a little faster. I spotted the Grand National. It was painted with a shiny black, patent leather finish and sported a silver racing stripe. The number 42 was painted on the sides and the top. The car was sponsored by Donnelly's Repair and Replacement, so that logo was painted on the car as well. There was not one piece of chrome on the vehicle—even the bumpers were black. The usual painted-on-headlights were absent too. It was all just black. That lack of chrome made the car look very cool, very fast and very dangerous. It was a vehicle that would turn heads as it drove past. The boys had done a wonderful job on it.

The other cars lined up. All of them were sponsored by local businesses who thought that advertising on the track was good for them. They're probably right. Race fans are loyal. The cars revved their engines, and the crowd grew quiet. The pace car led off with the pack following for one lap then it pulled into the pits, the green flag came down and they were off. The crowd rose to its feet and cheered wildly. I jumped to my feet and joined them. It felt good to scream and yell!

Billy drove like a champ, and at the end of three laps it was evident that he'd be in the front of the pack when it came time to race.

There were about twenty-five other cars in the heat. This was the first race for the Grand National, but it ran like a winner. Our track is a three-quarter of a mile oval, known as a short track, and it's a dirt track not asphalt. Races on dirt tracks aren't as fast as races on asphalt, and there's been talk in recent years about paving the track. But the drivers seem to like the challenge of dirt and always vote the paving idea down. We may not be NASCAR sanctioned, but we're proud of our track and our sport.

The Powder Puff race was great, with about ten cars all done up with girly colors and sponsored by businesses that cater to women: dress shops, beauty shops, shoe stores and the like. The female drivers are not just fooling around though. Those girls can drive. Sometimes there's some real cut-throat maneuvering. On a majority of race days there're as many yellow flags for wrecks in the Powder Puff race as there are for the main event. The final tally was three yellow flags and one wreck with no injuries. The car sponsored by a local beauty emporium, Curl Up And Dye, won.

The Teen Challenge was a good race as well. Again not as many cars participated as there'd be in the main event. The fifteen or sixteen drivers who ran were serious about their sport and were good drivers. It wouldn't be long before they would be running in the big race for bigger prize money. The race was uneventful—no wrecks, no flags—and that was alright with everyone. Watching grown people tangle on the track was scary enough. Watching young drivers crash would curl your hair.

I have to admit that the Run What You Brung race was almost always my favorite. People from the audience who wanted to race put their names into a hat. Six cars are picked at random to race the street car they had driven to the track. These cars are not stock cars, and the drivers are certainly not stock car drivers. Although many of them think that they are. The race that day was between an old VW bug, a late model Mustang, a vintage GTO, a Fiesta, a small pickup truck and a Thing.

The drivers sat at the starting line behind the pace car and revved their engines, then the pace car moved and all six cars took off. At least most of them did. The Thing just sort of leapt off the line then seemed to coast along at a rather sedate speed.

The track was sprayed down with water between races to keep

down the dust, but it also made the track a bit more slippery. The cars were all over the track, tending to slide in the dirt, which was exciting. No one spun out, and I guess that was due to the fact that the street cars had tires with tread which held them to the track a bit better than the stock cars. Still the cars swerved like crazy and ran up the outside of the track which put them in serious danger of colliding with the wall. Fortunately none did.

The crowd laughed and cheered the drivers on, giving them encouragement for their bravery. The race came down to the Mustang and the GTO with the GTO finally taking and keeping the lead.

You may not believe that it takes real skill and nerves of steel to drive around an oval track at high rates of speed for twenty five laps, but our amateurs proved that it does. Watching how badly some of the street car's racers ran the track made me appreciate the pros, or in our case, the semi-pros. It was fun to watch, and the winner got a trophy, a small cash prize and a victory lap as well.

At last it was time for the race we had all come to see. It'd be a twenty-five lap race like the others had been, but it'd be faster and more exciting. The pace car did one lap with the other cars following as before, the green flag came down and the cars shot into high speed. Billy drove like a demon. He shot every gap, avoided each attempt to cut him off, and maneuvered around all the wrecks. There were plenty of those—there always are. Usually no one's hurt, by some miracle. The wrecks are always exciting, but some of the near misses will take your breath away too.

There were several times that a car was spinning out of control on the track, and all the other cars miraculously missed hitting it as they sped around the track. There was one spectacular three-car tangle where the cars just bumped each other then got locked together. They all did a long spin all hooked together. Other cars swerved like mad to get out of the way. Finally, the trio spun out on the grass in the center of the track. Two of the cars rejoined the race but the third limped into the pits. It was wonderfully exciting.

There were lots of spinouts with cars sliding around and kicking up big clouds of dust, some barely missed spinning into the pits. That gets the adrenaline pumping. The pits are set inside the track and they're open—no buildings. I guess that makes it easy to get in and out. It also makes the pit crews targets for out-of-control cars. That's why it's surrounded by those big water barrel barriers like you see on the interstate. There are gaps in the barrier for the cars to enter and exit, so it's a pretty safe arrangement.

Billy was fearless. He managed to get a two-lap lead on every other car. There was a red Trans Am with a gold racing stripe, number 16, which tried to narrow that lead. It wasn't a car I recognized, but it was sponsored by a dry cleaner over in Dixon. The car might be new to our track, but the driver knew his business. He was really pouring on the speed trying to catch up to Billy. By the time we got to lap fifteen, the race was between Billy and the Trans Am. There were still many other cars on the track, but I didn't think any of them had a chance of taking the lead away from Billy, except for number 16.

By lap nineteen, the Trans Am driver was getting desperate or maybe just mad because he rolled up behind Billy and tapped his back bumper. Billy swerved a bit, laid a little more speed on and pulled away by a few feet. Then the Trans Am pulled to Billy's left and tried to force Billy into the wall. People in the stands were yelling and cussing the driver of the Trans Am. Everyone wanted to see Billy win, plus it's considered poor sportsmanship to cause a wreck deliberately. That behavior can also get you fined by the track, can cause you to lose points so you have to start farther back in the pack at the next race, and repeated offenses can even get you banned from the track entirely.

Billy hit his brakes and dropped back behind the Trans Am then came up on the Trans Am's left. The driver must have thought that Billy was going to try and push him into the wall because he hit his brakes and dropped back. Billy sped away from him. The Trans Am picked up speed again, passing a bright green Mustang, which he clipped causing it to spin out. Three other cars hit the Mustang. The Trans Am never slowed down. The yellow flag came up and everyone held their spot in the race, biding their time until the Mustang and the other cars were off the track. It took two full laps to get the Mustang into the pits, then the green flag came down again.

The Trans Am kicked in with some real speed, taking several serious chances on the track, barely missing three more cars. He caught up to Billy on the Grand National's passenger side, swerved and tapped Billy in the back quarter-panel. Billy swerved to try and get away from the Trans Am, over compensated and went into a spin.

The Grand National spun like a big black and silver top, around and around, and slid into the grassy area right outside of the pits narrowly missing one of the barriers. Even with the barriers in place, pit crews scattered to get out of the way. I held my breath and prayed that Billy wouldn't hit one. That would not only take him out of the running, but he might get hurt as well. Just because a driver is strapped in with a web and there's no glass in the car, he can still get hurt—sometimes killed.

After what seemed like a week, Billy righted the spin and flew back onto the track with a red-hot vengeance. He went after the Trans Am like an avenging angel. I had a moment when I knew the other driver looked over his shoulder and saw his doom chasing him. After that the race was over—Billy ran the other driver into the ground and finished the race a half a lap ahead of everyone else.

The checkered flag came down as Billy crossed the finish line first, and we all lost our minds. We yelled and screamed and hugged and jumped up and down and cried. This was more than a race, more than a victory for Billy and Sammy. This was an affirmation of Chick's life, and we cheered for him. Mars stepped round Connell and grabbed me in a bear hug. We cried like babies on each other.

"I'm sorry, I'm sorry I scared you," I sobbed.

"I love you," she sobbed back to me.

Connell put one hand on my shoulder and one hand on Mars' shoulder, and the three of us stood locked in a tiny bubble of love in the middle of the insanely cheering crowd.

Billy took his victory lap while pumping his fist in the air through the windshield space. After a moment, I could hear the pit crews yelling something that I couldn't make out. Soon the cry moved into the stands and more and more of the crowd took it up. It was a chant. Everybody in the stands was yelling: "THIS WIN'S FOR CHICK!"

It was a breathtaking moment, and I looked around for Chick, sure he was there somewhere. Sure enough, I spotted him standing next to Sammy in the pits. I clutched Mars' arm so tightly that she gasped.

"What?"

I pointed to Sammy.

"Chick. He's right there next to Sammy. He's watching Billy take his lap."

I could barely talk because I was so choked up. Mars looked where I pointed. Chick turned and looked at me and he smiled. I waved and sat down, not trusting my knees to support me any longer.

The wild jubilation continued, but I decided that I needed to pee and wash my tear-stained face. I turned to Mars to see if she wanted to make the trip with me, but she was in what seemed like a very serious conversation with Connell. I picked up my bag and headed to the potty. Behind me the crowd was still cheering wildly. I grinned through my tears as I walked up the steps to the concourse where the bathrooms and concession stands were housed. It was deserted up there since everybody was watching the race, but that meant no line at the bathroom! I did my business, washed my hands and was wiping my face when the bathroom door opened. I didn't think to turn around and check out who had just entered. I was too concerned with cleaning my face. A man appeared in the mirror behind me.

"Hey, pal," I said to his reflection, "this is the ladies."

The lights went out.

CHAPTER 24

?

My first thought as I swam up toward consciousness was: Wow, that was a hell of a party! I feel like death on a cracker! I lay there for several more minutes just cataloging the multiple aches and pains in my body: head splitting, shoulder really hurting, face aching. On a pain scale of 1 to 10, I was a 17-1/2.

What the hell had I been doing? The last time I felt this ghastly was the night of senior prom. I drank an unknown amount of Boone's Farm Strawberry Hill wine, decided to climb the water tower down by the railroad tracks and fell when I was about halfway up. My brothers carried me home, and my sisters put me to bed. My parents pretended they knew nothing about it. Lucky, for me I didn't break anything but my pride.

Other thoughts began to crowd up behind that one. My head was roaring in pain, but I didn't remember going to a party…maybe I drank so much that I had a blackout…that was a bad sign. Uncle John used to have blackouts and he ended up in rehab…four times or was it five…

I woke up again, and I realized that I was lying in an awkward position. My hands were practically between my knees, and I was on my side—not the side I usually sleep on, either. Why did my bed feel like concrete? My cheek hurt and felt abraded from the contact with the bed. That made no sense at all. I have 1000 thread-count sheets. God, thinking hurt!

I decided that I was brave enough to open my eyes to see how bad off I really was. When I did, I found my vision was blurry and murky. I could barely see the room that I was in—that was a bad sign too. Maybe I'd been drinking bad "shine." I always heard that could make you go blind. Regardless of my state of possible blindness, I was fairly certain I wasn't in my own home or in my own bed…

I woke up again—oh man, that was not good. Every time I shut my eyes, I passed out. I wondered vaguely how many times that had happened. I decided the key to making that stop would be to stop closing my eyes. Maybe moving would help too, so I struggled to get in to a sitting position. I found that I couldn't use my hands. What in this blue-eyed world was wrong with me? Was I paralyzed? Real fear began to gnaw at me. My blurry gaze traveled down to my hands, and I saw that they were bound together with duct tape.

Oh my God, oh my God, oh my God. That was a very bad sign. Bad people had me. I started to hyperventilate from the panic. Calm down, I told myself. Think. My chest hurt like I was having a heart attack, but I was sure it was just panic. My mind was spinning like a hamster on a freakin' wheel. I tried to get a grip on my rising panic. But it was hard to calm down when I looked at my hands. The duct tape was so tight, my fingers looked swollen around my rings.

I needed to get loose fast for many reasons, but the most pressing reason was so I didn't lose a finger or three. The second reason that I needed to get free was the bad guys would be back soon. It was at that moment I realized my mouth was duct-taped as well. I must have really been out of it not to notice that first. There are several ways to get duct tape off your mouth. None of them are fun. I just knew that it had to come off, so I could breathe better. I felt like I was suffocating.

I could feel panic growing inside me and quickly gave myself a stern talking to: Panic will get you dead; get hold of yourself; use your brain, that's why God gave it to you." That sort of thing. I concentrated on breathing for a minute, not so easy with a big piece of duct tape over your mouth. I slowly sucked air in through my nose then exhaled through my nose, many times. When I had a grip on myself I examined my situation. I appeared to be in a below-ground basement, no windows, just small vents up close to the ceiling. Great.

I twisted around a bit to get a look at the ceiling. There was nothing above me but duct work, pipes and one lone light bulb. The light wasn't on, so the only light I was getting was from the vents. That explained the murky quality of the lighting. It also told me it was still daylight. This was not a basement I recognized. I had no idea where I was. I couldn't hear street sounds, but it might be that outside sound was muffled since I was underground. If I couldn't hear anything from the outside, it was a sure bet nothing from the outside could hear me. It was looking worse by the minute. I asked St. Jude to help because this sure looked like an impossible cause.

My hands were positioned in front of me, thank God. That meant whoever put me here was not a pro, or was sloppy or lazy. Any of those reasons worked out for me. I was on my side and my hands were almost in my lap. I took a second look at them and confirmed my initial assessment of how God-awfully bad they were swollen. I hoped they still worked when all was said and done.

I raised my bound hands to my mouth and grappled with the tape. It wasn't easy. My fingers were so swollen they looked like sausages, and I had a hard time getting purchase on the tape. Plus, I was starting to sweat with fear and panic, and that just made getting the damn tape off my face harder. My fingers kept slipping off the tape. I cried in frustration, but I didn't give up, I kept trying.

I'd promised Mars I'd be the godmother to her children, and I had to get out of the basement to fulfill that promise. I felt sick like I was about to vomit. That tape had to come off. It wasn't my fate to choke to death on my own puke in some damn dungeon!

After what seemed like three weeks, I got one corner of the tape in between my fingers, closed my eyes and yanked. Have you ever had to yell in your head because you didn't dare make any noise? OH FUCK ME!!!!!! screamed over and over in your head is not terribly satisfying, but it had to do. I breathed some more and then I yanked again. GOD!!!! That hurt, but the tape was off my mouth. I wondered if I had any lips left. They burned like fire. At least if I didn't make it, there was lots of DNA on that tape to prove this was where I'd been held prisoner.

I lay there a minute or two, gasping in large quantities of air and trying not to cry out loud from the pain that was racking my body and trying to hold down the rising panic. I still felt nauseated, but breathing through my mouth helped a bit. As I re-oxygenated my body and tried not to puke, I spent the time wondering where I was, who had me and how long before they came back. No answers there, except I was positive that it was the bad guys that had murdered Chick. Daddy always says "Knowledge is power. Tally up what you know, it'll save your life. Don't worry about what you don't know."

First, I was hurt but not dead. That meant they wanted me alive. That was really all I knew, and it sure as hell wasn't much. They wanted me alive. Why? Because they thought I had info they needed, or I had info about them that I could share with others. What did I know? Hmmm. My mind was blank. Maybe that was caused by the blow to my head. I was pretty sure that was the source of a good deal of my pain. Someone had knocked me in the head. Thank God for my good hard Irish noggin.

As I lay there scared out of my freakin' mind, a memory floated to the surface of my mangled mind. I remembered the race and the man in the bathroom. He was one of the men I'd seen with Donna! They'd told her they'd find out how much of a threat I was. It was all coming back to me now, and I knew I had to get the hell out of that basement!

I listened for sounds from the upstairs for a full minute and heard nothing. I took that as a good sign. Maybe. They thought I was down for the count and didn't leave a guard. Maybe. They underestimated me, I hoped. Where were they? Assuming they hadn't just stepped out onto the porch for a smoke, what were they doing?

My thought was they were out sniffing around town, doing some reconnaissance. They figured that I had information on them, and they wanted to know if I had shared it. They were of course right on both counts. I had a hard time believing that they'd get anyone to cooperate and tell them a damn thing. Who the hell could they ask that wouldn't get suspicious.

They could hang out in bars and eavesdrop on conversations. That'd get them squat. In that case they'd think that I hadn't shared my knowledge and simply come back to shoot me in the head. After which they would dump my body in a deep hole.

I found myself hoping that they didn't discover that I'd shared my information with anyone, or other people would soon join me in the basement. I took a moment to say another prayer, this time to St. Anthony. This seemed like a fairly lost place I was in, so he seemed like the man for the job.

I started to work on the duct tape wrapped around my wrists using my teeth. At first I let my fear rule me and worried at the tape frantically like a dog with a very good bone. But removing tape in this manner is a process that takes a while, depending on how many layers of tape your abductors use, how sharp your teeth are and how desperate you are to get loose. I was pretty damn desperate, and I have good oral hygiene.

I added sore teeth and aching jaws to my list of pains. If I survived this, tomorrow I'd really hurt. I forced myself to slow down and work through the layers of sticky tape.

I had to stop and rest every few minutes. It was hard work. I also wanted to listen just in case my captors had returned. It would suck to have them find me halfway free. In case anyone ever asks you, duct tape tastes like ass. Suddenly I felt some blood flow into my hands and it hurt, God Almighty, it hurt! I almost peed on myself. But the new pain lifted my spirits. I knew I was making progress. I worked faster and tried not to get manic. I was really starting to get mad though. Mad is much better than hysterical. I swore that if I got out of there, I was gonna totally and completely ruin someone's day!

Ripping and tearing duct tape, pausing to breath and listen, sweating like a whore on dollar day, crying and leaking snot, all were things that enhanced the experience. My head throbbed like there was a little man with a ball-peen hammer inside, trying to beat his way out. Plus I was hungry and had to pee. Not to mention being more scared than I had ever been in my life. All and all, not a couple of hours of my life that I ever care to relive or even remember. Finally the last bit of duct tape parted and I was free. I almost cried out from the relief. But I clamped my jaws shut and held the sound inside. I rolled on to my back and panted for a moment or two, then I began to suck in air and thanked any saints or angels who were listening.

After a few euphoric moments, I realized my ankles were bound. That brought me back down to earth. At least I wouldn't have to chew through those restraints. I flexed my fingers and rotated my wrists. Damn it hurt! I felt more tears spring into my eyes. I feared that my fingers would never work right again, that my hands were damaged beyond repair, that I had nerve damage! Ruthlessly, I knocked those thoughts out of my head and got a grip. I couldn't afford despair.

I sat up, kind of. It's not so easy to do when your ankles are taped together. You don't have to try it at home, just take my word for it. I wiggled around, and I think I passed out again, but finally I rolled back on my side, put both hands on the concrete and leveled myself into a sitting position. I had to sit and rest for a minute because of the pain in my hands, head and shoulders. Crap, I was convinced that it must be the slowest escape in the history of escapes! My brain was screaming for me to hurry but I couldn't. As I rested I surveyed my adorable sundress. It was torn and stained and rucked up around my waist. It was destined for the rag pile, if I escaped. If not, it would be my shroud.

After what seemed like a month, I began to work on my ankles with my pathetic hands. Luckily the more I worked, the better my hands seemed to get. The blood was finally flowing better. I only hoped the swelling would go down, and I wouldn't have to get my rings cut off my fingers. With every move I made, patches of skin were scraped off on the rough concrete and only added to my litany of woes.

With each layer of tape I removed, I discovered a new one just below it. The bastards must have used an entire roll of tape on me—it just seemed endless. Finally, I jerked the last piece of tape off my ankles and tossed it away. I wanted to dance a jig but thought it was wiser just to see if I could stand on my feet. That didn't happen right away. There wasn't enough feeling in my legs and feet to risk doing that. It would be pathetic to chew through the duct tape just to break my leg trying to stand up.

I pulled off my rather mangled sandals, so I could get to my feet. I massaged my feet and ankles for a few precious minutes to try and restore the feeling. I hate that pins-and-needles feeling you get when the blood begins to flow through your veins again. It made me want to scream. Instead I just kept rubbing. I tried not to wonder where the bad guys were or when they might come back. That was fruitless and only led to heightened panic.

When my hands were more or less working, I decided to let my legs recover on their own and explored my head. It hurt so bad I wondered if it was cracked. But the Maher hardheadedness is near legendary. The back of my head was bloody—the blood dried and stiff. That would take a while to wash out. It felt like a lot of blood. I poked around a bit looking for a soft place or indentations. Maybe a concussion, probably not cracked. I felt nauseous but hadn't vomited, so most likely I'd recover from the head trauma. Any good news was welcome. My head was bloody but not busted. I didn't seem to be too damaged. Good news.

I decided it was time to try standing up, but when I tried I found I couldn't do it. So I rolled over onto my stomach and raised myself to my hands and knees. I stopped and breathed for a minute because my head hurt so much worse in this new position. I think I actually saw stars. I may even have passed out again. I pushed myself up with my hands, which made my poor abused appendages hurt even more. I took that opportunity to put my sandals back on. It hurt. My feet and ankles were swollen, but if I was going to escape, I needed footwear.

After all the effort to get to my feet, standing was not so great. My legs felt heavy, my head hurt about a bazillion times worse, I was dizzy and as a bonus, I wanted to puke even more than before. That confirmed my lay diagnosis of concussion. Despite a growing need to sit back down and put my head between my knees, I knew that I couldn't afford to waste time when my kidnappers could return at any minute. That thought sent a shot of adrenalin that ran from my heart all the way to my knees. I had to keep moving. Move. Move. Move. I had to escape.

I looked around the dank basement. I needed a way out or I needed a weapon. I wanted both. The stairs were in front of me, running straight up along one side of the wall. They looked steep and crummy and unreliable. I wasn't even sure I could climb a single step, but I sure as hell meant to try. I staggered over and pulled myself up the steps one at a time. This simple act took what seemed to be hours but could actually have been weeks. I had to stop and regroup every three or four steps, and it took ages before I made it to the top. I carefully put my hand on the doorknob and started to turn it. It was locked, I wasn't really surprised, just a touch disappointed.

I slowly made my way back down the steps. My legs were still not working so great, and I was extremely unsteady. I couldn't afford to take a tumble, which would be the end of my escape attempt and most likely the end of me. So I hung on to the railing and prayed my way down. When I finally reached the bottom I started to work my way around the walls searching for anything I could use to free myself. What I wouldn't have given for a good crowbar. I could feel the panic starting to grow inside me again. I needed to get pissed off, so I wouldn't flip out. Some son-of-a-bitch, maybe plural, had hit me in the head, trussed me up like a Christmas turkey, thrown me in a damn dark basement and left me there to die or worse. That did piss me off, help clear my head a bit and push back the panic.

The basement was a bitter disappointment—it was so very clean. No dynamite or gasoline or guns or bombs or even a tiny dab of C4 with which to make bombs. What kind of homicidal maniac kept such a tidy hideout? I kept groping around grumbling until I found a pile of trash in a corner. I carefully sifted through it and found a plethora of empty beer bottles, discarded nails, bent screws, pieces of metal and the head off a broken hammer. It appeared to be the leftovers from construction. It was a jackpot. I might not be able to build a bomb, but I was fairly certain I could build something that would ruin a bad guy's day.

A little light went off in my head and I hatched a lovely evil plan. I retrieved all the pieces of duct tape that had been used on me and carried that up to the second step from the top. I wrapped all the pieces together to form a long rope. I wrapped the hammer head in the tape and swung it up to break the single light bulb. My plan required darkness to be successful. It took me five tries before the bulb broke and glass rained down on me. By the time I had completed that part of my plan, I was winded and exhausted, but I didn't stop moving.

Next I wrapped and knotted my homemade rope to the railing on one side of the steps and tied it to the hand rail on the other side. Duct tape is tough. I hoped it was strong enough to trip a bad guy too.

Back down the steps I went where I gathered as much debris as I could carry and climbed to the top step. There I spread the nuts, bolts, nails and other detritus evenly across the step. I went back down and gathered another pile of trash and carried it back up and spread that across the next step. I repeated the procedure on the next step, and the next and the next.

I was moving slowly and was still unsteady. I was wet to my socks with sweat before I was finished with my task. But I'd stopped crying. At last all the nuts and bolts and other debris was scattered across the steps. I allowed myself to lean against the cool concrete wall at the bottom of the stairs for a moment, but I knew I dared not rest long.

The longer it took me to complete my tasks, the more anxious I became that someone would return and catch me half finished with my plans. I was shaking with anxiety. I turned, picked up my trusty hammer head, listened to make sure I was still alone and broke every beer bottle. I tried to be quiet with the breaking, but it sounded like a bomb each time. I stopped to listen after I broke each one.

I scattered the glass in a fan configuration on the concrete floor from the bottom step reaching out to about three feet away. I figured if a person tripped on the steps and fell, that would be about as far away from the bottom step as he'd fall. Trying to be logical when you're scared, sweaty, concussed and in serious pain isn't easy. I thought it was a good idea, but my thinking was suffering from a fuzzy and possibly damaged brain.

I finished my task, making sure that all the sharp points were exposed. No one had come running to investigate the noise—another good sign, unless they just meant to leave me here to starve. Nice thought. I stood, straightened my aching back and surveyed my battleground. It looked good and I was satisfied with the results, maybe even gleeful. I wanted to see some blood today other than my own.

The stairs were the only place to hide, so I scooted under them and hunkered down to wait on my prey. I knew that sooner or later someone would show up to check on me. If that didn't happen, I thought I could pry the door open with the hammer. Probably. I had a lot of adrenalin flowing right now. There was new blood flowing from my poor hands too. I'd tried to be careful but had still managed to cut myself up some. I didn't think I'd bleed to death from the wounds, but they stung like crazy.

I must have nodded off. I found myself slumped over and drooling. Yep, definitely a concussion. I may have been out a long time because it was dark down in the basement. Of course, not knowing what time of day I got stuck in the charming place made it hard to gauge time.

I realized what had awakened me—the sound of footsteps over my head. My heart started to race. I could hear muffled voices too. There were two voices. Please, Mother Mary, let them both come down the steps to check on me. I knew that was a bit of a stretch, but I could pray. I got a tighter grip on the hammer head, holding it in my fist like a knife. My hands still hurt, but they were working well enough to knock somebody's brains out, and that was all I could ask for right now. That and for my aim to be true. Really, I could ask for a lot. Like getting out of here with my skin intact, a hot bath, a good meal, chocolate, good sex, a long life—lots of things.

"Go check on the bitch. You hit her pretty hard, you mighta killed her," said a gruff voice.

I couldn't be positive through the floor, but I thought the voice belonged to Joe. He didn't sound concerned at all that I might be dead. He was just stating a fact. I decided immediately I'd enjoy hitting him with my hammer.

"I don't see how it matters how hard I hit her. She's dead anyhow. Now or later, it don't much matter," said another voice.

I was willing to bet that was Marty. What a sweetheart he was. I added him to the list of people that I would like to damage.

"She mighta told someone what she knows, and we need to know who and how much. Just because we didn't find out nothin' in town, don't mean she didn't run her mouth. We gotta cover our asses here, and we need to know how much information is floating around," Joe snapped impatiently. "So let's wake her up, so we can ask her some questions."

"Right, right, right. I got it," growled Marty.

I could hear his footsteps moving overhead as he reached toward the basement door. I broke out in a sweat. Beads ran down between my breasts and rolled down my spine. I wiped my hands off, adjusted my grip on the hammer and got ready to spring into action. I knew this would be my only chance to escape in one piece. It was probably a rotten chance, but beggars can't be choosers. I intended to go down fighting.

Marty opened the wooden door while he was talking over his shoulder to his partner.

"You always complain about how I do things." He switched on a flashlight but wasn't moving. "You're never satisfied."

"Go the hell on," Joe demanded. His footsteps moved away from the basement door.

"Can we have a little fun with her before we kill her? She's got a great rack."

Marty didn't wait for an answer but stepped out. He was chuckling to himself at his own great wit when he tripped on the improvised rope and lost his balance. He danced around for a moment as he tried to regain his footing. That was when he hit the debris on the step and was launched into space.

"WHAT THE FUCK!" he shouted.

Then he hit more steps and more debris, and it was all over but the shouting. Man oh man could he shout and cuss. He was stunning! I wished I had paper and pen to record the new and exciting use of language. He rolled a couple of times on the trip down, bounced on a couple of steps, and then he was truly airborne. He landed on the glass, and the screaming ratcheted up the scale. He abruptly stopped screaming. Joe came running.

"What the hell's wrong with you? Jesus Christ!" he shouted.

He could probably see his pal lying at the bottom of the steps but not the reason for the fall. The light was too dim. The flashlight had landed halfway across the basement with the light pointing toward the opposite wall. Joe was apparently too agitated to flip the light switch on because he came down the stairs fast and fell like a ton of bricks, somersaulting all the way down. It was beautiful. I was smiling, I couldn't help myself. He cursed and yelled too. He'd been carrying a gun because I heard the unmistakable sound of a weapon hitting the concrete floor.

Joe didn't hit much of the glass thanks to his pal Marty who covered a good portion of it. He also was not knocked out. Damn. I knew I could fix that. I darted over to his crumpled, cursing, bleeding body and hit him in the head with the hammer. What a horrible, wet sound that made. I wondered for a nano-second if I killed him. Then I realized I really didn't care.

I bent over and checked his pulse. He still had one. I looked at Marty. There was a lot of blood. It was on his hands, his clothes, the floor, just everywhere and it continued to flow. Good. I gave him a love tap with the hammer too. Not just for pay-back but because I wanted to make sure he stayed out for a while. Then I ran across the basement and retrieved the flashlight and used that to find the gun. It was a nice little snub-nose .38, looked to be in pretty good shape and it was fully loaded. Excellent.

I considered shooting them both as a parting gesture and realized that I couldn't do it. I was a wimp. I climbed over the assholes and carefully made my way up the steps. As I neared the top, I saw it was totally dark outside. Great. I had no freakin' idea where I was and now I'd have to complete my escape in the dark. At least I got to hit people in the head with a hammer. That thought perked me right up. I locked the basement door behind me. That should take them out of the equation, since I'd taken the means of escape with me—my trusty and now bloody hammer.

The stairs came out into a kitchen that was mostly dark, with a pool of light at one end. I crept through the house in case anyone else was there. If there were others, they could be lying in wait for me. I had that weird coppery taste in my mouth, and I was really shaking like a leaf in a gale.

The pool of light turned out to be a lantern. Odd. I found a light switch and flipped it, nothing. I stupidly flipped it several more times. Why do people do that? I guess it's because we're just so accustomed to having electricity at our fingertips that we can't believe it when the lights don't work. I was disgusted that I had expended so much energy to disable the basement light bulb that didn't work in the first place.

I switched off the flashlight and shoved it in between my breasts then picked up the lantern with my left hand. I didn't want to leave anything I could use behind. I began to explore the house. It was small and it only took a few minutes to search every inch of it. There was no one else hiding and waiting to get me, thank God. I didn't realize how scared I was until I knew I was alone and there was no other bad guys waiting to bash me in the head again. That was when the reaction hit me and I began to really shake, I thought my joints would pop loose. I leaned on the kitchen counter for a minute and breathed deep cleansing breaths to help me get a grip.

When I calmed down a bit I realized that in my search I didn't find a phone. I didn't think to check the pockets of the bad guys for cell phones. I decided that I sure as hell was not going back into the basement again. No siree! I looked out the kitchen window and saw a car in the driveway. I saw no other lights from houses anywhere around me. Where the hell was I?

Where ever I was, it was time to get the hell out of Dodge, I decided. I took one more look around the kitchen. No keys were in sight, so unless they were still in the car, those too were in someone's pants pocket, in the basement. Dammit, why hadn't I searched them? Well, after all, this was my very first escape, so I couldn't beat myself up too much. On the negative side, I was on foot, hurt, and lost. On the plus side, I had a hammer, a Maglight, a lantern and most importantly a gun. I wasn't empty handed.

I was fairly familiar with Simpson County, so unless I'd been carried to another county I should be able to find my way home. It was also possible that someone had noticed I was missing, and even now a search could be underway. Okay, no more stalling. It was time to go. God, I really needed to pee. I wasn't going to take the chance of peeing in the house. I'd find a nice tree once I'd put some distance between me and the place.

I went out the kitchen door in a crouch with the gun ready and made my way to the car. I checked for keys or anything else I could use. Nothing. I found the trunk release by the brake pedal, hit it and scrambled around to the partially opened truck. Lo and behold, I found my purse! I rummaged through it and found my phone. There was also my Beretta, mace and a pair of handcuffs. Now I felt truly invincible! I flipped open my phone and discovered there were no bars, at all. Where the hell was I, on the moon? Quickly I placed the .38 and the hammer in my purse. It's a big purse. I resolved in that moment to never carry a tiny purse again, no matter the occasion. I was feeling better. I searched a bit more and found my holster! Now I was ready for anything.

I swung my purse over my left shoulder and winced. That hurt. I wondered if the shoulder was dislocated. It sure hurt and it wasn't working so good either. I put the lantern in the trunk. The flashlight would serve me better. I reached my hand out to close the trunk and saw car lights behind me. Shit! There was a little rise between me and the lights but in a second or two the driver would see me. The car was coming behind me, so that meant there had to be a road back that way. I ran like a rabbit away from the oncoming lights and the house. I saw a tree line and went for it. I didn't dare turn on the flashlight, so I was running in the pitch dark over uneven ground in freakin' sandals! Why the hell was I wearing sandals? I swore to God that if I survived this I would never wear sandals again. I also prayed I wouldn't find a gopher hole that would end my flight.

I made it to the trees just as the new car pulled in behind the parked car. The driver cut the lights and got out. It was too dark to get a good look at him. He looked in the trunk, closed it while muttering under his breath. He went into the house, and I could hear him calling for his buddies. New Guy didn't have a flashlight. Good. Time for me to high-tail it!

There was a tiny sliver of a moon and that was good and bad. It was good because the bad guys couldn't see me. It was bad because I couldn't see them either. I thought maybe I could swing around and find the road that I was sure was off to my right. But when they started looking for me, they'd look on the road. At least I had a head start and I'd hear them coming. When I heard a car it was just a matter of finding some cover. Simple.

I picked my way through the trees, fell several times and banged myself up some more. I couldn't go very fast, but I wasn't dragging my feet either. I was also trying to be quiet. It was so silent and still that I knew every grunt and groan would carry. My flight or fight mechanism was urging for speed, but I told it in no uncertain terms to shut the hell up.

After about two minutes I heard shouting but couldn't make out the words, just the emotion. Someone was extremely pissed. I kept moving. I heard the kitchen door open and slam against the wall behind it, running feet, the car trunk open and shut and more running feet. New Guy had decided to fetch the lantern. Dammit, I should have broken it. I heard more shouting inside, then the shouting seemed to be outside again. I heard a second voice, not as loud as the other. That meant one of the thugs in the basement had recovered enough to help in the search. Keep moving, I urged myself.

Finally, the sounds behind me faded, and I started trying to angle my way toward the road. After a few more hours, I found the road. Hooray! Truthfully, I had only been at it for maybe fifteen minutes. It just seemed like hours. Now the dilemma was which direction should I take? I turned all around in a circle and couldn't see lights anywhere. At that point I could only hope that one direction was as good as the other.

I chanced the Maglight for a second and found the road was blacktopped. Thank you, Jesus! Now years of jogging would really pay off. I put the gun and flashlight down and pulled my purse strap over my head, put the strap on my right shoulder so the bag rested on my left hip. It hurt like hell, but I needed to secure the bag and be able to use my right hand. I put the flashlight in the bag with just the tip sticking out and zipped the bag to hold the light steady. I angled the bag down so the light would shine on the road as I ran. The weight of my left arm would hold everything down. It wasn't good for much else at the moment. My right hand was free in case I needed to shoot someone. It wasn't perfect but I thought it might work.

I'd never in my life shot anyone, but I knew that might change. I might not be able to shoot two unconscious guys in cold blood, but if they came after me I thought I'd be up for the task. I was scared, injured and mad as a hornet—a bad combination. If it came down to me or them, it was definitely gonna be me. I started running.

About five minutes later I heard a car. Damn, I knew it was them. What were the freakin' odds they would choose the same direction? Oh yeah, 50-50. I switched off the Maglight and headed back into the trees. I wanted good cover before they reached me, and I only had a few seconds to hide. The headlights lit up the dark road. They were driving slowly, and as they reached my hiding place I could hear them talking. They were riding with the windows down, listening for me.

"What makes you think she went this way," said a familiar voice.

Joe had recovered to join the search. Obviously, I hadn't hit him hard enough. I misgauged the hardness of his head. If I got the opportunity, I'd correct that mistake.

"If we don't find signs of her soon, we can assume she went the other way and turn around. She can't have gotten far on foot."

New Guy sounded smarter than Joe. He'd be the one I'd shoot first. They moved on slowly. I crouched down farther and waited. When their taillights disappeared down a hill, I started moving again. I wanted to stay in the woods this time because I knew they'd be back, but the road would get me farther faster. I chose fast.

About ten minutes later I heard the car coming back toward me. As luck would have it, the trees were thinner in this stretch. Crap. I switched off the Maglight and moved farther from the road. The land sloped a bit. I got as far from the blacktop as I dared and lay down on the ground, face down with my hands under me. I did my best to hide all of my white skin from sight. I froze and didn't move. I believed my best chance was to stay frozen. "I am the ground, I am the ground, I am the ground," I thought frantically.

The car was crawling now and the lantern was swinging over the woods. Maybe now was the time to move, I thought just as I heard Joe shout.

"Hey, I think I saw something odd about twenty feet back. Back up, back up!"

New Guy threw the car into reverse.

Joe shouted, "THERE!"

New Guy hit the brakes, and I popped up like a turkey timer, squeezed off one wild shot and hot-footed it deeper into the woods.

There was a lot of yelling behind me, but I didn't think I'd hit anyone. I concentrated on getting away.

I wasn't being careful or quiet now, just running as fast as I dared in the uneven and unfamiliar terrain. I heard car doors slam and bodies charging headlong through the underbrush behind me. I tried to keep my breathing steady—pulling in air, not gasping—a trick I had learned over the years for long distance running. I could hear Joe yelling at me.

"Bitch, you're gonna die slow and be beggin' me to kill you before I'm done. I can keep you alive for days..."

And so on and so forth. There was lots of it but you get the drift. He was mad as hell, and he was trying to scare me into making a mistake or giving up. Or maybe he was just mad as hell and venting. All he accomplished was to make me move faster. I believed him when he said he'd cut off my eyelids, so I could see everything else he was going to do to me. I refused to panic.

I skirted around the trunk of a large sycamore tree and ran into Chick. I stopped dead in my tracks. Chick had a worried look on his faintly luminous face.

"Quick, TisTis, over here's a dead tree leaning on a oak, you can climb on one and shinny up the other," he said and pointed.

I could see a bit because he was glowing, and sure enough I spotted the trees and started moving in that direction.

"God bless you, Chick Donnelly," I whispered fervently.

I slipping the pistol in my bag and made for the tree.

"Hurry, TisTis, they're right behind ya."

He was right. I could hear them blundering through the undergrowth. They weren't dressed for hiking through the woods, and if I was any judge, by the sounds of labored breathing I heard, they weren't in any shape for it either. Better for me.

I ran up the fallen tree, reached the upright tree, grabbed a low branch and pulled myself up. WOW! My shoulder exploded in pain. I literally saw stars. But I didn't stop even though my slick-bottomed sandals threatened to slide off every branch. I kept climbing. There needed to be lots of branches and lots of leaves between me and my pursuers.

If you're not a tree climber, then know it's not as easy as it looks. You have to pull your weight up with your arms and balance on branches that are round. The object is to get as high as possible without falling. I was doing the feat in the dark, burdened with a full purse, injured, scared shitless and in a freaking dress and sandals. The dress seemed to catch on every branch and the sandals that I had thought to be so darling had become a nightmare. My hands began to sweat, and that only added to my difficulties.

Despite my handicaps I was doing pretty well until I wrapped my good arm around the branch above me, reached up with my injured arm and my foot slipped. There I was dangling by one arm probably twenty feet above the ground. I barely managed to stop myself from screaming with the pain. I refused to look down as I got a grip on the branch and managed to pull myself to relative safety. I tried to quiet my breathing by taking several slow breaths when I wanted to gasp the air into my lungs. After a few seconds I gritted my teeth and continued to climb.

I was about thirty feet up the tree when I heard them coming. They were incredibly close. I was afraid to try for any more height in case they might notice branches shaking where there was no wind. I was also afraid I might make a noise, or worse, slip and fall. So I sat on a nice branch and leaned against the tree trunk for support. That made be feel a bit more stable. I quietly dug into my bag and pulled the gun out. Then I slung the purse behind me and got ready to shoot people. Chick sat on the branch beside me. He put his finger to his lips. Really?!! As if I need anyone to tell me to be quiet. A few heartbeats later I saw the lantern light beam swinging back and forth as they searched for me.

"She has to be here somewhere. Maybe she went to ground and is hiding, not running."

That was New Guy and he sounded exasperated.

Joe said, "That bitch thinks she's so smart. When I find her I'm gonna cut her into little pieces starting with her toes!" He was breathing hard now.

"Apparently, she's smarter than you and Marty since she managed to escape and almost killed you both in the process."

New Guy was getting fed up.

"You telling me you woulda seen the trap she set and not fallen ass over tea kettle? Huh? You think you're smarter than me and Marty? Huh? You so smart you wanna hunt for her by yourself? Huh?

'Cuz I can sure as hell go back to the car and leave you standing here."

Joe was getting a full head of steam up. Unfortunately, he was building that head of steam right under the tree where I was sitting. I prayed they'd stop arguing and move along. Go fight under another tree, fall into a hole, anything—just go away. Maybe get eaten by a bear. I liked that one. Except that there are no bears in my part of Tennessee.

"*Don't worry, TisTis,*" Chick said.

He almost scared me out of the tree. I was engrossed in the tableau below me and had forgotten about him sitting right here next to me.

"*These boys are city slickers and not so good in the woods. 'Sides most humans and animals don't look up when they're tracking somethin', and I bet these boys won't either.*"

I didn't answer, just held my breath, waited and prayed he was right. I nodded at Chick to let him know I'd heard him and tried not to look worried. I had to wonder if that was successful. I debated with myself about the wisdom of shooting them while they stood beneath me. I could probably get away with a self-defense plea, so that was a pro. But I wasn't sure I could get them both before one of them got me, which was a con. I held still.

"Calm down, just calm down. We're all on edge here, and I was just blowing off some steam. We have to keep looking. You know that giving up is not an option for anyone, right?"

New Guy was being reasonable now. I guessed he really needed Joe to help him. They began to move again and that gave me a bit of hope. Maybe I'd see another sun rise after all.

"*TisTis, that one boy, the one with the lantern is the same one that was driving the Hummer last week,*" Chick said.

The bad guys were still not far enough away for me to feel safe making noise, so I just nodded. I sat there and wondered if anyone was looking for me yet. I was pretty sure they were. It was full dark and that meant I'd been missing for hours. I wasn't sure who to pray to, St. Jude or St. Anthony. Maybe both since I was in what looked like an impossible situation, and I was sure as hell lost. I strained to hear sounds in the woods around me and heard nothing.

"Chick," I whispered, "where are we?"

"Oh not too far off I-Forty, near that new housing development that hadn't been finished yet, near Bootstrap Road," he answered. *"The one where the developers ran out of money."*

I nodded. That made sense. I didn't see any lights around me because no one lived in the development. I was still in the county but about 30 minutes out of town. No one was going to ride to the rescue any time soon.

"I think they're far enough away for me to climb down. I'm gonna move slow and keep low until I can find the road. Maybe I can find a human to take pity on me and give me a ride back to town."

"I'll do a little scouting and see which way they went," Chick said.

"Good, 'cuz which ever direction they went in, I'm going the other way."

I climbed down from the tree, which seemed to be an even harder process than climbing up had been. I froze when I reached the ground. I strained to hear, but still there were no sounds anywhere. I thought the road was off to my right, so I moved that way. I wasn't ready to get on the road yet. I needed to see where my stalkers were. I drew my gun and clicked the safety off. I wanted to be ready. You really have to be careful walking in the woods at night with a loaded gun and the safety turned off. It's too easy to trip and accidentally discharge the gun. So usually only stupid people do such a thing. I knew all that. I also knew that if the bad guys got the drop on me, I wanted to go down shooting.

Suddenly, Chick appeared right in front of me. *"TisTis, behind you!"* he shouted.

I turned and fired without a thought. The bullet hit Joe, and he went down screaming. I knew that would bring New Guy, so I turned to run and slammed right into the bastard. We both went down in a heap, and I lost my grip on the Beretta. Damn! New Guy grabbed a handful of my hair, and I punched him in the face. He punched me back. It felt like my jaw shattered and I screamed. The bastard hadn't lost his gun, and he pointed it at my face. In the dim light, the barrel of the gun looked like a cannon as I stared into it. He sat up and loomed over me.

"Hold still and shut up, Ms. Maher. You've been quite a thorn in my side tonight, and you've led us on a merry chase through the countryside. I do not prefer the countryside, and so I am decidedly out of sorts, as you can imagine. Since you know entirely too much and have seen our faces, I'm afraid that you must be taken out of the equation."

As he pontificated, I was carefully searching the ground beside me for a weapon of some kind.

"God damn it, Rick, I think I'm bleeding to death here. That bitch gut shot me," Joe groaned.

"In a moment, Joe, first I have to take care of Ms. Maher."

Rick flicked his eyes toward Joe for just a second. In that second my hand closed around a good-sized rock, and I hit Rick harder than I've ever hit anyone in my life. The gun went off. I wasn't hit, but I wouldn't be hearing in my left ear for some time. Rick hit the ground and I hit him again, several times. I had to force myself to stop. I wanted the bastard to lie down. I felt around for my gun or his.

"You crazy bitch, I'm gonna kill you," snarled Joe.

I located my bag and rooted around in it until I found my phone. I flipped it open, still no bars—what the hell! I looked at Rick who was bleeding, a lot. Maybe I'd killed him. I climbed to my feet and stood over Rick just looking at him, then something snapped and I lost my mind. I started kicking him and screaming.

"You bastard!"

Kick.

"How outta sorts are ya now?"

Kick. Then there were several more kicks.

"You crazy bitch!" Joe growled at me.

God, it hurt to talk. Something was very wrong with my jaw. I sat down again and dug the flashlight out of my bag. I ran it over Joe who was lying on his side and bleeding a lot. I gave him a short mirthless laugh.

"I don't think you'll be killing me tonight. So you can shut the hell up before I finish what I started."

Of course, he didn't shut up but continued to threaten and call me names. After a short search I found both guns, which lightened my mood to no end. I had a dilemma. I wanted to secure these two goons, so they could be found later. Joe wasn't going anywhere, but Rick might recover soon. He might wake up and run away. I could handcuff Rick to Joe, but I didn't want to get too close to him. Joe was, in my opinion, way too mad and way too feisty for me to get near. In the end I handcuffed Rick to himself. I cuffed his right hand to his left leg. Let's see him make an escape like that. I felt stupidly pleased with myself—so much so that I began to laugh and couldn't stop. I bent over to try and get a grip. A little voice in my head told me I was having a hysterical reaction. That didn't help me stop. I think Joe quit talking while I was laughing so wildly. I think I might've scared him. When I straightened back up, the world was spinning and Joe was staring at me with wide eyes. I held my light on Joe and pointed my gun at him.

"Joe, you be real still. If you move I'll shoot you again. Understand?"

He nodded.

"Well, Joe, I'll send the sheriff back for you. Maybe he'll get here before the wolves eat you."

God Almighty, it hurt to talk! I walked away on unsteady legs and left Joe yelling after me. I didn't bother to tell him that we don't have wolves in my part of Tennessee. I chuckled to myself as I picked my way through the woods. Suddenly, Chick was there beside me, and I felt ridiculously comforted by his presence.

"Hang on, TisTis, the road's this way. You're doing good."

About 30 minutes later, I found the road. I had run much farther than I'd thought during my escape. I picked up a rock and marked the tree where I left the woods, I thought I could find my way back to the place where I had left my kidnappers. I walked for what seemed like hours, but it might've been much less. I didn't jog, I was too tired and beat up and too drained. It hurt to walk, and each step vibrated in my jaw and made me whimper. I could barely put one foot in front of the other. Plus I was fairly sure that running was out of the question since I had destroyed my sandals. I could feel them flopping on my feet as I walked. I stopped walking and kicked them off out of fear that I'd trip.

At some point as I dragged myself down the road, I had the bright idea that I should holster the gun I was carrying. I doubted that anyone would give a ride to a bedraggled, bloody woman with a gun in her hand. It took me several minutes digging in my bag to find the holster. It took forever to struggle into it with my really painful shoulder, but after an eternity I did it and finally holstered the Beretta.

"Better," I said.

Chick nodded and we kept walking. A moment later I heard a car behind me and resisted the impulse to run back into the woods. I was pretty sure none of the bad guys were in any shape to drive and this would be a friendly. I stopped walking, put one hand on my gun just in case I was mistaken, and stood in the middle of the road. It was an F-10 pickup, which was a good sign.

The driver slowed down and stopped about a hundred yards from me. I took a chance and walked slowly toward the truck. The driver leaned out of the window. "Tess Maher? Is that you, girl? You been on the news. The whole damn county is ahunting ya!"

The relief was so great that I fell to my knees and just knelt in the middle of the road with tears running down my face. Chick stood beside me.

CHAPTER 25
MONDAY

I must have passed out because the next thing I knew I was waking up again. It had become a habit—a bad one. This time, however, there was a pillow under my head, and I felt kinda drunk. My body hurt in many places, but the pain was sort of fuzzy and far away. When I opened my eyes I saw most of my family sitting around in what could only be a hospital room. The dead giveaway was the white walls and the machinery that made weird beeping noises. The sky that I could see through the window was pearly grey. It was barely daylight.

"Hey, ya'll," I muttered.

Holy Mary Mother of God! It hurt to talk! Everyone looked up at me, and Mommy started to cry.

"Oh God, Mommy, please don't do that. I think I'm alright or I will be." I couldn't open my mouth, and my words came out slurred and muffled.

"They shot you and beat you up and kidnapped you. I just knew you were dead." She began to cry harder and Daddy pulled her close to him.

You have to understand, this is a woman who rarely cries. It was daunting to watch, and it made me feel guilty to be the cause of her tears.

Dugan said, "You disappeared. We all thought you went to the bathroom. But when you didn't come back, we started searching for you everywhere and couldn't find you."

"Connell went to the parking lot, and your car was there but you weren't," said Michelene.

"That's when we knew you hadn't left under your own steam— that someone had taken you," Moira said in shaky voice.

"I did go to the bathroom, and a guy named Marty came in behind me and knocked me in the head. Am I hurt bad?" I asked.

Moira said, "You have a concussion, a couple of broken ribs, a cracked jaw—so please try not to talk too much—a severely bruised shoulder and a furrow over your right ear about an inch long caused by a bullet."

"Wow, I didn't know he shot me. I thought he missed. Holy crap, he really shot me? That bastard! I'm not hearing so good from that ear either, and why can't I open my mouth."

"Your hearing will get better. Your jaw is wired shut. That'll get better too," Moira assured me.

"Holy shit!" I exclaimed. "What about the bad guys. One was left in the house they were using for a hideout, and I left the other two in the woods bleeding. They could be dead by now. Is my jaw wired shut? I can't open my mouth?"

Everybody laughed but Mommy.

"Yes, honey, you're wired together," answered Moira. "Quit talking so much, I told you."

"Holy shit! I'm wired together?"

That brought more laughter from the peanut gallery.

"We found 'em, all alive, no thanks to you. I had to send for dogs to track 'em. They're all here in the hospital, under guard. The TBI agents still think they're drug dealers and this whole episode is about revenge." Connell was not a happy boy.

"But still it's illegal to kidnap someone no matter the reasons, so they'll be charged, right?" I asked. "They won't get away with it, right?"

"Oh, they'll be charged with as much as I can throw at 'em. But the real problem is that we still got no connection between them and Donna and no real proof yet they killed Chick."

Now I understood why my brother was pissed.

"We'll get it," I assured him, "just as soon as I have a bit of a nap."

Okay, I gotta say that passing out and waking up got old as hell. It made my head hurt worse or maybe that was the concussion or the bullet wound. It's also disconcerting to find drool running down your chin. Ick. The next time I woke up it was dark outside, and Mars was sitting next to my bed.

"Hey, babe," I whispered with my gravelly voice.

"Oh, Jesus!"

She threw herself across me and hugged and kissed me. I started laughing even though she was hurting me. Mars pulled back and stared at me.

"How the hell can you laugh? We all thought you were dead. When I walked out in the parking lot and saw your car sitting there, I knew they had you. I thought my heart was gonna fall out of my chest. I thought they'd kill you." She started to sob.

"Oh God, don't cry, sugar. I know you were scared, but I'm a hard bitch to kill and I'm still here." I hugged her to me with my good arm. Talking was still a misery. That hadn't improved while I slept.

"I just kept thinking about the last time I saw you and how I acted like a bitch to you."

"Mars you were pissed at me and you were right to be pissed. Funny, isn't it?"

"What?"

"That all ya'll yelled at me about being careful and not going off alone and telling everyone where I was all the time, and then these bastards grabbed me from the middle of a crowd in broad daylight on a freakin' Sunday afternoon!"

Mars raised her head from my chest. "These boys weren't afraid of being caught," she said as she wiped her face.

"I've come to that conclusion myself. But now that they're caught, let's see who will go post their bail. Won't that be interesting?"

"Hmmm, it will be. Oh, Lyle and Boyd were here earlier, but you were sleeping and wouldn't wake up for them. They left kind of in a huff."

"Damn, how rude of me to inconvenience them by being unconscious! We've got to get a plan of action together and bust this thing wide open, so they'll go away and leave us all in peace to bury our dead. Can you hand me that glass of water, please. I'm so dry."

"Sure." Mars got the water and held the straw to my mouth. It tasted like the nectar of the gods. "Do you have any ideas?"

"Thanks. As a matter of fact I do. Hey, Mars, what day is this?"

"It's Monday."

"Wow, I've lost an entire day. The last thing I remember, the sun was coming up. I guess it could be worse, I could be dead. Would you call Connell and see if he can come over? I think we better get a game plan together and now. Please."

While Mars was talking to Connell, I tried to get my thoughts in order. Not easy considering what I'd been through. Did you know that when you have a concussion it's because your brain has been slammed around the inside of your skull? Your brain is swollen and bruised, and that makes it very hard to think. I still couldn't believe that I'd been shot. I tried to get pissed about it and couldn't, probably because they were slipping something in my IV bag. That needed to stop and right now. I needed a clear head.

"He was on his way over before I called. He'll be here in about a minute," Mars informed me.

I stared at her. There was something important that I was trying to remember about her and Connell at the racetrack. I couldn't get hold of it. It would come back, I hoped. A nurse came in.

"How're we doing?" she asked.

Why do they always talk in the plural?

"Better I think. Could we stop the pain killers or sleep meds or whatever you have me on? I think I can do without them."

She looked at me like I had suddenly grown another head.

"Honey, your doctor has to order that. He'll be here in the mornin' to take a look at you, and you can ask him then. He's just tryin' to keep you comfortable. You're also on an anti-biotic and you need it too."

She smiled as if she had just solved all the world's problems. I grimaced back and she took my pulse. Connell walked in and sighed.

"Is that how they get you to shut up around here, by wiring your jaw together? We should've thought of that years ago."

I made the signs for "asshole" and smiled around the nurse. Sign language is so handy.

"Hey, Connell," said the nurse.

She had sugar dripping out of her mouth. All women react to him that way—by smiling and talking in sweet tones. That's why he's so spoiled.

"Hey, Margie, howudoin'? How's Het and the boys?"

Margie's smile widened. "They're all just fine, and I'll tell 'em you was asking after 'em."

It was then everything fell into place for me, and I realized I knew her.

"Margie Simms," I said. "I'm sorry I didn't realize who you were. It must be the head injury. I may have come off a little testy."

"No, honey not at all. You've been through an ordeal, but thank the good Lord you're safe and mostly healthy. Now you try and get some rest." She looked at Mars and Connell, "You two need to go on soon. The more she sleeps, the quicker she'll mend."

She bustled out of the room. I watched her go and turned my attention to Mars and Connell.

"We gotta work fast before Nurse Ratchet comes back and tosses ya'll out of the room."

Connell and Mars pulled chairs up to the bedside.

"Whacha thinkin'?" asked Connell.

"Well, I think that the three bad guys won't tell you if it's day or night outside much less how they're hip deep in this mess. Have they been charged yet?"

My brain was clicking through ideas to bring this mess to a satisfactory conclusion. Okay, so I didn't get to shoot everyone, because that really would've been a satisfactory outcome to my way of thinking. Oh well, I had to take what I could get.

"They've been charged but not arraigned in front of a judge yet," said Connell.

"That's because they're laid up in the hospital with a wide variety of injuries. You damn near killed them," Mars said and then she smiled. I smiled back at her.

Connell nodded. "Deep cuts, lacerations, contusions, broken bones, a gunshot wound, and the guy you hit with the rock is still unconscious. There's a bettin' pool on whether or not he'll ever come around."

I smiled. "His name's Rick and he's a pontificating, self-important asshat who underestimated me. Frighteningly, I think that he might be the brains of the outfit."

"What about the other two?" my brother asked.

I chuckled, "I think that two villages somewhere are both missing an idiot."

Connell smiled. "I think that Donna's our weakest link. I'm gonna bring her in based on the anonymous documents I received. Then I'll squeeze her and see if I can get her to break."

"Anonymous documents? What anonymous documents?" Mars wanted to know.

Connell and I both looked at Mars.

"Plausible deniability," I said.

"Someone has delivered documents to the sheriff's office that cast Donna Maples in a bad light. Now they could be false documents of course. We don't know that yet," Connell said. He somehow managed to keep a straight face, bless him.

"Wow," said Mars looking at me, "so that's what you were doing running around in the middle of the night like a ninja? You've been a very naughty girl."

I decided to ignore that.

"What if she's not as weak as we think she is and she holds it together?"

"I get the judge to issue a subpoena for her computer, and call Jim Burns to crack it open like a hickory nut." Connell smiled.

"Jim's the best. He can even find things that she may have erased." Mars was enthusiastic about this plan.

"Yeah, I guess. That way just takes longer. I want this mess over and done with and the four of them in jail. And I want Aggroco to suffer too. They're at the bottom of this," I groused.

"It will all come out alright, have faith," said Mars as she reached over and patted me on the arm.

"Oh, I got faith. I'm just grumpy and tired of talking with my jaws shut. It's hard to do and it hurts."

They moved to each side of my bed and patted me and smiled at me.

"Look we better get going. It would look bad for the sheriff to get booted from the hospital."

He leaned over and kissed me on the forehead.

"Connell, what about the fourth guy?"

"Fourth guy?"

"There were four guys who ambushed us at the house—I counted 'em. I shot one, three of 'em are here in the hospital."

"I think I'll get a warrant in the morning to go have a look-see out at the Cove. I've been meanin' to do that but had other priorities. Maybe I'll find a Hummer and a fourth guy."

"Promise me that you'll wait until I can get out of here to bring Donna in for questioning. I've got to be there to listen. I've earned it. Promise." I almost begged him.

"Promise, if you'll go to sleep and behave and not drive the nurses crazy."

"Go to sleep. I'll be here in the morning, and we'll see when they plan on springing you," Mars said and she kissed me too.

Then the two of them exchanged a funny look over me. I couldn't understand what that look meant, but it was about secrets and promises. They each wore an identical tiny smile too. They were up to something, but I knew it would do me no good to ask. They thought I was physically hurt, and maybe mentally too, and they'd try and protect me. Fine, I'd find out sooner or later. I always do. As I drifted off I realized how much my jaw hurt even with the pain medication in my IV bag. I started to tell them that maybe I'd keep the pain meds for another minute or two but passed out before I could. I think they were still standing there sharing that secret look when I did.

CHAPTER 26
TUESDAY

Mars showed up the next morning as promised. The doctor was giving me my marching orders when she came in. He was young and handsome. His thick, chestnut-colored hair was combed back from his face, and his hazel eyes were focused on me. He could play a doctor on TV. He was very sincere and made me believe that he cared about my welfare. He was also a guy who wouldn't be at Simpson County General long but would be moving on to a bigger hospital and more money. It was difficult to concentrate on what he was saying because I was looking at his beautiful, full lips. The arrival of my best friend snapped me out of my fantasies.

"Ms. Maher, you have several severe injuries, and just the total number of injuries is serious. You need complete bed rest for at least three more days. I'd like to see you at that time to make any further determinations and decisions. The MRI showed us that your shoulder isn't dislocated, but I still want you to wear an immobilizer until I see you again."

He looked very stern. I thought to myself that I'd like to see him too, naked.

"I understand that I'm pretty banged up, but none of my injuries are life threatening, right?"

"Correct, but your body has taken quite a lot of abuse, and you need to be good to it. How's the pain level?"

I did a quick system check. I hurt, that was for sure, but it was bearable. Of course that might have been the drugs talking.

"Not too bad, but I still have meds in me so it's hard to judge."

"There's a notation on your chart from last night that you requested to terminate the pain medication." He studied the chart in his hands.

"True, so how about if we terminate the meds, and let me see if I can live with the pain."

"How about this. We'll stop the meds, and I'll prescribe you pain meds that you can decide to use or not. If you promise to go home and go to bed, I'll sign the paperwork that will get you kicked out of here."

He smiled at me and I felt much better. He had a lovely smile with even, pearly white teeth. He reached over to the IV bag and turned some gizmo.

"You do have someone to take care of you?"

"My mother, grandmother and father."

"Good, I'll get the paperwork started, and you'll be out of here by lunch time. How does that sound to you?"

"Great! Dr. Jonas, this is my best friend Marcella Price. She'll be taking me home. Marcella, this is Dr. Jonas."

Mars smiled her zillion kilowatt smile at the doctor, and they shook hands.

"Ms. Price, I'm pleased to meet you. Take good care of our girl here. She's had a hard time. Make her rest and take the rest of her medications."

"Doctor, I'll do my best, but she's as stubborn as a mule."

I frowned and took exception to that statement, but before I could voice my displeasure the doctor spoke up.

"I'm sure she is, but if she gives you any trouble just bring her back here, and I'll have her tortured day and night by nursing students. They love to draw blood and administer enemas."

"Ya'll do realize that I'm right here?" I said.

"You can count on me, Doctor," Mars said. Her tone was evil and conspiratorial.

The doctor I had thought was so handsome turned and smiled at me, and I realized that he was rather plain and unremarkable to look at—maybe even homely. I did not smile back at him. When he had sailed out of my room I narrowed my eyes at Mars.

"Hey, you're supposed to be on my side!"

"I would've promised him anything to get you out of here. Connell wants to bring Donna in as soon as he can, and he promised you that you could listen in on the conversation."

I blew out a breath. "Good God, help me get dressed. Wait a minute, where are my clothes?"

"Shot to hell. We're gonna have to burn them. But I brought you something to wear—never fear."

She held up a shopping bag. I upended it on my bed, and there was my Liz Phair tee-shirt, underwear, socks and my favorite jeans.

My running shoes were in the bag too, thank God.

"Thank you, Mars, and especially thanks for the shoes. As God is my witness, I'll never wear sandals again!"

Mars laughed at me. "Oh Scarlett, eventually you'll wear them again when the pain of this disaster has faded and you find a cute pair on sale."

I shook my head which hurt, and I resolved not to do that ever again. I got dressed fast, since I was a little worried the good doctor might change his mind. Just as Mars tied my shoes, he came back with my release and something else.

"Now don't forget anything I've told you. Your health and recovery depends on you following orders. An aide will be here in a moment with the wheelchair, and I'll see you in three days. Book the appointment with my office today. I want you to get these prescriptions filled on your way home and take all of the antibiotics and steroids. Take the pain meds as needed."

"Yes sir, doctor sir. I will be a good girl," I promised and saluted him.

He handed me a card with his name and number, and the prescriptions. He unwrapped a sling-looking thing and helped me into it. It hurt to move my arm.

"Oww! You sure this is only bruised? It hurts so bad, I want to cry when I move it."

"This is exactly why I want you to wear this at all times, except in the shower. Okay?"

I nodded and the doctor left me in peace. Just as he left, a pimply faced, pudgy orderly in scrubs showed up with the promised wheelchair.

"Your chariot awaits, madam."

I love a comedian. I looked around to make sure that I wasn't forgetting anything, but only saw my bag, which Mars picked up.

"I can't believe that you aren't going to argue about being forced to ride in a wheelchair," she said.

"Well, I feel like hammered dammit. I'm not sure I could make it to the parking lot by myself, and so I'm going to ride in comfort." I lowered myself gingerly into the seat. "Less humiliating than falling on my face halfway to your car. Lay on, McDuff."

Being pushed around in a wheelchair is a weird experience.

You're moving but you have absolutely no control of the experience. I figured the kid knew what he was doing, so I tried not to worry over much. Within minutes we were in the parking lot, and he even helped to get me in the Thunderbird. Not an easy feat in my condition.

"I should've brought something else to take you home in. I didn't think about how hard it would be for you to get in and get out. I could've brought your Jeep or your dad's car."

Mars looked worried as she helped load me in the sports car.

I winced. I couldn't help it, the process hurt. I breathed a sigh of relief when I was seated. Mars hovered around me trying to figure out how to help.

"Mars, you're dithering. I'm fine."

I looked at the orderly's name tag. "Thanks for your help, Johnny. I appreciate it."

"Just one of the many services we offer. Come back anytime." He grinned and headed back into the hospital.

I had to laugh. That was funny whether he meant for it to be or not.

"Hurry, let's get over to the jail and see what happens," I suggested.

"We're going to park in the back and go in the back door. That way no one will see you, especially Donna. I don't know if the TBI agents are in the jail today, but we sure want to avoid them," Mars said.

I couldn't argue with that logic. The less people who saw me the better.

"For real. I wonder if Connell has even been allowed to talk to the three stooges."

"One of 'em's still out. How many times did you hit him with the rock?"

"I wasn't counting... Many."

I shook my head at the memory. We pulled up behind the jail, and I started to get out.

"Wait, let me help you," said Mars.

Again I wasn't inclined to argue. She helped me out and to the door, which was unlocked—that was unusual. It was kept locked, but Connell knew we were coming. Once inside, I headed straight to the observation room.

"Mars," I said over my shoulder, "secure the door."

We made our way quietly down the hall without being seen. The door to the observation room was unlocked too, so we went in and made ourselves to home.

There were several chairs in front of the two-way mirror, and on the other side of the mirror was a room with a long table and several more chairs. Donna Maples was sitting at the table facing us. Connell stood opposite her with his back to us. He couldn't know we were here yet, so I called him. He took his phone out of his pocket.

"Maher."

"We're here," I said in a low voice.

"Very good, I'll sign that report as soon as I finish with this interrogation."

He hung up, and Mars and I settled in for the show. I wished we'd brought some popcorn because I knew it was going to be entertaining.

"Donna, I'm afraid that we have a very serious problem."

"I have no idea what you're talking about, Sheriff. We don't have a problem, but I think that you're going to have one. I don't like being commanded to report to your office."

Donna seemed cool and collected and just a bit snotty. I wondered how long that would last when she realized just how screwed she was. Her perfect ruby lips were pinched in an ugly pucker.

"Well, you're here because it's come to the attention of my office that you've been using your position to help facilitate the sales of property in exchange for monetary compensation."

You could have heard a pin drop. She never batted an eye, just stared straight at Connell.

"Again, I have no idea what you're talking about, so if we're done here, I have to get to the office. But don't think for a red hot minute that you're going to get away with these draconian tactics. I think I'll be having a little chat with the mayor over lunch about your witch hunt." She stood up.

"Sit. Down." Connell's voice was low and menacing.

She narrowed her eyes at him, but she sat back down. "How dare you take that tone with me?"

Connell took several pieces of paper from a file folder that he was holding and threw them on the table.

"This is how I dare. Take a good look Donna because this is evidence that'll put your ass in a sling that neither you nor your brother-in-law will be able to get you out of. You've broken the law, and I mean for you to pay for it."

Donna looked at the papers that were strewn across the table. She was a hell of a poker player, I'll give her that. The only reaction she had was the slightest widening of her eyes. If I hadn't been looking for tells I would've missed it.

She laughed derisively. "You could've gotten that anywhere. It's obviously edited or cut and pasted. Someone's trying to cause trouble for me with this lame attempt. Whatever, it's still false and now I'm leaving." She stood up again.

Connell leaned in close to her. "This is the only chance you'll have to come clean and get in front of this thing."

"Fuck you, Connell Maher."

She flounced out of the room. My brother turned to the two-way mirror and shrugged at us.

"Hmmm, that went well," I observed.

"Yep," Mars agreed.

Connell walked into the little room where we were standing. "That went well."

"Yeah, I just said that. Now what do we do?" I asked.

"Now I go and see the judge, and you two are gonna make yourselves scarce. There's no tellin' when Boyd and Lyle will pop in. They're in and out of here like dogs pissin' in snow."

He was frustrated, and I couldn't blame him. We had all piled way too much hope on Donna crumbling and giving us a break in the case. Still I had to laugh at the image his phrase had conjured for me. I have a ridiculous imagination, and when people say things I see pictures in my head. From that moment on, Boyd would be a large stupid-looking bloodhound and Lyle, a Jack Russell terrier. Not that bloodhounds are stupid, they're not. It's just the long nose and droopy ears and sad-looking eyes. I realized that Connell and Mars were staring at me.

"Sorry, Connell, I know how much you love them and their high-handed ways. I think I need lunch, so will you call us as soon as you get the subpoena? We won't be far away. I think the Red Dog is calling my name." I laughed again.

"As soon as. You okay?"

"Yeah, I just had an image of Boyd and Lyle as dogs. Although it could be the drugs still, but you know I'm a little crazy even without them." I smiled at him and loved him for the worry he had for me. "Really I'm pretty good."

We exited the tiny room and were walking down the hall when we ran smack into the aforementioned TBI agents. Awesome. I was willing to just walk on by, but Lyle put her hand on my chest and stopped me. I stood there and stared down at her hand.

"You might want to move that, or you're gonna be drawin' back a nub." My voice was low and level—no anger, just stating facts.

"Agent Lyle." Boyd sounded like he was reminding her that she dropped something, not like she was committing assault.

She let her hand fall but continued to glare at me.

I pinned her with an ugly look. "Touch me again, and I'll happily go to jail for stompin' your ass."

I started to step around her, but Boyd's voice brought me up short.

"What are you doing here, Ms. Maher?" he asked.

I decided that being a smart ass was the way to go. "I was born here."

"Here in the sheriff's office?" he clarified.

"Oh, well I came over straight from the hospital to see what was happenin' with the charges on the guys who kidnapped and tried to kill me. As you might imagine, I am just a tad bit anxious to see them go to jail."

Boyd looked thoughtful for a moment, but he seemed to accept what I said. "Oh, I can see that you would be concerned. When you double-cross criminals they have a tendency to become violent. It would seem there really is no honor among thieves."

"There's a distinct possibility that the three wounded men will bring charges against you," Lyle snarled at me.

"Wow, if I was them, I'd be ashamed to admit that a girl beat me up." I smiled when I said it. Which hurt like hell.

"Are you admitting it?" Lyle asked in a condescending tone.

She was really pushing me, but I knew better than to take that bait. I chuckled right in her ugly little pinched-up face. She took a menacing step toward me, but Boyd stepped between us.

"Who's the young woman that just left here, Sheriff?" he asked.

I laughed some more. "That's Donna Maples, the county tax assessor. She probably brought cookies or brownies or something sweet for Connell." I cupped my hand to one side of my mouth like I was about to tell a secret. "She's been trying to court Connell for some time now," I said. My tone of voice was low, then I laughed as if it were a huge joke.

I was being remarkably jolly for a woman just out of the hospital. Connell had the grace to look annoyed at the whole thing.

"Something I can do for you today?" he asked Boyd.

"We have a few more interviews today and will be using your interrogation room," Boyd answered.

Not "we'd like to" or "may we" or "is it convenient"—just a statement of fact that they would be taking over the room. I hope they brought their own coffee supply because I doubted there'd be any for them in this building.

"Happy to oblige."

Connell walked away from the agents with Mars and me following in his wake like two little puppies. My little puppy heart was beating kinda fast, I have to admit. We went into Connell's office and I sank into a chair. I was tired all of a sudden.

"Think they bought my story?" I asked.

"I doubt it," said Connell. "You suck at lying."

He sat down behind his desk and hit the intercom button. Mars snickered.

"Only 'cuz you know me so well," I complained. "I don't have that problem with strangers."

"Yeah, Connell," said Mavis in response.

"Mavis, please run down Judge Smiley, and then find out if he'll see me. I need a couple of search warrants."

"Will do. By the by, them two TBIs are in the building."

"Oh I know, I've already had that pleasure. Call me as soon as."

Connell leaned back in his chair and huffed out a breath. "Well so much for making yourselves scarce."

"It wasn't my fault. Now what?"

"Now we wait," he answered.

"One of those search warrants for the Cove property?" I asked. "Will that cause a problem with Boyd and Lyle?

"Nope, seems there was an anonymous call to the office awhile ago about some loud activity and strange comings and goings out at Coleman Cove."

"I'm hungry," I complained.

Connell and Mars actually laughed at me.

"What? I am, I haven't had anything but JELLO since lunch on Sunday, and I had to suck that between my teeth. I need to keep my strength up. I've lost blood, ya know."

"Something from the Red Dog okay with you?" Connell asked.

I nodded pitiably and tried to look extra sad.

"I gotta pee."

I walked across the hall and realized that the last time I used a public restroom I was kidnapped, held hostage, chased through the woods and nearly killed. I shivered all over. I peed the quickest pee ever in my life. I was washing my hands and made the mistake of looking in the mirror.

"HOLY SHIT!" I yelled.

I looked like a train wreck. My face was a mass of scratches, my jaw was black and blue, and it looked like both my eyes were going to turn black. There was a bandage on the side of my head right over my ear. I couldn't help myself. I had to see it. I gently lifted the bandage away from my head and gasped when I realized that a huge patch of my hair had been shaved. I started to hyperventilate.

"Son of a BITCH! I shoulda killed him!"

I couldn't stop staring at the mess my head was in. That would take forever to grow back. Meanwhile, I'd look like some kind of a lopsided idiot. The black stitches running over my ear just added to the horror I was seeing. The antiseptic or whatever they had used at the hospital was an orange-red color and had stained my skin. I looked like Jack the Freakin' Ripper had paid me a visit. I started to cry. Fifteen seconds later the absurdity of my reaction hit me, and I began to laugh. After everything that had happened to me, I was freaking out over a little hair loss. I dried my face and hands and went back to Connell's office.

"Did you know they shaved my head?" I asked.

"They had to stitch your head up," Connell said.

"I totally get that, but they shaved my head."

"Only a little bit, I'm sure," Mars assured me.

"Well it sure doesn't look like a little bit. If I shaved the other side to match I could start a new style."

"Lunch will be here any minute. Darlene promised to fix you something very special." Mars sounded like she was talking to a three-year-old who was about to pitch a fit.

"It's okay. You don't have to talk me down off the ledge. I already had my moment in the bathroom. I swear though, I'm gonna stop using public bathrooms. Bad things keep happening to me in them."

Darlene and Brian walked in at that moment and they had food. That was fast! I forgot all about my hair.

"Oh, Sis," Brian said just as Darlene said, "Oh, honey."

They put the food down and hugged me, gently.

"Bless your heart," said Darlene. "How bad are you hurtin'?"

"Not too bad, but I still have pain killers in my system. I'm tired though," I admitted.

Brian hugged me to him again. I could feel his heart beating. He drew a deep breath. "You had us all scared to death. Tess, I haven't always been the best brother, but you know that I love you, and I'd do anything for you, right."

"Stop it, you're gonna make me cry. I love you too." I squeezed him a little. "What did you bring me?"

Darlene pulled a large to-go cup out of the box and held it out to me. I raised a questioning eyebrow at her.

"What's this?"

"It's a triple-chocolate-fudge-mint-double-thick milkshake, with protein powder." Darlene smiled at me and pushed the cup in to my hand.

"What else did you bring?" I knew I wouldn't like the answer.

"That's all for you because you can't have solid food, honey. Your jaw is wired shut. Did you forget?"

"Well not exactly 'cuz I'm talking through my teeth, but I guess I didn't think about eating." I blew out a breath. "Great."

She handed me a spoon. We all settled down, and I hungrily watched everyone else scarf down Reuben sandwiches with lovely, loaded potato skins. I tried to content myself with my milkshake. It was after all a particularly delightful milkshake. But it wasn't real food. I wondered silently how long it would be until I could taste real food again and decided that I just really didn't want to know.

Mavis came in the door. "Them TBIs want me to call and order 'em some lunch, but for the last couple of days no one in town'll deliver if they know it's for them. Whadda you want me to do?"

"I'll take care of it," Connell grumbled.

He wiped his mouth and left the room. Mavis went back to her desk and presumably her own lunch.

"I hear food is not the only thing they're having trouble getting," said Brian. "No one will sell them anything. They had to go down to Beasley to get gas yesterday. They tried to buy gas at Chick's and Sammy told them the pumps were down." He smiled. Beasley was a larger town down the highway about 10 miles from Medicine Springs.

"Nobody speaks to them unless they have too. The entire town is giving them the cold shoulder," said Darlene. "It'd be sad if it wasn't so funny or so well-deserved."

"Yep, this town has closed ranks against them. Not just because they're accusing you, Tess, but because they've been so high-handed and downright ugly in how they approached people. They've not shown respect or common courtesy to anyone," Mars said.

If I had to guess, I say she'd been interviewed and it hadn't gone well.

Connell came back with an evil little smile on his face. "I told them the truth, and boy, are they pissed."

"Connell," Mavis said over the intercom. "The judge is in his chambers and said he'll see you if you make it quick."

Connell spun on his heel and took off.

About 30 minutes later a ruckus came in the front door. We all poked our heads out into the hall. The ruckus turned out to be Connell and Donna. Connell was carrying a computer, and Donna was yelling at him. He was ignoring her. She followed and yapped at his heels like an enraged poodle. We ducked back into the office as they came closer, but we peeked around the door.

"You can't do this! I'll have your job for this, Connell Maher! Where are you taking my computer? This is not legal! Are you crazy? Answer me! Do I have to call my brother-in-law to make you quit? Stop ignoring me!"

There was a lot more ranting, but it all followed the same theme. I do so enjoy it when people claim that you can't do something at the very moment in which you are doing it. Baffling.

Connell stopped and turned to look at her.

"I have a warrant for this computer and for any computers at your house. Joel is on his way out there now. Judge Smiley signed the warrant. If you want to yell at somebody I suggest that you yell at him because I'm tired of hearing your voice."

"I promise..." Donna began.

Connell held up one hand to silence her.

"If you don't go away right now, I'm gonna lock you in a cell, I promise you."

He stared her down for about 30 seconds, and she finally turned tail and practically ran toward the front door. Connell looked in at us.

"I'm gonna take this to Mark's office. Will one of you call Jim Burns and see if he can come over here and have a look at this computer. Tell him there might be more than one."

He walked away. Mars took out her phone to call Jim. I followed Connell.

"You know she's probably erased the incriminating files, right?" I asked.

"Probably." He set the computer down on Mark's desk. "I have faith that Jim can find those files, no matter what she's done with 'em."

"She's pretty good at coverin' her tracks, Connell. There's no tellin' what she was able to accomplish in the last hour or so." I frowned and winced. Damn it hurt!

Joel walked in with a laptop, and Jim Burns was on his heels. Jim must have sprinted over to show up that fast.

"Joel. Jim." Connell nodded at each man in greeting. "These are the computers I want you to take a look at, Jim. There're most likely files on here that have been deleted. I need those files found yesterday."

Joel placed the laptop on the desk next to the tower. I realized that both men were staring at me, then I remembered that I looked like a survivor from the Texas Chainsaw Massacre.

"Hey, ya'll." I said through clenched teeth and smiled. "It looks worse than it actually is."

"Somehow I can't believe that. You look like you got hit by a

Mack truck, in the face," Jim said. He continued to stare at me.

"Yeah," agreed Joel.

"You bring any other files from her place?" Connell asked.

Joel shook his head. "I checked around for files and didn't find anything. I reckon that most of her paperwork stays at the office."

"Right, well take the warrant and go over there and start looking for anything that ties her to Aggroco or the land sales out at the Cove. She's gonna piss and whine. Ignore her and do your job. If she really gets in your way, arrest her for obstruction."

"Yes sir, on my way to get my ass chewed on, sir. Tess, you get on the mend quick now."

He hurried out to his fate. I sure wouldn't want to be the one searching Donna's office.

"Jim, the same for you but without the whining. Find any files marked Aggroco, Cove properties and anything to do with money paid to her by outside sources. I have some copies of emails that I'll give you. Find 'em for me."

"I'll do my best, but depending on how computer savvy she is, this could take days." He sat down at Mark's desk and hooked Donna's tower up to Mark's monitor. "Do you know her password?"

I almost let the cat out of the bag, but I bit my tongue just in the nick of time. It simply wouldn't do for anyone to know that I knew her password. I just stood there with a blank look on my face.

Jim looked up from the computer. "No? Oh well, good thing I have a handy gizmo to help out with that little problem. I'll yell if I find anything, but don't hold your breath, okay?"

Connell and I went back to his office. Brian and Darlene had gone back to work, but Mars was there working on her Blackberry.

"Looking at porn?" I queried.

She never looked up. "Chinese lesbian midget girl-on-girl porn." She said it with a straight face and I had to laugh. "Nosey, if you have to know, it's work stuff. I do have to make a living after all. I can't spend all my time worrying about and babysitting you."

"Wow and I thought you liked me." I took a seat. Mars stuck her tongue out at me. "Oh, very mature," I said in a mock stern voice.

"Connell?" Mavis' voice came over the intercom.

"Yes, Mavis?" Connell answered.

"There's a call on line two that you need to take. It's some lawyer from California, and he wants to talk about them three yahoos what kidnapped Tess."

"Got it." He picked up the phone and punched the button. "This is Sheriff Maher."

He listened for a full minute.

"Well, the men in question are being charged with a variety of crimes: kidnapping, assault and attempted murder. They're recuperating in the hospital here. Their injuries are severe but probably not life threatening. They're under arrest but haven't been arraigned yet since they're in the hospital, so bail hasn't been set at this time. It's highly unlikely that any judge in this county will set bail, since I'll do my best to convince the DA that these men pose a flight risk."

He listened for another minute.

"Well no, they weren't injured while being arrested. They were injured by the woman they kidnapped while she was making her escape. I'd say your boys picked on the wrong woman."

I snickered. I couldn't help it. Connell cut me a "shut-up" look.

"Well you can do that if you want, but it won't make the process go any faster—wheels of justice and all that. Uh huh, uh huh. Then I reckon we'll see you then."

Connell hung up without saying good-bye.

"So I guess we have a big time city lawyer descending on us?" I asked.

"Yep, and he's gonna experience culture shock when he gets here. This is a very well-paid and well-connected lawyer who's used to throwin' his weight around. He's gonna find out that a fella who is too big for his britches will get cut down to size." Connell grinned his poker grin.

"Still you look worried," I said.

"Look at it this way. You're beat up. The three alleged assailants are beat up. They're actually in worse shape than you. There's no proof they took you by force. It's a 'he said, she said'. A case could be made for a fallin' out amongst thieves."

"Good God! Connell, I can't believe that!" Mars said.

I closed my eyes and just sat there stunned. Connell was right. This could turn on a dime. What a never-ending nightmare! At that instant I realized that we didn't have days for Jim Burns to find the files on that computer. He had to find them now. We needed as much proof as possible as fast as possible to tie the three thugs to Aggroco and to Chick's murder.

"I'm whipped. I need to go home." I looked at Mars and she nodded. "Call me if you get a break on this, please." I stood up and kissed my brother.

"You know I will," he assured me. "Try not to worry. We'll build a case against Donna that'll lead to everythin' else breakin' loose. We can do this without gettin' crossways with Boyd and Lyle."

"I think that ship has sailed," I muttered.

Connell looked at Mars. "Can I talk to you for a minute?"

She nodded and they stepped out into the hall. I was pretty sure their conversation was about me but I didn't care. At that point all I could care about was saving my ass and taking a nap. My eyes locked on Connell's keys lying on his desk. In that moment I committed an act that I knew I might live to regret and then stepped into the hallway.

"I need my bed, ya'll," I said.

Mars and Connell smiled an identical smile at me which confirmed my suspicions about the topic of conversation.

"See ya later, love ya, bye," Connell said and hugged me.

We were out the back door and climbing into the car before Mars said a word. "So what are we really doing?"

I grinned at her the best I could. She just knows me too well. "First we are going to the hospital. I need to pay a visit to my kidnappers. Then we're going to my office. I wanna set Jewels to work on finding a connection between the bad guys and Aggroco. We need proof that they're employed by that company. Somebody's payin' them and unless they're getting' cash, there's a paper trail. Then we're going to my house. There's a little item there that I need to retrieve.

"Oh, is that all? So are you going to tell me what that item is? Mars cocked an eye at me.

"If I don't tell you, then you never have to lie under oath."

"Oh, great! Just what I wanted to hear." She rolled her eyes at me and started the car.

CHAPTER 27

We got to the hospital, and I had Mars drop me off at the front door.

"I won't be long. Just sit tight."

"I know you are about to do something illegal."

"I don't think it's illegal—probably questionable and maybe unethical, possibly even immoral—but not illegal."

She made an ugly face at me as I struggled out of the car. I really was tired. There was nothing in the world I wanted more than three weeks of sleep and a pedicure.

It was simple to find the rooms where my playmates were housed. The hospital is small, with only two stories. I simply looked up and down hallways until I spotted a sheriff's deputy standing guard. I figured that Connell wouldn't leave the three men unattended even though they were badly hurt. You can never gauge another person's determination, and you had to know that these guys wouldn't want to stick around if they could help it. I'd have crawled through broken glass to escape the legal troubles that were about to fall on them.

I limped down the hall. As I got closer I realized that the deputy standing guard was Andy King. He'd worked for my father and had retired several years ago. Connell used him when the staff was shorthanded. It was a win-win situation. Andy made a little extra money, and Connell had an experienced man he could trust on the job.

"Hey, Andy," I said.

He looked up from the book he was reading and grinned then frowned.

"Tess, you look like Hell's Half Acre. Howya feelin'?"

"About like what you see. Andy, I wanna take a look at the men."

"Tess, I don't have no orders to let you in."

"Please, Andy, I need to see them. Right now they're monsters in my head. I need to lay eyes on 'em and realize that they're only humans—mean and dangerous—but humans nonetheless. If I don't I know I won't sleep. Please, let me do this."

He didn't say anything for a few seconds, then he reached out and put his hand on my good shoulder. "I understand. They're drugged up and cuffed, so I don't reckon they can do you no harm. Don't you do them none neither."

"I won't, cross my heart. You can check on their health when I'm done." I started to open the door but turned back to Andy. "Did the one guy wake up yet?"

"He come 'round for a few minutes 'bout lunch time."

"Good, I think."

I pushed the door open and went into the darkened room. The three were in the same room—it was a four-bed ward. They were all sleeping. Beside each bed was a wardrobe where personal belongings were kept. That was my goal.

I rifled the first one next to the bed of Joe. Not an easy task with the damn immobilizer on me. I spared a single glance at the patient and decided with glee that he looked worse than I did. I located his wallet and laid everything in it on the bedside table. I took my phone out and snapped pictures of everything.

I went through the same routine with the other two and got my first real look at Marty. He was a mess, just as you would expect someone to be who'd fallen down a flight of stairs and landed in glass.

Rick's head was swathed in bandages, his eyes were black and his breathing was shallow. As it turned out, I decided I was glad none of them were dead by my hand. Funny, huh?

I completed my mission, restored everything to rights and stuck my head out the door.

"Andy, would you come in here and be my witness that I left 'em all in good health."

"Glad to." He entered the room and looked at each man, checked the monitors and nodded at me. "You left 'em in better shape than they deserve." He narrowed his eyes as he examined me closer. "You need to be in bed too."

"Soon, Andy, I promise. Thank you, and I have one more favor."

"Don't mention to no one that I saw you?"

"Don't lie. Just don't bring it up if you can help it."

He smiled and winked. "Girl, you just won't do."

I smiled back at him and made my exit to find a very antsy Mars waiting for me.

"Jesus, I thought you'd never get back."

"Mars, I don't think I was in there any longer than twenty minutes.

She started the car and we headed to my office.

"It sure seemed longer than that. Did you get what you needed?"

"Oh yeah. Who knew that bad guys carry many forms of identification? I figured there'd be no IDs, and the labels would be missing from all of their clothing, but no. They all look like hell too."

"Connell's going to throw a hissy fit when he finds out you went in there, you know."

I sighed. "I hope that he won't find out for days and days. Mars, this California lawyer will be here tomorrow. There's every chance in the world that he'll get bail for these boys or bring charges against me. We don't have much time to solve this."

"I know."

She parked in front of my office and we went in. I felt like I was sleep walking. I had to get my appointed rounds finished, so I could lie down. I opened the door to the office. Jewels looked up and saw me.

"Dear God!" She jumped up from her desk and grabbed me in a hug. "You could've been killed." She cried all over me.

"I'm gonna be fine," I assured her.

"Oh my God, you can't talk! Is your jaw broken? Oh my God!" she wailed.

"Yes. Jewels, darlin', I need for you to get a grip. There's serious work to do. We have to find the links between the three guys who kidnapped me and Aggroco. So you're gonna run all the information in the world down about them. I wanna know who their kindergarten teachers were—if they even have kindergarten in reform school—rap sheets, credit reports, everything."

Jewels drew a shaky breath. "Okay, what do I have to work with?"

I smiled and took out my phone. "I think you'll find everything you need in here. Do we have any straws?"

"Maybe, I'll look and see. Why?" She looked puzzled but at least she had quit crying.

"Well, we're gonna find out if I can drink coffee through a straw." I found out that you can, you just have to be careful that it isn't too hot.

Mars and I chilled out in my office while Jewels took the information off my phone. Within ten minutes or so, we were ready to roll again.

I kissed Jewels. "Thanks for doing this. Text me as soon as you find the info we need," I said and hugged her.

"I will if you'll please go home and get some rest."

I nodded my head. I hated to lie to Jewels outright.

"Okay, so what are we doing at your house?" Mars asked.

I leaned my head back on the seat and blew out a breath. It would have been nice to take a short nap, but Mars deserved an explanation.

"Okay, Jim says it might take days to find the deleted files on Donna's computer. The California lawyer will be here tomorrow. We don't have days. We need for him to find the files now, so charges can be pressed all the way around. We're not even close to being out of the woods yet."

Mars nodded, "I agree. But you have a plan."

I smiled. "As a matter of fact, I do. But this is gonna be tricky. My family'll be all over me with tea and sympathy. I need to go back to town and back to Connell's office. They'll chain me to my bed if they realize what I intend."

"But you can't just disappear from the house. YaYa'll have a coronary, and your mother will spend the rest of her days making you feel guilty."

"True enough. She has raised guilt to a fine art form."

I thought about my best options for a minute or two.

"Then I'll have to get Daddy to be my cohort in crime. He understands that sometimes you have to do what you have to do. This has to be done today without fail. My life depends on it."

"I know and that's why I'm helping you, otherwise I'd handcuff you to the bedpost myself. Are you going to tell me the plan or not?"

"Mars, I might get burned on this, and I sure don't want to endanger you. This isn't like the scrapes we used to get into as kids. This is real do not pass go do not collect two hundred dollars but go directly to jail stuff."

"You've always been able to fall into manure and come up smelling like a rose. I trust you to do that now. I'm with you on this."

We pulled up to the house and Daddy came out to greet us.

"Glad you're home, my girl. Your mother thinks you need to be in bed."

He helped me out of the car and hugged me. I hugged back, which felt so good and made me feel so safe. I leaned into him and pulled a little of his strength into me.

"I know and I'm bone tired, Daddy, but I can't lie down yet. There're still several things I need to do to clear my name and catch the bad guys, things that can't wait for me to get a good night's sleep. Events are moving fast, maybe faster than I can get ahead of, but I have to try."

I looked up at him hoping that he understood. He nodded and held me at arm's length.

"First, tell me that what you're plannin' isn't dangerous."

I sighed, "I don't think it's dangerous."

He looked at Mars, and she nodded her head as if she agreed with my assessment of the situation. Daddy drew a deep breath and nodded back at her.

"What do you need me to do?" he asked.

"Keep Mommy off my back while I run an errand. She's gonna have a conniption if she finds out I've left the house."

"And after the errand?" he asked.

"I promise I'll come straight home and crawl into my bed and stay there."

"Then I think an early cocktail hour is called for."

He grinned at me and Mars, and I laughed out loud. The three of us went in through the kitchen, and I tried to prepare myself for the greeting I knew was coming. Mommy and YaYa were all over me like white on rice. They hugged me and kissed me and looked into my eyes and made *tsk tsk* sounds over my bruises.

"Hey really, I'm not too bad, all things considered."

Mommy pursed her lips. "I suppose you're right. You could be dead in a ditch somewhere, and I'd never know what happened to you." She hugged me again.

"Maggie, let the girl sit down. She's practically swayin' on her feet." Daddy steered me to a chair at the table.

The escape took much longer than I hoped it would. Mommy and YaYa had a zillion questions. They tried to feed me and were horrified that I couldn't eat. They fixed me tea and tried to give me coffee.

"You want a drink, kid?" YaYa asked.

I hung in as long as I could, but finally I'd enough. "Maybe later, YaYa. For now I gotta go and lie down. I love you and I'll see you in the morning, okay?"

"I think that Martinis are called for," Daddy announced. He winked at me as Mars and I ducked out.

The stairs were a bitch to navigate, and I said as much. "Jesus, these stairs are gonna kill me."

"Only a few more. Come on, you can do it," Mars encouraged me.

We got to my room and I fell on my bed.

"Oh God, this feels so good."

"Well, don't let it be too good to you. We have work to do."

I sighed, "You're right. Mars, I can't do another flight of stairs. Please do this for me."

"What exactly am I doing?"

"There's a thumb drive hidden upstairs and I need it. If you stand in front of the chimney with your back toward this end of the house, on the right hand side of the chimney there's a secret compartment. On the corner, three bricks up from the floor, there's a loose brick. Work it out and get the thumb drive."

Mars raised her brows at me. "You have a secret hidden compartment in your house? Why?"

"I didn't create it. I just found it one rainy afternoon."

"You have a secret hiding place and you never told me about it? What else have you hidden from me? Who else knows about it?"

"Me and now you, and you have to promise not to tell. It'd take a month of Sundays for anyone to search this house and find it. It's perfect. Honest to God, I never told you because we never needed a hiding place, and I just kinda forgot about it."

She just shook her head and walked out. I thought a short nap was called for and so I took one.

I woke up about twelve seconds later to the sight of a pink thumb drive, decorated with skull and crossbones, dangling in my face.

"I think I dozed off. That's the one." I sat up and rubbed my eyes.

"Let's go."

Mars put her hands on my chest and pushed me back down on the bed. "Hold on there, Calamity Jane. What's in this thing, and what're you going to do with it?"

I puffed out my cheeks and expelled a breath. "Look, I don't want to drag you down the well with me. The less you know, the safer you'll be."

"Not good enough. Tell me."

I huffed out a breath. "Well, let's just say that, hypothetically, there could be copies of files pertaining to an ongoing investigation that may have been deleted from a suspect's computer on that drive."

Mars looked at the innocent looking thumb drive as if it were a tarantula. "Holy crap! The missing files from Donna's computer are on this?"

"I didn't say that." I held up one finger to emphasize my point.

"Okay, so what are you going to do with this?"

"Well, it might be a good idea, hypothetically, to reintroduce the missing files to the suspect's computer so that they could be easily found."

Mars looked at me with huge eyes and slowly raised her eyebrows almost to her hairline. "You intend to go into the sheriff's office, plug this drive into a confiscated computer and restore the missing files?"

"I never said that."

"In broad daylight, under the nose of the TBI, your brother and Miss Mavis? Have you lost your mind? Are you insane? Were you ever sane? Are you gonna tap dance and juggle chainsaws while you do it just to make it more fun?"

"Now you see why I didn't want to tell you? Besides the fact you'll be an accessory, I knew you'd yell at me. By the way, you shouldn't yell at me, I've had a terrible trauma."

"You're about to have another one! You promised your father that your *errand* wasn't dangerous."

"It's only dangerous if Boyd or Lyle catch me in the act. In that case I go to prison and everyone will know where I'll be every night for the next fifteen years."

Mars actually sputtered for about five second, then she was silent for another five. "What do you need me to do?"

"Drive, sit in the car and be my lookout. No, wait, that's not what I want. I want you to drive me downtown and drop me at my office."

Mars quirked one eyebrow at me. "Why."

"So you can pass a polygraph."

"Jesus Christ on a bicycle! Okay let's go."

"I suggest we go down the steps to the computer room and out the front door. We'll have to circle around the entire house, but it gives us less chance of being seen."

We tiptoed out like little guilty mice, circled the house and stopped by the back door.

"They're going to suspect something if I take off without saying good-bye," Mars whispered.

I knew she was right so I nodded. She went in the back door to make her farewells, and I walked on around to her car. I got in and ducked down—not easy, let me tell you. A minute or so later Mars joined me. She was smiling.

"Your mom is already on her third Martini, and I think your dad is mixin' them extra strong."

You know how sometimes you dread something so very much, your palms sweat and your stomach churns with acid and you start to twitch. That's how the entire ride to town was for me. I kept thinking what would happen to me if I got caught. I weighed that against what would happen to me if I failed to pull this off. Either way I was screwed. That meant my only hope was to do this crazy act and not get caught. I had to be invisible. Any hint that I had touched the computer or tampered with evidence and I was toast. By the time we reached town more than my palms were sweating. Of course riding crouched in the seat only added to my discomfort.

"Mars, drop me off at the back door of my building. After that I want you to go somewhere public, someplace where lots of people will see you. Talk to folks so that they'll remember you were there. In forty-five minutes, come to the back door of my building. I don't want anyone to see us together."

She nodded and looked extremely unhappy.

"Look I don't like doing this—leaving you, I mean. Maybe I can help."

"You are helpin'. I'm tryin' to cover your ass here. Let me do it."

It's very difficult to sound bossy when you are scrunched into a ball in the floor board of a tiny car, but I managed.

"Fine, but I don't have to like it."

She hit the brakes and came to a halt. I mouthed a kiss at her and slipped out of the car. I walked down the alleys until I got to the jail. The back door was locked, but I had a key. I'd stolen it off Connell's ring earlier. My motto is always, be prepared. I unlocked the door and ghosted inside, I looked up the hall and it was empty. I stood for several seconds and listened. It was late in the afternoon and the place was quiet. I tiptoed up the hall to Mark's office, opened the door and slipped inside. I put my back to the door and breathed a big sigh of relief. So far so good.

The computer was waiting for me, just like I knew it would be. There was no way that Connell would let the thing out of his sight now. I sat down and flipped it on, gave it a few seconds to warm up and plugged in the thumb drive. After that it was a matter of minutes before the erased files were no longer erased. I turned the computer off and wiped my fingerprints away. Then I listened at the door for signs of life. I heard voices and it sounded as if they were coming my way. I began to sweat again. It was Boyd and Lyle and they were arguing.

"I think that everyone in this town is part of a conspiracy to protect Tess Maher," Lyle said.

"Well, we can't arrest the entire town, so we have to find someone who'll crack this for us. Someone who when squeezed will admit that Maher and Donnelly were selling drugs. So far all we have is an anonymous tip and our own suspicions," Boyd grumbled.

I closed my eyes and willed them to be gone. I couldn't believe they were still on the drug dealer idea. That was about as stupid a thing as I had ever witnessed. It's a fact though that sometimes law enforcement can be blind. They get an idea and build the case around it, fitting pieces into the scenario with a hammer. Blessedly, my two pains in the ass moved on past the door and toward the front. I released the breath I'd been holding.

I gave them five minute by the clock to get out of the building. Then I snuck out of Mark's office and into Connell's. His key ring was in his desk drawer where I returned the purloined key. I checked to see if the coast was clear and headed out the back door. I scooted down the alley to my office. I didn't go inside the building. I didn't want Jewels to see me and ask questions. I stood just inside the building by the back door and waited for Mars. Forty-five minutes on the dot from the time she dropped me off, I heard her car pull up. I walked out the back door, got in her car, scrunched down in the seat and we took off.

"Now I understand what anti-climactic means."

Mars never said a word, just took me home and tucked me into bed.

CHAPTER 28
WEDNESDAY

My chirping cell phone jarred me out of a deep and sound sleep. I growled at it. This had better be good. I grabbed it off the nightstand and looked at the text.

Get down here now if you want to see the show.

It was from Connell. Show time! I swung my feet out of bed and tried to stand up. I fell back onto the bed.

"SHIT!"

That hurt. I had forgotten how badly I was banged up. Stupidly, I tried the entire procedure again more slowly and favoring just about everything. There was much regret that Mars and I hadn't had a chance to fill the pain killer prescription yesterday. I wasn't sure that I could drive or even get dressed by myself.

I struggled into a tee-shirt and jeans and tried to do something with my hair. I had showered the night before and washed my hair four times trying to get the blood and the orange-red medicine stuff out. I gave it up as hopeless and finally just stuck a baseball cap over the whole mess. I looked like a fugitive from a stalker movie. The cap didn't really fit over the bandage, my bruises were even more spectacular, the scratches were Technicolor, and I had enormous bags under my eyes. Even my hair looked sad and beat-up. Yep, I made this look good. I limped down the stairs to find my parents and grandmother having breakfast.

"I have to go into town. I need a driver. I don't think I can shift gears and besides I don't really know where my car is." I sat down a little too heavily and winced.

"Are you insane?" Mommy asked.

"Why do people keep asking me that?"

"Maybe it's because you keep doing insane things, kiddo," YaYa said.

I laughed and rubbed my hands through my hair, forgetting the bullet wound and my shoulder. "Ow, really ow." To say that it hurt is an understatement in the extreme. I barely restrained myself from screaming.

"You see, you're not fit to leave the house. Go back to bed. Do you have any pain killers?" Mommy was frowning at me.

"Connell's about to break this whole thing. I have to be there. I need a ride. Please don't fight me on this," I begged.

"I'll take you," Daddy said.

"Ed, she's not fit to take to a dog fight. You can't be serious," Mommy protested.

"She has to see this through," Daddy declared.

Mommy looked at me, and the worry was evident in her eyes. She stood up, nodded and hugged me. YaYa followed suit.

"I'll be fine and I'll call you as soon as there's anything to tell."

I kissed them both and left them standing there in the kitchen with identical worried looks on their faces. Daddy and I got in the SUV and headed for town.

"What do you know?" he asked.

"I don't know anything, but I suspect a lot. I suspect that my errand from yesterday has born a delightful fruit. I suspect that Connell is about to drop the hammer on Donna. I suspect that Donna is about to have an apoplectic seizure. Thanks for takin' the heat off me, by the way."

"You owe your mother for one monster hangover you know. So you got a message from Connell?"

"Right, he sent a text telling me to get to town because the show was about to begin. That has to mean that Jim Burns, you know him, the computer guy, found the missing files that tie Donna to the bad guys. He's gonna haul her in for questioning, and he knows how bad I want to be there."

"Then we should hurry. I'd hate to keep the wheels of justice waitin'."

He accelerated and we flew down the road. I hung on for dear life.

My phone chirped to warn me that I had a text message. It was from Mars.

Where r u?

Omw 2 town connell sent for me its showtime come on

Yeehaw!! On my way.

I chuckled at her message. Daddy looked at me.

"Oh, it was Mars. She's gonna meet us at the jail."

"Good, the more the merrier I say."

"I have butterflies in my stomach," I admitted. "What if Donna won't break?"

"We keep tryin' until we break her or one of the fellas in the hospital. There're ways to do this short of water boardin', you know." He smiled. "We can threaten any of them with you, which should be enough to get 'em to talk."

"Hardy, har, har, very funny. Wow, I think my brain just kicked in. I need to get hold of Jewels," I said.

I texted: Jewels where are u?

Office

Any info on the bad guys?

Yep

On my way

"Daddy we need to make a detour to my office. We may have something that will help break Donna or maybe the bad guys. I set Jewels to diggin' for dirt yesterday, and it seems she may have found some."

In short order we arrived at my office building and hurried inside—or in my case, more like hobbled inside. Jewels was waiting at her desk when we entered the office. She smiled and her eyes twinkled.

"I think I have something you'll like. Boss, you look even worse today."

I laughed because I knew it was true.

Jewels laid three folders on the desk. "First, we have Martin 'Marty' Greenly. This is the guy who fell down the stairs. Marty has been in and out of trouble since he was in the third grade, and I'm not kiddin'. His juvenile record may be sealed, but plenty of people have lots of bad things to say about young Marty. From age eighteen on, he has an impressive rap sheet: B and E, extortion, arson, insurance fraud, assault—actually an impressive number of assaults. For the past five years he's been working for a company called California Holdings. They have his job title listed as Acquisitions Manager. Since he went to work for California Holdings, he's had no arrests."

"Fascinatin'." I said. "What else?"

"Joseph 'Joe' McKenzie, the guy you shot. Whereas Marty is

stupid and mean, Joe is smart and mean. He killed a guy over a pack of cigarettes when he was just fifteen. He was acquitted on a technicality and has been careful not to get caught since. The general sense from all reports—and there are many—is that Joe is the wet-work guy. Good at his job and good at not getting caught. He's a pro. He's suspected in a dozen murders, but there's never been enough evidence to bring him to trial. He works for a company called Insure Products. He's listed as Head of Security. Since his employment four years ago he has not had so much as a parking ticket."

I started to run my hands through my hair again but remembered my shoulder and head just in the nick of time. I dropped my hands to my side.

"Wow, nice to know that even hired killers are subject to the laws of gravity and lead poisoning," I said.

I tried to sound flippant, but the idea that I had tangled with a professional murderer made my blood run cold. The fact that I had tangled with him and won to tell about it didn't make me feel better. This was the guy who alluded to taking care of the problem. He meant Chick.

"Number three, Richard 'Rick' Journey. Rick likes to talk people out of things such as their money. He's smart, silver-tongued and usually employed as a front man. He's been arrested only three times—all for fraud. The info says he can handle himself in a fight, he likes to think that he's smarter than everybody else and he's probably the brains of the outfit."

"Except that I knocked his brains out."

Jewels looked at me and she smiled.

"Why yes, you did. Rick's employed by a company called, Pacific Home, where he's listed as a Public Relations Specialist. Since his employment seven years ago he's had no arrests. You beginnin' to see a pattern here?"

"Sho' 'nuff," I answered.

"You saved the best for last, haven't you, Juliet? Now you're gonna tell us who owns these three companies," Daddy said.

"Well, it took a bit of digging," she admitted. "I called my husband last night and had him bring me dinner so I could keep lookin'. There're many shell companies inside of dummy corporations inside of holding entities, but when you get to the bottom of the pile, there you will find Aggroco."

I made the *ta-da* sound. "This is it! Jewels, my darlin', you have cracked the case." I kissed her on both cheeks. "Thank you, thank you," I gushed.

She blushed. "I was just doing my job."

"My daughter doesn't pay you enough, Juliet. You're worth your weight in gold," Daddy praised her.

"Hey, be careful, you'll give her a big head." I smiled. "Okay, I'm sure you've made copies of all this, so I'll take these files over to the sheriff. I'll bet he can make good use of them."

Daddy and I entered the sheriff's office and were greeted by Mavis.

"Hello, Sheriff, Tess. Big happenin's 'round here, but I reckon ya'll know that. Connell's waiting in his office."

Daddy walked around the partition and kissed Miss Mavis on her wrinkled cheek. She grinned.

"Girl, you still look like a wild cat had holt of you."

I grinned back at her, and we went to Connell's office where he was indeed waiting on us. He grinned when he saw us.

"Jim found the files this morning." He looked at me. "Don't guess you know anything about that?"

I shook my head and tried to look innocent. He eyed me like he wasn't buying what I was peddling.

"Anyway, everything that we need to connect Donna to Aggroco is here. She was bribed to use her office to smooth the way for the company to purchase the land at the Cove which is against the law. If I can use that to scare her, she may give up her friends over at the hospital."

I drew the three folders out of my bag.

"This may help you even more."

I dropped them on his desk.

"Gimme the Cliffs Notes," Connell said as he thumbed through the files.

"Well all three of 'em have lengthy criminal records, they're employed by three different companies and none of them have had so much as a jay-walking citation since they joined their current employment. All three of the companies can be traced back to

Aggroco. Connect that!"

"Think I will," he said and stood up. "You wanna watch?"

"Oh hell yeah."

We stepped into the hall, and a man in a very expensive suit with a very expensive hair cut almost ran into us.

"Sheriff Maher?" he asked.

Both Daddy and Connell answered simultaneously, "Yes."

Then Daddy laughed, "Sorry, old habits you know."

"What can I do for you?" asked Connell.

The man produced an elegantly embossed business card and passed it to Connell.

"I am J. Steven Vickers of Young, Brothers and Vickers out of Los Angeles, California. I'd like to talk to you about the three men you have in custody and who are currently patients in the hospital. I want to get them out of the hospital, in front of a judge, get bail and fly them home. This needs to be facilitated today, so how do we get that ball rolling?"

Connell didn't say a word for about ten seconds, just stared at the guy as if the lawyer had grown another head.

"Well, I reckon you're about to find out how it feels to want. Get yourself a room, get settled in, pick up a couple of magazines 'cuz you're gonna be here awhile."

"Sheriff, these men are grievously wounded and far from home. They're in pain and frightened. Can you not show some sympathy?"

"Mister, the only place you are gonna find sympathy in this town is in the dictionary between shit and syphilis. The library's two blocks that way." Connell jerked his thumb in the right direction. "Now if you'll excuse me, I have work to attend to."

"Sheriff, I don't think you understand who you're dealing with here. Don't make this any harder than it has to be. My client employs these men. I have been retained to deal with this matter, and the client can either be very grateful to you or very displeased with you."

"I don't think you understand. Your boys are staying where they are. If you continue to annoy me, I'll throw you into a cell for obstruction. As a bonus, I'll go out of my way to make sure that everyone you know or have ever met will also be unhappy with me. While I have you locked up, I'm gonna try and decide if what you just said to me is a threat or the offer of a bribe, and I'll let you know how

I intend to handle that. Now get out of my jail."

"I'll be filing a motion today for the release of my clients," J. Steven Vickers said.

There was an icy note in his voice. I think that he thought he was intimidating Connell.

Connell chuckled. "You have fun with that. Let me know how it works out for ya."

We left the California lawyer, in his $3000.00 suit, standing there looking perplexed. I'd say he was a man who was accustomed to people saying "ribbit" when he said jump and couldn't figure out what had just happened.

Daddy and I went into the observation room, and Connell entered the interrogation room like he owned it. Donna was sitting at the table with her face all snarled up like she just swallowed something that tasted nasty. She cut him an ugly look.

"Joel dragged me in here as if I were a common criminal." She spat the words at Connell.

"Well, Donna, you're a criminal, but as far as I can tell you're not common."

Mars eased into the observation room, and before she could shut the door, the mayor came in behind her. I knew he couldn't be happy about this. Donna was his sister-in-law and a political appointee. If this went the way I knew it was going to go, it could hurt him in the next election. Plus I believed that he had real affection for her. He seemed surprised to see us at first but quickly composed himself and nodded to all of us. He stared at me for a moment before he turned his attention to the interrogation room.

I felt bad for him. Stan Wynne was a nice guy and a good mayor. He doesn't look like your usual politician. He's short and round, and his dark hair is thinning, leaving him with a bald spot in the back. Behind the horn-rimmed glasses there are intelligent eyes that seemed to see deep into a person, and he was perpetually in a good mood. Except for that moment, his face had extra lines that hadn't been there the last time I'd seen him.

In the other room, Donna was staring at Connell, and her mouth was all twisted up like she was going to spit at him.

"You are out of your mind. What exactly are you accusing me of? Be careful what you say next or you'll be lookin' at a slander suit."

"Donna, it's only slander if it isn't true."

Connell dropped several files on the table in front of her.

"This first file is a series of emails between you and several different people at a company called Aggroco. These emails prove that you accepted bribes from that company."

He opened the folder so that she could see the emails. One of her eyebrows rose up almost to her hair line as she stared at the papers like they were snakes.

"That's, that's…" She swallowed, hard. "That's not possible I del… I mean that's impossible because no such exchange ever took place. I don't know where you got those but they are forgeries." She was breathing hard like she had run a mile.

"You tried to delete them, but nothing ever really gets erased from a computer. You can hide it, but you can't make it go away. It took a while to find, but here they are. Now let me explain what this means for you and your future happiness. You've taken a bribe, and in this state that means prison, probably for a long time. You won't be nearly so cute and perky as you are now when you get out. The food is bad—lots of carbs, so it'll be difficult to maintain your girlish figure. Medical and dental care isn't great either. You may meet some women that take a real dislike to you and are willin' to show it in many terrible ways. You may meet some women who take an extreme like to you, and you won't like that outcome either. Once you get out, it's gonna be very hard to get a job. No one trusts a person who betrays her employer by taking bribes—or ex-cons, in general."

"You're makin' all this up. I never did any such of a thing. You're out to get me for some reason, I don't know why, I've never done anything to you. I only ever wanted to love you and make a life with you. Why are you treatin' me this way?"

"I'm treatin' you this way because you're a criminal," Connell snapped.

"I'm not a criminal. I'm on the Downtown Beautification Council, I go to church, I cut my grass, I work for the county and the mayor is my brother-in-law!"

"You took a bribe."

"NO! I never did. That's a black lie that someone has brought against me. You call Stan right now. He'll come over here and straighten this out." She drew a breath as if to try and regain her composure. "I'll have your job for this!"

"Donna, I have emails here that spell out everything you did for Aggroco and the exact amount of money they offered you. Did they pay you yet?"

"Yes. No. I mean there's nothin' to pay me for. They inquired about property that would make a good investment for them here, and I found the properties at the Cove for them. That's all. It was PR for the town and money and jobs. That's all. Everybody profited."

"Especially you, Donna, you profited to the tune of a million and a half dollars."

"No, not true."

"Yep, you're lookin' at the proof. I also have someone checkin' into that number." He pointed to a piece of paper. "It looks like a bank account number. We'll know soon enough."

Donna drew herself up and cast a steely look at Connell. "I think you're insane, and I am gonna leave right now."

"It all worked out so well, didn't it? The company paid you for doing your job, you had a nest egg, the vacant land was sold and jobs were comin'. It was great. Here's what you don't know. The land and the water are tainted, poisoned. Anything grown on that land would be poisoned as well. Maybe not enough to kill anyone, but it could damage them in many different ways, from heart disease to infertility. Aggroco knew that. They did the tests and found out. That's why they told you to keep the sale quiet, not to tell anyone. They intended to hide the truth in some way."

Donna's eyes were wide and her bottom lip began to tremble. "No, no, no." She shook her head in denial.

"Yes, they knew. They sent four men here to make sure things went smoothly: to keep an eye on you and make sure that no one was the wiser about the land. That's when Chick got caught up in the mess. Such an odd string of events really. They were out at the Cove and ran over something that caused a slow leak in a tire. They took the vehicle into Chick's, and he noticed the red clay in the tire treads and commented that they must have been out to the Cove. They decided he knew too much when really he had no idea what the truth was. They murdered him, Donna. Your friend, neighbor and school mate. They murdered Chick without a backwards glance. They blew his heart out of his chest."

Donna just stared at Connell and shook her head.

"Yes, and that means you're an accessory to murder, Donna. The bribery charge will get you about fifteen years, but conspiracy to commit murder and maybe accessory after the fact could get you life. On top of that, these men attacked my family in their home and critically wounded Mark. The prosecutor may ask for the death penalty."

She just kept shaking her head. Tears were swimming in her eyes, but no words came out of her mouth. She folded her arms across her chest and continued to stare at Connell.

"Donna, help yourself out, get in front of this, tell me everything you know and I promise I'll help you. I know you never meant for anything bad to happen. You didn't know the land was bad, or that these fellas would commit murder. Let me help you."

Connell stood there for a full minute waiting for Donna to speak. Finally, when she didn't, he walked out of the room. He left the files on the table. Donna didn't even watch him leave. She just sat there dumbfounded as if she could not figure out how it had come to this. Connell came into the observation room and looked at all of us.

"She needs to tell us everything, so we can tie those three guys to Chick's murder. We don't have enough unless she confesses. All we have now is her for bribery, and somebody can bring a suit against Aggroco for bribin' a public official. The other three will walk."

The mayor shook his head and looked down at his feet. "Oh God, this is a mess. I can't believe what I'm hearin'. Why would she do such a thing?"

"Sometimes money is hard to turn down," Daddy said.

"I'll call my wife, Beverly. Maybe she can talk some sense into Donna. But I need to be honest with her. If Donna cooperates can we get her immunity?"

Connell nodded and Stan stepped into the hallway.

My breath caught in my throat, and I felt like my heart would explode out of my chest. "Immunity?! They murdered Chick!"

Mars reached over and grabbed my hand.

"No, you can't do this." My breathing was ragged and I wanted to cry. "Please, no." I looked around at all the faces, and I felt helpless to stop what I knew was coming.

"Sis, we need her to make the case for murder. Otherwise we've got a kidnappin' charge we can't prove, an attack at the house that's questionable. It's all circumstantial or your word against theirs. We need her, whatever it takes, we need her."

I fought tears and panic. "She knew about the land, she knew. Maybe not till the other day, but they told her the tests had to be falsified. This is wrong," I said. Tears escaped from my eyes. "Wrong." I said again. I sucked in several breaths. "I want her to go to the electric chair. I wanna be there when they throw the switch."

I wiped my eyes on the collar of my shirt and sniffed. I walked out and passed the mayor who was deep in an intense phone conversation. I slammed into the bathroom and hit the wall with my fist. It hurt and I didn't care. I was so furious. Mars came in behind me.

"She's gonna get away with this."

Mars shrugged. "In fairness, she didn't know."

"DON'T YOU DARE DEFEND THAT BITCH!" I screamed at her.

"I'm not defending her. I'm just saying she didn't know about the murder. She didn't pull the trigger."

"She's guilty as homemade sin! If she wasn't a greedy whore, then Aggroco would've gone somewhere else, these bastards wouldn't have come here and Chick would still be alive. He'd still be alive, Mars, he'd still be alive."

Mars put her arms around me and held me while I cried like my heart was broken. I suppose it was at that.

We stayed in the bathroom until Connell stuck his head in the door. "Beverly's here."

We all trooped back into the observation room. Beverly went into the other room and sat down across from her sister. Beverly and Donna looked so much alike but Beverly never stood in the spotlight. It was always Donna who was the cheerleader, the homecoming queen, the beauty pageant winner. I wondered at that moment if Beverly resented Donna. The sad look on her face told me no.

"Donna, honey, you have to tell Connell what he wants to know. That's the best thing for you, you know it."

Donna didn't speak or even look at her sister. She just kept staring at the files on the table.

"They're gonna put you in prison forever if you don't cooperate. If you cooperate and help them get a murder charge against those three men, Connell assured me that you'd get immunity from prosecution. That means..."

"I know what it means." Donna snapped. "I am not stupid. I've never been stupid. That's why I can't believe I'm in this fix."

"Donna, just tell him."

"Beverly, shut up. They don't have anything. Oh, a few emails between me and Aggroco. So what? The Chamber of Commerce would applaud me for bringing this kind of commerce to town. I'll probably get a citizens award. Besides I don't know anything about these three men or murder."

"Connell is buildin' a case against you. Chick was his best friend, so he's gonna be all over this like a dog with a ham bone. He's gonna send you to prison. Donna, I don't want my boys to have to visit their aunt through a glass wall. Please tell him."

Donna was silent.

"Donna, please. Why would you even get involved in this? I don't understand. You have a good life, a good job and lots of friends. Why, Donna?"

"What the hell do you know Miss Married-to-the-mayor-with-two-perfect-kids? I'm the pretty one, the talented one, the charming one, the smart one. Yet I end up in a shitty job making shitty money with no husband, no kids and no future. Then these California people contact me like a fairy godmother with offers of money—lots and lots of money. More money than I could ever earn in this shit hole. Enough for me to go someplace warm and sit on a beach, maybe find a rich husband and have a real life! Enough to get away from you."

"Honey, you had a life."

"No, I did not but I could've had one. All they wanted me to do was my job. It was all so easy."

"But you took a bribe."

"No one would've ever known if those three idiots hadn't panicked and murdered Chick. I still can't believe they did that. That stupid Joe telling me to go home and take something for my nerves like murder was nothing and I was being hysterical. I wouldn't be in this mess if Aggroco hadn't sent morons here to complete the land deal. Why am I always surrounded by fools?" She slammed her hand down on the table causing Beverly to jump.

Connell looked around the room. "I think we've got enough."

He left us and went into the interrogation room.

"Beverly, if you'll excuse us, I need to talk to your sister."

Beverly cast an imploring look at her sister, but Donna ignored her. Beverly left the room crying. Stan opened the door of the observation room and drew Beverly in with the rest of us.

"I don't know if I can bear to watch this," she said.

Stan patted her shoulder and held her hand. I felt sorry for her. I put myself in her place and knew how horrible I'd feel if that were one of my siblings in the other room.

"Donna," Connell said, "you need to listen to me. I'm chargin' you with acceptin' a bribe, accessory before and after the fact for conspiracy to commit murder, four counts of attempted murder and kidnapping."

Donna looked at him and smiled.

"You have nothing, no proof. You're bluffin', Connell. What did I ever see in you?"

"Donna, you just confessed your involvement in the crimes to your sister. It's all recorded. I'll take it to the judge and bring the indictment against you today, before dinnertime. I'll have the indictments against your co-conspirators as well."

"How? OH MY GOD! You were listenin' to a private conversation between me and my sister? That can't be legal! I didn't admit anything to anyone! You bastard!" She screamed. "YOU BASTARD!"

Connell was calm and collected.

"Would you like for me to play the tape for you?"

"Go to hell."

"Donna, write down everything that happened. If you do I'll see that your testimony is used as state's evidence against Greenly, McKenzie and Journey. Plus, you have to further promise, in writing, that you'll help us build a case against Aggroco for conspiracy to defraud and public endangerment."

He pushed a notepad and a pen across the table. Donna stared at them for a good long time, then slowly she reached across and picked them up.

"I don't go to jail if I help you?" she asked.

"You get immunity from prosecution for conspiracy, bribery, kidnapping and murder. You have to testify. I'm gonna further suggest some kind of protective custody for you."

"You're still a bastard and I hate you."

She began to write, and everyone in the observation room let out a collective sigh of relief. Except for me. I wasn't relieved. I was mad and sad and hurt. I felt betrayed. I wanted to scream, curse, throw things, get drunk and beat the hell out of Donna. Instead I walked out of the room and out of the jail.

Mars, Connell and Daddy found me about twenty minutes later in the small park that sits inside the town square. I was sitting on the edge of the large fountain with my feet in the water, being miserable.

"Hey," Mars said and sat down next to me.

"Hey."

"How're you feeling," she asked.

"Like a bitch. I made this all about me." I covered my face with my hand. "I'm sorry, I just lost it. How did it go, where do we stand?" I asked through my fingers.

"She gave us everything. She's willing to testify that she was bribed by Aggroco, that Greenly, McKenzie and Journey held secret meetings with her and that they told her they had murdered Chick to keep him quiet. She also admitted that the bad guys told her the land was tainted and the tests would have to be falsified," Connell said.

"That's good, very good." While I had sat there by myself, I decided to stop being a baby and join the team. "Now what?" I asked.

"I've called Johnny Johnson and asked him to start turnin' out the indictments on the men. He's hungry to prosecute them. I think that even with their high-priced lawyer, we've got enough evidence to convict. Johnny's agreed to give Donna immunity if she testifies. He's also gatherin' information to see what we can do with Aggroco, what charges we can bring against them," Connell said.

"Johnny's a great district attorney and if anybody can tie this up, he can. You done good, brother. Don't let my titty-baby fit fool ya. You were patient and relentless. Ya done real good."

Mars looked at Connell and smiled her million dollar smile.

"You did."

That triggered a memory for me in which the two of them were locked in a look and oblivious to everyone else around them. A light bulb went off. That was at the drag races and again at the hospital. If I didn't know better, I'd say something was up with these two. How funny would that be?

When I woke up the next day, the sun was already high in the sky, and I knew I'd missed breakfast. I stretched and it hurt. As a matter of fact, I might have felt worse than the day before. I took my time with my morning ablutions. I had no particular place to be. I thought about the whole horrible tragedy from beginning to end as I showered. It had been eleven days since Chick was murdered. We knew why and by whom and still it didn't make me feel any better. I had hoped it would. How foolish of me. I was toweling my hair dry when I heard Mars in my bedroom.

"Hey, girl," she called.

I cracked open the bathroom door. "Good morning."

Mars laughed. "Hardly morning."

She stared at me for a few seconds. "Honey child, you look like a dog's dinner. It's a good thing my momma sent you a bottle of Bruise Begone Brew. She gets it from a shop in Nashville." She held up a blue bottle.

I looked at it warily. "What'll it do?"

"It'll help the bruises heal faster, so you won't scare all the small children in town."

"Nice, very nice. You say the sweetest things to me."

"Here, just let me do this."

She grabbed a face cloth and dragged me from the bathroom. I took a seat on my bed while she soaked the cloth in the liquid. When she held it on my shoulder, it was cold but not unpleasant. I patted the place next to me and Mars sat down.

"Best friend, what's going on between you and my brother?"

She looked like a deer caught in a headlight for a second. "I don't know."

"You don't know or you won't tell?"

"Don't know. We've been around each other more in these last few days than ever before since we were kids. The more time I spend with him the more I realize how much I like his sense of humor, his ethics, the way his brain works, his political views—and he's cute.

We just seem to end up in corners discussing this case. So I don't know. I like him as a guy—not just as your brother but as a guy that I'm attracted to, you know?" She shrugged her shoulders at me.

"But you've known him all your life. You see him all the time. How come nothing ever blossomed before?"

"Don't go talking about blossoming. I've no idea what this is, if it's even anything. I don't know how he feels about me. He may still see me as an annoying little sister tag-a-long." She blew out a frustrated sigh. "Besides, as adults one of us always seemed to be in a relationship, and after Carol Ann left town, he's been as anti-social as a badger with hemorrhoids."

I nodded. "Yep, ever since the bitch-who-must-not-be-named kicked his guts out, he's become a monk. I don't think he's had one date. He thought she was it, Mars. She was the love of his life, his soul mate, the future mother of his future children. Then he caught her with that used car salesman from over in Only. He was devastated."

"I heard they got married."

"God, I hope so and she'll stay gone. I've always been afraid that she'd come back, and in a moment of weakness he'd let her move back into his place."

"Regardless, as this progresses—if this progresses—I'll keep you posted." She took my hand. "If this progresses, are you okay with it?" She looked worried.

I threw my good arm around her and kissed her cheek. "Yes."

Mars and I wandered into the empty kitchen. She threw some fruit and yogurt and God knows what else into the blender for me, then she made a sandwich for herself as the contents of the blender whirled around.

I had just settled myself at the table when Daddy came in and said, "There's going to be action in the courthouse in about an hour. You game?"

I smiled my pathetic smile at him. "Am I ever! Let me drink this concoction then I can get dressed and we'll go."

"Your mother and grandmother want to go as well." He grinned.

I rolled my eyes at that idea and sucked down the drink Mars offered me.

Forty-five minutes later we were all sitting in Judge Smiley's courtroom. When I say all, I mean all. It seems that my siblings had all dropped whatever they were doing to come and watch the show. Jewels had closed the office, and she was sitting with Mars and me. It was a packed court.

"All rise for the Honorable Judge Larry Smiley," intoned the bailiff.

We all obeyed. Judge Smiley was aptly named. He was a large man—not fat, just big like the former football player that he was. His hair was blond and curly and he had lots of it. His blue eyes always seemed to hold a twinkle, and he smiled, a lot. Judge Smiley came in and sat on the bench. Today he was not smiling.

"This court is now in session. Please attend and keep silent," the bailiff said.

The judge looked out over the crowd.

"Well it seems that we have a full house for a Thursday afternoon. Mr. Johnson, you would like these three men, Greenly, McKenzie and Journey bound over to the grand jury for trial." He looked at the paperwork on his desk even though I was pretty sure he'd already seen them. "These are some very serious charges. I will assume that you have proof to back this up?" the judge said.

"Yes, Your Honor, we do," Johnny Johnson replied.

"You're the defense attorney for these men?" Judge Smiley asked the California lawyer.

The big suit had on a different suit than before, no less expensive though, and an oily smile to go with it.

"Yes, Your Honor, I am J. Steven Vickers. Your Honor, I do not feel that there is enough evidence to hold my clients for trial."

"Really, well since I am the judge here, I reckon I'll decide." He looked back at the paperwork. "So it says that we have a witness who is willing to testify that all of these charges are correct. Do we have anything else that will corroborate her testimony?"

"We do, Your Honor, we have the statement of Tessely Anne Marie Maher in regard to the attack on the Maher home and her own kidnapping. Former sheriff Edward Maher, Margaret Maher, Marguerite Morgan and the current sheriff Maher will also testify to the attack on the family home. Deputy Mark Jenkins was also wounded when he responded to the call at the Maher home, and we anticipate that he will recover enough to give testimony. We also have the testimony of Donna Eloise Maples pertaining to the murder, conspiracy and fraud," Johnny said.

Judge Smiley looked at me and nodded. I didn't remember making a statement and my puzzlement must have shown on my face.

"You are willing to testify, Ms. Maher?" he asked.

Mars leaned over and whispered, "You gave Connell a statement while you were in the hospital."

"Yes, Your Honor, I'll testify." I nodded vigorously which was painful.

"Then it is the opinion of this court that the three men, Greenly, McKenzie and Journey shall be bound over to the grand jury for trial on all charges, the trial to take place as soon as possible."

The judge raised the gavel.

"Your Honor!" Vickers was on his feet. "Your Honor, I request that you set bail for my clients."

"Your Honor," said Johnson, "my office considers them a flight risk and asks that given the severity of the charges, no bail be set and the defendants be remanded for trial."

"Your Honor, these men are grievously injured. They need to be in California where they can be properly cared for," said Vickers.

"Are you saying we have inferior medical care in our city?" Smiley asked with narrowed eyes.

"Of course not, Your Honor, I just believe that they'll mend faster in familiar surroundings. These are men that are employed by top-notch companies and have a good reputation in their communities. They'll be in court for the trial, I assure you."

"Your Honor, these are men with lengthy arrest records, and we're not really sure who employs them. But we do mean to find out," said Johnson. "As a matter of fact, I'm sure that many things will come out during the trial that will be truly interesting."

"Uh huh, these men are hereby bound over for trial. They are likewise denied bail." Judge Smiley banged the gavel.

Vickers turned to Johnson. "I intend to ask for a change of venue as I'm sure my clients cannot get a fair trial in this one-horse town."

He was haughty and looked down his nose at Johnny. He must have thought he was dealing with a hayseed. Johnny was dressed in a cheap off the rack suit that was probably twenty years old while sporting a rather lackluster haircut and wearing cowboy boots.

Johnny just smiled at the California lawyer. "You do whatever you think you're big enough to do, Slick, and rest assured that I'll fight you tooth and nail every step of the way. The best outcome you can hope for is to save your clients from the electric chair, 'cuz I mean to prove 'em guilty of all charges."

"You may rest assured that I'll grind you and this kangaroo court into dust. I'll tie you up in motions. My clients will be exonerated because you'll be so exhausted from the paperwork that I bury you under, Mr. District Attorney, you won't be able to do your job."

Johnny smiled an evil little smile. "Bring it, Big City, you'll find out what this little country mouse can do."

Vickers snapped his briefcase shut and made his exit but not without glaring at me and Connell.

"Wow, that was worth the price of admission," said YaYa.

We all agreed with her.

"So what do you really think, Johnny?" I asked.

"I think that if Donna really cooperates and with your testimony and the rest of your family, then we have a solid case. Plus, Connell tells me that he found a corpse buried out at the Cove. It's been shipped to Nashville. He also impounded the Hummer. Seems it's a treasure trove of damning evidence. We've sent the guns and bullets we found up to Nashville too, so they can run ballistics. I really think these boys thought they were playin' with a bunch of hicks, so they weren't particularly careful to cover their tracks. Don't worry, Tess, we've got 'em. Just the pictures of you will convince the jury of the guilt of these men."

"That explains where the fourth guy got off to. Seems like a lot happens when I sleep late. Wait, pictures?" I asked.

"We took pictures while you were in the hospital," Mars said.

"Well, I hope you got my best side," I quipped.

"I suggest that we get some more. You're looking even more amazingly Technicolored today. We wanna dazzle the jury with the injuries you suffered at the hands of the defendants," Johnny smiled.

"We'll get more pictures," Mars offered.

We all left the courthouse in an elevated mood until we saw the TBI agents, Boyd and Lyle standing at the foot of the steps. They looked like they'd been sucking lemons.

"Sheriff, a word if you please," said Boyd in a noticeably snotty and authoritarian tone.

We all followed Connell down the steps and moved to one side but stayed within earshot. No one wanted to miss a word of that conversation.

"You were told to stay out of the investigation of Charles Donnelly's death, yet you've persisted in sticking your nose into it. You've been warned several times, and now it seems that you've brought charges against the three men confined to the hospital for his death. Do you deny this?" Boyd was fit to be tied.

"Well, Agent, I was investigatin' another matter altogether, and somehow the two investigations just intersected. Now here we are." Connell didn't smile but I know he wanted to and badly.

"We've informed our superiors of your actions, Sheriff Maher, and we intend to bring charges against you for interfering in an agency investigation and tampering with evidence. You'll be lucky if you don't go to jail, but I can guarantee you won't remain sheriff here when we're done with you," Lyle snarled.

"I want every scrap of paper pertaining to this investigation in my hands by lunchtime. Do you understand me? No one is bringing charges against those three for the death of Donnelly. This is a bureau matter—period. I intend to comb through everything and find the discrepancies. You're covering for your sister, and we all know it. You may not just lose your job, you may be charged as an accessory to murder." Boyd was practically foaming at the mouth, and his face was red as a beet.

"Excuse me." Johnny sounded so polite.

"And who would you be?" Lyle snapped.

"Well, I would be the district attorney for Simpson County. I find myself wanting an explanation for your little fit." Johnny stared a hole through Boyd.

"If you're the D.A. then you should know that we, Agent Lyle and I, have been investigating the death of Charles Donnelly. We have compelling evidence that Donnelly and Tess Maher were dealing drugs in this county, and after a falling out, Maher murdered Donnelly or caused him to be murdered," Boyd said.

Johnny just burst out laughing. "Are you kiddin' me?" He

laughed some more, and the harder he laughed the redder Boyd got.

"There's nothing funny in this matter," Lyle said. "This is murder we're talking about."

"This is nonsense and incompetence we're talking about." Johnny quit laughing. "I've seen everything in this case. I like these California boys for the murder of Chick, plus the murder of one of their own boys and the kidnapping of Tess Maher. I don't know what the two of you've been sniffin', but you better taper off."

"The fourth man was shot by Tess Maher by her own admission, so she's responsible for his death. I won't argue this further. The chief of the TBI will settle this in short order, and I wouldn't want to be any of you when he gets done," Boyd threatened.

Johnny smiled. "Hicky Hickson? Well I think I'll give ole Hicky a call and see if we can't work this out. By work it out, I mean he calls you and tells you to come back to Nashville and let us tend to our own cat killing down here."

"Why would Chief Hickson take your word for this over the word of two of his own agents? Agents who are highly decorated and whom he has personally trained?" asked Lyle in an incredibly haughty tone.

"Well, I've got embarrassing naked pictures of Hicky with a pig taken one night during a beer bash our sophomore year at UT. Those pictures always get me almost anything I want. And right now, what I want is to see the backside of you two." Johnny smiled a charming smile.

For a brief moment I thought that Boyd was going to burst into flame or that the earth would open up and swallow him like Rumpelstiltskin in the fairytale. Sadly, neither of those things happened. Boyd and Lyle just stood there in disbelief with their mouths open. Boyd turned on his heel and stormed away.

Lyle shot all of us one last ugly look. "You haven't heard the last of this." Her voice was dripping with venom. Then she too stormed away and caught up with Boyd.

"You really have a naked picture of the chief of the TBI with a pig?" I asked.

Johnny watched the retreating backs of the two TBI agents. "Oh hell no. It's a goat—pig just makes the story funnier."

He laughed at his own joke and we all joined in with him. For the first time in many days I felt hopeful.

My phone rang and rousted me out of troubled sleep. I had been dreaming about Chick, and I awoke with tears in my eyes. I reached for the phone and hit the message button before I realized it wasn't a text.

"Hello," I said somewhat groggily.

"Morning, sis," said Connell.

"What's up?" I rubbed my eyes and tried to wake up. I needed coffee.

"The California lawyer wasn't kidding when he threatened to bury us in paperwork. So far he's holding at a dozen motions, and it is only eight a.m. He must've had someone in California up since three to get all this done, typed and faxed to him."

"So what does that mean to us?" I could feel knots already forming in my stomach.

"It means that he'll drag us around and around to try and get his way. He'll unleash a bigger flood of documents and do everything else he can think of to slow us down. He wants his boys sprung from the hospital as soon as they're able to travel. He won't get that. When they get out of the hospital they'll go straight into Club Maher. He wants bail. I promise you that he won't get that, but there'll be a fight over it. He wants to negotiate the charges—not happening. The charges stand as they are. No reduction is possible. He wants a change of venue. Any lawyer in his right mind would give his left arm for that."

"Reckon he'll get it?"

"I reckon he will. He'll take the appeal way beyond me and Johnny and Judge Smiley. Any reasonable outsider will look at the case, see the facts and draw the conclusion that in this town you wouldn't be able to find twelve people who didn't know Chick or you. We might be able to keep it in the county though."

"So that just means that we go to wherever they have the trial and testify. We'll stand a good chance of getting a conviction, right. Please tell me that I'm right."

"You're right. We have Donna, and that's going to carry a lot of weight even when the jury finds out that she's trading her testimony for immunity. Then we have you, and you'll testify to the reasons they kidnapped you. We have the gun. It was in the Quonset hut. At least I'm pretty sure it's the gun. It's a thirty-aught-six."

"It'd be nice to top all of that off with a confession from one of those bastards. It all feels pretty thin to me. We have bullets and a gun that we can't match ballistics with because we never found the slug that killed Chick. So the caliber is an educated guess. It all seems pretty circumstantial," I grumbled.

"You're forgetting Donna."

"I'd like to, but you're right. What're you gonna do with her until the trial? She can't go back to her old job as if nothing had happened. Truthfully, I wouldn't be surprised, given the history of Aggroco, if something unpleasant and permanent didn't happen to her."

"We've thought about that. I also worry that she might just take off for parts unknown. So she's in the jail under protective custody. The county doesn't have the funds for any other accommodations, so she's gonna be my guest for a while."

I fell back on my bed. "Oh God, that sucks for you," I said.

Connell chuckled. "Actually I think it sucks for Donna. Every day, three times a day, Mavis's gonna take meals to Donna. Nobody can cut a person down to size like Mavis. She'll have Donna crying like a three-year-old on a daily basis."

"So even though she's getting immunity, she's still gonna have to sit in a jail cell?"

"Yep."

"I like that. Connell, when you find out about the dead bad guy, if I killed him, let me know, okay?"

"You got it."

I tried to make myself look presentable after I got off the phone since I had a full day ahead of me, but really it was impossible. The bruises were fading a bit, so now they were a sickly shade of yellow and green to add to the rather spectacular purple and blue. It was a lovely look. I gave up. When I got downstairs, I was still mulling the information from Connell around in my brain.

"Morning," I greeted my family members.

"Morning, Glory," said YaYa.

"You look a little better this morning," my mother offered.

I smiled and it hurt. "I've been using some stuff that Ms. Price gave me for bruises. Looks like it's helping."

"Coffee?" Daddy asked.

"Only if you have straws."

I was struck by inspiration at that moment and ended up making myself a coffee/espresso/vanilla ice cream yummy liquid breakfast. I sat down at the table.

"Connell had lots of info for me this morning." Everyone looked at me. "He thinks that the lawyers will get a change of venue. There're gonna be several trials too. I guess I hadn't thought about that."

"How many?" YaYa asked while waving her fork in the air.

I ticked the items off on my fingers. "I reckon each one of the bad guys will have separate trials for murder, kidnapping, conspiracy to commit murder, assault with the intent to commit murder and attempted murder. That last one is for Mark, who is slowly recovering by the way."

"Good God, that's three trials, and they each could last for months!" Mommy said. "You want juice?"

"Nope, don't want to ruin my coffee buzz."

"Speaking of Connell, I think I see his car coming in the drive," Daddy said.

"Most likely. He said he was coming to pick me up." I took a big sip of my drink. "The ME released Chick today, and they're bringing him down to Mathews and Sons. We're going to Chick's house to pick out his clothes."

I suddenly wished there was rum in my yummy coffee drink. Today was going to suck.

Connell came in the kitchen door and greeted everyone. Mommy poured him coffee and he sat down at the table. He looked tired.

"Son, you look tired," Mommy also observed.

"Well I guess I am, but I can sleep soon. Tess tell ya'll they released Chick?"

Everyone nodded.

"I've seen the preliminary report, and the findings bear out what we initially thought. Chick was shot from approximately two hundred yards away. A single bullet entered his back between the fourth and fifth vertebra and exited his chest through his heart. Death was virtually instantaneous. He never knew what hit him. But thanks to the coroner, we suspect it was a round from a thirty-aught-six, the same caliber of gun we found in the Quonset hut at the Cove."

"How do you think the trials will go?" Daddy asked.

"I think the California lawyer will argue for and get a change of venue. I think that the three defendants will likely get the death penalty, and it will take twenty years for any of them to be executed." Connell sounded disgusted. I was too.

"And that Donna Maples gets away with what she done?" YaYa asked.

"Not exactly," I said. "She's in the jail till this is over, and Miss Mavis is gonna torment her every day."

"Fine by me. Mavis will have her steppin' and fetchin' in no time flat. Mavis's got six grown sons who all walk small around her. Nothin' less than Donna deserves too. Never could stand that girl always thinkin' she was so high and mighty. I always thought she was no count," YaYa declared.

"What about Aggroco? Will anyone bring charges against them? Or do they get away with the crimes they committed too?" I asked.

"Johnny has gone to the state attorney general and asked for indictments to be brought against the company for fraud, bribery of a public official, conspiracy and accessory to murder before and after the fact. Everyone involved agrees that the bribery charge is easily proven since we have the emails, but it will be harder to prove that they sanctioned the murder. Getting that charge to stick will be just about impossible, unless we get one of the three peckerwoods to roll over. I don't think that'll happen but we'll see. Finish your breakfast, baby sis, we got stuff to do."

I put the rest of my drink in a roadie, kissed everyone good-bye, and Connell and I headed to Chick's house to pick out clothes for his funeral. I knew it wouldn't be difficult to decide on the outfit. Chick only had one suit.

The ride to Chick's was silent. I guess that neither of us had much to say, and we were both dreading the sad duty. We arrived at Chick's house, and there was a note on the door: CONTENTS INSPECTED BY THE TENNESSEE BUREAU OF INVESTIGATION. Connell used the key he had received from Buzzy, and we let ourselves in the front door.

Have you ever thought about what the people who come to take possession of your belongings when you die will find? I'm morbid and I've thought about it. That's why I try to keep my space neat and the fast food wrappers out of the floorboard of my car.

Chick's house was quiet and sad as if it knew that Chick would never be coming back. Everything was neat and tidy. Except for the layer of dust, anyone would have thought that Chick had only left that morning. My chest hurt as I walked through the rooms that he had occupied. There were lots of pictures of his family and friends on the wall. I looked at the one where my sibs and Chick and I went down the Ocoee River in a raft. My mouth was open because I was screaming like a banshee.

Connell walked behind me looking at the pictures and the mementos and trophies that Chick had collected over his too short lifetime. I went into the bedroom and began to sift through Chick's closet.

"You reckon we should buy him a new suit?"

Connell laughed at me. "If he isn't already haunting you, he will be. He only had one suit for a reason 'cuz that's all he needed. It was for weddin's and for funerals. He'd shit a squealin' worm if we went out and spent good money on a new one."

He turned and started going through drawers. I pulled out Chick's one good suit then found a tie and shirt that I thought would look good together. I turned to find Connell with socks and underwear in his hands. He was looking at them as if he couldn't quite figure out what they were.

"This sucks," I whispered.

"Yep."

I took the socks and underwear from Connell and stuffed them in the pockets of Chick's suit. I didn't want to lose anything on the way to the funeral home.

"I think we need pictures," I said as we walked back through the living room.

"Okay, that's a good idea."

Connell started taking pictures down from the wall and setting them on the coffee table. I could see that he was being very picky about the ones he took down. I thought he needed to do this himself, so I busied myself by taking the pictures out of their frames and stacking them.

"You know it's weird. This is my house now, and I keep looking around expecting Chick to walk in the door and ask me what the hell I'm doing."

"Yeah. What are you gonna do with this place?"

Connell shrugged. "I've got my own place and I'm comfortable there. Besides I just don't think I could live here. It has too many memories. I guess I could rent it out or sell it." He sighed and I felt like my heart was breaking.

"We can drop off the suit, then I can run over to Meyerton to get foam core so we can mount the pictures. I think the school supply place ought to have that."

"You aren't supposed to leave town, remember," he said without looking at me.

"Are you serious? It's only ten miles down the freakin' road?! I thought when my new best friends told me not to leave town they meant I shouldn't go to Bora Bora! Besides does that still count? I mean, the case is solved. We solved it."

"It isn't official yet and they don't like you. They like you even less than they did before, since you're the main reason the case is solved and you proved them wrong. We caught the bastards who murdered Chick and have essentially left them standing around with their dicks in their hands." He pulled a few more photos from the top of the bookcase.

"Well, I'm still going to Meyerton. I'll wear a hat and dark glasses, and I'll drive real fast. They'll never know," I said grinning.

Connell just smiled and shook his head. Five minutes later we were in the car and headed back to town. Connell stayed at the funeral home while I made a run to buy the foam core. I did drive really fast, so I guess I was a little nervous about Boyd and Lyle. I had a lot to think about on that short trip. We had solved the murder of my best friend. We had caught the bad guys, and they would go to trial and get convicted without a doubt. Donna would walk. Aggroco would most likely get a slap on the wrist. So if you're keeping score I'd say we won, but it wasn't a slam dunk. I was a little depressed about it. I brooded all the way to Meyerton and back again. I can really brood when I put my mind to it.

The rest of the day was spent at the funeral home accepting delivery of flowers and greeting people who dropped in to pay their respects. I got creative with the food. There was just so much of it, I had to stack it and spread it all over the kitchen area. In the South, whether it's a marrying or burying, there's always potato salad, and there was a lot of it in that kitchen. No one would have to cook for days.

I got the mounting boards and attached pictures to them, starting with the youngest Chick picture and ending with the one from last summer when we all went camping in the Smokies. My entire family was in the picture, and in the middle stood Chick with a big goofy smile on his face. I tried not to sob as I worked.

We had opted for an open coffin for the vigil. Open coffins depress me, but people seem to be able to get closure better if they actually see the body. Makes it more real, I suppose. I preferred the pictures so I could remember him as he was, not laying still and cold.

Connell found me in the kitchen. "Sis."

I looked up from my task. "What's up?"

"I've been talking to Chad Mathews about how to proceed. He and his dad think that we should hold the funeral until Sunday. That gives them more time to get the word out. The obit will go in the paper tomorrow, and the radio station will run the information as a bulletin. No one wants to miss the funeral, and lots of people have to work on Saturday. What do you think?"

I hadn't thought about the actual funeral. I was just putting one foot in front of the other and trying to keep busy. "I think that's a good idea."

He nodded and started to leave. "By the way, the fourth guy died from blunt force trauma to the head. You didn't kill him."

"I think I'm glad. Even under the circumstances I think I'm glad that I didn't kill anyone."

Connell nodded and left me to my work. My family arrived a bit later. The rest of that day and night is a blur to me. People, food, tears, talking, laughing, pictures, stories, comfort given and taken have all merged into one long sleepless bad dream. Sometime that evening Chick was rolled into the viewing room. The sight of his body lying in the coffin knocked all rational thought from my head, and I was swallowed by a terrible black grief.

CHAPTER 31
SUNDAY

On Sunday morning I went to the funeral home. I decided that I'd wait with Chick until he was transported to Our Savior Methodist Church for the funeral service. I don't think that I shared my intentions with anyone, but Saturday was a complete misty memory for me, so there was no telling. I ran into the elder Mathews as I came in, he greeted me and went about his work. I sat for what seemed to be a considerably long time before the younger Mathews came and told me that they would be taking Chick to the church now. My heart seemed to be beating in a funny way in my chest.

"Tess, we're going to seal the coffin now. Do you want to go into the other room?" Chad asked me. His tone was kind and sincere.

"No, I'll stay."

He patted me on the shoulder and moved toward the coffin. I followed him and stood looking at Chick, a sight I never thought to see.

"Chick, we caught 'em. We'll get a conviction. I did my best, but not as good as I wanted," I said softly.

He looked like he was asleep. Tears rolled down my face, but I didn't care.

"It wasn't supposed to be like this Chick. I'm so sorry."

I heard footsteps and turned to see Connell walking across the room. He joined me at the coffin and kissed me on the forehead. Then he looked down at Chick. He didn't say a word, but a silent tear slid down his cheek. I slipped my hand into his, and we stood there lost in thought and grief. Then the moment was over. We stepped back and Connell nodded to Chad who closed the lid and sealed it. My chest hurt and I tried not to sob out loud.

Connell helped load Chick in the hearse. We followed it to the church in Connell's car. The lot was already filling up with mourners. It looked like everyone in town would show up for the service, which was not surprising.

"Connell?"

"Yep."

"Who's guarding Donna today?" I knew he was shorthanded still, and everyone in town would want to be at the funeral.

"Funny you would ask that. Johnny not only got Boyd and Lyle recalled to Nashville but got a favor as well. They'll be leaving tomorrow. Today they're babysitting for me. Believe me when I tell you they're not happy campers."

I smiled at that.

My brothers and Sammy and Billy were the pallbearers for Chick. They were waiting for us. The men lifted Chick from the hearse and carried him through the crowd and into the church. The vestibule was full of mourners, and every single pew was packed.

The choir sang and they sounded like angels. The words spoken were beautiful and promised that the afterlife was glorious. We were comforted because Chick was in the arms of God and reunited with his loved ones who had passed. We were told we must not grieve but should rejoice. I found it hard to rejoice as I sat there and thought of the large gaping hole in my life that once held Chick. Connell rose and gave the eulogy for Chick. He said good things, funny things, told stories and reminded us of all the good things that Chick had done and how much he would be missed.

My right side was suddenly cold and I looked over to see Chick next to me. This time I didn't start or yelp or even twitch—I expected him. He was looking at Connell.

"*Gosh, I feel like Tom Sawyer spying on his own funeral. Connell looks so sad.*"

I had to smile. What a thing to say.

"Except you really are dead," I whispered.

"*Lots of flowers, and ya'll did a good job picking out the pictures. TisTis, I know you did the best you could to catch my killers. You almost got yourself killed in the process. Don't fret. It'll all come out alright.*"

"What do you know that I don't?"

He didn't answer but disappeared from my side to reappear standing next to Connell. Connell must have sensed something because he stopped speaking in mid-sentence and looked right at Chick. Connell finished his speech, then the minister told us to go in peace.

The coffin was reloaded into the hearse for the trip to the

cemetery. I rode with Connell.

"You know that Chick was standing there at the podium with you, right?" I said.

"Yeah, my left side got cold for no reason, and I could smell his aftershave. I knew he was there."

"He said we did good with the case and the pictures we chose for the funeral, and that we shouldn't worry, everything would come out alright."

"Wonder what he knows that we don't?"

"I asked the same thing but he didn't enlighten me."

I looked behind us and realized the procession was incredibly long. I figured everyone who came to the funeral was also coming to the cemetery too. Wow, that was impressive. I had a speech to read at the gravesite and spent the trip going over it. It would be difficult enough to get through it without tripping over the words too.

Connell parked the car. I leaned over and kissed him before he could get out. He hugged me for a second then went to the hearse. My brothers and friends unloaded the coffin and carried it to the gravesite. It took forever for all the people to park their cars and make their way to the grave. There were literally hundreds and hundreds of people.

Reverend Chris stepped up to the open grave and blessed the earth that would receive Chick's body. When he was done, he motioned me forward. I prayed for the strength to get through this. What had seemed like such a good idea, now seemed quite the opposite to me. Still I rose, squared my shoulders and went to the stand by Chick's coffin. I'd chosen a poem to read that spoke to my feelings about Chick. I'd cut and pasted it into a pretty book so it would look nice as I stood before all those people. I cleared my throat before I began to read.

My New Reality

I long to hear your sweet voice again,
But you are gone, lost on the wind.
My heart is broken into pieces,
The pain comes in waves, never ceases.

I walk so alone in this wide world,
My thoughts and feelings are in a swirl.

My soul is empty and without joy,
No matter the measures I employ.

You're tucked in a corner of my mind,
To all else, everyone, I am blind.
I reach out a thousand times a day,
I dream of you, I cry and I pray.

To touch you, to hold you one more time,
To have an instant when you are mine,
To share the trials and joys of my life,
But all I have is sadness and strife.

I love you now and will for always,
I search for you in streets and byways.
But you are not there for me to find,
And so you live only in my mind.

You're my joy, my soul, my life, my heart,
How do I go on? How do I start?
Don't forget me, love me from afar.
I look up and see you in a star.

I'll ever hear your voice in the breeze,
As it moves and rustles through the trees
In the sun as it shines on my face
I feel you everywhere, every place.

Dearest one, I pray you love me still,
Forever, and that you always will.

I promise you that by the time I was finished, there wasn't a dry eye in the house. That's the way it should be too. We should all cry when a good person leaves this world. I walked back to my seat under the awning amidst the sniffling and outright weeping.

Chick's coffin was lowered into the hole, and the men who were paid to bury Chick stepped forward with shovels. My brother stood up, took off his jacket, handed it to me and stepped up to the grave. He took a shovel from one of the gravediggers and started to throw dirt onto Chick's coffin. One by one, each of my brothers and Sammy and Billy did the same thing. The grave diggers moved out of the way and stood beneath a tree to watch the men in suits bury their friend. Isn't it funny how weird things stand out in emotional moments like that. I kept looking at everyone's shoes. They all had nice shoes on and they were standing in dirt. I kept thinking what a mess that was going to be to clean. My heart finished breaking at that moment.

As Chick's friends shoveled dirt into the grave, not one person in the crowd made a sound except for crying. No one spoke a word. We all just watched. It was the most amazing tribute to the man that we all loved. I sobbed as silently as it was humanly possible to do. Why do we do that? Why do we try and be quiet in our grief? Why don't we wail and cry and scream our sorrow out? Michelene reached over and clasped my hand. I looked and realized that my family was all holding hands.

Finally, the men finished and handed the shovels back to the grave diggers. The minister said a few more words and thanked everyone for coming. All the people sat transfixed as if by a spell for a full minute. Then the spell was broken and the crowd began to break up. Many of them would be heading to our house for the wake. I saw Mommy, Daddy and YaYa walking slowly to the car. They wanted to beat the crowd to the house to make sure everything was ready for company.

Sammy walked over to his truck and came back with a bottle and a stack of Dixie Cups. He poured each of us a shot of Tullemore Dew. I took mine from him.

"Pour one more, Sammy," I said.

He did and I took it to Chick's grave and set it amongst the overwhelming ocean of flowers. As I walked back to my family and friends I saw Chick standing under the same tree the grave diggers had sheltered beneath. I smiled at him and raised my cup.

"I love you, Chick Donnelly."

I drank my shot and I watched as Chick faded until he was gone.

End Note

*Page 175 cites material from the following document prepared by Interstate Technology and Regulatory Cooperation (ITRC) Work Group, Enhanced *In Situ* Biodenitrification Work Team:

Technology Overview: Emerging Technologies for Enhanced *In Situ* Biodenitrification (EISBD) of Nitrate-Contaminated Ground Water, June 2000

While I am citing materials produced by ITRC (Section 2.3), this work of fiction is not an official ITRC training course and this work as a whole has not been reviewed or approved by ITRC. More information regarding the work of ITRC may be found at www.itrcweb.org.

Disclaimer

ITRC Materials do not necessarily address all applicable health and safety risks and precautions with respect to particular materials, conditions, or procedures in specific applications of any technology. Consequently, ITRC recommends consulting applicable standards, laws, regulations, suppliers of materials, and material safety data sheets for information concerning safety and health risks and precautions and compliance with then-applicable laws and regulations. ITRC, ERIS and ECOS shall not be liable in the event of any conflict between information in ITRC Materials and such laws, regulations, and/or other ordinances. The content in ITRC Materials may be revised or withdrawn at any time without prior notice.

ITRC, ERIS, and ECOS make no representations or warranties, express or implied, with respect to information in ITRC Materials and specifically disclaim all warranties to the fullest extent permitted by law (including, but not limited to, merchantability or fitness for a particular purpose). ITRC, ERIS, and ECOS will not accept liability for damages of any kind that result from acting upon or using this information.

ITRC, ERIS, and ECOS do not endorse or recommend the use of specific technology or technology provider through ITRC Materials. Reference to technologies, products, or services offered by other parties does not constitute a guarantee by ITRC, ERIS, and ECOS of the quality or value of those technologies, products, or services. Information in ITRC Materials is for general reference only; it should not be construed as definitive guidance for any specific site and is not a substitute for consultation with qualified professional advisors.

About the Author

Tish Owen is an ole Southern girl, born and bred by her very Southern mother, a Yankee father and his Irish mother. She grew up Catholic, and in the South that was a rarity. So she has a bit of a different take on the world and how things work. She spent most of her childhood running in the woods and playing make believe—a good foundation for a writer. She is blunt, funny, hard-working, sarcastic, irreverent, opinionated, polite to her elders, expects children to behave, likes dogs, cats, horses and birds—isn't such a fan of snakes. She lives in Nashville with her husband, her ninety-seven-year-old mother, a rat terrier, two cats and an African Grey.